Dear Reader,

For more than twenty-five years, *New York Times* and *USA TODAY* bestselling author Kathleen Eagle has been beloved by readers and critics alike.

Eagle is known for her strong voice, compelling characters and highly emotional plots, and with this 2-in-1 volume, we are proud to present two of her novels that exemplify just that. In *Defender,* the unlikely hero is Gideon Defender, a man who is intimately aware of the distinction between us and them, between have and have not, between the things he can touch but never keep. Raina McKenny, the woman who chose Gideon's brother over him, returns to the reservation after fifteen years and sets off an emotional and political firestorm. As a non-Native raising a son registered with the band, Raina's return provokes a custody battle. Desperate not to lose her child, she looks to Gideon for help. But while he'd do anything to be her hero this time, as the band's tribal leader it is his duty to uphold the band's law. Adding to the powder keg is the reignited passion between Gideon and Raina, a contentious treaty issue that threatens to turn violent and an explosive secret that will change Gideon's world forever.

In *Broomstick Cowboy,* we have another man caught by duty, this time to his dead best friend, Kenny. The word *responsibility* makes Tate Harrison shudder, but he just can't turn his back on Kenny's widow. Amy Becker would never admit to needing help, but she's barely holding on. She's pregnant, her ranch is on the verge of failing and her young son is desperate for a male role model. Tate promises to get Amy through the winter, and come spring he'll be back on the rodeo circuit. As winter deepens, though, Tate slowly begins to understand the appeal of a true home—a place of love and warmth, a place where he is needed and valued, a place where he could find peace and happiness. But this is *Kenny's* home, *Kenny's* family—can he honor his friend's memory and still claim Amy and her children as his own?

Gideon and Tate are real heroes—they have flaws and edges and doubts—but you'll fall in love with them just as surely as these heroines do.

Happy reading,

The Editors,

Harlequin Books

KATHLEEN EAGLE

published her first book, a Romance Writers of America Golden Heart Award winner, with Silhouette Books in 1984. Since then she has published more than forty books, including historical and contemporary, series and single title, earning her nearly every award in the industry. Her books have consistently appeared on regional and national bestseller lists, including the *USA TODAY* list and the *New York Times* extended bestseller list.

Kathleen lives in Minnesota with her husband, who is Lakota Sioux. They have three grown children and three lively grandchildren.

New York Times and USA TODAY Bestselling Author

KATHLEEN EAGLE

A CERTAIN KIND *of* HERO

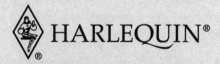

HARLEQUIN®

TORONTO • NEW YORK • LONDON
AMSTERDAM • PARIS • SYDNEY • HAMBURG
STOCKHOLM • ATHENS • TOKYO • MILAN • MADRID
PRAGUE • WARSAW • BUDAPEST • AUCKLAND

Recycling programs
for this product may
not exist in your area.

ISBN-13: 978-0-373-18917-5

A CERTAIN KIND OF HERO

Copyright © 2010 by Harlequin Books S.A.

The publisher acknowledges the copyright holder of the individual works
as follows:

DEFENDER
Copyright © 1994 by Kathleen Eagle

BROOMSTICK COWBOY
Copyright © 1993 by Kathleen Eagle

CONTENTS

Remembering Lillian, Phyllis and Barbara with love.

DEFENDER

Prologue

Gideon Defender instinctively hit the deck at the sound of gunfire. The first person he'd learned to defend was himself, and this wasn't the first time he'd had to eat a little dirt in the process.

"Damn." Tribal game warden Carl Earlie dropped to his knees at Gideon's side. "Don't see nothin', but my ears are ringing pretty good. How close would you say that came?"

"Too close for comfort." Another bullet zinged over Gideon's head, scattering chunks of oak bark as it ricocheted off the trees. He grabbed the back of Carl's belt and jerked him down. "Eeeez, that forty-acre forehead of yours makes a nice, shiny target."

Carl's eyes widened. "You think they're shootin' at *us?*"

"You know anything else that's in season this time of year besides Indians?"

Carl thought about it, then turned down the corners of his mouth and shook his head. "Naw, you're gettin' paranoid,

Chief. Nobody's out to shoot us." Flashing a quick grin, he stuck his head way up on his scrawny neck, looking around like some big-eyed ring-necked duck. "You know what I think is—" Another shot rang out, and the duck became a turtle. "I think I got a job to do. Somebody's poachin'."

"Just stay down, Carl." Gideon spared him a warning glance. "And don't call me 'Chief'."

"Sorry. If they heard that, I guess you'd be the one they'd aim for, huh?"

"Not if they're poachers. Poachers'd go after you first, mistaking you for a moose."

"Get outta here, Ch—"

Gideon touched his fingers to his lips and cocked one ear toward the sound of footsteps. Glimpsing the sprinting shooter, they exchanged nods, scrambled to their feet and followed. To anyone who didn't know him, it would have been surprising that a man of Carl's considerable girth was able to move nearly as quickly and almost as quietly as Gideon did, but they shared the heritage of native woodsmen.

"Taking a little venison, Marvin?" Gideon asked as they approached the man.

Marvin Strikes Many stepped between his challengers and his kill as he tucked the butt of his rifle into his armpit and carefully pointed the barrel at the ground. "My kids are hungry."

"It's fishing season," Carl said. "And you're a damn good fisherman."

"I saw this buck, and I happened to have my rifle along, so I took a shot." Marvin threw his shoulders back and wedged his thumb between his overlapping belly and the waistband of his jeans, assuming a cocksure, hip-shot stance. There was something about the combination of skinny legs and droopy gut that ruined the effect, but Marvin seemed oblivious to that fact. "You call yourselves Chippewa, but you talk about licenses and seasons, just like the whites. I have a right to take this meat home to my family."

Gideon eyed the deer carcass. He almost wished he could let the man take the meat and go his way. A few years ago, that was exactly what he would have done. But these days he couldn't pick and choose on a whim. The tribal chairman's hat was a tight fit for a man who was used to taking some pretty broad liberties. He'd spent most of his life doing things his own way and telling anyone who didn't like it to go to hell. Nowadays he had to choose his words more carefully, even though he couched them in the same tone he'd always used when he was challenged. What was once considered offensive was now authoritative.

"You have to go by the rules, Marvin. The Pine Lake Band has rules."

"And the state has rules," Marvin recited. "And the feds have rules." He shifted his weight from one foot to the other. "You gonna slap me with a fine, Carl?"

"Got to, Marvin, you know that."

"The Strikes Many family has its own rules. The Pine Lake Band doesn't speak for us." Marvin jabbed his forefinger in Gideon's direction. "You might be chairman of the Pine Lake Band, but you've got no say over the Strikes Many clan, Defender. We're White River, and we didn't ask to be put in with you guys."

"*We* didn't invite *you,* either," Carl said.

"All right, all right." Gideon didn't like being pointed at, especially by a man toting a hunting rifle. Times like this he wanted to throw the damn chairman's hat back into the ring, land one punch and walk away.

But he took a deep breath and calmly made his case. "The fact is, the feds included your clan in the Pine Lake Band,

Marvin. That all happened way before my time, so I had nothing to do with it. You wanna complain to somebody about your tribal affiliation, complain to the Bureau of Indian Affairs. Let me know if you get anywhere with them. Meanwhile, I'm tribal chairman, and I've got some say over you."

"You didn't get *my* vote." Marvin gave a smug nod, convinced he'd just delivered a crushing blow. "Nobody did. Election Day, I said the hell with you guys, and I just stayed home."

"Well, we sure missed you, Marvin. Tell you what—next time around, why don't you run against me?"

"Run for chairman of Pine Lake?" He gave a mirthless hoot. "Might as well run for chairman of the Pine Ridge Sioux."

"C'mon, Marvin, we're related closer than *that*. We're all Chippewa, right?" Silently cursing himself for sounding exactly like a politician, Gideon indicated the deer with a quick chinjerk. "Let's dress this guy out. We'll give the meat to some of the elders."

"I gotta take your rifle, Marvin." Carl held out his hand. Reluctantly, Marvin surrendered his weapon. "Could be worse. I could impound your pickup."

"One game warden's just as bad as another, doesn't matter whether he works for the tribe or the state." Marvin unsheathed his hunting knife and wagged it at Gideon. "You think you're gonna make this deal with the state, selling our treaty rights down the river, you can think again."

"Point that thing somewhere else, Marvin, or I'll break it in half. Now, you know that all we're trying to do is work a compromise just like other bands have done. We're not selling anything. But either way, you've got to get it through your head that you can't do this." He nodded toward the carcass. "We've always had some kind of rules for the hunt. *Always.*"

Carl laid a conciliatory hand on Marvin's shoulder. "Hell, man, we thought somebody was shootin' at *us.*"

"I didn't know you were within range."

"Thank God for small favors," Gideon muttered. He unsnapped the knife sheath that was fastened to his own belt. "Give me a hand here, Carl."

"We'll take care of this," Carl said, offering an insider's smile. "You've got business to tend to over at the lodge, right? You don't wanna keep the pretty lady waitin' too long."

"She's my *sister-in-law,* Carl," Gideon protested.

"I know that, but your brother's dead. Been dead awhile now. And the way I remember it, you saw her first."

"If anybody ever wants to write my life story, I'll tell 'em to give you a call. You remember more than I do." He had to walk away from that infuriating grin. Carl had known him too damn long. "And that chapter would only run about a page and a half."

"Yeah, right." Carl's gesture invited Marvin to start the gutting process. "You've been stallin' around long enough, Chief. Go tend to your business now."

"Quit calling me—" Gideon turned and cocked a finger in Carl's direction, but he couldn't quite keep a straight face in the presence of that cock-eyed grin *"—Chief!"*

Chapter 1

Her name was Raina, but perched on a ladder-back oak chair in the rustic lobby of Pine Lake Lodge, she was all sunshine. She could easily have been the solitary woman in one of those stippled paintings, the kind that seemed to equate fair women, white dresses and blue water with pure serenity. The lodge's big front window framed her quite nicely, with the lake in the background. Streaming through the glass, the afternoon sunlight embroidered her dark blond hair with threads of gold. She wore a flowered sundress and a straw hat with a big sunflower tacked to the band. Beneath the droopy yellow brim, all Gideon could see of her face was pink nose, pink lips and small white chin.

Standing in the dark shadows of the lounge, he tuned out the jangle of the slot machines at his back as he watched her flip through the magazine that lay open on her lap. Her lips moved slightly as some noteworthy bit of information caught her eye. Despite the passage of more time than Gideon had the heart to mark, the sweetly familiar habit hinted of the same old Raina. Soft and yielding, those lips had given him much pleasure the few times he'd been permitted to taste them. But in recent years she had pressed them only against his cheek and only briefly, then smiled and made some polite remark about being glad to see him.

Only snatches of her first words ever registered with him. She had a way of bombarding his senses, and it usually took him a moment to get his mental bearings. But this time he'd gotten the drop on her. This time, much like a time long past, he'd been the one to see her first....

She looked like a fish out of water—a goldfish that had somehow escaped the confines of a giant crystal brandy snifter and fallen into a shot glass. Seated on a stool in the company of two women who were polishing the bar with all four elbows, the lady with the big blue eyes seemed a mite uncomfortable. Gideon knew the other two—Kristy Reese and Charlotte Croix—both seasoned teachers, both single and neither a stranger to the Duck's Tail Tavern. But the young blonde was new to the north woods, and Gideon was an expert guide. He knew all about taking fish out of the water, and he hated watching them struggle.

He felt especially charitable tonight. After he loaded up the jukebox with quarters, he was going to take this one off the hook.

"How's the three-R's business lookin' this fall, ladies?" With a subtle nod he suggested to Charlotte that she move over one stool. "Have you filled up all those little desks yet?"

"Gideon." Charlotte smiled, gave a quick, knowing glance at Gideon's chosen target, then obligingly vacated the stool to give him a clear shot. "It's been a while since we've seen you around here. Did you venture out of the woods just to check up on us?"

"If this is still the same Duck's Tail, I'm not out of the woods yet." He claimed his seat, acknowledging Charlotte's collaboration with another nod, this one more deliberate, more courteous. "Came in to see if we pulled in any new faces this year. Not that it isn't a pleasure to see the old faces, too. Well, not *old* faces," he amended with a deferential smile. "Returning faces. Friendly faces of old acquaintances who shouldn't be forgot."

"Nor offended when they can introduce you to a pretty new face," Kristy said. "Raina McKenny, meet Gideon Defender. If you ever get the urge for a real wilderness experience, Gideon's your man."

Charlotte's chortle nearly caused her to choke on her drink. She recovered with a rejoinder that got a giggle out of Kristy. "He has an excellent reputation for satisfying all kinds of wild urges."

Charlotte was trying hard to sound like the voice of experience, which gave Gideon his chance for a good laugh. With a mischievous sparkle in his eyes, he nodded in her direction. "This one's hoping I might take a run at hers someday."

The remark drew an indignant scowl, but his order for another round made the proper amends.

"Care to dance, Raina?"

"Well, I…"

Gideon waited while she exchanged meaningful glances with her companions. It wasn't like she was asking permission—after all, this was what they'd come for, right? To meet guys. It was more like, *Any last words of warning, girls? Any particular aberrations I should be apprised of before I take the plunge?*

When neither of them came up with anything, she slid off the stool and looked up at him.

Gideon cupped his hand under her elbow. "Nothing wild, I promise. I just stuck all my money in the jukebox. I picked all slow tunes."

Her tentative smile seemed real enough. "Is that supposed to be reassuring?"

"It's supposed to be romantic. I've been in the woods a long time, and I've had nothing but all-male fishing parties all summer." Locking her gaze with his, he took her hands and slid them over his shoulders, as though he were putting on a necklace. "I was about ready to put on an apron and dance with one of them, like they used to do in the old days at the trappers' rendezvous."

"You enjoy dancing that much?" He'd put both his arms around her. She promptly withdrew his left one and made him do the tea-spout pose with her. "I was taught this way."

"Really? How about this?" He made a silly face and started them rocking side to side.

"Are you serious?"

"Hell, no. Just trying to make you smile." And this time her smile came easily. "There. That took some of the tension out of your shoulders. I could feel it." He spread his hand over the middle of her back, pulling her closer. "Damn, guess I shouldn't have mentioned it. You stiffened up again."

Casting him an apologetic glance, she made a deliberate attempt to relax. "I don't know anyone here very well yet. I'm really not very…good at this sort of thing."

"Not much of a barfly?" She shook her pretty head, and he chuckled. "Not much nightlife in a small town. You from the Twin Cities?"

"Yes."

"Teacher, right?" She gave a tight nod. "First year?"

Another nod. He pulled in the teapot spout and held her hand against his shoulder. This time she didn't object. He figured he'd hit on a compromise.

"What made you decide to start your career at Pine Lake Indian Reservation, of all places?"

"They offered me a job."

"Not your first choice, huh?"

"I wanted to start out in a small school, and I've always loved the northern part of the state." She glanced up at him, still unsure, but clearly, as far as he was concerned, attracted. "And I wanted to come to a reservation."

"Really." He slid his hand down her spine and let it rest at the small of her back. He led with his hips. She wanted to follow merely with her feet, but he was having none of that, and he could feel it the minute her hips stopped resisting the rhythm. He smiled and settled in. She was going to give him a run for his money, but he would reach the payoff window eventually. "Well, here you are. How do you like our music?"

"It's—" she drew a shallow breath and gave a soft sigh "—familiar."

"You've heard this one somewhere before?" She nodded. "How about our dancing?" She looked up. He indicated the two of them with a suggestive chinjerk. "*Our* dancing."

"I like it," she confessed. Unwilling to lose the ground he'd gained, he drew her only a fraction of an inch closer. She acknowledged his restraint with a smile. "I like it very much."

He had held her close on the dance floor, touched his cheek to hers, and later that night he had tasted her lips. And in the months that followed he'd found himself, much to his surprise, going for broke. Not only had he tried to make it with her, he'd also tried to make her love him. Unfortunately, he'd made a few mistakes. Maybe more than a few—he'd been good at that then. But he'd made up for it by introducing her to the Defender who could do no wrong—his brother, Jared.

When she finally looked up, she peered straight at him and smiled, as though she'd known he was there all along. His boot heels sounded an unhurried rhythm across the hardwood floor of the lobby. She closed the magazine, set it aside and slowly rose from the chair. He would greet her in the customary fashion, he thought. He would simply, properly shake her hand.

But her way was to greet him with a sisterly embrace and a peck on the cheek, and he gave in to it without objection. Her smile was easily mirrored, her greeting easy to echo, but her withdrawal came too quickly. His response lagged by a heartbeat. His hands lingered on her back just a little too long, and she beat him to the punch at stepping away.

"I wasn't sure you'd gotten my message," she said as she adjusted her hat. "It's not so easy to reach you."

"Easier than it used to be. I have an office indoors these days."

She nodded, and it bothered him that she seemed to smile only on cue, her eyes devoid of anything but the recognition of the rudiments of an acquaintanceship, an acknowledgment of the fact that they had seen each other only occasionally over the years.

With a shrug he told himself to shift into the same gear. "But things have been pretty hectic lately, and I'm in and out. Actually, I got two messages this morning—one that you were coming, the other that you were here."

"It was kind of a spur-of-the-moment decision. I wanted to get away, but at first Peter didn't want to go on vacation at all. He didn't want to leave his friends." She sighed as she turned from him, snatching off the hat as though it had suddenly become troublesome. "You know how kids are at twelve, nearly thirteen. Suddenly their friends become their whole reason for living."

"Is he twelve already?" He didn't know why the number should hit him so hard. It was just a number. With a casual click of his tongue he tried to shoo the whole thing into an insulated mental box. "Almost a teenager. My God, that's really hard to believe."

"I know. I don't know where the time went. All of a sudden he's a young man, and I… Sometimes I just want my little boy back." She brushed her hair from her temple in a nervous gesture, then summoned a bright smile. "Anyway, we hit on this idea, that we would just come up here for a week or so and explore the woods. Try boating on a little bigger lake than we're used to and maybe do some fishing or something."

"Not your first choice, huh?" The echo of his old challenge made him chuckle. It made her blush, which at last added some real color to her smile and told him that she remembered, too. He laid his hand on her shoulder and offered a sympathetic squeeze, then a teasing jiggle. "Come on, Raina, when were you ever interested in fishing?"

"I've always enjoyed the water. And the woods," she averred amiably.

But his hand lingered on her shoulder and drew her in closer, not so much physically as intellectually. It seemed as though she sensed his willingness to be her ally. "Truthfully," she began quietly, "Peter doesn't really know any other kids that share his Native heritage. We live in the suburbs, you know, and he's definitely in the minority. He's beginning to have mixed feelings about his culture—doesn't seem to know whether to take a serious interest or to pretend to be—" her eyes shifted from his face to the front desk and back again, and she shrugged, unwilling to name an alternative "—something else, I guess. I don't know how to, um… Well, he's at that difficult age. With Jared gone…"

She spoke her husband's name so softly that Gideon could barely hear it. With Jared gone, what? he wondered. With Jared gone, Peter was probably the only Native left in the upscale suburb he'd lived in all his life. With Jared gone, Peter was surrounded by people who didn't look much like him, including his mother. So with Jared gone, just who was going to tell Peter to stay away from mirrors and he'd be fine? Jared, for all his smarts and all his talents, had been the Chippewa who was not a Chippewa. That was his chosen alternative. If he'd lived a little longer, Jared would have helped his son learn the ins and outs of avoiding mirrors. And, Gideon had to admit, nobody did it better. It had once been one of the many accomplishments Gideon had envied his brother.

Gideon shoved his hands into his back pockets and banished all negative thinking about his brother with a quick shake of his head. A dead brother could do no wrong. Respect was due his memory. Respect and then some.

"So where's Peter now? You brought him with you, didn't you?"

"He's up in the room, playing video games." She glanced at the wide staircase with its dark, rustic banister. "He insisted on bringing them along."

"He doesn't want to rough it too hard?"

She shook her head and gave him an indulgent, just-between-adults look.

He let it pass. The boy could have his video games and his hiking in the woods both, no problem. He could have a little taste of life on the rez, maybe use it in a school essay in the fall, and tell his friends all about how his uncle, the chairman of the Pine Lake Band of Chippewa, had taken him fishing. The boy was welcome to take all that back with him. And then some.

Respect, *and then some.*

No, Gideon didn't really give a damn about the boy bringing his video games. But he did give a damn about being ignored.

"It's been over two years, Raina. I haven't seen either of you since the funeral."

"You know where we live," she said breezily.

Too breezily. His flat stare was intended to remind her that he'd never been there. He was never invited.

He wasn't sure she got the point.

"You do get down to the Cities once in a while, don't you?" she asked. "I saw you on TV recently. You were in St. Paul, I believe."

"Meeting with some people from the Department of Natural Resources about this treaty issue."

Okay, maybe he was being a little stubborn. Going back to the Cities was never easy. The best way to avoid old haunts was to stick to a business agenda. He never looked anybody up. Never tried any of the restaurants people suggested, never even stayed overnight unless he had to. But when he did, there were times when… "I thought about calling you."

"I've thought about that, too. About coming back, about establishing some sort of ties." Too quickly, she added, "For Peter's sake."

"Of course. For Peter's sake." Too quickly, he smiled and gave an open-handed gesture. "So, for Pete's sake, here you are. And you look great, as always."

"You do, too. Your job seems to agree with you, Gideon."

"It agreed with me better when I was a hunting and fishing guide, working for a good outfitter. Back when I first met

you, I think that might have been the best job I'll ever have."
With a look, he told her that he didn't expect anyone else to
be impressed.

"Now, here I am, bucking tradition. Too young to be a tribal
leader. But they voted me in, so what the hell." He caught
himself patting his breast pocket for the cigarettes he'd given
up, and he nodded toward the restaurant. "Let's go get some
coffee."

She tipped her head in assent, and he gestured for her to
lead the way.

"Rumor has it that you're a refreshing change," she said
as the hostess seated them near a sunny window. "Quite
progressive, in fact." She declined the proffered menu. "Just
coffee for me, please."

"Yeah, well…" He spared the waitress a two-finger sign
and a nod. He was suddenly more interested in telling Raina
what he was about these days, since she'd brought it up. If she
hadn't been impressed back then, maybe she would be now.

Not that it mattered anymore. But just for the hell of it…

"The longer I hold this job, the more respect I gain for
traditional thinking. The only problem is, the rest of the world
doesn't get it." He braced his forearm on the edge of the table
and leaned closer. "They're into money power. They don't
understand traditional values. They don't have any respect
for spiritual power."

Raina nodded, her eyes alight with interest. "That's why
we're here. Peter needs to know more about what it means
to be Chippewa. Without Jared, I—" Her voice dropped into
that confessional tone again. "I'm kind of at a loss, because,
you know, *I'm* not…"

He watched her align her flatware with the edge of the
table, and he wondered which part of what she'd just said
embarrassed her. He didn't think it was the Chippewa

part—at least, he'd never gotten that impression from her before. Maybe it was her being at a loss for the insight she was seeking on Peter's behalf. Or maybe just being at a loss for her husband.

He shook his head and sighed. "For somebody who always had a knack for doing the right thing at the right time, my brother sure picked a bad time to check out."

"It wasn't his idea to have a heart attack." She raised her eyes to his and smiled softly. "I know you miss him as much as we do, Gideon."

He nodded once, almost imperceptibly. "So you're looking for Uncle Gideon to do a little straight-talking, man-to-man?" Less than comfortable with the assignment, he arched an eyebrow as he snatched a toothpick from the holder on the table, peeled off the cellophane and stuck the poor substitute for what he really wanted into the corner of his mouth. "Do you have any idea what I was like when I was twelve-goin'-on-twenty?"

"Hell on wheels would be my guess."

"And you'd be right on." His smile faded. "Peter knows he's adopted, right?"

"He's thrown that up to me once or twice lately. 'You're not my *real* mom.'" She leaned back as the coffee was served. "I try not to show it, but that one really hurts."

"I don't know much about kids, Raina. If I heard him say something like that, I'd probably…." Probably what? He'd hardly known his own father, so he was short on memorable examples. "Well, I'd probably say the wrong thing."

"I probably already have." She added cream to her coffee and stirred until the mixture was well past blended. "Listen, I know you're busy. I don't expect you to entertain us. I thought if Peter could meet some people, maybe some kids his age, and participate in some of the—"

"It might be a little risky." Avoiding her eyes, he sipped his coffee.

"Why?"

"Because he might run into—" He was tempted to say *more complications than culture,* but that would sound like a defeatist attitude. "Some problems, maybe. You never know. A lot of people are up in arms over this treaty issue. We don't have much land left, but we've got a treaty that says we've got major hunting and fishing rights, and we're suing the state over it. Even though there's precedence in our favor, the non-Indian landowners and the resorts and the sportsmen's groups are making all kinds of threats. The tourist trade is down this summer because of all the controversy." He wrapped both hands around the mug of coffee, took a deep breath and admitted with a sigh, "It's not a good time to learn about being an Indian."

"What *would* be a good time? When there is no controversy?"

He chuckled. "Good point. We'd need a time machine to take us back a few hundred years, wouldn't we? But I don't know about—" *Right here, right now.* What he should have told her was that he didn't have the time. That would settle it, at least for the time being.

But he had a strange feeling that the die had been cast and that there was no point in trying to change the numbers that had come up. They would just come back. Sooner or later, the same combination would turn up again. Raina, Peter and Gideon. Along with maybe a ghost or two.

Gideon glanced at the door, as though he were expecting someone to come through it and rescue him. Jared, maybe. The brother who did everything by the book. *Read it to me, brother. Where do I go from here?*

"It might be a better idea if we got together someplace else. Neutral territory."

"Neutral? I don't understand, Gideon. Am I unwelcome here? This was my husband's home."

He gestured with an exception-taking forefinger. "It was a place your husband put behind him, with very little time spent looking back."

"Not on my account. I never really understood why he stayed away. Believe me, I never asked him to. In fact, if he'd wanted to, I would have—"

"It doesn't matter anymore. We made our choices, the three of us, and it worked out the way it worked out." He leaned back in the booth, taking a moment to study her, to wonder what she would have done if he himself had asked her. Since he'd denied himself the chance, he didn't want to know the answer, but there had been many a time when he'd taken an awful kind of pleasure in torturing himself with that question, and others.

But those were the days when he'd taken his pleasure where he could get it. No more.

"So you're back again. Full circle, Raina." And she would find that things had changed some. Gideon had changed. He tipped the coffee mug, studied the contents as though he were reading tea leaves, then nodded. "You need a fishing guide, I guess I'm your man."

"I'm not asking you to just drop everything on such short notice. I mean, I know you're much too…"

"Too what?"

"Too busy now. I'm sure."

"You're not sure." He shook his head slowly, half smiling, taking a new and perverse pleasure in protracting her discomfort. "Not about me, Raina. You never were."

* * *

He tried to dismiss the uncomfortable sense of foreboding that plagued him as he followed her up the stairs. If he could handle himself around lawyers and politicians, he could surely deal with a twelve-year-old kid without getting warm in the face and sweaty in the palms. 'Course, maybe that was just a reaction to following Raina up the stairs. He had to remind himself that she wasn't taking him to her bedroom, the way he used to dream she would back when he was a man of large cravings and little character. She was asking him to do her a service, not to service her, and, damn his own hide, it was the least he could do.

But seeing the boy for the first time in over two years, actually seeing the boy with the controls of a child's game in his hands and what had to be man-size tennis shoes on his feet, was a real gut-twister. Before the boy even opened his mouth, he reminded Gideon of Jared. Spitting image, just in the way he moved his hands and the way he spared only a glance for the two people who had entered his domain when he was clearly occupied with important business. Like father, like son, Gideon told himself ironically. He found himself digging deep for an easy, breezy smile as he offered the boy a handshake.

"How's it going, Peter? You remember me?"

"Sure." One last jiggle of a button elicited an artificial explosion from the game. Peter gave a victorious nod, switched it off and accepted Gideon's greeting. "You're Uncle Gideon. You took my dad and me fishing once."

"Seems like a long time ago, doesn't it?"

"It was. I was just a little kid. I remember, though." Peter stepped back as he measured a foot and a half of space between his hands. "I caught a fish that was like *this long*."

"Close." Gideon shoved his hands in his pockets as he looked the boy over. Damn, he'd gotten tall. "The three of us had fun that time, didn't we?"

"Yeah, I guess it was pretty good."

"Wanna try it again?" With a gesture, Gideon invited Raina to join in the reunion. "Take your mom along this time?"

"I guess that's what we're here for." Peter shot his mother a sullen look. "It was this or else get dragged to someplace like Disney World."

"Peter actually chose Pine Lake over Disney World," Raina confirmed.

"Well, that doesn't surprise me. Lots of people choose Pine Lake over Disney World." Gideon clapped a hand on Peter's bony shoulder. "A born fisherman just naturally knows where to come for the best walleye fishing in the country."

"But we realize you have tribal business to attend to, Gideon, and Peter and I don't want to get in the way of your—"

"You won't be in my way." Gideon slid his hand away from the boy's shoulder, disappointed that his friendly gesture hadn't changed the guarded look in Peter's eyes. He turned to Raina. "But we've had a little trouble lately, just so you know. A couple of incidents down at the public boat landings made the local news."

"I haven't heard about any real violence," Raina said.

"No violence so far. Just some verbal confrontations between some of the so-called sportsmen's groups and some of our people." He shrugged. "Rednecks versus Indians. Same old story. A lot of name-calling. Some threats tossed back and forth. The kind of stuff you don't want your kids to hear." *Anybody's* kids, he thought, recalling the vulgar words thrown around like hot potatoes in a game no kid needed to be taught to play. "Adults setting the kind of example you wish kids didn't have to see."

"Kids know how to form their own opinions," Peter claimed.

"Anybody ever ask you for yours?" Gideon asked. He was inclined to try laying a friendly hand on Peter's shoulder again, but the look in the boy's eyes warned him not to push. "I mean, like your friends or your teachers at school? They know you're Chippewa, right?"

"They know I'm an Indian."

A distant look came into the boy's eyes. Gideon knew exactly what it meant, and he knew why Raina glanced away. She knew, too, but not from experience. And that was what troubled her most.

"Do they have a problem with that?" Gideon asked gently.

"No way, not my friends," Peter declared defensively. Then, with a shrug, he qualified his claim. "One guy asked me why Natives think they should have special fishing privileges, like higher limits and using spears and some kind of nets."

"Gill nets," Gideon supplied. "So what did you tell him?"

Peter shrugged again. "I told him I didn't know anything about any special privileges. I've only been fishing about three times in my entire life, and I used a pole." He looked to Gideon for confirmation. "I did, didn't I? I don't remember any weird kind of nets or anything."

"You used a rod and reel, and I had you casting pretty good for such a little guy."

"I can't exactly see me throwing a spear into the water like some kind of wild man."

Gideon laughed, even though, deep down, he hurt for

the boy's choice of words. "You're not much of a wild man, huh?"

"Maybe with a video game, but not a spear. Besides, from what I hear, if the Natives get to use spears and nets, pretty soon there won't be any walleye left in the lakes."

"Really?" Peter's assumptions echoed the accusations being bandied back and forth in the media and the halls of the Minnesota legislature lately. It chilled him to realize that it wasn't just the so-called sportsmen he had to worry about. It was the kids Peter's age who had no reason to question what they were hearing. The books from which they learned their history told a distorted story. Popular culture had turned his people into stereotypes and foolish-looking mascots. The critics were legion, and there were so few Native American voices left to be heard.

And for Peter, who was growing up surrounded by caricatures and critics, it must have been scary to hear all this stuff, then look in the mirror and see himself, living and breathing inside real Chippewa skin. It had to make him wonder, *What the hell is this all about?*

And Jared had neglected to leave the answer book behind.

Which left Gideon.

He gestured instructively. "Spearfishing is a sport that non-Indians indulge in during the winter, so they've made sure it's legal then. But spearfishing for our people is a food-gathering skill. We have traditionally practiced it in the spring for hundreds of years. And there are still plenty of walleye."

"Yeah, but they say there won't be if you guys get your way." Hearing himself, Peter instinctively looked to his mother for help, then shook his head, as though coming to his senses. "I mean, if you get this treaty settlement thing."

"Who says that?" Gideon asked.

Peter shrugged. "I don't know. Some of the guys whose families have lake cabins and stuff."

"What *they* say and what's true are often two different things. Our people have never endangered the fish, and we don't ever intend to."

Now it was time, welcome or not, for Gideon to lay that friendly hand on Peter's shoulder again. The boy did, indeed, need him.

"I think your mother's right. It's time you did a little fishing with your uncle Gideon."

Chapter 2

Gideon had taken her fishing only once before. They'd had a good time together—the *best* of times. And the worst, as well. As she pulled on a comfortable pair of khaki slacks, Raina remembered how the day had begun all those years ago with an admonishment from her roommate, Paula, to "dress warm."

She had bundled up in her down-filled jacket and her insulated boots. The snow pants she'd borrowed were so thickly padded that she could barely bend her knees as she climbed into Gideon's battered green pickup. Lifting her onto the blanket-covered seat was like tossing an armload of satin pillows onto an army cot, he'd teased.

Oh, she remembered that deep, rich chuckle close to her ear. She couldn't have worn enough layers to protect her from the quick shiver that exciting sound had sent shimmying from the side of her neck to the tips of her toes. Gideon had always had a way with shivers, a way that continually challenged her to anticipate his next move. It had been a talent too titillating, too unpredictable.

It had scared her silly.

And silly was the way she remembered behaving when she'd ventured reluctantly onto the frozen lake. The glare from the distant winter sun had nearly snow-blinded her. Despite Gideon's assurances that the ice was well over a foot thick, she hadn't been able to forget that it wasn't all ice. That there was still water down there somewhere. Deep, cold, breath-stealing water that would swallow her up if her foot found a patch of thin ice….

"It could happen," Raina insisted. She tested her footing and found that, sure enough, ice was ice, and it was slippery. "I've read about shifting currents, treacherous weak spots."

"I've got a treacherous weak spot, darlin'." He was unloading fishing gear from his pickup, but he managed to shift the tackle box and cooler to one arm so he could steady her with the other. "Deep down in my heart, and I think it's got your name on it."

"What a line." She laughed as she slipped her arm around his waist. "So corny it's actually sweet," she quipped, playfully bumping hips with him as they slip-slid toward the little fishing shack he'd said belonged to a friend of his.

"Mmm. Sweet corn makes a good side dish, don't you think?"

"What's the main dish?"

"You are."

She looked up, feigning surprise.

He dropped a quick kiss on her pouty mouth. "Come on, now, you should've seen that one coming."

"I did. I decided to accommodate you, since you're the host."

"Guide," he corrected. "The man who's gonna show you the way, sweetheart."

"The way to…?"

"Heaven." He gave a sly wink as he shoved a key into the padlock on the door. "Or supper. Take your pick."

She was tempted to tell him that she really wanted heaven. Might as well admit it right off the bat. Everything about him said sexy. The way he walked, the way he laughed, the way he wore his jeans, everything. The trouble was, Raina was wary of heights. She believed in working her way up, testing all the footholds along the way. Meanwhile, she wanted a third choice. She liked the word *maybe*. Maybe later, in a few weeks or months, after they'd shared lots of suppers and made commitments, maybe *then*…. Heaven sounded awfully good to her.

With Gideon, nothing came easily, not even a simple supper. He did make ice fishing look simple, even with a spear, which required a larger hole than the icehouse would allow. So he dazzled her with his skill several yards away from the house, and then they took his catch inside. She was surprised to find that the little house actually had chairs and a card table inside. There was a small heater, and Gideon had brought a camp stove for cooking. Once he'd gotten the appliances going, he squatted next to a hole that had been drilled in the middle of the floor and began chipping away at the ice that had formed since the last time the icehouse had been used.

"What's that for?" Raina asked. "Don't we have enough?"

"No appreciation for the sport," he complained to the hole in the ice. "This is our excuse for being out here. Otherwise we look pretty stupid, sitting out here in the middle of a frozen lake." He grinned up at her, his hands braced on his knees as he prepared to stand. "Officially, it's your line that's going down here. I'm giving you the chance to catch the big one, darlin', so you can brag to your friends."

"A hook at the end of a line is my best chance," she agreed. "Obviously I'll never have your talent for spearing."

"It takes practice. Either that or you have to be born to it." He stood, ducking to avoid bumping his head on the low roof. His baiting smile loomed over her. "As you've probably heard, some of us just naturally come complete with the necessary equipment."

"You might find this hard to believe," she said, returning a coy smile, "but some of *us* are perfectly content to let you carry that particular burden around with you constantly."

He chuckled appreciatively as he rummaged through his tackle box, and she figured she was racking up points for her side. He handed her several pieces of tackle.

"Ah, yes." She looked them over, ostensibly weighing them in her hands. "The hook, line and sinker are so much less cumbersome."

"Maybe." Going about the business of setting a line, he sank into an ice-fisherman's crouch. "But I'll bet you're gonna ask me to bait yours for you."

She returned the bits of tackle he'd given her, with a prim "If you insist." She didn't know what to do with the stuff, anyway. She unzipped her jacket.

"Here, I'll trade you."

It surprised her when he produced a pint of whiskey from his box of supplies, sampled it, then extended it her way. "Help yourself. Warm yourself up inside."

"I'm fine, thanks." She wasn't sure what bothered her about it. Maybe it was just the idea of nipping from a bottle, or the fact that she'd felt as though she were on a roll with her clever repartee and suddenly he'd suggested a different kind of fun. The kind that made her nervous. "A little too warm, in fact."

"Nice and cozy, isn't it?"

He didn't seem to notice the change in her tone. Which was fine. She didn't want him to. She wasn't a kid anymore, and he surely wasn't. In fact, she found it hard to imagine that he ever had been.

He took another drink, then pointed with the bottle toward the hole. "Your job is to watch that line. I'll fry up the first course while you catch the second." Again he offered the whiskey. "Maybe *you* haven't heard, but this is part of the fun of ice fishing."

"I don't know how you can drink it straight like that," she said, shaking the bottle off with a grimace.

"Your trusty guide will show you how." He took a longer sip this time. "Easy as sin, once you get past the initial burn."

"With sin, the burn comes later, doesn't it?"

"When I find out, I'll give you a holler." His naughty grin was enticing. "All it takes is one belt to chase the chill."

"I'm not cold." In answer to that grin of his, her indulgent smile probably looked prudish. "Neither are you."

"No, but I'm sinful." And it didn't bother him one bit. Neither did her prudishness. He favored her with another of his charming winks. "And you're not quite sure whether it turns you on or scares the hell out of you."

Rather than admit to both, she stood silent, and he went about his cooking. She was more interested in watching Gideon than watching the fishing line. His broad shoulders seemed to fill one whole side of the ice shack. His size dwarfed the little camp stove over which he happily busied himself cooking their meal. The truth was that every move he made turned her on, even the occasional nip he took from the bottle. He probably didn't realize that in high school she'd had a reputation for being somewhat aloof. She glanced at the hole in the ice and smiled to herself. The term "cold fish" had been bandied about, actually. Not that it mattered, since she'd dated only boys she could count on to be, well, almost as scrupulous in their behavior as she was.

All right, the truth was that the boys with the *un*scrupulous reputations never asked her out. Not that they hadn't flirted with her once in a while, and not that she hadn't occasionally flirted back. But going out with her would have been a waste of a precious Friday night with the family car.

Apparently her reputation hadn't preceded her when she'd come to Pine Lake. The thought almost made her laugh out loud, and the joke was on her, for imagining a locker-room network that extended this far. It was time to grow up, she told herself. Time to stop playing games. Time to try a different kind of…

"You've got a bite there, daydreamer."

"What?"

Arms folded over his chest, Gideon stood there grinning down at her. "If you weren't afraid to touch the thing, you'd have felt it."

"What thing?"

"The *long* thing—" the look in his eyes grew deliciously devilish "—that I dropped in the hole for you, sweetheart." He chuckled. "Your hook, line and sinker."

"Oh." She reached for the line. "What should I do? Pull on it?"

"Too late now. You lost him. You scared him away with that word *pull*." He sucked air through his teeth, as if the word pained him. "Use a light touch, honey. Jigging works better." He turned back to his cooking, clucking his tongue in mock disgust. "Remember that when he gives you another chance."

In the end they had to make do with his catch, which made the freshest-tasting fish dinner Raina had ever eaten. She took off her snow pants and used them for a chair cushion, and she and Gideon played cards and listened to country music on the radio. Gideon got a little tight and played the ham, crooning along with every tune while he slapped his cards on the folding table with a flourish and beat her three hands of whist out of five.

Then he pulled her onto his lap and started in with some playful kissing. Together they quickly heated up the icehouse. Before she knew what was happening she was straddling him, and he was holding her hips steady while he rocked himself in her cradle, pushed her jacket aside, opened her shirt and suckled her breast until she moaned with exquisite pleasure.

"Pretty as an angel," he muttered, then nuzzled her hair aside from her ear and whispered, "but are you willing to give the devil his due?"

"What devil?"

"You're sittin' on his lap, honey."

"I doubt that." She combed his long, thick hair back from his temples with her fingers. His hair was as black and as beautiful as a raven's wing. "I'll buy 'sinner,' but not 'devil.'"

"Sold," he said softly as he unsnapped her jeans. "To the lady with the shiny halo."

"No, I'm not…no." Her zipper was halfway down before she stayed his hand with hers. But he turned her hand and pressed it against his own zipper and let her feel the hard bulge straining beneath it.

"You wanna pull on something, pull on my belt buckle, okay?" He slipped his hand inside her jeans, and the zipper gave the rest of the way. He tucked his thumb over the top of her panties. "Do this to me," he entreated, his breath warm against her neck.

"Gideon, we can't. Not now." She tipped her head back and gulped cool air. The plywood ceiling seemed so close. "Not... here."

"Not here and now?" His hand stirred at her waist. His low voice sounded somehow menacing. "Or not you and me?"

She slid her hand away from his lap and put her arms over his shoulders. Her pulse was racing so wildly, she wasn't sure she could achieve her indulgent, goddess-of-good-sense smile, but she gave it a shot.

"Have you drunk enough to make you forget that the floor is made of ice here?"

"No." The heated look he gave her was far from contrite. "I'm not drunk."

"I didn't say you were." She wanted him to kiss her. Just kiss her, and maybe... "Gideon, don't look at me like that. It scares me."

"I want to make love to you." He tightened his hand at her waist, and the heat in his eyes made her mouth go dry. "Why would that scare you?"

"If you could see the look in your eyes..."

"I'm hungry for you, Raina."

"It's more than that."

There was a predatory gleam in his eyes, and she suspected the whiskey was responsible for that. She liked having control, and this man threatened to take that from her. He made her scare herself. He made her want to let go, just for a moment. And something told her that a moment would be all it would take. He belonged to the wilderness and the wildlife. And Raina's world was much too tame for him.

"I could make it much more." He nuzzled the promise into

the valley between her breasts and made her catch her breath. "I could make you hungry for me."

He already had, but she wouldn't indulge herself. Not with icy water lapping at a hole in a floor of ice in a rickety shack in the middle of a frozen lake in the middle of absolutely nowhere. Lord!

Her hands trembled as she pushed against him. "Please don't do this, Gideon."

She slid off his lap awkwardly. His hand shot out, but only to keep her from stumbling into the hole in the ice. "Watch your step, little girl."

"I'm not a little girl."

"My mistake," he muttered, eyeing the breasts that were only partially curtained by her open shirt.

"But I'm certainly not…" Not what? She felt foolish. He was fully dressed. She was the one totally disheveled, panting, on the verge of screaming and moaning at the same time.

"Check your other line, honey." He nodded toward the hole in the ice. "The name of the game is catch and release."

"I'm not playing a game," she said.

"Neither am I."

That was all it took with Gideon Defender. "Please don't." The words seemed to drive him back into the woods.

They had run into each other at a party a few weeks later, and he had introduced her to his brother. Then he'd stepped aside and quietly watched, as though he were testing for her reaction. It was a move she'd resented, and she'd told him so, the same night she'd told him that Jared had asked her out and she'd accepted. He'd expressed no surprise, offered no objections, mentioned no regrets. Not that it would have mattered, since she'd made up her mind. But it had hurt. Just a little.

Jared had never asked her how she'd felt about his brother. Other than a certain physical resemblance, the two brothers had little in common. Jared had a different brand of charm. More practiced, perhaps. More polished. He had gone to the University of Minnesota in Minneapolis, while Gideon had, for the most part, preferred to stay in the north country among the people he'd grown up with, in touch with the life he knew. In the end, Jared had chosen Raina's world. And Raina had chosen Jared.

They'd both wanted children, and when a pregnancy hadn't occurred soon enough to suit Jared, they had adopted Peter. Raina hadn't questioned the decision when Jared announced that the opportunity for a baby had unexpectedly presented itself. His low sperm count was an issue he neither wanted to discuss nor fret about. He'd had some childhood health problems that he didn't care to discuss, either. They had been blessed with a perfectly beautiful son, and all was well.

For a time after that they had been a fairly typical suburban family. Raina had quit her job to stay home with Peter until he started school, and then she'd only worked outside their home part-time, while Jared had worked too hard. He'd found less and less time to be at home as his time, unbeknownst to him, slipped away quickly. Eventually there had been no chance for visits to Pine Lake, and then suddenly, irrevocably, the time was gone.

At least, *his* time was gone. At first Raina had had to remind herself that hers was not. But not lately. Ever since adolescence had overtaken her son and transformed him like some kind of fairy-tale curse, she had no trouble remembering that she had miles to go and challenges to meet.

Like another fishing trip with Gideon.

"Are you ready, Peter?" He'd been in the bathroom forever. A year ago, sixty seconds in the shower and he was out. "You know, your hair doesn't have to be perfect. We're going out *fishing*. Uncle Gideon said he'd pick us up at the dock in—"

The door finally opened, and her son deigned to emerge. His beautiful black hair was still wet, so she assumed that the new pimple on his chin was the reason for the stormy look in his eyes. He was hoping for *hair* on his chin, he'd informed her a few weeks ago when she'd tried to tell him that the occasional pimple was not the end of the world. A man's beard, he'd said. Not a wimpy zit.

Raina was not ready for either development. Not quite yet.

"Why don't you just call him Gideon?" Peter's scowl was ominous. "He's not your uncle."

"He's *your* uncle. He's your father's brother."

"Yeah, well…where did you hide the damn hair dryer?"

"Peter, please don't talk like that." She handed him the blow-dryer, and he mumbled his thanks. "You told me that this was where you wanted to come. We're here. The next step is to venture beyond this room."

"It's been a long time since I've been up this way." Barefoot and so far dressed only in his favorite ripped-knee jeans, he plopped on the rumpled bed he'd claimed as his, then fell back as though he'd just run a marathon. "I mean, I was just a kid. I don't know *him*. I don't know anybody here, and I feel like I'm supposed to. It's weird."

"I know." She sat down beside him and patted one knobby knee. "You miss your dad."

"You always wanna blame everything on that." He pushed up on his elbows and looked her in the eye. "It's *not* that."

"Tell me what's wrong, then."

"Nothing's wrong. Why does something always have to be wrong? I just—" Dramatically he flopped back down again. "It isn't like what I thought it was gonna be."

"You haven't been out of the room yet." She knew it was no use to ask what he was looking for. He didn't know. "Let's go see what it's going to be like. Give it a chance. If it's no good, we'll go home."

He sat up. "Is there a damn plug around here?"

There went her chance to use the bathroom. "Try—"

"Following the lamp cord, I know." He dived for the head of the bed and tossed pillows over his shoulder like an overgrown pup burying a bone.

She laughed and shook her head when he announced, "Pay dirt." Then he flopped on his belly and hung his head over the side of the bed, brushing his hair forward. "You know what, though?" He tucked his chin and turned to look at her upside down. "He seems pretty cool."

"Who?"

She held out her hand for the dryer, making an offer she hoped would hurry things along. It was the kind of thing he might have asked her to do for him a year or so ago. Now he might be offended. Then again, he might take her up on it. She never knew which way he was going to jump next.

"Uncle Gideon." He plunked the dryer in her hand. "*Gideon*. You know what Dad told me once? That his brother got all the looks, and he got the brains."

"Your father said that?" She turned the machine on low and directed it at his nape, gently finger-combing his hair and feeling favored by his willingness to confide a remembrance, and to still let her coddle him once in a while.

So Gideon had all the looks, huh? He was the younger of the two, but physically, Gideon was the big brother. He'd certainly never shared Jared's taste for expensive clothes, and she remembered Jared teasing Gideon about his need for a barber once. His hair wasn't as long as it used to be, but it was still shoulder-length, still an attractive expression of his own personality. But nothing, surely, that Jared would covet in any way.

"That was a strange thing for him to say. Your dad was very handsome, and Gideon is…" She shrugged. "Gideon is Gideon."

Peter peeked up at her. "What's that supposed to mean?"

"It means it's been a long time since I've been up this way, too." She smiled and turned the dryer on full blast.

Gideon was waiting, as promised. He was sitting at the end of one of the lodge's boat docks, basking in the sun and chatting with a boy about Peter's age. Below their dangling tennis shoes was a fishing boat with cushioned chairs and two outboard motors—one for trolling.

Gideon turned when he heard footfalls treading the planks. They were late, and Raina half expected him to check his watch and ask where they'd been. But he smiled as he hopped to his feet and tapped the boy on the shoulder, coaxing him to follow suit. Raina liked the way the spokes at the corners of his eyes made his smile seem even brighter, and the easy way he handled himself put everyone else at ease, too. From the look of him, it appeared that the years had been kinder to Gideon than they had been to his brother. But then, maybe it was true, Raina thought. Maybe Gideon had all the looks.

"This is Oscar Thompson. He's been camped out in my office ever since I told him I was thinking about going fishing pretty soon." The two boys shook hands. "That was last May, wasn't it, Oscar?"

Oscar shrugged. "Before school was out."

"See there? And here we're going fishing already. Fishing lesson number one—" Gideon squinted into the sun and brandished a finger "—patience. Everyone wants to go fishing with me, because everyone knows…"

"He's got a good boat," Oscar put in.

"...that ol' Gideon knows exactly where to go lookin' for Mr. Walleye. Plus, I've got some extra tackle."

He took a pair of aviator-style sunglasses from his pocket, put them on as though he were preparing to read a sign and made a production of surveying Raina from head to toe. "So, I see Mom's wearing the proper fishing attire, all nicely coordinated. Matching shoes and hat."

Raina compared his cutoffs and T-shirt with her neatly pressed yellow blouse and khaki slacks. "Heck, I'm casual," she said. "Don't you like my fishing hat?"

"It's very...yellow. But I think we can fix that in a real hurry. Right, boys?"

The round of male chuckles would have bothered her if it hadn't been exactly what she'd come looking for. For Peter's sake, of course.

"What about a license?" Gideon asked.

"License?"

"Fishing license. See, the three of us are okay because we have tribal ID." He arched an eyebrow in Peter's direction. "You brought yours along, I hope?"

Peter cast an accusatory glance at the person he considered responsible for the boring technical details of his adolescent life—his mother—as he reported, "I didn't know I had one."

"You do," she said. "I brought it."

"You've got yourself a good assistant there, kid. If you're smart, you'll pay her well." He turned to Raina. "But no fishing license, huh?"

She shook her head.

He shook his, too. "And you look just all heartbroken about it. We can get you one over at the tackle shop."

"I'll just go along for the ride this time."

"Good woman." Gideon clapped a hand on each boy's shoulder. "Then we're set."

Raina let the *good woman* comment go unchallenged. She didn't want to question anything, justify anything or fish for anything. Just going along for the ride was exactly what the doctor had ordered. It was early evening, the best time of a summer's day. The sun's slanted rays became bright flashes in the water. When the boat was moving, she could close her eyes and catch the wind in her face while her hand trailed in the cool wake. When they anchored in the shallows, she could simply enjoy her son's growing excitement for the relaxing sport as Gideon patiently tutored his casting arm.

"Good catch." Gideon gave Peter a shoulder slap of approval. "Now take him off the hook and throw him back."

Peter looked up in near horror. "Throw him *back?*"

"We're fishing for supper for the four of us." Gideon appraised the small wriggling crappie that Peter had just pulled proudly from the water. "That's guy's not worth bothering with. We want nice, pan-sized—"

"Gideon, I think that's a wonderful fish!" Raina sharpened her bright tone with a defensive edge. "A beautiful fish. I think we should have it stuffed and mounted."

"This isn't like bronzing his baby shoes, Raina. We're looking for food." He nodded toward the cooler containing the fish Oscar had already caught. "Right, Pete?"

"I guess so." Peter looked at his catch again. "He's too small, huh?"

Those motherly instincts would not rest. A quick justification tingled on the tip of Raina's tongue.

But Gideon headed her off with a warning glance. "Put him down in the water and see if he's gonna make it. We don't return dead fish to the lake."

Peter complied, his face brightening when, revived by the

water, the little fish flipped its tail and swam away. "There, see?" Gideon watched the boy's first catch in six years head out to the middle of the lake. He promised himself it wouldn't be the last one for this season. Not by a long shot. "He's a survivor, like us. If we catch you next year, brother fish, you'll make a fine meal."

They dropped their lines again. Once Peter had caught a pan-worthy fish, Gideon put in at the public boat landing, where he would take his boat out of the water. There was no one else waiting to use the boat ramp, and his pickup and trailer were parked in the public parking lot. Soon he would be cooking up a meal for Raina and the boys. Soon he would be able to show her that he had a little place of his own now. He'd been looking forward to this day for a long time.

Gideon cut the motor, while Oscar took up his assigned post in the bow and prepared to catch a mooring. As the boat drifted toward the dock, Gideon smelled trouble. The odor came from the four young men who were hanging out right where Gideon planned to step ashore. The signs were all there—the four accusatory stares, the folded arms, the set of the jaws. The gist of the quick comments passed among them was easily interpreted visually—Gideon didn't need to hear those words. He had heard it all before.

"I'll tie her up, Oscar," Gideon said quietly.

But it was too late to switch places. "I've got it," Oscar muttered, reaching for a piling as the boat drifted in to the dock.

They could have been ordinary boaters or fishermen—and most days they probably were. They sure didn't look like anybody's idea of a gang, but the tough-kid posturing was there—the insolence, the confidence in bully power.

The first man to speak wore a Redskins T-shirt. "You got any illegal nets in there, chief?"

"Do you know who you're talking to?" Oscar looked up, scowling as he slipped the nylon rope around the post. "He *is* the chief."

"I don't give a damn if he's Tonto himself," the man said as he adjusted the bill of his Twins cap. "You guys out spearing fish today?"

"Nobody's spearing any fish." Gideon grabbed the piling, planted one foot on the dock and rose to tower over the gang's spokesman.

"Oh, yeah? So you claim." The man stepped back, his friends covering his flanks as he jabbed a finger at Gideon. "You guys better drop this little plan to get special privileges for yourselves. There's no way you're gonna start netting and spearing in these waters. The sports fishermen in this state won't stand for it."

"You're in my way," Gideon said calmly.

"No, you're in my way." The man settled one hand on his hip, but on the other hand, that finger was still jabbing. "You're trying real hard to get in *my* way."

Gideon returned a level stare. "This gesture shows me that you have no manners. Touch me with it, and you will have no finger."

The man sniggered, then checked to make sure he wasn't alone and sniggered again. But the finger came down.

This was a public landing. Gideon had half a notion to punch this blockhead's lights out. He could take him easy, and the three jerks backing him to boot. A few years back there would have been no question. Just impulse. But now, besides the fact that he had a woman and two kids with him, he had to remember who he was and what he stood for.

Damn. Standing for more than just Gideon Defender could be a royal pain sometimes. He couldn't walk away and leave Raina and the boys with the boat as long as these guys were standing there. He was going to have to back down and take the boat back to the lodge rather than load it up here and take his guests up the road to his cabin. He didn't have his own dock. Couldn't afford it. This was prime tourist territory. Thanks to all the damn treaties, the Pine Lake Band was land poor. Three thousand meager acres and some hunting and fishing rights were all they could call their own. The only dock space they actually owned was at the lodge.

Public landing? Hell.

"You need any help getting your boat out of the water, Gideon?"

No one had noticed the timely appearance of Bill Lucas, a conservation officer with the Minnesota Department of Natural Resources. The gang of four didn't seem too pleased when they turned to find him walking up behind them.

But Gideon was glad to hear his old friend's voice. "Not if these boys would just step aside so I can go get my pickup."

Bill's uniform probably had something to do with the way the small crowd parted for him. "You boys have a problem with that?"

"No problem at all," the Redskins fan said, "unless they're taking more than their rightful limit."

"How does that concern you? I don't see a badge on any of you."

"I own a cabin on this lake." The claim was made by one of the three backups. "Along with my dad, that is. That's how it concerns me. All this talk of the state cuttin' some kinda deal with the Indians, I was just tellin' this one here, we're not gonna stand for any gill nets, and none of their spearfishing, either."

"You talk to your legislator about it. You call the attorney general's office," Bill suggested. "You don't bother these people. This is a public landing. We don't want any—"

The Twins cap got another adjustment as its wearer did some more posturing. "We just want to let 'em know what's comin' down the pike if they don't drop this thing. You remember the violence in Wisconsin over the same issue."

"We're trying to avoid the kind of trouble they had over treaty rights in Wisconsin." Bill glanced his friend's way. "Gideon here's Chippewa. He can go over to Wisconsin and do all the spearfishing and gill netting the law allows."

"Yeah, well, go on over to Wisconsin, then, 'cause you ain't gettin' anywhere with that here." The four started edging away as the summer cabin owner made his final point, driving his finger toward the dock like a nail. "We won't stand for it here."

His buddy added his concurrence—a quick glare and another adjustment of the baseball cap—and the four sauntered down the dock toward a club cab four-wheel drive pickup that was parked at the end.

"His family's probably been coming up to their summer cabin on the lake for what—two, three generations?" Gideon's gesture was one of empty-handed frustration. "You know how long *my* family's lived on this lake year-round? You know how many generations, Bill?"

"No, do you?" Bill raised his palms and chuckled as he shook his head. "No, don't answer that. You'll be reciting the whole history for me again."

"For you guys it's history, for us it's tradition."

"Either way, anybody can see you've got a good case." Bill shrugged. "Anybody with an open mind, that is. Seems like the more we talk this compromise up, the more guys like that dig in their heels. Never gonna change his mind."

"Then we'll end up in court."

Bill nodded. The department recognized that possibility. And dreaded the likely outcome.

Gideon turned his attention to the boat and the three people who were waiting for him. He leaned down to offer Raina a hand.

"Catch anything?" Bill asked Oscar, who was still in charge of mooring the boat.

Oscar smiled. "Supper."

And that had always been just what fishing meant to Gideon's people. Supper.

Chapter 3

Supper was a joint project. Gideon had done some shopping with the intention of pleasing his guests at any cost. Raina was amused by the choice of skim milk or whole, butter or margarine, white potatoes or red. "Or rice. If anyone hates potatoes, I've got rice." He offered every salad leaf imaginable, whole wheat or white bread, three flavors of ice cream, for which he was sorry he didn't have any marshmallow cream.

"Marshmallow cream?" Peter pretended instant nausea.

"Hey, that stuff's good, man," Oscar said.

"Are you starting a restaurant?" Raina wondered with an appreciative smile.

Gideon shrugged. "I know kids have sensitive taste buds."

"I'll eat anything," Oscar promised. And he did. He ate *everything*.

"Me too." But Peter asked for *his* fish—the one he'd caught himself—red potatoes and blue cheese on his salad.

The blue cheese was one request Gideon hadn't anticipated. "Next time," he promised.

Raina liked his house, and she made a point of telling him so. It had no feminine touches and didn't need any. Made of logs and furnished with a functional combination of old chairs and new stereo equipment, it was comfortable. And it was Gideon.

After supper he and Raina sat on the little screened porch at the back of the house, enjoying the chorus of crickets, listening to the water lapping at the shoreline, sharing coffee. He had a view of the lake, which glistened with the pink and purple shades of twilight, but he possessed no pricey piece of lakeshore. He didn't have much of a yard, but he was within shouting distance of the end of the neighbor's dock, where the boys sat, dangling their feet in the water like Tom Sawyer and Huck Finn.

"When you guys get tired of donating blood, there's a can of repellent up here," he called out. Through the dusky shadows, he smiled at Raina. "Specially formulated to ward off the Minnesota state bird."

"Mosquitos?"

"Want some? I think there's a hole in the screen somewhere." She shook her head. "Not your scent, huh? Yours is more flowery." He leaned across the arms of the wicker chairs they occupied, the arm of his touching the arm of hers, and drew a deep breath. Another mistake, he thought, as his blood rushed to harden his sex. That scent was all it took. "The same one you always wore."

"One bottle lasts me a long time," she said, as though it might possibly be a relic from years past. "Actually, I haven't worn it in a while. I haven't been dressing up much, or..." It sounded like an apology. "Perfume is one of the frivolities I'd all but given up lately."

"Nice touch for a fishing expedition." He wanted to keep his thoughts to himself, so he teased, "Classy bait."

"It wasn't—"

"Intentional, I know." It was working its magic on him, anyway. "I don't know what to make of this visit, Raina. After all this time, you suddenly show up with—"

"Peter. I came for Peter's sake." By way of apology, she touched his arm. "That's becoming a familiar refrain for me, isn't it? And it's not the whole truth." Her sigh seemed distant in the near darkness. "I never intended to stay away. I enjoyed teaching here. We had friends here, and Jared's family, of course. I suggested to him once that we leave the rat race and come back here. I thought maybe he'd like to offer the Pine Lake Band his legal services, and I could go back to teaching." She sighed and shook her head, remembering her husband's answer. "'You can't go home again,' he'd say. And that always bothered me."

"Why?"

"Because I was afraid it was because of me that he stayed away. Because of me that he was so—" she waved her hand, the gesture evaporating into the shadows "—driven to succeed. And that's what killed him. That's what—"

"Are you looking for credit or blame?" His tone sounded sharper than he'd intended. He tempered it. "Either way, you're way off base. Jared was always ambitious. I'm surprised he came back here when he did, even for a short time." He remembered Jared's explanation. The high school history teacher had quit in the middle of the school year, and Jared needed to earn some money so he could continue with law school. "But if he hadn't, he wouldn't have met you."

"If you hadn't introduced us…"

"It might have prolonged the agony for, what, another week?" He'd told himself they would have met, anyway, even though she was an elementary schoolteacher. For some reason, Gideon had wanted it to be *his* idea when she met his brother.

"What agony?"

"You and me." He chuckled, remembering. "Fire and ice."

"You were the one who had a thing for ice."

"You bet I did."

"And a thing for fire*water*."

"That, too," he admitted quietly. "Which wasn't your style. And neither was I."

"Nor I yours. So you introduced me to your brother."

After several moments of seemingly respectful silence, he asked, "Do you miss him, Raina?"

She turned, ready to challenge his insolence, but the words dissolved on the tip of her tongue when she saw the distant look in his eyes. And the sadness.

"Do you ever think you hear his voice and go looking out the window, just for a second actually expecting him to be there?"

"Your voice sounds exactly like his on the phone." She remembered his call early one morning. No hello, no name, just a voice, a continuation of a dream. He'd said he was sending her some old yearbooks. She'd struggled to find more than a two-word answer. "A bit unsettling in kind of a bittersweet way," she told him now in the hope that, if he remembered, he would forgive her reticence after the fact.

But he had other recollections to share.

"We were close when we were kids, up until he went away to boarding school. They wanted me to go, too, but..." He shook his head, the way he had back then. "No way. I'd heard all about how strict those teachers were. Make you study so hard you get cross-eyed. When Jared had to get glasses, I got to say 'I told you so.' I don't know why, but he really liked that. Studied so hard he had to have glasses."

Gideon slid down and rested his head against the back of the chair. "He was there for three or four years before they sent him home. They found out he had a heart murmur, and I guess he'd been sick with pneumonia, and they were scared something might happen to him. He looked okay to me. All I know is, it nearly killed him right then, 'cause he was making straight *A*'s. He said the school here was too easy for him." Gideon shook his head slowly, rolling it back and forth against the chair. "Damn show-off. Too *easy* for him. I was lucky to graduate."

"He said you hated school."

"He was right. Damn desks were too small."

"He thought he'd outgrown his heart problem," she recalled. "At least, that was what he told me."

"He knew it all, my brother. Knew all there was to know about everything. Damn walking encyclopedia." He turned his head her way. "I used to think he could probably walk on water and recite the Bible backwards if he wanted to. And it was the kind of thing he just might do if somebody challenged him to." His smile was a bright spot in the dark. "Me, I couldn't see taking up a challenge unless there was some fun in it."

"We saw so little of you after we were married, Gideon." She looked him in the eye, challenging him for the truth. "Why was that?"

"You were busy, and I was…you know, knockin' around." He turned his attention to the ceiling. "You think you've got all the time in the world, you know? You tell yourself, maybe next summer, maybe Christmas. Last time I talked to him, I called to tell him I was running for chairman. I thought, if I got elected, we'd kinda be—" with a wave of a hand, he minimized the notion "—on equal footing in a way."

"In what way?"

"I don't know. Importance, I guess. Here we're like an apple and an orange, but I'm thinkin'"—" He cut off the comparison so abruptly, she thought he'd bitten his tongue. "Forget I said apple. I didn't mean apple. I'd give anything just to have one day back—one *hour*."

"What's wrong with 'apple'?"

"You know, red on the outside, white on the inside. Some of the more traditional members of the band get disgusted when—" He gave a quick shrug. "I remember calling him that a time or two, along with a few other things. I had no right to judge my brother. Right now, today, I'd like to hear some of his answers. But damn him, he took them all with him."

"Tribal law wasn't his field," Raina said quietly.

"Doesn't matter. He'd have the answers. He always did. *Good* answers, not just bull—"

"I miss him, too, Gideon." There, she thought. She'd finally answered his original question. She'd made him work for it, too. It was the biggest chunk of himself he'd ever shared with her. He'd earned some trust. "So does Peter. Peter has so many questions about so many things. Things I only know about secondhand."

"Because you're a woman?"

"And because I'm not Chippewa." She sighed. "And also, I guess, because I know very little about his background. Jared was able to make all the arrangements through the tribal court, even though he was born in a Minneapolis hospital. That's where we got him. He was so little, so…" Her wistful smile faded. "Anyway, I know he needs…someone like you." She shook her head. "No—*you*. He needs you, Gideon. You're his uncle. You *are* Chippewa, and you're—"

"Hell, lately some people have called *me* 'apple.' Taste of my old insult, comin' back at me." He chuckled humorlessly. "Anyway, I can't replace—"

"We're not looking for a replacement," she assured him. "Or answers, really. Peter needs to learn how to find his own answers."

"What does he want to know? Who his parents are?" He peered at her, his eyes burning with the question. Abruptly he turned away. "The answer to that is you and Jared."

"He knows he's adopted."

"He knows you raised him. That makes you his mother."

"He needs to learn more about his Native heritage, Gideon. And with Jared gone…"

"Jared didn't know his heritage from—" Jared had answers, but not *those* answers, damn it. Those were the answers Gideon had. At least, he had *some*. A few. "Look, Raina, the problem is that this whole treaty rights issue is pretty dicey right now, and people are circling their wagons up here." He chuckled. "Some analogy, huh?"

"It's an interesting choice of words."

"These are interesting times. It can be tricky just figuring out who your friends are. Tell you what—we'll take in the powwow tomorrow, give Peter a taste of smoked fish and frybread. How's that?"

"Will you take us canoeing before we go?"

"I could," he supposed. "With a canoe you can avoid the boat landings. One of these days I'm liable to blow my cool and bash somebody's face in. Then I'd sure as hell make the front page of every newspaper in the state. And not the way I'd want to."

She touched the back of his hand with her cool fingertips. "After what I saw today, I don't know how you've resisted this long."

"No choice." Her soft touch had the same effect on him

as her scent had. Old reflex, he told himself. The evening shadows covered for him nicely. "Anything I do reflects on the people. Gotta mind my manners." He smiled playfully. "Mostly."

"I won't ask what 'mostly' means."

It meant that as long as he was playing the gentleman escort, he would behave himself and dress the part. Gideon's idea of dressing up coincided in some ways with Raina's. He broke out a bottle of men's cologne that reminded him of the north woods on a chilly spring evening. He thought he could detect a hint of spruce, a touch of balsam and a splash of fresh water from a swift, icy current. And he wore his dress shoes—moccasins with floral beadwork—and his hair-pipe choker with the abalone shell tickling his Adam's apple. The small leather bag he wore tucked inside his shirt was generally not for show, but the beaded belt was.

Damn, he felt good-looking.

It was too hot for the sport jacket he usually wore for official occasions. And the jeans, well…short or long, jeans were always Gideon.

The powwow was held in a traditional circular bowery. The focus was music and dancing, and the costumes splashed color in every corner of the fairgrounds. The prizes for the dance contests drew dancers from out of state, and even though styles had blended in recent years, Gideon was able to point out the differences between the American Chippewa and the Canadian Cree moccasins, both with floral beadwork. He noted the Ojibwa influence on the local Dakota designs, as opposed to those of their Western Lakota cousins. There were even visitors from the Southwest, and Raina was impressed with Gideon's knowledge of Zuni, Hopi and Navaho silver work, which was available for sale at some of the stands.

Peter was interested in everything that was going on around him—the costumes, the dance steps, the people, the food—but Raina could tell he was feeling a little awkward. He was like a saddle horse's colt catching a glimpse of a herd of mustangs. Was this really who he was? If he left his mother's side, would those strangers let him run with them, or would they kick up their heels in his face and leave him standing there looking stupid?

"What do you like to eat, Peter?" Gideon asked as they approached the chow wagon. "Corn dogs or Indian tacos?"

Peter checked the list of choices on the sign next to the sliding window. "What's frybread?"

Gideon's glance told Raina that she'd neglected her son's culinary education.

"I don't know how to make it," she explained.

"You take a bunch of bread dough, smash it down, cut a piece off—" his quick hands made air frybread as he explained "—make a slit, drop it in hot lard…." He peered through the window. "You got any fresh frybread in there, Ron? I mean *fresh*." Shoving his hand into his pocket for money, Gideon turned to relay the cook's nod to the outside world. Then, in competition with the fan inside, he shouted into the window again. "We've got a guy out here who's never had frybread."

A round, sweaty, bespectacled face appeared in the window, followed by a paper plate with the sought-after sample. Ron adjusted his glasses and gave Peter the once-over. "*This* guy's never had *frybread?*"

"Boarding-school kid," Gideon said as he pushed some bills across the counter. With a conspiratorial wink, he handed Peter the plate. "Spends all his summers at Disney World."

"Geez, poor little guy. What did he cut his teeth on?"

"Mouse tail."

Peter nearly choked on his first mouthful of frybread.

Gideon laughed and slapped him on the back. "If you like this part, we'll have the works. Indian tacos. How about it?" Peter nodded, and Gideon ordered three.

"Two for me," said a voice at Gideon's back.

"Marvin, hey." Gideon wasn't sure Marvin Strikes Many would accept his handshake. But it was powwow time, time to socialize, so Marvin relented.

Gideon breathed a sigh of relief. He wanted everything to go smoothly today. No politics, no taking any stands. He shoved his hands in his back pockets and grinned. "Is your oldest boy around? I've got someone I want him to meet. My brother Jared's boy, Peter."

Peter was a little slow on the uptake with the older man's proffered handshake, but he had a mouthful of frybread to contend with.

"And this is Raina, Peter's mother."

Marvin nodded, then gave a gesture toward the bowery, where the afternoon elimination rounds were taking place in the dance contests. "Tom's over dancing right now. Competing in men's traditional. It's his first year in twelve-to-eighteen."

"Is that Arlen Skinner judging?" Gideon frowned slightly, craning his neck to get a look past the lineup of younger boys dressed in colorful double bustles, waiting outside the circle for their turn to dance. "Haven't seen him around in a while."

"Some of us parents got together and asked him to come out and judge the dance contests," Marvin reported with a clear sense of satisfaction. "Arlen's one of the real traditionals. He knows how it's supposed to be done."

Gideon watched the old man take one of the boys aside and demonstrate a dance step, shuffling his moccasins in the grass.

"He sure does. It's good when the old ones do the teaching." He glanced Peter's way and gave an instructional nod. "It's good when the young ones pay attention to them."

"Arlen can still bring a buck down with an arrow."

"He uses a compound bow," Gideon pointed out as he indicated, again with a nod, that Marvin should help himself to the first two plates of Indian tacos Ron had served up.

"Nothing wrong with taking advantage of an improvement." Marvin handed his money through the window and claimed the plates. "But Arlen still knows his culture. Knows his rights, too." Hands full, he nodded his goodbyes and headed for the bowery.

"Good seeing you, Marvin," Gideon said to the man's heels. "Glad you've got no hard feelings over that deer."

Marvin plunked his plates on a bleacher seat, turned and watched the threesome wander from the chow wagon to the pop stand before he took exception to Gideon's assumption under his breath.

"What're you mutterin' about, nephew? Complainin' about the judging?" Arlen Skinner gave a dry laugh as he hiked his arthritic bones up to the plank seating and pulled a cigarette from his shirt pocket. "Your boy did real good."

"We've been working on his costume. Can you use some chow?"

The old man shook his head. "Could use a match, *ninininqwanis.*"

Marvin fished in his jeans pocket for a match for the man who called him his nephew. With his free hand he waved his son down. "Got something over here for you to eat."

He offered Arlen a light, but his attention strayed back to the motley trio at the pop stand. Motley from his perspective, anyway. "What do you think of how Defender's doing as chairman?"

"I don't pay much attention to politics." Arlen blew a stream of smoke and turned a cursory glance toward the man who held Marvin's interest. He registered his reaction with a grunt. "Looks like he's got himself a pretty white girlfriend."

"That's his brother's wife," Marvin informed him. "His brother Jared. The one that moved to the city and died of a heart attack."

"You mean the lawyer? That's his wife?" Arlen pulled the cigarette from his mouth and took another look. "She don't look Indian."

"Nope." Marvin wagged his head. "The boy sure takes after his dad."

"His dad?" Arlen squinted, staring harder now in a manner that would have been rude, had it not been necessary. "You're talking about the lawyer? The lawyer was that boy's dad?"

"Hardly looks like a half-breed."

"If that's Jared Defender's boy, and if that's his only son, then he's no half-breed. He's my grandson." Arlen took another drag on his cigarette, squinting through the smoke for a last look before he finally turned away, muttering, "The one my daughter gave away."

Chapter 4

Gideon had promised to bring his canoe over to the lodge the following morning, and they planned to launch their outing from there. Raina had popped down to the little grocery store early and put together a picnic lunch, but she was beginning to think she would have to make a second trip if Gideon didn't show up soon. Peter had already eaten half the fruit she'd bought. He was working on a banana when Gideon called to say he would be a few minutes late. What he'd planned as a quick stop at his office was turning into a little more than that, he explained. Raina graciously refrained from mentioning that he'd long since passed a few minutes. Instead, she told him not to worry about it.

"He says he really wants to go, and we'll be doing him a favor if we hang in and wait," Raina reported as she hung up the phone.

"Jeez, Mom, he's like the president of the tribe. He's probably got a lot of stuff going on all the time." Peter dropped the banana peel into the wastebasket, propped his feet up on the chair opposite the one he occupied and checked the grocery bag for another selection. "I wonder what Mark and Eric would say if I told them my uncle was a tribal chief."

"I'm surprised you haven't told them," she said absently as she turned for a backward inspection of her outfit in the mirror. She wasn't sure she liked the way the blue looked tucked into the white. "Can you see my shirt through these shorts?"

"Kinda." Peter was more interested in slurping every drop of juice dripping from the plum he'd just bitten into. "It came up in a class once." His mouth was still half-full, so the words sounded juicy. "Social studies." He swallowed and licked his lips. "We were talking about current events. One of the other guys heard the name Defender on the news and asked if I was related. I said I didn't know."

"Why did you say that?"

"'Cause I don't." He shrugged and popped the rest of the plum into his mouth. After he spat the pit into the wastebasket, he allowed, "Not by blood, anyway. Figured I can say I'm related, or I can say I'm not. Depends on how you look at it and who's askin'."

"What would you say now?" she wondered, the shorts forgotten.

He had to think about that one. "I guess I *feel* like he's my uncle."

"Good." She tried to ruffle his hair, but he leaned away. "Did you enjoy the powwow?" she asked.

"Sure, it was okay." He reached for a magazine that was lying on the table next to the grocery bag. "I think I'd like to try spearfishing."

"It's legal during the ice-fishing season," Raina recalled.

"Maybe this winter we can come back and ask your uncle Gideon to—"

"Oscar says the best time for spearing is in the spring." After a quick scrutiny, he tossed the schedule aside and snatched up another banana. "He says there's supposed to be a big celebration, traditional ceremonies, stuff like that. And there will be, once all this argument about who's got the say over how Indians do their fishing is settled. Oscar says it's a treaty right, and it's got nothing to do with state laws."

"They're working on some sort of compromise so that the Chippewa can resume the practice peacefully, without—"

The knock at the door prompted another mirror check, which confirmed Peter's assessment. The blue *did* show through the white shorts. "Too late now," Raina muttered on her way to the door.

But the man on the other side was not the one she was expecting. This one was wearing a uniform, a sidearm and a badge.

"Mrs. Defender?"

"I'm Raina Defender, yes."

"Cletus Sam. I'm a tribal police officer." He nodded politely, then glanced over her head, into the room. "I'm looking for Peter Defender. I'm carrying a court order for his—"

Court order? Raina folded her arms, squared her shoulders and took a wide stance in the doorway. "Peter hasn't done anything. He's been with me ever since we got here."

The officer produced a piece of paper with an official letterhead. "The judge issued an order for him to be taken into the custody of—"

"Custody?" Raina stepped back into the room, instinctively falling back to protect her child as she examined the document with Peter's name on it, signed by Judge Gerald Half. The

names registered clearly enough, although the judge's was not familiar to her, but the rest made no sense.

She scanned the document again, but her eyes were working faster than her brain. "What does this mean—'the terms of the Indian Child Welfare Act,' and this part about biological family members?"

"May I come in, ma'am?"

Raina gave a tentative nod. "I don't have the papers with me, but I assure you that I can prove that I am legally Peter's mother."

"All I know is the boy is an enrolled member of the Pine Lake Band of Chippewa."

"Yes, he is. So was my husband. We adopted Peter when he was a baby, and it was all perfectly leg—"

"Are you Peter?"

The policeman turned to the table, where the boy sat with the first bite of his second banana still in his mouth, looking from one adult to the other in total confusion. He nodded hesitantly.

"You wanna come with me?" Officer Sam asked, as gently as he might have petitioned a much younger child. "We're just goin' over to see Judge Half, over to the court."

"I didn't do anything," the boy said quietly.

"Nobody says you did, Peter. The judge will explain." Officer Sam nodded to Raina and spoke just as quietly. "You can sure come, too, ma'am."

But Raina's voice was on the rise. "Gideon Defender is Peter's uncle. He'll straighten this whole thing out as soon as he hears—"

"Maybe he will, Mrs. Defender. But the court is separate from the chairman, so I've got to do like the judge told me." He gestured toward the paper, which was still in Raina's hand. "Gideon's office is right across the street, though, so you can go right on over there and see what he has to say. I mean, it's not like anybody wants to do any—"

"I'm interested in hearing what this *judge* has to say." She perused the document again, but the words wouldn't stay in focus, and the paper seemed to burn her fingers. "This is ridiculous. Peter has nothing to do with welfare, or whatever that act is supposed to mean."

She stared at the man, hoping to convince him, searching for the magic words that would make such perfect sense that he would take his paper and go back where he'd come from. "I'm the one who's raised him. I'm his *mother*."

"Yes, ma'am." The officer turned to Peter again. "Nobody is going to hurt you, son. You're not in any trouble. The judge just wants to see you in his office. He'll explain everything."

She was doing all right until the judge asked her to wait outside his office while he talked with Peter. "I have no jurisdiction over you," the portly man with bulldog jowls explained. "Only the boy."

Over her objections, Cletus Sam directed her to a chair, but it was on the other side of the door to the room she ought to be in. The room where Peter was. This was not defensible. She definitely had parental rights. *Legal* rights.

Gideon's blue pickup was parked across the street. Right across the street! Surely he could see what was going on here. Why wasn't he doing something about this? Raina fumed to herself. Getting herself in a huff expanded her confidence as she marched past his assistant and through the door labeled Chairman's Office.

Taken off guard, the assistant was a little late in sliding her chair back from her desk. "You can't walk in without—"

Standing next to his desk with a handful of papers, Gideon turned in surprise. Dressed in a T-shirt and cutoffs, he clearly hadn't planned to spend the morning on official business. He looked poised, in fact, to set the rest aside.

"Gideon, thank God," she breathed.

He smiled sheepishly as he selected one paper and put the rest in a desk tray. "I'm sorry to keep you waiting, Raina. I think that phone has eyes. I ought to know better than to—"

"Gideon, what in heaven's name is going on?" She closed the door and approached him tentatively. "Did you know that your judge sent a policeman over to the lodge to arrest Peter this morning?"

Gideon's eyes widened incredulously. "*Arrest…*Peter?"

"Yes." She nodded once, then shook her head in confusion. "Well, take him into custody because of some child welfare law that says he can just take *my* son into *his* custody. I don't understand how—"

"Where is he now? Where is Peter?"

She gestured with an unsteady hand. "Right across the street." In two strides he was at her side, turning her toward the door while she was still sputtering, "You have to *do* something, Gideon."

On his way past his assistant's desk he tossed a letter under her nose. "You know what to do with this, Rosie?"

"Sure. Slam-dunk it into file thirteen."

"No, you send out the standard reply. The Pine Lake Band has no intention of depleting the lake of all the fish, which were here before the Chippewa, who were here long before the North Woods Anglers Club started its annual fishing derby, *which* we wouldn't dream of interfering with, et cetera, et cetera." Half of him was guiding Raina toward the outside door, the other half reaching back, still pointing to the letter. "Those guys spend a lot of money at the casino."

"They say they're going to *boycott* the casino," Rosie

pointed out. "Maybe you ought to call this guy, or else maybe—"

"Tell them we hope they'll reconsider. Just say—"

"Excuse me, Gideon." Raina tugged on his arm. "Peter doesn't understand what's going on any more than I do, and he's probably scared."

"Thanks, Rosie. Gotta see what the hell's goin' on across the way here."

Gideon opened the front door and ushered Raina into the late morning sunlight. "The Indian Child Welfare Act," he explained as they walked. "That's the law they're probably talking about. It's a federal law, and in Minnesota there's also a state law. The idea is to keep the children from being taken away from the tribe."

"What are you talking about, Gideon? We adopted Peter when he was a baby. Jared and I—"

"He's Chippewa. Somebody must have taken a notion to file a complaint of some kind."

"A *complaint?*"

They waited at the curb, both of them watching a car cruise by. The driver gave a nod, and Gideon returned the greeting. Then he turned to Raina. "I'm not sure why anyone would in this case, but you might need an attorney. We'll have to—"

"There's nothing to complain about. That judge has no right to take my son. Gideon, did you say something, or did someone approach you about—"

He shook his head. "I didn't know anything about this. As long as Jared was alive, there was no problem. Now, maybe there could be." He sighed as he stepped off the curb, thoughtfully eyeing the sign across the street that said LAW AND ORDER: Pine Lake Band of Chippewa. "Let's go see what kind of a problem. And how big."

They found Peter and Arlen Skinner occupying two chairs

in the judge's chambers, exchanging sidelong glances as though neither was quite sure what to make of the other. Raina didn't know what to make of any of it, but she was relieved to find that Peter hardly looked scared, although he did still look confused. At Gideon's request, the judge admitted her into the office. He introduced the old man, Arlen Skinner, as Peter's grandfather.

"Grandfather?" Raina echoed softly, trying the word out on her own tongue. She knew she was supposed to approach an elder with a respectful handshake, but her feet wouldn't move. She knew she wasn't supposed to stare, but she couldn't help it.

Peter's biological grandfather?

"Here's the paperwork on this so far." The judge handed Gideon a file folder.

"Why didn't you talk to me about this before you served any papers, Judge?" Gideon looked the documents over, but he had a good idea what they would say. "This was some pretty fast work."

"Since the boy was in the neighborhood, seemed like the sensible thing to do was serve the papers first, ask questions later." The judge exchanged nods of previously determined agreement with the old man sitting quietly in the corner chair. "Peter here is a member of the Pine Lake Chippewa. He was enrolled by Tomasina Skinner, his birth mother. She didn't name his father. She's got him down as half Chippewa, so apparently his father wasn't a member of the band."

"Is she…" Raina glanced from the judge's face to Gideon's and back again. "Is she trying to take him back now?"

"My daughter was killed in a car wreck," Arlen said evenly. "Eight, nine years ago now."

"Judge, my husband and I adopted Peter when he was a baby. Jared actually made the initial arrangements, but I understand that Peter's mother—" The words, coming from her own mouth, stunned her. *She* was Peter's mother.

She turned slowly, like a player just enlisted for blindman's buff. A rising mire of uncertainty threatened to engulf her as she thrust her pleading gesture first in the judge's direction, then briefly toward the old man. But finally, as though she were awakening, recovering a full awareness of herself, she drew her hand back to her own chest.

"I…" She injected her voice with what starch she could muster and explained softly, "*I* was told that Tomasina, whom we never actually met, was allowed to choose the…to *choose* adoptive parents for Peter, and she chose us. We were looking for a child to adopt, and because Jared was Chippewa, we were…we were…"

She hated her senseless emotionalism when what she needed was coolness and poise. She cleared her throat and forbade her voice to crack.

"We were even… We gave him his name and everything."

She didn't have to do this, she told herself. There was no need to plead her case to these people, especially since the look in Arlen's eyes was decidedly unmoved. *Don't even try,* she wanted to say, but she was afraid.

"It was all perfectly legal," she insisted quietly instead. She turned to Gideon, whose familiar face did not threaten her composure. "After all, Jared was an attorney, wasn't he, Gideon? So it *all* has to be in order, because Jared never left any loose ends."

She took the slight bob of Gideon's chin as an endorsement. She turned to the judge, and calmly she concluded, "I know I'm a single parent now, but Peter is legally my own son."

Judge Half was unruffled. "The boy's also Arlen's grandson."

Son and grandson were not the same, Raina told herself, which enabled her to recover her manners and offer the old man a belated handshake. Arlen Skinner briefly permitted the courtesy, then withdrew his hand.

"Forgive me. I'm happy to meet you, Mr. Skinner. And I'm more than willing to…" She smiled at her son and fell back on her mother's prerogative to speak for him. "I know Peter's very glad to meet his grandfather, too. He never knew Jared's father, and mine is…"

Peter lowered his eyes and restlessly braced his hands on his knees.

Gideon was watching Peter.

Judge Half was surveying the order he had issued.

"All right, what's really going on here?" Raina demanded quietly. "Why did you send a policeman after my son?"

"Arlen asked the court to claim custody of his grandson on his behalf." The judge's dark eyes conceded nothing, deeply impregnated as they were with the power of Solomon. "Peter is Chippewa."

"So was my husband. Gideon's brother." She spun around, seeking his help. "Gideon?"

But he appeared to be studying the blank side of the document the judge held in his hand. "I'm guessing the tribal court is exercising its right to claim custody of a Pine Lake Chippewa child living in a non-Indian home." He looked up. "Right, Judge?"

"That's right." Judge Half extended his beefy hand toward Raina. "I understand how you feel—"

"Gideon, whose side are you on? Peter is your…" Her hands curled into fists as she remembered Peter's claim. He could be related or not related—whichever he chose. Maybe Gideon saw it the same way.

But she did not. She was Peter's mother. Period.

"We'll call our attorney and get this whole thing straightened out today, Peter. I'm not going to let them do this."

"I guess the question of whose side you're on—" Judge Half glanced sidelong at Gideon "—might be on a lot of people's minds, Mr. Chairman."

Gideon sighed. "The boy lost his—" He swallowed hard and cast a quick look ceilingward. "He lost his father just two years ago." He drilled Judge Half with a challenging stare. "We'd be hard-pressed to take him away from the only living parent he's ever known, wouldn't we, Judge? Hell, he's twelve years old. This is no time to be meddling in his—" Abruptly he turned his attention across the room. "You ready to raise another teenager, Arlen?"

"Marvin Strikes Many pointed him out to me at the celebration." The old man shifted in his chair, spreading his hands wide. "I didn't interfere with my daughter's decision to give her baby up for adoption, even though I didn't think it was right. She said the baby would go to a good Indian home. Jared Defender, she said, so I thought, okay. A good Indian home. I was sorry when I heard he'd passed away. I wasn't doin' too good myself then, so I didn't get to his funeral or nothin'. I never knew he was married to a white woman. Never thought to ask." He spared Raina a quick glance, then spoke to the judge. "I keep to myself, mostly. Never pay much attention to other people's business unless it crosses over into mine somehow."

Judge Half folded his arms over his chest. "Did Tomasina tell you much about the boy's real father?"

Arlen shook his head. "She wouldn't say who it was. All she ever said was, 'This is what he wants, too. Give the kid half a chance,' she said. I thought maybe she got some money out of it or something, because she always wanted to move to the big city, and that's what she up and did." He grunted with disgust and shook his head again. "But now, I don't think it's right, my grandson being raised by a white woman."

"What's wrong with a *white* woman?" Raina demanded, the trepidation gone from her voice. "I'm a good mother, and Peter is my son. You can't take my *son*. I don't care what this crazy law—"

"Raina." Gideon touched her arm. "Believe me, the judge has the authority to take this matter—"

She shook him off. "I *won't* give up my son!"

"I know." His hand dropped to his side. "Under the circumstances, I'm sure some kind of compromise—"

"Compromise!" Raina clipped, as sharply indignant as any mother cat surrounded by males threatening to devour her young.

"Sounds a lot like the word *settlement*," Arlen muttered. "Which is a word some of us are getting pretty tired of hearing."

"Let's not confuse *that* issue with this one," Gideon said. He rested one hand low on his hip and nodded toward the court order still held menacingly in the judge's hand. "What are we lookin' at here, Judge? Temporary custody while the lawyers cinch up their briefs, right? I'm the boy's uncle, and I'm also a resident of Pine Lake and an enrolled member of the band. I'd say I'm a good prospect, wouldn't you?"

"You want me to appoint you his guardian?"

Raina stepped forward. "Peter doesn't need—"

As a subtle warning, Gideon laid his hand on Raina's shoulder. "Temporarily."

"Hey, I gotta get back to school by September," Peter put in. It was his first real comment, and it surprised Raina that getting back to school was his first concern. But she was relieved to hear him speak up so sensibly for going home.

"We'll have time to get in some fishing, maybe a little

camping before school starts," Gideon said. He slid Raina a glance that said *trust me,* while he turned his negotiations from the judge to Peter, skillfully including Arlen in the verbal circle he was drawing. "Your grandfather can teach you to dance like us. That's what you came up here for, right? To learn about your culture?"

All the while he kept his hand on Raina's shoulder.

She'd never known Gideon to be such a smooth talker. For the first time she could see a commonality between brothers. She noted that Arlen hadn't refused the suggestion yet.

Gideon sidled quickly over to Peter, tapped him on the arm with the back of his hand and inveigled some more. "So here you've got yourself a grandfather into the bargain. Pretty cool, huh?"

"Pretty damn confusing," Peter grumbled as he stood slowly. He looked up at Gideon, implicitly accepting him as an ally. "Can these guys really…uh…take me away from Mom?"

Raina closed her eyes briefly, clamping down on the terrible burning in her throat. She would not lose it now. *She would not.*

"Judge Half is a fair man, Peter. He's got to sort though all the claims and the circumstances." He laid his hand on the boy's shoulder. "You're right, it's confusing, but we'll get it straightened out. It'll just take a little time." Gideon turned to the man who had the final say. "What about it, Judge?"

"You're her brother-in-law," Arlen injected. "I don't know if that's such a good idea."

"I'm the tribal chairman, Arlen. It's not like I'm gonna skip town."

Arlen looked at Raina, then turned to the judge. "Maybe she might try to take off with him or something."

"Take off!" Raina ignored the look of warning in Gideon's

eyes. "If we leave, we won't be *taking off*. We have every right to leave here whenever—"

"Nobody's gonna take off," Gideon, the self-appointed voice of reason, insisted. "You don't mind staying with me for a while, do you, Peter? Your mom will be staying at the lodge."

Peter looked at each face in the room, one at a time. Finally he shrugged, then gave his head a quick shake. Unsure, uncomfortable, even a little unsteady, he was willing to defer to the man with the plan. At least Uncle Gideon—*Uncle* sounded better all the time—was not a stranger.

Gideon kept a judicious distance from Raina, but his eyes sought hers, and he offered quiet reassurance. "It'll work out."

She glared at him.

He glanced away. "You got something you want me to sign, Judge?"

The judge produced another document, which he filled out and finally slid across the desk for Gideon's signature.

"I wish my dad was here," Peter said as he assumed a detached stance from which to observe the proceedings. "He knew everything there was to know about the law. You'd hand him a court order, he'd hand you an injunction—" he snapped his fingers "—like that."

Gideon looked up, a trace of regret in his eyes, and he smiled. "Guess you'll have to settle for me. I'm no lawyer, but I know a little bit about a lot of things." He nodded toward Arlen, who hadn't moved from his chair. "Kinda like your grandfather."

"I know it's not right for her to take him away," Arlen said stubbornly. He folded his arms and shifted in his chair. The look in his eyes said this was only round one. "You'll need your Indian ways," he told Peter. "You'll be a man soon."

"But I don't know if I want to *live* up here. Summer might be okay, but—" Peter looked at the judge. "Don't I have something to say about all this?"

"Sure you do." Judge Half slipped the paper with Gideon's signature on it into his file. "Everybody gets a say in my court." He nodded in Arlen's direction. "I want you to spend some time with your grandfather, too, now that you two have finally met. You'll see to that, Gideon? And meanwhile, I've got to study up on your background a little bit. I'm just a judge. I'm not a lawyer, either. Like the chairman, I don't know everything there is to know about anything." He brandished the file. "Got some studyin' up to do."

Raina's brain was as wobbly as the hindquarters of a rhino shot with a tranquilizer gun. She hadn't seen the blow coming, and she was still reeling from it. Gideon kept telling her to stay cool, but his voice seemed distant. Peter had little to say, except that he didn't mind riding in Gideon's pickup "to keep up appearances," while his mother followed them back to the lodge in her car.

There they set about packing up Peter's clothes.

"You got a TV that I can hook this up to?" Peter showed Gideon the controls to his video game.

Gideon shoved his hands into his pockets as he scanned the cords. "I have a TV, but it's not new. Will it still work?"

"Probably." Peter glanced at Raina.

Without even seeing it, she could feel that visual check-in from child to mother, that won't-it-Mom? look. Sitting on the bed, carefully folding each shirt, she looked up. There was an unspoken concern in her son's eyes, as though he were seeing her differently as he prepared to take his first significant leave of her, and it scared her.

But he smiled at her as he reported, "At home I have my own TV."

"I don't watch TV much," Gideon said. "It's yours for the duration."

"Yeah." Peter reached behind the TV and unplugged his equipment. "Whatever that means."

"It means until this custody thing gets straightened out," Gideon said. "It gets complicated, doesn't it, being an Indian?"

"Hey, I'm just minding my own business, eatin' a banana, and in comes this cop." Twirling the cord like a lasso, Peter nodded toward the door. "Pretty soon I've got a grandfather named Arlen Skinner, who tells me his daughter was my mother, and her name was Tomasina, and she's dead, and then my uncle gets to be my guardian, just *temporarily….*" He turned to Raina, giving her a puzzled look. "And I'm wondering, how come I never knew any of this stuff?"

"I didn't know about your grandfather," Raina said. She laid her hand atop the pile of folded shirts, splaying her fingers over the soft cotton. "The adoption—your adoption—was a private arrangement, which is perfectly legal in this state. Your dad handled the technical end of it, and when the time came, we both went to the hospital to get you." A warm surge of nostalgia flooded her as she recalled cradling her baby in her arms for the first time. So much beautiful black hair, she'd said. Such tiny, delicate fingernails.

"I remember the caseworker's name was Susan something, but I was never told your birth mother's name. I've often thought about her and wondered—" She shook the speculations away. She now knew the answer to the final question. *Wondered what ever happened to her.*

"We were given some medical information, but that's about all. I was just so glad to…" Raina looked at her son and smiled.

"I was just so glad you were ours, Peter. Maybe I was afraid to rock the boat, I don't know. But I've never deliberately kept anything from you. I've answered all your questions as best I could."

She picked up the shirts and rose from the bed. Gideon and Peter both watched her every move, as though they were suddenly fascinated by her ability to pack a bag. As though they'd forgotten that mothers did such things. "That's why we came, remember?" she continued. "To answer some of your questions. If I'd known about your grandfather, I would have told you. And I have no idea whether your dad knew about him." With a glance she invited Gideon to answer for his brother.

But he skirted the invitation with a shrug. "Arlen's never been what you'd call a sociable fellow."

"Is he as mean as he looks?" Peter wondered.

"He just looks *old,*" Gideon said. "And he *is* old." That was about all he could say for sure about the man, besides the fact that he was a "traditional," and he was reclusive, even among his own people. What little contact he'd ever had with Arlen Skinner had been accidental and had always made Gideon feel a bit uneasy.

"No, I don't think he's mean." Even now he had to make a concerted effort to shake off the uneasy feeling. He'd long since learned to arrest such feelings by distancing himself from personal ties. He could put Arlen into perspective by thinking of him as one of the elders. One whose realities dwelled, for the most part, in the past. One who remained behind as a reminder. One who deserved respect.

"Arlen's lost a lot over the years," Gideon said. "The older people remember how the land was appropriated by waves of newcomers. Around here, it wasn't so much the land but the timber they wanted first. Villages were a nuisance to the loggers, and logging drove the game away, anyway, so some of the bands agreed to move farther north. Our little band resisted.

"This is prime real estate." Gideon glanced out the window at the lakeshore below. "But we didn't know anything about real estate. We just knew we belonged here. We couldn't keep the miners out next, or the farmers, but in those days the United States didn't care that much about the hunting and fishing, so they said, 'We'll pay you for the land, but you can keep on hunting and gathering on it.'" He shook his head and chuckled at the irony of it all. "None of our people ever saw much of the money. Coincidentally, the Chippewa owed the white traders almost exactly the amount the government was paying for the land. So why not cut the red tape and send the money directly to the creditors? Makes sense." His full mouth turned down at the corners, and he nodded in a parody of understanding. "Eliminated a whole step. Went down in history as an early attempt to make government carry out its duties efficiently. But the Chippewa didn't much care for the way it worked out, so we've seen more than our share of red tape ever since.

"Anyway, with all the logging and the farming, the game kinda disappeared, so the Chippewa had some pretty hungry times. Most of the bands were relocated, but some families hung tough here by the lake. Guys like Arlen remember real well that after the loggers and the traders and the farmers, along came the weekend sportsmen, then the lake cabins. We didn't have much land left by then, but we still had our hunting and fishing rights. People like Arlen, the older ones, they just kept to themselves and watched over what was left."

As Gideon watched now. Long, silent moments passed as he watched a fishing boat head out from the lodge. Evidently Pine Lake had become everybody's current ideal recreation spot.

"What do you think he wants, Gideon?"

"Arlen?" Gideon turned from the window to find both Raina and Peter looking to him anxiously for the answer. He felt a little foolish. Maybe they didn't see any connection between his story and Arlen's demands. Maybe for them there wasn't any. "Guess he wants a grandson. *His* grandson."

"Which means—" Raina gestured, hopeful of something simple and straightforward "—visits, right? He wants to be able to see Peter periodically, the way…the way grandparents do. The way they *should.* I have no problem with that, and I'm sure Peter—"

"I'd like to get to know him," Peter chimed in. "As long as he's not as mean as he looks. Heck, I guess that's how I'm gonna look when I get to be old, you know? I'm gonna look a lot like him. I'm *related* to him by blood." A first for Peter, that much clearly impressed him. "Maybe he could come and watch some of my swim meets this year. Some of the guys' grandparents come all the time."

"You're a swimmer?" Gideon smiled. It was the phrase *related to him by blood* that got to him. And pride, and a strong sense of the circle. Maybe his sad historical tale had played a part in prompting this show of optimism.

"Yeah. Swimming and soccer." Peter turned to his mother. "I gotta be back by the time soccer practice starts. You remember the date?"

"I have it written on the calendar." She shot Gideon a look that pleaded for reassurance. *He'll be back in time, won't he? Tell him he will, and tell me this will all be settled and we'll be on our way home soon.*

Home, Gideon reflected. His idea of home was a far cry from Raina's. Not better. Not worse. Just *different,* and the difference would take some serious getting used to for Peter, if it came to that.

"How about taking Oscar out in my canoe?" Gideon suggested. "He's been bugging me again this morning."

"All four of us?"

"Four would be crowded," Gideon acknowledged as he crossed the room to lay claim to the large duffel bag Raina was zipping shut. "You're a swimmer. Oscar's a paddler. Between the two of you, the important bases are covered."

Raina glanced up. "You've got something else to do?"

"Some calls to make."

"Yes," she said, as if she'd just remembered. "I guess I do, too."

"Hey, you're comin' over to my place with us. I'm responsible for him for—" Gideon shrugged apologetically "—probably for just a few days. Nobody said you can't be with us while I have, uh…"

"Custody of my son," she said bluntly.

"I'm his uncle," he reminded her, feeling the pressure of stretching his light tone beyond anything he felt. "Could be worse."

"You're also the tribal chairman. You ought to have some…"

"Pull?" The notion made him chuckle. "Tell you what, we're gonna take Peter's stuff over to my place and pick Oscar up on the way." He laid his hand on Peter's shoulder, carefully, as though he were testing the boy's forbearance. Peter lifted his eyes to meet Gideon's, offering tentative trust. The big hand tightened in a gesture of reassurance. "Then we'll see how much pull this guy can manage on a canoe paddle. What's your event?"

"Event?"

"Isn't that what you call it in swimming?"

"Butterfly and breaststroke."

"Hey, I'll bet you can paddle that thing all the way to Canada."

* * *

They had shared Raina's picnic lunch on Gideon's porch. Afterward, the boys had gone out in the canoe, and the phone calls to the attorneys had been made. Independently, the counsel for the Pine Lake Band and Raina's lawyer came up with similar pronouncements. It sounded like a "sticky" situation.

"*Sticky* just means they're gonna charge more." Gideon opened the refrigerator door and gestured for Raina to stash the remaining lunch meat inside.

"Easy for you to say. Yours is on retainer." She offered him the last of the plums. When he shook his head, she tucked the fruit into the crisper. "Did he sound as confident as mine sounded doubtful?"

"Our attorney has dealt with the issue before. Yours probably hasn't."

"I've heard about it, of course, but I'm not sure I under-stand…*completely.*" She closed the refrigerator door, leaned back against it and stared him down across the narrow width of his kitchen. "You explain it, Gideon. Just what is it we're dealing with?"

He braced the heels of his hands on the edge of the sink behind him and took a deep breath, as though he'd been backed into a corner and now had to make an official statement. "The Indian Child Welfare Act was passed in 1978, and basically what it says is that the tribal court has the right to—" he lifted one shoulder, as though the right were self-evident "—become involved the way it just has. Used to be that Native American children were being siphoned away from their people, first into boarding schools, then non-Native foster homes and adoptions.

"Finally, the people said, 'no more.'" He tilted his head slightly, his eyes looking for the kind of understanding that ordinarily would have come naturally to her. Quietly, he told her, "They said, 'You take our kids away, we've got nothing left.' So recently they passed the law to protect Native families and to preserve the integrity of Native American nations."

"This all sounds very—" she sighed, gesturing impatiently "—philosophical and political and…and it sounds like an interesting topic for discussion, but this is *my child* we're talking about."

"I know." He laid his hand on her shoulder in a gesture that was pure brotherly love. "I can't see the judge taking him out of a good home after almost thirteen years."

"He could do that?"

"I don't know." Technically, the answer was yes, but the judge's *will* to do it was another question, and of that possibility, Gideon could honestly say, "I don't know."

"What do you mean, you don't know? You're a tribal leader now, for God's sake. If you don't know, who *does?* If you can't do anything about this, who—"

"Raina." Gently he squeezed her shoulder, then let his hand fall to his side. "This is a complicated issue. We're going to take it one step at a time, and—for Peter's sake—you're going to stay calm."

But he took half a step back, because her defensive stare accused him of taking something from her. "I think the judge is going to want Peter to have a chance to get to know his grandfather, but I don't think he'll decide to turn the boy's whole world upside down, take him out of school, take him away from—" he glanced at the top of the refrigerator and the cabinet above it, searching the high places in his kitchen for some assurance to offer "—his mother. I just can't see him doing that now."

"Excuse me, but I'd like to hear something a little more

decisive, a little more positive, than what sounds like a cloudy forecast from your crystal ball."

Stung by her sarcasm, he shrugged. "Call your lawyer back, then."

"I didn't like…what I heard in his voice…." Tears welled in her eyes, and her voice came dangerously near cracking. Her lips trembled as she drew a deep breath, searching for something that would steady her. "…any better."

What he saw in her eyes embarrassed him, and he glanced away. It wasn't easy for her to admit to a fear that might bleed her of her strength. He was afraid to touch her. He was afraid that if she fell apart and the pieces of her scattered across the floor, he wouldn't be able to put them together. He wanted to fix things for her, but he didn't know how. Arlen Skinner saw her as an outsider, and she sure as hell looked like one.

But this was Raina—Peter's mother, Jared's widow and Gideon's…

Gideon's *what?*

Sister-in-law. That was enough. She was family. The Indian way, he needed no more explanation, no other excuse. It didn't matter who he was or what office he held, she was family, just like Peter, and she deserved his protection, his care, all the comfort he could give her. He took both her shoulders in his hands, effectively pinning her to the refrigerator. *Ask me,* he willed. *Care, comfort, the strength in my body—they're yours for the asking.*

But that was not what she asked. She lifted her chin, her eyes pleading with him to use his power on her behalf, whatever power he had to steer the course of events.

Her silent, desperate plea clawed at his heart. The power she wanted didn't extend to her. It was for Peter and Oscar, even Arlen. But it was not for Raina. He was the chairman of the Pine Lake Band of *Chippewa.* And there was nothing he could honestly say to allay a white woman's fear. There was no promise he could make—honestly—and there was precious little he could give her in exchange for her tears.

He pulled her away from the refrigerator, drew her close until her shirtfront touched his, until he could feel the small, delicate impressions of her breasts through the layers of cloth. He slid his hands over her shoulders slowly, maintaining the lock his eyes had on hers, giving her fair notice, ample warning. Her eyes slid closed, and a tear escaped. One sparkling tear slipped down her cheek. He caught it on his tongue, tasted its wonderful saltiness, murmured something about her liking this better, this would be better, this would be...

A kiss. That was all. There was power in it for him, but little promise for her. Maybe she knew that. Maybe she didn't. When he felt her arms encircle him, he didn't care either way. All he wanted was the taste of her sweet mouth deep inside his, the feel of her tongue against his, and the dampness— the dampness of tears and kisses and opportunities long ago denied him. But the need for more than that swelled low in him, slow in him, gathering strength from the response her lips made, moving with his. His soft, involuntary groan expressed the depth of his need. He held her tight and pressed himself against her, letting her feel what he had to give. This and more, his hungry mouth promised. Don't be afraid. Don't...

Raina tore her mouth away on a desperate gasp. "Oh, no, not this." Her quick, frantic breaths fluttered against the base of his throat. She clung to him even as she denied him. "Gideon, we can't let this happen."

He drew back slowly, thinking—hoping—he hadn't heard her right. They'd put their arms around each other and shared a kiss, for God's sake. It tasted good. It felt good. It was what they both needed. What could be wrong with something that felt this right?

"Peter," she began as she sidled away, still gripping him at the waist for support. "Peter might…"

A thousand retorts raced through his mind, but he allowed none to pass his tongue. He couldn't afford to. The state his head was in right now, he couldn't be sure which one would cut itself loose first. Something about her or himself or the two of them together. Or something about Peter. Or Jared. God help them all, he thought as he finally stepped back. With everything that had happened already, this was a tangled mess.

But the kiss was right. That was all he knew. No matter what the source of confusion in her eyes, no matter how much fear and hurt glittered in them like glass splinters, there was a glimmer of something within her tears that told him the kiss was right.

We can't let this happen?

Didn't she realize it was more than fifteen years too late for that?

Chapter 5

Raina returned to Pine Lake after spending two days tying up loose ends at home. Her neighbor couldn't be expected to take care of the place indefinitely, which was exactly the kind of time frame Raina was looking at now. *"Indian time."* It was the leisurely pace Jared had been determined to put behind him when he'd left the reservation. He'd often complained that the stereotypes hounded him—the notion that "Indians" never got anything done on time. That if they showed up at all they were always late. Good workers once they got started, but undependable. Unpredictable. Inconsistent.

She'd heard all the modifiers and qualifiers, too, and she'd watched her husband try to ignore them whenever speaking up might cause a rift with someone with whom he did business. She'd watched him try to change minds that didn't want to be changed, to try—without offending anybody—to kick holes in cherished images and long-held assumptions. All he'd gotten in return for his efforts, besides a lot of stress, was the occasional, presumably complimentary observation, that he certainly had come a long way from those roots of his.

Roots like *Indian time*. There had been many times when she'd wished Jared could slow down and smell the roses, maybe rediscover the meaning of Indian time. But he'd set his course for changing times, and he'd followed it religiously to the end.

He'd left her with more house than she and Peter could manage easily. She'd been inclined to sell it, but friends had advised her not to make any major changes immediately after her husband's death. Now she hired a lawn-care service and a home-security agency to tend it while she was gone. She couldn't say how long it would be. All she knew was that she had to stay close to her son. She had to accede to someone else's terms, to someone else's schedule—or lack of one. All things in good time. On the reservation, good time meant Indian time. And the reality was that, no matter what her husband had endeavored to be, her son was physically, legally, undeniably, Chippewa.

But he was also a twelve-year-old boy, and he was hell-bent on acting like one. When Raina returned to Pine Lake, she learned that Peter was "on restriction" for the weekend.

And, for the first time in over two years, she hadn't been the one to make the decree.

"Whose restriction?" she demanded. "The court's?"

"Mine," Gideon said simply as he passed Peter the potatoes he'd helped prepare for supper. "Since my experience with kids is pretty limited, I'm not used to sleeping with one eye open." He arched an eyebrow over that one eye, and Peter quickly lowered his. "But I'm learning fast."

Raina sighed. She'd thought her son had learned his lesson the last time he'd tried using the basement window instead of the door for an exit. "Did you sneak out again, Peter?"

"Me and Oscar did." He served himself a generous helping of potatoes. "We went to check out the casino, but they carded us, so we just hung out. This place is really quiet at three in the morning."

She gave Gideon a look of apology. "I forgot to warn you that Peter is a night owl."

"I've been known to do some hootin' with the owls myself." Gideon sawed on his well-done beef with a table knife. "I know all the haunts around here and probably a few tricks you haven't thought of yet, Peter. So I'm way ahead of you."

"Did you get grounded, too?" Peter asked.

"Didn't get caught too often." Gideon glanced at Raina. "Didn't have anyone out looking for me. My dad wasn't around, and my mom wasn't up to it." He turned a hard look Peter's way, tapping a forefinger on the table to make what he hoped would be a memorable point. "So when I *did* get caught, I got searched, handcuffed and hauled off to jail."

"For what?"

"Petty stuff. Kid mischief." He nodded confidently. "Mistakes you're too smart to make, Peter. Myself, I was a slow learner."

"Seems like you turned out okay."

Gideon leaned back in his chair and put his hand to his mouth. His eyes shifted from Peter's face to Raina's and back again as he wiggled his front tooth until it came loose with a click. He withdrew it and showed them the empty space.

Raina's eyes widened. Peter laughed, as thoroughly delighted as he had been when he was six years old and Gideon had magically produced a quarter from his ear.

"My goodness, Gideon, I'd never have known," Raina marveled.

"You would have if you'd seen me about ten years back, when I couldn't afford a false one." He popped the tooth back in place and smiled, as splendidly as ever. "Indian Health Service doesn't cover the cosmetic stuff."

"How'd it happen?" Peter wanted to know.

"Lost it in a fight. It could have been worse. It could have been an ear or an eye." Gideon pointed the blunt-tipped knife Peter's way in passing, then set it back to work on his meat. "There's a lot of bad stuff going on after dark. A lot of ways to get hurt."

"Around here?" the twelve-year-old voice of experience scoffed. "This place is like the outback at night. You oughta try the Cities."

"I have." Gideon noticed the question in Raina's eyes. He shrugged. "If a guy's looking for trouble, he'll find it wherever he goes," he said before he took a bite of meat. But the question hung in the air until he dismissed it without looking up from his plate. "I lived in St. Paul for a while. Didn't like it much."

"We didn't know you were living so close by."

An old wound melted away when he looked into Raina's eyes and saw honest bewilderment. He smiled wistfully. The *we* part wasn't exactly true, but it was good to know that she didn't realize that. And that *she* hadn't known.

He'd said he didn't want her to know, but he'd often wondered whether Jared had mentioned it to her after all. Gideon had needed his brother then, but he'd never been able to say it in so many words. He'd also thought a lot about his brother's wife. He'd thought about the baby they'd adopted, the home they'd made for themselves, the family he wanted to be part of in some small way. Staying away had never been harder than it was then.

She read it in his eyes—at least, some of it. "Jared didn't tell me. Were you there for…?"

"I was only there for a short time. It didn't work out."

Nothing had been working for him then. With an abrupt gesture he dismissed the recollection and turned to Peter. "So you see, big city or backwoods, you're probably not gonna come up with too many tricks I haven't tried. You might as well save yourself the trouble."

"Like you're just about to tell me you wish you had," Peter supposed, challenging Gideon to a stare-down. "You did your own growing up, and you did it your way. Why don't you leave me alone and let me do mine?"

"Why don't I?" Out of a hundred reasons, he was supposed to pick the best one right there on the spot. "Because your dad was my brother, and your mom…" He'd taken the first easy choice, then skidded when he hit the hard part.

With a wave of his fork he backpedaled, settling on what was indisputable, figuring he was entitled to all the prerogatives of the man in charge. "Because I signed some papers saying I wouldn't. At least, not for the time being."

"Yeah, well, I don't see why they let you just—" Peter slid his mother a help-me-out-here glance "—take over on me all of a sudden."

"I should've seen this coming, I guess." Gideon pushed peas and carrots across his plate with an ineffectual fork. "This legal hassle. I should have realized that, with Jared gone, something like this might come up."

"Yeah, well…" With perceptiveness honed by years of parent-handling, Peter recognized Gideon's self-doubt as the chink in the fortress. "This is supposed to be temporary, and you act like you think you can be my dad. Like you can just tell me what to do." Seizing the moment, he fired his zinger. "But you can't. My dad *would've seen* this coming, and he wouldn't be letting any of it happen."

Gideon took the blow with a level stare. "What would he

have done if he'd caught you sneaking out at night? Anything different from what I'm doing?"

"That's not exactly the point."

"It *is* exactly the point." It really wasn't, but Gideon decided to make it the point by virtue of the authority Judge Half had unwittingly vested in him. "I'll stand in for him the best I can as long as…"

Raina and Peter were both staring at him now, wondering if he knew something they didn't. *As long as* what?

He went for the open-ended option, hoping it covered the bases innocuously. "As long as need be."

Now drop it, he warned Peter with a paternal look that seemed to come naturally, without a lick of practice.

"We talked about paying your grandfather a visit," Gideon said, easing smoothly into a different subject. No less sticky, just different. "You still wanna do that, Peter?"

"I guess so."

Gideon turned the offer over to Raina. "We were just waiting for you to get back so you could go along if you'd like to."

The suggestion clearly surprised her. "Do you think I'd be welcome?"

"I think we need to try to get along." Gideon spared Peter a patently inclusive glance. "With each other and with the old man. I'm betting that a genuine, friendly overture will earn you some points with the judge."

"Earn *me* some points?" Raina's look challenged him, and her follow-up smacked him hard. "You're maneuvering on my behalf, Gideon? When I'm not even part of your constituency?"

Surprised less by the remark itself than by the way it stung, he sighed. "Just trying to pour a little oil on the water, that's all."

* * *

Arlen Skinner lived in a three-room house tucked deep in the woods at the end of a gravel road that turned into a dirt track about three-quarters of a mile before it became part of his side yard. Visitors couldn't call ahead, since Arlen had no phone, but Gideon assured Peter that his grandfather was usually home. And that there were people checking on him regularly.

One of the programs Gideon had started since he'd taken office involved adding a home-visiting assignment, not only to the duties of the tribal health workers, but also for the tribal employees whose jobs had them traveling the reservation byways. People like game warden Carl Earlie paid routine visits to the tribal elders.

At a time when increasing numbers of the younger generation of Chippewa were looking for off-reservation opportunities, elders like Arlen Skinner were not to be ignored by Gideon's administration. Even though profits from the casino had made it possible to provide housing for many of the elderly within the small town of Pine Lake itself, Arlen preferred to stay in his own house, isolated as it was. Gideon was a strong advocate for respecting the elders' reluctance to change the way they'd always lived. He paid as many personal calls as he could, mostly for his own benefit, he was quick to say, for there was much to be learned.

But he had always seen that Arlen was on someone else's route rather than his own.

The old man was sitting on his porch, his chair tipped back against the weathered siding on the front of the house. He was surrounded by wood shavings, plastic pails and bundles of willow and birch, and he was working with strips of birch bark. He looked up as the three expectant visitors approached.

Lowering the front legs of his folding chair to the plank porch, he nodded a solemn acknowledgment of their presence.

Clearly neither side knew what to expect of this meeting.

Gideon reached past the steps and wordlessly offered a handsɪ.ake. Raina knew well enough to follow suit, but Peter, suddenly reluctant to take center stage, hung back.

"Shake hands with your grandfather, Peter," Gideon instructed.

Peter promptly complied, stubbing the rubber toe of his tennis shoe on his way up the wooden steps.

"Do you speak Ojibwa?"

"No—" Awkwardly stuck for a way to address this newfound relative, Peter tried, "Sir."

"Call me *nimishoomis*," the old man said, then translated, "'Grandfather.' I'm not a 'sir.'"

"Nimishoomis," Peter repeated carefully.

"Can you make coffee, *ninaoshishan?*"

Peter didn't need a translation. He knew that he was being addressed grandfather to grandson. "You mean like in a coffeemaker?"

"I mean like on a stove. Show him," the old man ordered Gideon. "You won't have any trouble finding the kitchen. Everything you need is there. When you come out, bring yourselves some chairs." He waved a strip of bark toward a folded chair leaning against the house and offered Raina an invitation by way of a nod. "I have one here for Mrs. Defender."

She opened the paint-splattered chair and set it next to the small, green Formica-topped kitchen table that was spread with Arlen's work-in-progress. Gideon ushered Peter into the house. The door closed softly behind them as Raina took her seat across from their host.

"Raina," she said quietly, perching like a shy forest creature on the edge of the folding chair.

Arlen spared her a questioning look.

"My name…" She cleared her throat nervously as she folded her hands in her lap, feeling a bit like the girl with the impeccable school record who'd been called to the principal's office. She took a deep breath and offered a tentative smile. There was no call, she told herself, to feel nervous. "Please call me Raina."

"Raina," Arlen said, testing the name out much the way Peter had done with the Ojibwa word he'd been given.

"Rain, with an *a* on the end."

"That could almost be an Indian name." It might have been a compliment, but there was no smile on his slash of a mouth. Only a hint of one, maybe, in the dark depths of his eyes. "Rain, with an *a* on the end," he echoed. "I know some people by the name of *Reyna,* but they're not 'rain with an *a* on the end.' They're Indian, though. Part Indian, anyway."

He eyed her curiously.

She fidgeted, the backs of her thighs sticking uncomfortably to the metal chair. She smacked her knee, flattening a mosquito, and regretted her choice of walking shorts for this outing.

"Do you have a great-great-grandmother way back who was part Indian or something? Maybe your grandmother named you after her." One corner of his mouth turned up just slightly. "Raina."

"None that I know of," she said airily, offering him her own smile and hoping to set an example. "I used to teach at the Pine Lake School, though. Back when I first met my husband. Does that…help?"

He slid a strip of bark between his fingers, considered her face and finally nodded once.

"Jared," she supplied obligingly. "My husband. Did you know him?"

"Not really. I knew his dad, long time ago. I used to stay with my wife's people." He tipped his chin in a vaguely westerly direction, pursing his lips as though his idle hands were too busy to make the gesture. "Over by where they got that new school now. She was from the Strikes Many clan. After she died, I came back here. But I lost track of those Defender kids. This one moved to the Cities. That one got to be chairman somehow." He shrugged. "I lost track."

"Do you have other children besides—" unsure of the reference, she gentled her voice to the point of near downiness "—besides Tomasina?"

"Two sons," he reported. "Both went away, looking for jobs. One other daughter, married one of them Oglalas, moved to South Dakota. Peter's mother was the youngest." She could tell he was testing her. When she didn't take exception to his choice of the word *mother,* he confided, "The wildest, looks like."

"Do you have other grandchildren?"

"Five. Don't see any of them that much." He couldn't quite hide the fact that he felt slighted. He shifted in his chair. "So you used to be a schoolteacher. And your husband was a big-shot lawyer?"

"I wouldn't say he was a big shot. He worked very hard." Gently, as was her way, she added, "And he died very young."

"A lot of Indians die too young." His dry chuckle might have seemed inappropriate had Raina not experienced the cruel irony firsthand. "They don't want to listen to us *old* Indians. They don't ask us how we keep livin' so long, 'cause they got their own ideas. They want to go live like white men. They say it's more fun for them."

Raina nodded. "Jared just worked too hard. Twelve, fifteen-hour days sometimes… His heart…"

"Was he too busy to make babies?"

"No." Curiously, she did not find his question intrusive, nor did she mind answering it. "We did try. It just didn't work out for us until…until Jared found out about Peter."

The old man grunted. "I told my girl it wasn't right, giving her baby away. She told me he was going to an Indian home, so I just let it go. She always had to do things her own way. Then she told me the name—that Defender that got to be a big-time lawyer down in Minneapolis. I knew he was probably giving her money, but I didn't say anything."

"Well, we *offered,* but…" She didn't like the turn the conversation was taking. "Maybe some for expenses. I'm not sure. Jared handled all the details of the adoption, but it wasn't like…like we *bought* Peter or anything." Whatever the arrangements had been, Raina felt that she owed Tomasina Skinner a debt of unending gratitude, regardless of whether her father approved.

She braced her hand on the edge of the table, leaned closer and entrusted him with the simple heart of her cause. "I've been Peter's mother since he was six days old, Mr. Skinner. I love him very much."

He nodded and pointed toward the end of the table. "Hand me that pail of water there. This bark has to be soaked."

She jumped at the chance to accommodate him and to talk about something else. "What are you making? Will this be—"

"Who wants coffee?" Gideon appeared at the door, steam rising from the melamine cups he carried, one in each hand.

Peter came next. With his free hand he held the door for

Gideon, who served Raina one of the cups and kept the other for himself. Peter's cup was for his grandfather.

"Don't hardly keep any pop around." Arlen nodded his thanks, then sipped noisily, his grimace a sign that the coffee was especially hot. "Mmm, good and strong. Next time you come, I'll have some pop for you, *ninaoshishan*. What kind do you like?"

"Any kind." A long, narrow, bark-covered bowl on the table caught Peter's attention. He touched one of the clothespins that held the lining in place. "What're you making?"

"Winnowing baskets," Arlen said. "Good birch-bark baskets. That one's drying."

"They're for ricing," Gideon put in.

Arlen set his cup down. "You like wild rice?" he asked Peter as he gathered several pieces of bark for the pail Raina had set next to him.

"It's okay. We don't have it much."

"I do make wild-rice stuffing sometimes," Raina put in quickly.

"We're going to teach her how to bait her own hooks next. We'll get her trained." Gideon slid Raina a teasing smile, then nodded toward Peter. "This guy's gonna make a hell of a good fisherman. He caught a nice walleye the other day." He held up his hands to show Arlen, measuring generously. "That sucker was two pounds, easy."

"Bigger than that," Peter insisted, moving Gideon's left hand another inch. He grinned, ignoring the dubious look on Gideon's face. "More like that, yeah."

"Born fisherman," the boy's grandfather said.

As Arlen demonstrated the basket-making process, he described how the baskets would be used during the early autumn wild-rice harvest, when the Chippewa would exercise another of their treaty rights. It was an important source of income for him and for many others. He lamented the competition from the cultivated varieties of wild rice, which was not rice at all, but truly a lake-grass grain, and he noted that the "farm stuff" was not to be mistaken for the real thing.

"Real wild rice is longer, lighter in color, tastes better, and it's gathered in baskets like these by real Indians in real canoes. Right, Arlen?" Gideon said.

"Big difference. Big, big difference." He wagged a gnarled finger and gave Raina the hint of a smile. "You remember this when you make your stuffing next time."

When it was almost time to go, Peter helped Raina clear away cups and led the way inside. "I'll show you how we made the coffee, right on the stove. I didn't know you could do that. I thought if you didn't use a coffeemaker, you had to use instant. Remember how Dad hated instant?"

Gideon watched them disappear into the house, then turned to Arlen, who offered him a cigarette. Gideon told himself he didn't want to be rude. Besides, he figured he owed himself one. Arlen leaned forward in his chair as Gideon struck a match on his thumbnail and offered him first touch of the flame.

"What do you think of your grandson?" Gideon squinted past the smoke as he renewed his acquaintance with the gritty pleasure of the first long, deep drag from a good cigarette. "He seems like a pretty well-adjusted kid, doesn't he?"

"Adjusted to what?" Arlen's smoke mingled in the air with Gideon's. "He has some things to learn yet."

"Well, sure, he's not quite thirteen."

"Things about who he is and where he comes from."

"That's why they came up here, Arlen. Raina doesn't want to keep him away from us. She wants him to learn those things."

The old man gave the woman's purpose some thought as he smoked a little more. Finally he shook his head. "It's no good, Indians moving to the city."

Gideon studied his cigarette. He couldn't argue that point. It hadn't been that good for his brother, but it was all Jared had ever wanted. "The good life" meant different things to different people, and Native Americans were people, just like everyone else. They paid their money and took their chances, and they deserved the chance to choose.

"You've let well enough alone until now, Arlen. Why stir this up when the boy's almost grown?"

"Seeing him with her," the old man recalled. "No offense to your sister-in-law, but when I seen him with her, I knew it wasn't right."

Gideon understood how the old man must have felt, seeing the boy for the first time, and then having Marvin Strikes Many on hand with just the right goad. Something like, *Your grandson's being raised by a white woman, and Gideon Defender's the one to blame.*

"Now that you've met her, what do you think?"

"I think she's still white." Arlen appeared to be studying the toes of his moccasins. "Like I said, no offense, but I think you're forgetting, just because she's your sister-in-law."

"She's a good mother. You can see that."

"I can see that she cares for my grandson," he allowed. "But a boy his age needs a man to help raise him. And a Chippewa boy needs—"

"My father was dead by the time I was his age, and Peter's—" Gideon closed his eyes briefly. The taste of cigarette smoke turned acrid in his mouth. "Peter's is, too."

The door behind them opened, and Raina emerged, still praising Peter's first efforts at stove-top coffee making.

Arlen looked up as Peter stepped out behind her. "You

would like wild rice the way I make it, *ninaoshishan*. The rice I have gathered myself."

Peter touched the unfinished edge of the basket on the table. "I wouldn't mind learning how to make these. They look pretty cool."

"It looks something like that basket you made for me for Mother's Day when you were about seven years old," Raina said proudly.

"That was just a grade-school project." He shrugged off his achievement as a pale comparison. "The teacher did half of it, and she was following directions out of a book."

"That's what schoolteachers do." Raina offered a maternal pat on the shoulder. "They get ideas from books. There's nothing wrong with that."

"Nothing wrong with learning the old ways, either," Gideon said. "Put the old ways together with a few new ideas, you never know. You might end up with the best of both worlds."

"Or you might lose out." After directing it first at Peter, Arlen deftly transferred his admonishment toward Gideon. "You might lose everything, just like we've *been* doing for the last hundred years. We've been compromising." The old man took a last puff on his cigarette, then spat the smoke in disgust as he pressed the butt into a jar lid on the table. He eyed Gideon dispassionately. "You're too young to be a tribal leader. That's why I never voted for you."

Gideon shook his head, chuckling. "No beatin' around the bush, this guy." He followed Arlen's example, putting out his cigarette in the jar lid. The end of a smoke signaled the end of a visit. "That's all right, Arlen. Man's gotta vote his conscience."

"Maybe you ought to think about teaching up here again,"

Arlen told Raina. "Maybe your brother-in-law could get you a job."

"I've always loved this place." She turned to her son. Reading him came less easily these days, but it was a mother's habit, and one she wasn't ready to break. "I don't think Peter wants to change schools."

Content to let the supposition stand, Peter tested the spring on one of the clothespins holding the bark to the basket frame, then eased it back into place.

"Next time you come back, we'll make a sweat," Arlen told Peter. "We'll smoke the pipe together."

Peter glanced at his mother, who was dead set against smoking, then his uncle, who had supposedly quit, and finally his grandfather, who had offered him the forbidden right there in front of their faces. He'd never had a grandfather before, but he'd heard there could be interesting benefits.

He smiled. "That'd be cool."

"Good." The old man rose from the chair slowly, easing his stiff joints into motion. "I will give you something, then. A gift from your grandfather."

At Gideon's house that evening, Raina wasn't asked to stay for supper. She was simply included. But Peter had a place at Gideon's table and a towel in Gideon's bathroom. They showed Raina the room they had fixed up for Peter downstairs, next to the den, where the video games were now hooked up to the TV. Gideon had borrowed a rollaway from the lodge, and Peter had apparently acquired some fishing tackle. Raina didn't ask about it. Seeing it shelved in "Peter's room" near "Peter's bed" angered her a little, but it frightened her more.

Peter had a room elsewhere, she reminded herself. He *had* a bed—a bigger one than this, made up with the bedding she had chosen for it in the subtle colors he tended to choose for his clothes. He liked blue denim and brown corduroy, not the gaudy plaid that covered the rollaway. It hadn't been more than two weeks since Raina had pulled a plaid shirt off a rack in a department store, and Peter had said, "No way. I'm not wearin' *that*."

She was thinking of all those things as she helped Gideon put the last of the dishes away. She hadn't been much help, actually. Peter had taken out the trash, then bounded down the steps to use the TV in "his" den. Raina dried a few dishes and handed them to Gideon. She could have guessed where they might go, since the pine cupboards in the kitchen were few in number.

But whenever he had them open, she paid less attention to what was inside than to the unconscious ease with which Gideon took to such mundane chores. Gideon Defender putting his dishes away in his kitchen, filling the coffeepot with water, clamping an opener on a can and releasing the homey scent of fresh coffee. Remarkable, she thought as she watched the strong hand that was a natural at wood-chopping and paddle-wielding turn the crank on a kitchen device.

She'd never pictured him in *his* kitchen. She'd never imagined him in such domestic surroundings. In her mind, he was part of the wild life, both outdoors and, less frequently, in honky-tonks and poolrooms. She'd always been fascinated by the wildness she perceived to be intrinsic in him. Barely controlled, barely controllable, Gideon's very nature was like a curious passageway that lured her with the promise of something new and exciting at the end. She'd always approached excitement cautiously, one shoulder leaning in its direction, the other aimed for a last-minute escape.

But she remembered that, in the end, it was Gideon who had backed away. Maybe that was the way of wildness, she had decided. And in her mind she had consigned all wildness to a world quite different from hers, a world full of risk-taking and privation. She hadn't expected it to live in a place with dishes and cupboards, nor to make room in that place for her child. She should have felt comfortable with it, now that she could see for herself how unexpectedly familiar so much of it was. But she felt like an outsider. And that scared her.

"You've been pretty quiet," Gideon observed as he handed her a cup of the coffee he'd just made. "I thought some decaf might go down easy right about now."

She told herself it would be easier if she stopped letting his every move surprise her, and she murmured her thanks.

"Mii gwech," he said with a warm smile. "You remember. *Mii gwech?* Thanks?"

"Mii gwech," she repeated softly. They faced each other across the small kitchen, each with a countertop to lean against, each with cup in hand. "You speak Ojibwa fluently, don't you?"

"Mmm-hmm." He sipped his coffee. "I get stumped when people ask me to spell it, though. I speak it, but I don't write it."

"I don't think Jared knew much of the language at all."

"See, I'm one up on him. But don't tell Peter. I don't want to spoil anything for him." He glanced away. "The dad who knew everything. That was Jared. The man who could do no wrong."

"Was that the way you saw him, too?"

He glanced at her curiously, then dismissed the question by changing the subject entirely. "What did you think of Arlen's suggestion? The one about coming back here to teach."

"It's a little late in the year to start applying for teaching jobs."

"There are still a couple of openings. I checked."

"And you'd put in a good word for me?" He nodded. "A

few days ago you were discouraging an extended stay," she reminded him. "You said the political climate had rendered relations a bit—" the pause was mostly for effect, because she did remember "—*dicey* was the word you used."

"That was then," he quipped, his tone suddenly as flat as hers was sharp. "This is now."

"Yes." An outsider, she told herself, needed to be sharp. *Stay* sharp. Mix in a little sarcasm. "And what a difference a day makes, hmm? A little controversy over a few fish suddenly seems rather insignificant."

"Not to me." He studied her with expressionless eyes. "Not to *us*."

"And my son is now court-ordered to be one of *you*."

"He always was."

"I don't mean culturally. I never disputed that. I mean politically."

"It's one and the same." He drew a deep breath, still watching her, waiting with less than his usual patience for her to stop skirting the issue.

"You haven't answered my question, Raina. I don't know what your lawyer told you, but *I'm* telling you there's a good possibility that Judge Half will rule that Arlen deserves *some* time with his grandson and vice versa. I don't know how much time, and I don't know how he'll suggest you work it. I just know that the precedent is pretty well established."

Sharp, she told herself. Stay sharp. But she glanced away, the threat of too much truth blunting her will. "Yes, that's what my lawyer said."

"You won't lose him," he said.

The hope that he knew something she didn't brought her eyes back to his, wordlessly asking for a promise.

"No one's going to take him away from you." He couldn't stop himself. When she looked at him that way, he had to give

her what she wanted. "That's not gonna happen. I won't—"
He swallowed hard, looking elsewhere for help—the bright
light above the sink, the shiny faucet, the dish drainer. "Well,
the *judge* won't let that happen. He knows it's too late to take
the boy back."

"You really think so?"

"Yeah." He nodded persuasively. "I can't see that happening
now."

"I've thought about trying to get my old job back here." She
offered a tentative smile. "I checked, too. They need a fourth-
grade teacher. I just don't know whether it would be good for
Peter. Jared didn't think much of the schools up here."

"He didn't think much of the *life* up here." Gideon stared
into his cup. "But as it turned out, life in the fast lane didn't
agree with him all that well, either."

"He used to say that *you* were the one looking for fast…
oh, fast thrills or something."

"That's *cheap* thrills." His brow furrowed as he made a
pretense of searching for the right words. "A fast buck and a
faster woman. I think that about sums up my brother's favorite
assessment of my basic needs."

"He never spoke unkindly of you, Gideon. Sometimes I
thought he envied you your—" she shrugged, glancing around
her as if some piece of it might be found in his kitchen "—your
freewheeling life-style."

"My 'freewheeling life-style,'" Gideon repeated with a dry
chuckle. "Right. Nothing about my life appealed to Jared.
'The good life'—that's what Jared wanted. The American
dream, looming off in the distance at the end of that fast lane."
He shook his head, raising his coffee cup as though he were
toasting her. "I had nothing he envied. He had goals—I had
needs. Big difference between the two."

"You don't think Jared had needs?"

"They were always met." His eyes conveyed the full weight of his meaning. "Always."

"And yours?"

He answered with a look, smoldering in silence.

"Gideon, I have to ask you something." But she had to glance away before she withered beneath the heat in his dark eyes. "Something I've thought about often over the years, but never—" She bit her lip, hesitating as she looked up at him again and sought his indulgence. "I never asked, even though I told myself there was a good chance the truth would ease my mind. But the prospect of opening a ruinous can of worms was always enough of a deterrent."

Before she went on, she stepped to the back of the kitchen and quietly closed the door at the top of the basement steps.

His eyes followed her every move.

She took a deep breath as she came back to him, speaking softly, steadily. "I have a feeling you know more about the circumstances of Peter's adoption than I do."

"What do you mean?"

"Specifically," she began carefully, "about Peter's biological father." She looked up, looked him straight in the eye. "Was it Jared?"

He was thunderstruck. "Jared?"

She squared her shoulders, preparing herself to hear the truth, whatever it was. "Did Jared have an affair with Tomasina Skinner?"

"That's a hell of a thing for you to ask me, Raina." He suddenly looked confused, even hurt. "My brother's dead. Why would you even…?" He shook his head, staring at her as though she'd just popped out of the floor. "Why would you think that?"

"Most people wait years for an adoption. Our was almost too easy." She wasn't going to let his reaction alter her course.

"I said that to Jared once, just…just wondering how it came about. He said that being an Indian was an advantage for a change."

"That and being a lawyer."

"But it was all so—" Too good to be true, too wonderful to question. "One day he knew where we could get a baby, and the next day we had Peter."

"Didn't happen quite that fast."

"But Jared had had very little contact with the reservation since we left, as far as I knew. He seemed to go out of his way to avoid…"

"Avoid…what?" Gideon's smile did not reach his eyes. "Or should I say *who?*"

"All things that reminded him of this place, I guess. Once he'd left it behind him, he kept saying he didn't want to look back."

"You guys wanted a baby," Gideon recalled for her, and she nodded, acknowledging that much. "Jared said he had a low sperm count. It was like he was confessing some terrible personal secret when he told me, like he'd found out he was missing—" For lack of acceptable words, he used those he once scoffed at. "'What separates the men from the boys,' I think he said. I thought he meant he couldn't get it—" His gesture, turning out to be as awkward as any word he could have chosen, ended in a frustrated slap to his own thigh. "You know, I thought he meant he couldn't perform."

"Perform?" She shook her head. "His sperm count was below average, but it wouldn't have been impossible for him to father a child…or for me, except for my…"

"He said you had a problem, too, but he didn't get—" *Personal* was the word that came to mind. The idea grated on him, but it had seemed as though once she'd become Jared's wife, nothing about Raina had been any of Gideon's damn business. He settled on "Technical."

"I have a tipped uterus," she told him. "Which isn't the end of the world, either, but with the combination of the two..."

"He couldn't *produce*. Couldn't get you pregnant."

Her eyes turned icy. "Sounds like you're talking about breeding stock instead of people."

He knew it did, just as he knew that the pleasure he took in making such a statement was of a pretty perverse nature. *Jared couldn't get the job done.* "So you're thinking he managed to get another woman pregnant."

"The thought did occur to me, yes."

"Are you jealous?"

"Jealous!" She scowled. "My husband is dead, for heaven's sake."

"They're both dead, *for heaven's sake*." He lowered his voice and persisted. "Are you jealous?"

"No." She had the look of a woman who'd swallowed the first half of a dose of bitter medicine and was still determined to take the rest. "But I think I'm entitled to the truth. Did he confide in you?"

"I just told you what he confided."

"That's not what I'm asking." She sighed, then recited with exaggerated patience, "I know he's not here to defend himself, and I know you don't want to betray his memory in any way. Or his trust, or your sacred oath, or whatever." She laid her hand on his arm, found it rigid, and her touch turned to subtle stroking. "But it can't change anything now, can it?"

His throat went dry. "Not for him."

"Then tell me, Gideon." The pressure on his arm became insistent. "Did Jared have an affair with Peter's mother?"

His memory, his trust, a damned sacred oath? Did she imagine he had a suit of shining armor on, too?

Gideon shook his head and turned away.

Chapter 6

She followed him to the back porch, where she waited, watching him light up the second cigarette he'd had in as many years. The second in a single day. The red ash glowed steadily in the dark as he filled his lungs, seeking the insidious calm of an internal haze. Gideon held his breath, mixed with the smoke, willing it to do its damage the way it always had, the way so many things had. If it felt good now, it would hurt later. But he could take it. Hell, he was tough.

But Raina wasn't. She was a good woman, but she wasn't tough. Jared hadn't been tough, either. He'd been smart, but not tough. And Peter...well, Peter was still young yet. Soft and malleable. With any luck he would end up good and smart, loving and well loved, proud of his heritage and strong in every way. And with all that going for him, maybe he wouldn't have to be tough.

She stood behind him, waiting for her answer, and, damn his mean soul, he wanted to tell her *yes*. Yes, your husband was a sinner, too, and yes, he screwed up sometimes, and *yes, Raina, you married the wrong man.*

But he couldn't quite get the words out. He wasn't sure why. There was no one to dispute them, and they might have served him well.

For some equally mysterious reason, he couldn't tell her *no,* either.

"What difference does it make, Raina?"

There was no sound, and even though she had to be standing at least a foot away from him, he could feel her body stiffen. His first response to her question had seemed to confirm her suspicions, and she was wrestling with it. He could help her with that, he told himself. He could spare the living and let her think what she would of the dead. *I'm here for you,* he could say. He'd always known the truth would hurt, but whom would it hurt, and how?

"There's the chance that Jared's health problems might be hereditary," she suggested, almost timidly.

He stared through the screen into the night. The trees behind the house stood like dark, shadowy sentries, and in the distance, there were lights twinkling on the lake.

"Is that it?" he asked quietly. "Is that why you want to know whether Jared had an affair?"

"I'm asking you whether Jared was Peter's biological father."

"No, you're asking me whether Jared cheated on you." It was a question, Gideon realized, that a man had to answer for himself. All his brother could say was, "If he did, it's history. It doesn't matter anymore."

"Then he *did.*"

"I didn't say that." *Yes, you did. To her, you did.* "Hell, I don't know," he admitted, giving in with a sigh. "I wasn't living with him. You were."

"I know he kept a lot inside," she said. "That's just the way he was. And I guess we buried it with him."

"Digging it up now might not change anything, but it could hurt somebody."

"Who?" Her motherly nose smelled a threat. "Peter?"

"First you. Then maybe Peter. Old ghosts ought to be left in the closet, where they can't hurt innocent people."

"I *am* Peter's real mother," she insisted, as though she believed he needed persuading now, too. "No matter what the circumstances of his conception or his birth were, *I'm* his true mother. And as his mother, I'm responsible for his health and his well-being, so if there's any possibility that he's inherited some kind of—"

"Jared was not Peter's father," Gideon said, his tone carefully controlled, utterly flat. "Not…biologically."

He took another pull on the cigarette, looking for heat. He could have sworn his skin was coated with ice. When she'd brought up the subject, he'd walked, but not far enough. The complications were piling up so damn fast he just wanted to walk out the door, jump in the lake and dive to the bottom.

Instead, there in the dark, he faced her.

"Look, I knew you guys wanted a baby," he said carefully, because now it was his turn to do some mental wrestling with all those damn pieces of the past. "And I knew that Tomasina Skinner planned to give hers up, so I told Jared about it. Simple as that. The fact that Jared was registered with the Pine Lake Band, along with him being a lawyer, *made* it as simple as that. No problem with the tribal court, and Jared handled the paperwork in the state court, smooth as still waters." He turned away and dragged deeply on his cigarette. On a trail of smoke he added, "Then he went and died on us."

"Gideon, you can't fault him for—"

"Don't *you?*" He wanted somebody else to, besides him. "Sometimes? Don't you ever say, 'Damn it, Jared, what did you have to go and *die* for?'"

"In the last week, sure. Well, I guess there've been a few other times," she admitted. "But I know it's selfish for me to think that way, as though he had a choice."

"Maybe. But I get mad at him, anyway, for checkin' out so soon, leaving some things unsettled between us." He reached for the empty coffee can he'd left on the porch, thinking it would come in handy for something. He hadn't expected it to be an ashtray.

Damn the complications, he told himself.

But a picture of his brother formed in his mind, and it made him smile. "Guess we're both human, huh? But if ol' Jared's earned his wings—and knowing him, he did it summa cum laude—then I don't believe he'll be wasting eternity looking for ways to use anything we say against us. I think he's above all that now."

"Yes, he is," she said with a sigh. "And I'm left with a predicament that wouldn't be a problem if he were here."

She sank into one of the wicker porch chairs and began deliberating aloud. "I could move up here. That really wouldn't be a problem. The sensible thing for me to do is to apply for a job here. That way, whatever happens, I can adjust."

The hand she lifted toward him was the color of moonlight. "Peter's all I have, Gideon. Everything else is superfluous. Is it possible…could I lose him entirely?"

"Not as long as he breathes."

As quickly as he reached out from the shadows, her small hand disappeared between his, which were larger and darker and much, much warmer than hers. "Peter is just as surely your son as you are his mother. He's never gonna forget that."

"But…say if this treaty thing turns out badly for you, and

there's a lot of resentment over it, and the judge looks at me, and he sees a white woman who's your sister-in-law…"

"Don't be lookin' to buy trouble now," he warned, seating himself in the chair next to hers. "We've got enough to worry about. And I'm not going to let Peter become a political football. That I can promise you, Raina."

"Are you…on my side at all?"

"I am." He rubbed her hand, warming it between his. "Mostly because I'm on Peter's side." He cleared his throat of the bitter taste of having to qualify a promise that he wanted to give her outright. "He's lost Jared, too. I don't want to see him lose his mother."

"But the interests of the Pine Lake Band—"

"Are my responsibility." He felt her stiffen again, and he withdrew, leaning back into the shadows. "Make no mistake about that. I won't compromise the interests of the people. But Peter is one of the people. The fact that you're not isn't as important to me as the fact that he *is*."

"Is that supposed to be encouraging?"

"When you're talking to the chairman of our tribal band, yeah, it should be encouraging. I happen to think the judge will see it that way, too."

"What about Peter's uncle? What about my brother-in-law, my—" she gestured, searching, and her hand came to rest on his knee "—my old friend. I want to be able to talk to *him* without talking to the tribal chairman. Is that possible?"

"Depends on what you want to talk about."

"What I'm thinking. What I'm feeling. How worried I was the whole time I was gone, and how glad I am to be back." She paused. The way her hand stirred against his jeans was appealing in every sense he could imagine. "Can you take your chairman's hat off for a while and let me talk to Gideon?"

"I can take off anything you want," he told her. "Anything that's in your way."

"Shades of the Gideon Defender I used to know." There was an echo of relief in her laughter, a full range of appreciativeness in the way she patted his knee. "There must be a happy medium."

"Yeah." Gideon wasn't particularly amused. "His name was Jared."

Before she left, Raina went downstairs to say good-night to Peter. She found him asleep on the sofa in the den. She started to wake him, but Gideon was right behind her with a blanket.

"Let him sleep," he whispered as he covered the boy. "He's on vacation."

The only thing Gideon regretted was that Peter was too big for him to lift in his arms and carry into the bedroom without waking him. He could have done that the last time the boy had visited, when Peter was only six. He could have kissed him good-night then, too, the way Raina did.

And there had been a time before that when he would have kissed her good-night, a time when she would have expected him to. A time before the first time she'd said, *We can't let this happen.*

If she'd wanted him to kiss her this time, she might have lingered at the door. He knew she didn't feel right, leaving without her son. He could hear it in her voice. On the way to the front door, he'd kept his hands off the switches to avoid shining a rude light on her sadness, not because he hoped that in the dark she might reach out to him again, might turn and touch him somehow before she left for the night.

And she didn't, of course. He had something she wanted, but tonight it was not his kiss. She hardly paused at the threshold. She simply told him in passing that it would be her turn to make supper tomorrow, and she hurried out the door.

Gideon had changed a great deal in fifteen years. He wondered whether Raina realized that, and whether it mattered to her. He and Jared had never had much in common, but Gideon had respected his brother for what he'd made of himself. Even though he knew the feeling had not held true in reverse, he indulged himself in thinking that it might have, had Jared lived a little longer.

But what about Raina? With her back against the wall, she was talking about moving back onto his turf, and she wanted to know whose side he was on. He couldn't blame her for clinging to the notion that the world was made up of straight, rigid sides rather than curves that might bend and rebound, ebb and flow. They saw the world from different perspectives, just as he and Jared had.

Jared had clawed his way closer to Raina's vantage point, and Peter...well, Peter's parents had been handpicked, so that he might enjoy the advantages of having a Native father who had made it in the white world and a mother who truly wanted a baby.

Whose side was he on? When it came right down to the bare bones, hadn't he always been on her side? Hadn't he taken her emphatic *no* for an answer? Hadn't he stepped aside and stayed out of their lives? Hadn't he given her what she'd wanted, always? Maybe she still didn't see it that way, didn't even realize it, because she'd never bothered to inventory her allies. But he had been on her side even when he doubted the existence of sides.

And if there were sides, they were all curved. There were surely no straight lines, nothing to keep Raina's path parallel to, but separate from, his. The great distance between them had gradually, inevitably closed in on them again, for all things in life were, after all, circular.

But he was on Peter's side of the circle now, too. He had been there at the beginning, and now the years had rolled around an inner curve and bumped the boy up against him again. That was the way of things. Gideon had learned the hard way. If Jared had lived a little longer, smart as he was, he would have come to recognize the circle, too.

Early the next morning Gideon went downstairs to wake Peter for breakfast. When he found only a rumpled blanket and a sofa pillow, he swore to himself that the next time the boy tried this, he wouldn't make it out of the house without running smack into Gideon, even if it meant *he* had to take up sleeping on the sofa.

"Hey, Uncle Gideon, is it okay if I put a nail in this wall?"

The voice coming from Peter's bedroom glided over Gideon's ruffled feathers. He kept a lid on his sigh of relief and followed the sound, ready with a smile by the time he reached the doorway. Apparently sometime during the night Peter had opted for more comfortable sleeping arrangements and moved to his bed.

"You got something you want nailed down?"

Peter handed Gideon a leather-wrapped circlet about the size of a small plate. "I tried a tack, but it fell on my head this morning. *Nimishoomis* gave it to me. He made it himself." It looked like a large spider's web woven of sinew on a willow hoop. Blue and white feathers and beads dangled from the bottom of the hoop, and there was a loop at the top. "He told me to hang it over my bed."

"It's a dreamcatcher." Gideon examined the fine workmanship of the webbing. Peter couldn't ask for a better artisan to teach him than his grandfather. "Do you know what this is for?"

"To catch dreams?"

"The bad ones get caught in the web." Gideon fingered a blue bead woven into the lower portion of the web. "You see, like this little rascal here. But the good ones slip on through—" he demonstrated with sinuous, undulating fingers that took a plunge behind Peter's ear "—and into your head."

The boy laughed. "It's a nice decoration, anyway. I needed something to hang on the wall."

"You don't think it'll work?"

Peter's face formed a get-real expression.

"You've never had to worry about bad dreams?"

"I've had a few." Reclaiming his gift, he rolled his thumb over the blue bead. "Sometimes I dream that my dad's still alive. The only bad part is waking up and realizing it was just a dream." He lifted his bony shoulders in an exaggerated, heartstring-tugging shrug. "Then sometimes I dream that he's not dead yet, but I, like, *know* something bad's about to happen, and I want to stop it, but I can't."

Abruptly those big, black eyes looked up at Gideon, their innocence completely unguarded. "It's pretty stupid, you know? But it seems real, even after I wake up, at least for a minute or two. I really hate it when that happens."

"I know what you mean."

"You do?"

"Sure." He wanted to hug the boy, to take comfort with him after the fact. But he held back, laying a hand on his shoulder instead. "Sure I do. I've had dreams about him, too."

Peter hung his head, ostensibly studying the intricacies of the dreamcatcher. "Sometimes I don't want to sleep at night."

"I know how that is, too. A guy gets to be your age, he

starts feeling a little restless. Hungry for a little excitement."
That's when you go out and try to hunt up some kind of distraction.

Peter tapped Gideon's arm with his fist. "I suppose when a guy gets to be *your* age, the excitement's pretty much over for him, so he turns into a killjoy for the rest of us."

"How did we go from me sympathizing with you to you pushing me over the hill prematurely?"

"We were talking about dreams, and how a guy can wake up—" Peter's short-lived smile faded "—feeling kinda weird."

"You mean weird *scared,* or weird *weird?*"

"Weird like you see something in your dream, like maybe a picture you saw in a magazine or something." He risked a brief glance at Gideon's poker face. Seeing no sign of comprehension, he took the further risk of elaborating. "A magazine that you didn't buy yourself, but another guy maybe found in his dad's workshop. You know what I mean?"

"I'm pretty sure I get the picture."

"Really. Pictures like you can hardly *believe.* You know, it *is* kinda fun to draw mustaches and glasses, tattoos and stuff like that, on *most* of 'em, but then—" he popped a quick shrug "—maybe you leave one or two without any touch-ups…you know, artistically speaking…just because you kinda like them the way they are."

"Some of them aren't half-bad without the tattoos," Gideon allowed, hanging on dearly to that poker face. "A guy might even be half-tempted to tear one of those pages out of the magazine and stick it in his drawer."

"Nah, my mom's always putting my clothes away, so I can't keep anything private." Peter's careless drop onto the bed stretched the wheezing springs to their limit. "I mean, if I *wanted* to keep something like that around. Which I wouldn't, because sometimes if you go to sleep thinking about, say something in a picture, and you dream that, like, something happens, and you wake up, and you realize it was only a dream…" His voice dropped to the confessional level. "But something really happened."

"And your bed's wet," Gideon kindly finished for him.

"I'm not a baby." Peter's cheeks flashed like neon apples. "I don't wet the bed. Something *else* happened. What, do you think I'm a *baby?*"

"I think you're becoming a man, and men—"

"Ejaculate, I know. I mean, hell, I'm not a little *kid*. I know all about sex and stuff, but—" his hands flopped helplessly against the bed "—I wasn't *doing* anything."

Gideon sat down on the bed beside him, bracing his elbows on his knees and wondering who'd ordered him up this baptism by fire before breakfast. He'd just barely had time to get his toes wet.

After a couple of false starts, he spread his hands in a commiserating gesture. "You don't have to be *doing* anything."

At the news, Peter looked grief-stricken. "You mean it can happen, like, *anytime?*"

"It can happen in your sleep. It happens to all of us." Gideon's nod affirmed their fellowship as two healthy, normal males. "Mostly when we're your age. Before the excitement's pretty much over for us."

"It happened to you?"

"Sure."

God help him, he didn't want to mess this up. He had to give the boy credit for having the nerve to broach the subject with an adult instead of another kid his age. By the time he was Peter's age, he'd managed to gather such an encyclopedia of misinformation that he'd gone to the mirror one morning expecting to find that his eyes were turning green.

Peter was visibly relieved to learn that he wasn't alone in his predicament. He toyed with the dreamcatcher, rolling it between his palms. "What did you do about...the bed?"

"I cleaned it up."

"My mom would get pretty suspicious if I washed my own sheets."

"Your mom knows all about sex, too."

"She doesn't know about—" Peter's eyes flashed in horror. "I told you, I wasn't *doing* anything."

"I know what you're saying." *Anybody else's mom but yours. You don't want me to mention your mom and sex in the same sentence.* "At least you've got a washing machine. We didn't. No dryer, either. So I just kinda cleaned up a little, left the bed—" He glanced over his shoulder at the rumpled sheets. "You're not still letting your mom make your bed, are you?"

"Well, yeah."

"There's your problem. See, I never had my own room. I had to share. And nobody ever cleaned up after me. But I think if you take care of your own bed, put your own clothes away, keep things kinda straightened up, you'll have more privacy."

Peter had to think that one over.

And another one, as well. "You really think she knows about stuff like this? My mom?"

"You mean, sex?" Gideon smiled benevolently. "It's hard to imagine, isn't it?"

"Kinda." Peter shrugged. "Hell, she doesn't know anything about what it's like to be a *guy*."

"She knows what it's like to be a woman. That's pretty

damned hard for *me* to imagine." Gideon gave a quick cross-check. "How about you?"

"Imagine being a woman? Who'd want to be a woman?" He rolled his eyes at the very thought. "Or a girl. I wouldn't want to be a girl. Geez, that would *really* suck."

"I think women have it hard in a lot of ways, but the old way teaches us that women have strong power, and they must be respected for that. They have life-giving medicine."

"You mean, they can have babies. Big deal. I'm glad *we* don't have to get pregnant and stuff." Peter's boyish laugh sounded, blessedly, as giddy as any twelve-year-old girl's. "Imagine a pregnant soccer goalie."

Gideon grinned. "Is that your position? Goalie?"

"Yeah."

"I'd like to see you play sometime."

Peter nodded. Then he remembered the catch. "Maybe I won't be playing this fall, huh? If I have to stay here?"

"How would you feel about changing schools?"

"I wouldn't like it much." He examined the dreamcatcher, which seemed to have become a touchstone for serious consideration. "I guess one of my buddies is moving to Cleveland next month. His father got transferred."

"So you understand that it's a necessity sometimes?"

Without looking up, Peter nodded. "Is it going to be *this* time?"

"We'll try to take things as they come, okay? We'll work things out one step at a time."

"My mom's talking about applying for a job here."

"I know. You can be damn sure, whatever happens, she's gonna be right there with you."

"It was pretty nice of *nimishoomis* to make this for me." He lifted up the hoop and held it toward the window, letting the morning light flow through.

"You got that word down pretty good," Gideon allowed. "*Nimishoomis.* Do you take any languages in school?"

"I've had some French. I could learn Ojibwa easy." Peter closed one eye, sighting through the web. "So some dreams get caught in the web, huh? They just get stuck there, like, where everyone can see them?"

"Not *those* dreams. Only the bad ones." Gideon gave Peter's knee a playful sock with his knuckles. "The kind you were talking about? It lets those through. They're really not bad." He bounced the edge of his curled hand repeatedly on the boy's knee as he spoke. "Stuff happens to guys, stuff happens to girls. It evens out. It all works out pretty good in the end, you know, when you get older and you partner up with the right lady."

"So where's your lady?"

"We-ell, guess I must be doing something wrong. I've been dreaming about her since I was your age, but no partnership so far." Gideon shrugged. "Nothing lasting, anyway."

"Kind of a late bloomer, aren't you?" Peter offered the dreamcatcher as he elbowed Gideon's arm. "Maybe you'd better get *nimishoomis* to make you a few of these. Increase your odds before you *really* get too old."

"Trouble is, these only work when you're asleep. With my luck, I'll be meeting up with the ones that should have gotten caught in the web."

"Never know," Peter hinted, flashing an impish smile. "Maybe *you're* the one that got caught in *their* webs."

Chapter 7

Arlen wanted his grandson to spend a weekend with him. He'd been asked to judge more dance contests, and he was "kinda startin' to like the idea of pickin' the winners." He also liked the idea of an old man's grandson accompanying him to the powwow, listening closely to his words of wisdom, picking up a little Ojibwa language and a few dance steps along the way.

At first Gideon had been inclined to dismiss the idea, but he thought better of it after he'd put the suggestion to Peter, who was willing. By this time Peter had made friends with a couple of boys his age, including Marvin Strikes Many's son, Tom, who lived only a couple of miles from Arlen's cabin. It had been a few years since Arlen's own offspring had left home, and Gideon suspected that having a teenager around for a couple of days might be all it would take to convince Arlen to back off on his demands, to accept regular visits from his grandson rather than push for a change in Peter's custody.

Arlen was also just the man to encourage Peter's burgeoning interest in North American ways.

The trick would be to persuade Raina to give grandfather and grandson a little space without her supervision. In pursuit of that end—and maybe in the interest of getting away from any mention of the words *treaty rights* for a couple of days—he decided after supper one evening to ask her to share his own favorite space and a brief bit of time exclusively with him.

"Oh, it's been so long since I've been to the North Woods, Gideon, I'd love to go." Her smile was at once wishful and apologetic. "But I think Peter should go along with us. After all, he hardly knows Arlen. *I* hardly know Arlen."

Gideon handed her the after-supper cup of coffee that was becoming a nightly ritual, then took his seat beside her in what were becoming the his-and-hers chairs on the porch. "Would you consider leaving him with your own father for a couple of days?"

"Well, yes, but—"

"And your father lives where?"

"A retirement community in Arizona, which is why we haven't…which is why Peter doesn't—"

"Know *him* very well, either?" She nodded regretfully. He offered an accommodating comeback. "That's the way things are these days. People are free to find a climate that suits them, but the downside is that family members are scattered from hell to Texas."

Ease her into this, he told himself. He considered the various aspects of his plan as he sipped his coffee. He liked its prospects. It involved a fair amount of diplomacy, which was turning out to be one of his strong suits. If he played his cards right, he might be able to keep everyone happy.

"I think it might help your cause if you showed the judge

that you're willing to let him have a relationship with his grandfather."

"I am," she insisted. "I want that, for Peter's sake. I've said so." She glanced away. "But I'm not sure we should…"

"What?" By *we,* he knew she meant the two of them. "What are you afraid of, Raina?" She stared out at the lake. "Are you still afraid of me?" he asked carefully, barely disturbing the weight of her silence.

"I was never afraid of you." Her voice trailed off on the tail of her flimsy fib. "I just don't think I should go traipsing off…."

"With me."

"Without Peter."

"Peter will do just fine with his grandfather for a couple of days, and you'll be okay with me." He laid a hand over his heart and offered his most endearing smile. "Will you trust me on this one?"

She held up two fingers.

"What does that mean? Peace? Victory?"

"Two," she informed him. "Two counts you're asking me to trust you on."

He slid his palm over the two fingers, folding them back into her hand, his eyes inviting her to give in to her own fancy for a change, to stop questioning and submit. Enveloping her small hand in his, he brought both to rest on his thigh.

"You remember that place I told you about way back when?" For him it was a once-upon-a-time. It had no name or number. "I told you I'd take you to a special place come spring, a place you'd never want to leave."

"I remember. You called it Hidden Falls. We never got there."

"Come with me now."

He waited, his eyes daring her to accept, even though he

knew damn well he'd already lured her past her intent to refuse.

She drew her smile out slowly, but her answer glittered in her eyes.

Ordinarily it would have been next to impossible to get a permit to go into the wilderness area on such short notice, but having been a guide himself, Gideon had connections. All it took was a phone call to his old friend and former employer, camping outfitter Jim Collins, and everything was arranged. Jim had their canoe and supply packs ready. Gideon didn't need the detailed maps the outfitter also provided. Even Jim allowed that the "chief" of the Pine Lake Band of Chippewa knew the North Woods better than anyone.

But he did have one word of caution for Gideon. "There is one fishing party out there that… Well, maybe you'll just wanna keep an eye out and steer clear." The outfitter looked at Raina reflectively, then added an extra foam pad to the sleeping gear. "You wanna take special care when you're escorting a pretty lady, take a few extra precautions, add a little extra comfort."

"Keep 'em comin' back. Yeah, I remember." Gideon offered Raina her pick from the beef jerky jar on Jim's desk. When she declined, he helped himself. "So what's with this fishing party? What's their problem?"

Lean as a scarecrow, Jim gave a sardonic chuckle as he hitched up his ever-sagging jeans. "Nothing a little attitude adjustment wouldn't cure."

"Always give the client his due, Jim." Gideon tore into the strip of leathery meat with his back teeth. "Couple of weekend Daniel Boones who don't need a guide?"

"No, these two are regulars. Been coming up here for years.

Chuck Taylor and Daryl Weist. Did you ever run into them when you were working for us?"

"I don't remember taking them out back then, but I know I've run across those names recently." It was important to remember the names. The same ones showed up repeatedly on letters and petitions. He made a point of remembering the names of his adversaries, but he didn't want the faces fixed in his mind. The smug and incensed faces of people who showed up at public information meetings and statehouse-step rallies. "Those guys belong to a group called the North Woods Anglers Club," he told Jim. "Real vocal about their commitment to saving *the state's* natural resources."

"They also know everything there is to know about Indians." Jim slanted his friend a look that mixed amusement with disgust. "Why, they were telling me just yesterday how a compromise with the Pine Lake Band would be just like making a pact with the devil, since Indian fish and wildlife managers never bother to enforce the tribal regulations and quotas in the first place, and since they don't know, uh—" He grinned. "Don't know diddly-squat about wildlife management, anyway."

"Yeah, right," Gideon sneered. "Did they really say 'diddly-squat'?"

"Well, words that smelled the same." Jim tossed Gideon a waterproof bag emblazoned with the outfitting company's logo. "Compliments of the house."

"Thanks." Gideon opened the bag and started transferring the contents of his pockets.

"Besides," Jim went on, "these guys have read their history books, and they know damn well Chippewa don't really believe in civilized law. According to them, that's why the tribal courts routinely dismiss most of the cases that come before them."

"Can I count on that?" The irony of the claim almost made Raina laugh.

"You can count on not being tried in tribal court," Gideon told her. "Their jurisdiction doesn't cover you." He raised a warning hand. They had an agreement. "End of discussion."

"For now."

"So these guys gave you quite an earful." Gideon tucked his billfold into the self-sealing bag. "Where do you stand on the treaty issue, Jim?"

"On the side of good sense. The way I see it, you guys decide to go to court, you're gonna win. You *should* win. Just out of curiosity, I read a copy of the treaty. I'm no lawyer, but it looks to me like you could end up with half the fish and game harvest in that couple-million-acre—whaddyacallit?— ceded territory area if you take this thing to court. I think you oughta hang in there and go for the brass ring, man." With a shrug, Jim acknowledged that it was no risk to him to talk big. "'Course, my business is outside of that ceded territory."

"Yeah, well, if we could compromise, we might be able to keep the peace." Gideon sealed the bag, then nodded toward Raina. "Doesn't she get one of these, too?"

"Sure." Absently, Jim turned his attention to the supply shelves. The seat of his jeans drooped like an empty feedbag. "Besides—" for a moment he forgot what he was looking for, and his hand was still busy helping him expound "—there ain't enough of you to make a dent in that kind of haul. What've you got down there? A couple thousand Pine Lake Chippewa?"

"Twenty-five hundred, and most of the members are living off the reservation." Gideon noted with some amusement that Jim, all wound up in his discourse, had just given Raina two of the complimentary bags.

"Okay, so every man, woman and child goes out hunting

and fishing three hundred and sixty-five days a year, these guys still got nothing to worry about."

"They're worried about Indians getting something they don't have themselves, which would be a real turnabout, wouldn't it?" Gideon helped himself to another stick of beef jerky, using it as a pointer. "I'm worried about the threat of violence. Like you say, our numbers are small."

"The thing to remember is, these two guys didn't talk real nice."

Gideon opened his mouth, then closed it, the meat forgotten as he eyed Jim. "Did you have anything to say to them?"

"I told them I didn't think the settlement would hurt anything." Jim shrugged, flashing Gideon a look of apology. "Hell, those guys and their buddies are paying customers, Gideon. You know how that is. I ain't gonna argue with them *too* much."

"You can't change their minds, either. No point in trying."

"Just so you know they're out there." Jim took a sparring stance and playfully cuffed Gideon on the shoulder. "Hell, they mess with you, they'll learn a little something they probably ain't figured out yet. Like you don't wanna back Gideon Defender into no damn corner, that's for sure."

"Sounds like there's a story there," Raina said.

"Hot damn, you should have seen this guy." Jim hitched his jeans up on his skinny hips. He didn't seem to notice that the effort was wasted. "Playing pool down at the Duck's Tail, and some jerk tries to bad-mouth this ol' warrior for dancin' with the wrong, uh…." Jim flashed Gideon a querying glance.

"Don't tell me the whole thing blow-by-blow," Raina said, settling the question. "Just tell me exactly how many of his own teeth this man has left in his head."

"Never seen Gideon on the losin' end," Jim said. "But I'm sure he's sent a few dentists some business."

"Well, as my buddy Clint Eastwood said…" Gideon went snake-eyed, and his voice dropped to a husky whisper. "'I ain't like that no more.'"

Shoreline trees bowed close to the lapping lake, some dipping their leaves like women washing their hair. The morning sun cast its bright gems into tranquil waters as the canoe approached a family of loons, the two babies bobbing along behind their parents. The distinctive yodeling call carried across the water, answered in the distance by a similar song.

"Can you tell the male from the female?" Gideon asked, as though he was giving a test. The question was posed to her back, for it was Gideon's powerful paddling that provided most of the propulsion and steered the canoe, as well.

Raina got to play at paddling while she enjoyed the ever-changing view. "They look the same."

"Only the male does the yodeling. He's letting his neighbors know he's out strolling in his own backyard." Even as Gideon spoke, the loon changed its tune from the haunting yodel to a quavering tremolo. Abruptly it drew itself upright on the water, coiling its neck and stretching the fullness of its five-foot wingspan.

"My God, he's big." Raina's paddle froze in midair. "Gideon, I think he's angry."

"He's charging," Gideon said with a chuckle. "And we're paddling on past, Papa, so just relax."

"I had no idea they were that big. Boy, is he mad." She swiveled in her seat, amazed by the bird's ability to pull itself up in the water like a 747 taking to the air. "And their call always sounds so peaceful." The loon gave out another warning. "On CD."

"On CD?"

"'Sounds of Nature.' I use them to help me sleep." The loon's angry cry echoed across the water. "Whoa, I think they edited that one out."

"He's just letting us know he's there to protect his family. He helped incubate those chicks. Earlier in the season, he carried the little guys on his back a lot when Mama wanted to go diving."

"Diving?"

"Best diver there is." Gideon's paddle dripped across the canoe as he switched it to the other side. "We call him the *mahng*. Legend has it that once the world was all water. And *Chimaunido,* who is God, asked for a volunteer to dive to the bottom and bring up some mud, so that He could create the land. Otter, Beaver and Muskrat each tried and failed. *Mahng* was the only one who could hold his breath long enough and dive deep enough to get the job done. His bones are solid, so he's a much heavier bird than, say, the mallard. The air sacs under the loon's skin keep him afloat. When he wants to make a dive, he just lets the air out."

"What does he do with all that weight when he wants to fly?"

"He needs a good stretch of water for his runway. It takes some heavy-duty paddling and wing-flapping for him to get airborne, but once he's up, he can cruise over a hundred miles an hour."

The deep chuckle at Raina's back sent a shiver sluicing through her. Gideon always told his stories, even the fables, as though they explained some truth, great or small. Some truth about him, she thought. Some simple truth about the enigma that was Gideon Defender.

"Of course, he's in serious trouble on the ground. On land he can't take off and can't walk worth a damn, 'cause his legs are stuck way back on his body for diving." He stopped paddling, and she followed suit, letting the canoe drift. "So here's this creature who thrives only in water or in the air— land is his nemesis—but when *Chimaunido* says, 'Who'll help me make the land?' *mahng* turns out to be the right man for the job."

In the distance, the loon yodeled peacefully again.

"*Mahng* was given the dentalium shell necklace as a reward," Gideon concluded. "In our tribe, it's a sign of leadership. Only a leader may wear the *megis* necklace."

Raina turned, squinting into the sun. "So where's yours?"

"I have one."

"Really?"

"Would it surprise you to see me wear a necklace?" He smiled. "Feathers and beaded buckskins? Would it surprise you to hear me sing Indian? To see me dance in the traditional way?"

"No, of course not."

"I have the *megis* necklace, and the responsibility that goes with it. *Mahng* is like my brother."

Raina laughed softly. "You'd never guess that from the kind of welcome he just gave you."

"Guess I'm kinda like the prodigal brother." He dipped his paddle into the water again, but his eyes held hers. "Like I said, he was just protecting his wife and kids."

"Maybe *I'm* the threat," she muttered as she turned, facing forward. Maybe the bird could tell that she'd come from the city. Maybe she smelled of engine emissions, fluorocarbons and oil spills.

"I've read that acid rain and mercury might, umm…that they're a terrible threat to the loon." *Might do them in,* she'd almost said, but she didn't want to be an alarmist. Something could be done to reverse the threat. Something could *always* be done. "I can't imagine these woods without that sound."

"Without *mahng?*"

She felt his eyes on her, questioning her common sense. Without the loon, the North Woods would be desolate, but to Gideon, it was more than that.

"Without the diver, we'd have no place to lay our heads," he said. "No earth at all. Some might doubt that, but what they will tell you is that there is nothing to prove it. The stories mean nothing. They aren't scientific."

Another tremolo reverberated somewhere on the otherwise quiet waterway ahead of them.

"Doesn't that warning call sound like laughter to you? Kind of wild and desperate, like, 'Look around you, brother! Wake up and smell the rain!'"

Suddenly she could feel his breath against the back of her neck. She shivered, and he gave a deep, throaty chuckle. "The rain should smell like Raina," he said. "Clean and sweet. What would you do if I kissed you now?"

She closed her eyes and drew a deep, sharp breath. "Tip the canoe."

He chuckled again. "That's what I thought."

She heard him tuck his paddle in the rack. "Are we just going to drift?" she asked, her small voice floating on the water like the crystal notes from a music box. Every sound seemed to gain volume, in contrast with the quiet woods along the shore. It was midsummer, and birdsong had decreased with the season.

"I'm going to drop a line and catch us some lunch. What would you like with your mercury, honey? Bass? A little trout, perhaps?"

"Gideon!" She racked her paddle, stretched her legs and brushed her hands over her jeans. "Since I'm wearing plenty of sunblock, all I want is fresh sunshine with my lunch."

"Sure you don't wanna order up a little purified air-conditioning, maybe some bottled water?"

"No, but I do wish I'd thought of putting on a swimsuit under my jeans—even though I'd have to slather on the sunblock—but I was afraid of causing a stir—" she eyed him pointedly "—among the mosquitoes."

He made a pretense of taking a look around as he prepared his fishing gear. "Nothin' astir so far, except the damselflies."

Noting that the water's edge was alive with the black-winged creatures that looked like flying metallic green sticks, Raina almost missed Gideon's lazy appraisal of her casual, ordinary, hardly provocative man-tailored shirt and jeans.

His smile was both slow and appreciative. "And me."

Gideon didn't yet have lunch on the stringer, but he was in no hurry until another canoe appeared, disturbing their floating idyll. He cursed under his breath as he reeled in his line. A twelve-hundred-mile maze of waterways—interconnecting lakes and streams that the Park Service called canoe area wilderness, no motors allowed—and he had to run into two north-country good ol' boys. He knew damn well who they were. The hair standing up on the back of his neck told him that much.

They grinned and leered as they paddled closer. Whatever these boys had been drinking for breakfast wasn't part of Jim's supply pack. Regular clients of Jim's should have known better. Getting tanked on a canoe trip was a sure way to end up floating home facedown.

But it wasn't any of Gideon's business.

The interlopers slid off to the side, keeping their distance, but their voices carried well enough.

"Looky here, Chuck, these Indians do know something

about angling. All this time they had us thinkin' they couldn't catch nothin' without a spear or a net."

Gideon watched the tip of his own rod as he reeled in his line. The man in the front of the other canoe pulled in his paddle, laying it across his thighs.

"Hey, how's it goin' there, Chief? What are they bitin' on?"

"Frybread," Gideon quipped. He set his fishing rod down and picked up his paddle.

"No kidding?"

"Don't you recognize him, Daryl?"

The question had the man in front rubber-necking for clues while the bigger man wielded the rudder paddle, bending the course of the intruding canoe.

"He really is their chief," the big one called Chuck said. "He's the one they interviewed on TV. You know, when they talked about this settlement the politicians have cooked up."

"Sorry, boys, I'm unavailable for comment." Gideon sliced into the water with his paddle, and his canoe surged forward. "Enjoy the fishing."

"We will. Right, Daryl?"

"Damn straight. We always do, and we ain't gonna let nothin' change that."

"You might wanna put your life vests on," Gideon called out. Then he muttered, "Call yourselves sportsmen, you damn fools?"

"Don't worry about them, Gideon." Raina glanced back at him as she reached for her paddle.

"Force of habit. I'll paddle," he told her. "You just kinda casually keep an eye on those two turkeys over your shoulder. They make any sudden moves, you hit the deck."

She did a double take. "Sudden moves? Like what?"

"Like they're reaching for something." His deft, powerful

strokes had them skimming over the water. "You never know how hot under the collar those red necks of theirs are liable to get."

The watch she kept over her shoulder was anything but casual. Her eyes widened. "Oh, my God."

"What the—?" He reached for her even faster than he ducked. "I told you to—"

"It's just a cigarette." She stayed his hand on her shoulder. "He took out a cigarette. It's okay."

"The idea was to get down, not wait to find out what…" He shook his head as he switched his paddle from one side to the other. "Some of these guys are fanatics, Raina, which means you don't trust them when your back is turned."

"Okay, I'm watching your back, and they're—" her eyes shifted to his face, and she gave a snappy smile "—out of sight now."

Gideon kept paddling. They slipped through the water, both silent for a time. She didn't understand, and he didn't want her to. Bigotry didn't scare him much, except for her sake. He'd lived with it all his life. Usually it was more subtle. It was that all-knowing stare.

You're an Indian. We expect certain things.

People used to notice when he ordered shots with a beer chaser. Now they noticed when he ordered pop. Either way, he could almost hear what they were thinking. It wasn't so much that being noticed bothered him, but getting stares did. It was so damned disrespectful. But it had generally been a subtle kind of disrespect. Until lately. Until the Pine Lake Band of Chippewa had pointed out that the state had no jurisdiction over their treaty rights. Since then, he'd started to wonder whatever had happened to good, old-fashioned *subtle* prejudice.

No, it didn't scare him, except for *her* sake. But it did

embarrass him. Taunts from two jackasses who were probably too stupid to go on living should have meant no more to him than a little static on the radio. He congratulated himself for not launching himself at them headlong. They were bound to topple out before the day was over, and with no help from him.

But Raina had seen it. Raina had heard what they'd said. It was *their* disgrace, not his, but it chafed a raw place deep inside him, where a remnant of unearned shame had tied a terrible knot in his gut.

"I don't think they'll bother us now, do you?" Raina said finally.

"Probably not." He eased up on his paddling. "Likely the only shot they had in mind was verbal."

"Right." She tucked her knees and spun on her bottom, reversing herself on the canoe seat so that she could offer a face-to-face, glad-we-got-past-that-one smile. "Just a couple of pigheaded jerks, right?"

"Probably perfectly nice guys, as long as nobody mentions Indians or fishing rights." God, she was pretty. Her hair, cinched down by her billed cap, was poufed around her small ears and glistened in the sun like a counter display of gold jewelry. Her smile just naturally made *him* want to smile. "But I'll never witness that firsthand unless I do something about this Indian-looking face of mine."

"Don't you dare."

"What?"

"Change—" she leaned toward him, reaching for his smooth cheek "—anything."

"You like my face the way it is?"

"Yes." She nodded. "I always have."

"Oh yeah?" In one fluid motion he slid off his seat and moved toward her, balanced on the balls of his feet. The canoe drifted, its balance unaffected. "I've always liked yours, too." Smiling, he laid his hands on her knees as he knelt before her. "Which is something you've always known."

He slipped between her legs, bracing the insides of her knees against his hips. Thus bracketed, he took her chin in his hand. Her lips parted, and he covered her mouth with his. Her head fell back, and he deepened the kiss, making quick little stabs with his tongue. He felt her wind her hands into the loose front of his chambray shirt, brushing against his flat nipples and making them pucker, as though he'd gotten a blast of cool wind. He lowered his own hand, tracing the arch of her throat with his fingers as he withdrew his tongue to the corner of her mouth, then traced the slack seam of her lips with the tip.

"I like your mouth, Raina," he whispered against it. "Always have."

She clutched his shirt. "If those guys were to creep up on us now, they'd probably..."

"Probably what?" His mouth curved in a sly smile. "String me up to a tree?"

She gulped. "Say things."

"You've got that right. In this neck of the woods, they would 'say things' if they thought I might be messing with the wrong woman. But taking a walleye with a spear might just get me shot."

"It's not that I care what they have to say." She closed her eyes. "It's just that..."

"Whenever I get too close, it makes you nervous." He gave her lower lip a brief nibble. "Did my brother make you nervous?"

"You move so much more..." Pushing her fists against his chest, she gave her head a quick shake. He made a silent vow not to ask for any more comparisons between brothers.

She looked up at him. "Do you always cut right to the chase?"

"That was a kiss, honey. Nobody's chasing anybody." With a tip of his head, he reminded her of their surroundings. "You wanna run? You'll have to get wet first."

"You'd never catch me in the water. I'm the one who taught Peter to swim." She braced her hands on his brawny shoulders and taunted him with a coy smile. "I'm beginning to wonder whether you can even catch our lunch."

"A direct challenge to a man's rod—" he gave a naughty wink "—cannot be ignored. Consider yourself off the hook— for the time being."

Chapter 8

For lunch there was pan-fried lake trout. The aroma, wafting beneath their noses on wood smoke and pine-scented air, was so mouth-watering that when Gideon flopped the first fish on Raina's plate she pounced on it like a ravenous cat. It took some fast tongue-juggling to keep from getting burned. Oh, but the flavor was fresh and delicate. Even the bit of meat she dropped in her lap was too good to waste, and Gideon laughed when she snatched it up and popped it into her mouth.

"There's more," he offered.

"But not enough." Seated cross-legged on a slab of granite, she held out her plate for another serving. "I can't remember the last time I had fish this fresh."

"You should have married a fisherman."

"No fisherman ever proposed." It was an innocent remark, and true enough, considering she'd really known only one superlative fisherman in her life. And Gideon well knew who that was. She shrugged and added blithely, "I guess I should have become a fisherman myself, but I'd rather go along for the ride and let someone else do the actual hooking."

"Not being much of a hooker yourself."

"I'm better at procuring." She pulled a small fish bone from between her lips, the urge to smile brightening her eyes. "I'm hell on wheels with a shopping cart," she added finally, "but, mmm, this is really my favorite kind of eating."

"Mine too."

"Thank you for providing fire and food." She reached for his empty plate.

"Mind if I thump my chest and sound the call?"

"What call?"

"Mission accomplished. The male bragging call." He slipped his hands beneath his hair, laced his fingers together at his nape and leaned back against the trunk of a white birch. "As opposed to the mating call, which is sort of a 'heads up' warning."

"Heads—" she arched one eyebrow in disbelief "—up?"

"We're talking about mating calls." His eyes were alight with the pleasure he was taking in the natural way she played the game.

"You said *warning,* and you said—"

"Is it possible that behind this prim exterior lurks a naughty mind? I'm talking about the natural world here. I'm comparing me, man—fire and food provider—to—"

"Me, woman." She shifted the plates to her left hand and offered a handshake with the right. "Hearth tender and food preparer. Glad to meet you."

"You comedian," he said with a chuckle. "Me whipped. I wish you could paddle as well as you can joke around, you woman."

"No you don't. You hardly gave me a chance to do any serious paddling." This was turning out to be a traditional division of labor. He'd taught her to use sand, then water, on the plates for cleanup, which she did. But it was his turn to sit back and relax. She waggled a finger at him as she repacked the camp kitchen. "You're a one-man crew, Gideon Defender. A real loner."

"You think so?" He smiled as she approached. She stood over him, a shapely shadow blocking only half the sun. Still smiling, he squinted against the glare. "I've been told that I'm a people-pleaser. Always trying to be somebody's champion."

"Who told you that?"

"I don't know. Some counselor."

From where he sat, she appeared to drop from the sky and land beside him, perching on the incline of another slab of rock. "What counselor?"

Her curiosity bore the seed of caring. He could hear it in her voice. All he had to do was water it.

"The one who helped me get off the bottle." It had been a long time since he'd given any thought to talking with her about it. Suddenly he was thinking the time might be right, if he could just keep it light.

"When was this?"

"A while back." He wouldn't have expected her to remember dates, but she looked as though she were hearing about his infamous bout with the devil's brew for the first time. And for some probably very pathetic reason, he liked that cloud of concern in her eyes. "You didn't know?"

"No."

"Jared knew."

"He kept your confidence, then. He never told me."

"I don't know whose secret it was." He shrugged as he eased his spine a few inches up the tree trunk. "It wasn't mine. I never told him not to tell you."

"Maybe he thought you wanted it that way."

"Maybe he thought he'd have to come to the center for family week." He glanced away from the puzzled look in her eyes. "Like I asked him to. He said he didn't want to expose you to any truth-or-dare sessions."

"I would have gone," she assured him. "Or not. Whatever would have helped more."

"In the end I finally decided to help myself. Getting treatment only started the process." He rubbed the back of his neck and noted that she was hanging on his every word. His brother was dead, and here he was telling on him, when he had no right to lay blame at anyone else's door. "Jared was right, you know. Who knows what I would have said back then if I'd gotten the chance?"

"You can say whatever needs saying, Gideon. I'm no china doll. I can always talk back."

He chuckled. "Yeah, you've got a mouth on you, all right."

"Was that why you were living in the Cities?"

"No." *Damn you, Defender, a* yes *would be a whole lot simpler.* "Well, partly. I went down there to find a better-paying job, but I was…" *See how complicated it gets?* He jerked at an innocent blade of grass. "It was a long time ago. So now I'm doin' okay. I'm doin' *good,* actually. I'm trying to…"

Somehow he'd missed any sound of movement, but when he lifted his chin, she was there. His heart tripped over the soft light in her eyes and landed quivering at the mercy of her moist lips touching his. Her kiss was deliciously delicate, like a touch of morning dew, or a close encounter with a hummingbird's wing, hovering for a moment, then drifting away.

He half expected her to vanish with the blink of his startled eyes.

"What was that for?"

"For you." She sat back on her heels and braced her hands on her thighs, looking at him as though he were a bowl of flowers she'd just arranged. "For the man you are."

"You think you know who that is?"

"I think I'm learning. You have more patience than you used to have. More self-control. But you're still…" She reached out tentatively and plucked at his shirtsleeve. "You always had a very strong presence, Gideon. Very masterful. I think Jared found it a bit intimidating."

The incredible words stacked up one right behind the other, whap whap whap, like dominoes. He tumbled them with a laugh.

"You've gotta be kidding."

"Jared was older, but you were stronger," she insisted. "And I don't mean just physically. You were the one who took care of your mother when she was ill. Jared wanted to pay someone else to do it."

Gideon shrugged. Like he'd had a choice when the woman was *dying*. "She wanted to be home."

"I know she did. You're a very caring man, Gideon Defender." She sat down next to him, stretching her legs out beside his. Had she waggled her feet side to side, they would have touched him midcalf. "And you're a born leader."

As much as he enjoyed her praise, he still had to groan at the thought of him being a born anything. Hell-raiser, maybe. "Sometimes I think I'm just bluffing my way along as chairman. To hear Arlen Skinner and Marvin Strikes Many tell it, I got elected by default. My critics didn't bother to vote."

"You've made a lot of improvements," she pointed out, as though she'd taken inventory.

He told himself that he would have to remember how much credit this kicking-the-habit talk could earn him.

"How important is this treaty compromise to your program?"

"The compromise would be just that. A settlement. We'd gain a little land and some investment capital, and we'd return to some of our traditional practices without any interference from the state, which is what most of us want. In return, we'd give up some of our off-reservation treaty rights, which is what the state wants."

He'd told himself that he wanted to get away from this for a while, but he found that he didn't mind sorting it out for the umpteenth time with her as a sounding board.

"It's important because it might keep the peace. And it's important for our self-respect. Guys like those two we ran into this morning have been calling the shots long enough. It's a sport for them, and that whole scene this morning was part of the game. It's all about who's in control."

"They weren't." She sounded disgusted. "They were totally out of control, like those men at the dock the first time you took us out on Pine Lake."

"We've always fished and hunted for the same reason we gather rice and maple sap. For food. Traditionally, we fished with nets and spears. Those are the ways we were given to feed ourselves, and we value those ways. The reservations haven't changed that. The casinos haven't changed it, either." His gesture dismissed both would-be agents of change. "The reservations took away most of the land. The casinos bring in money. Big deal."

"Losing the land was no big deal?"

"We never owned it. We used it. And the treaty says we can still use it. We are who we are because of what Arlen called our Indian ways." He looked to her for acknowledgment.

"Remember? He told Peter he would need his Indian ways. Not just fishing or smoking the pipe, but *the way* things are done. And the way we use what we've been given. Does that make sense to you?"

"Yes. So far."

He couldn't blame her for reserving judgment. The jury was still out on how all this might affect her and Peter.

But he wanted her to understand that there was a lot to consider. "The only thing that changes is that sometimes people forget. You forget who you are, you start thinkin' you're nobody." He searched her eyes for some sign that she could imagine what it was like. *I'm talking about myself now, Raina. I'm talking about myself at twelve, and I'm talking about Peter at thirty-eight.* "Sometimes you lose sight of what's important. Then you lose your way."

"I can't imagine you losing your way." She laid her small hand on his thigh.

Incredibly, it weighed heavily on him.

She smiled. "I'll bet you know exactly where we are right now."

"You will, huh?" Relieved by the sudden switch in tone, he bobbed his chin, challengingly. "How much?"

"I'm betting on *you*."

"I know." He arched an eyebrow. "How much?"

"If you looked at a map, you would know exactly where we are right now. You could put your finger right on the exact spot." He raised both eyebrows. She lowered hers. "Couldn't you?"

He laughed. "Why do you think I told Jim to forget the map? Wouldn't do me a damn bit of good."

"Are we lost?"

Grinning, he tapped a fist on her knee. "We're on our way

to Hidden Falls, which is not on the map." He gave her a flirty wink. "I know *the way* there, and I know *the way* back."

"That's a relief."

"I haven't guided anyone astray up here yet." He nudged her shoulder with his. "'Course, there's always a first time."

"Oh, look!" She pointed to the lake. "Another loon." Her finger became an airbrush, tracing the big bird's graceful progress in the water.

Gideon watched, too. "See the white necklace? The stray shells scattered across his back?"

"You really have a necklace like that?"

"Sure do," he said proudly.

She studied him briefly, then shook her head. "Nah, you're not gonna get us lost. Not even as a joke. It would be too embarrassing for you."

He smiled mischievously. "But leading us astray is an altogether different matter."

Not a trace of their visit was left on the shore when Raina climbed into the canoe. Gideon lifted the bow, gave it a push and hopped aboard without even getting his feet wet. They paddled close to the shore, carried the canoe across a portage, then slipped into a rapid stream. The current eddied, and paddling was mostly a matter of controlling the canoe's direction. Gideon handled the craft so skillfully that all Raina had to do was enjoy the swift ride.

Another portage took them back into glassy water. Reflections of the pines stretched across the lake like long fingers. A beaver's cruising head blazed a trail through the lily pads close to shore, slipping through the water with a stick in its mouth. The white water lilies bobbed in the beaver's gently rippling wake.

They followed a stream that grew so narrow, it seemed to

hold no promise as a passage. But the next portage enabled them to bypass the stream's bottleneck, which was, in fact, the hidden falls he'd promised her. The water tumbled over a six-foot drop, splashing into a clear-water cove surrounded by massive red and white pine. The pine scent, the soothing sound of falling water, the choir of crickets, the occasional call of a loon blended into a lovely island of serenity.

Gideon set the canoe down near the water's edge. Most of the portage work had been his. Those brawny shoulders had been shaped in part by years of carrying a canoe over his head, and his height allowed few paddling partners to measure up to the task of assisting. He flexed his shoulders as he surveyed the spot he'd cherished in recent years only as a memory. Maybe his mind had improved on it a little.

"Not much of a falls, huh?"

"I wasn't expecting Niagara." Raina released the straps on the pack she'd been toting and lowered it to the ground. "It's a beautiful spot."

"I don't know whether Jim routes people this way now, but he didn't use to. Neither did I." He stretched, then used his fingers to iron the kinks out of his back. "We wanted it to stay like this."

"I'm the first?"

"Paddlers probably stumble on it once in a while. I haven't been here since…" He considered for a moment. "I don't know when. And you're the first person I've brought here."

"Can you believe it? A truly natural place." She lifted her arms, spun like a pinwheel, then faced him, exhilarated as she walked backward toward the water's edge. "It was like this a hundred years ago, and two hundred years ago, and back, back, back…."

"Whoa." His arm shot out, and he grabbed her hand. "You're about to back into the ice age."

"It's not that cold, is it?"

"Right now the water's about as warm as it ever gets."

"Can we go swimming?" Her face lit up, giving him a rare peek at the little girl in her. She lifted his hand toward the sky and danced under their arms, then ducked back and turned, drawing his arm around her waist as she backed up to him. "Do-si-do your partner," she sang merrily. "Can we have a campfire?"

"I can make it *feel* like we have a campfire."

She flashed a twinkling smile over her shoulder. "Hmm, yes, if memory serves—"

"I mean with a camp stove, which isn't as intrusive on the…" She looked a little disappointed, like a kid poised for a race and getting no takers. "Forget the memories, Raina." Close to her ear, his voice dropped for another husky imitation of his favorite Eastwood line. "'I ain't like that no more.'"

"Not at all?"

She turned slowly, and their eyes were suddenly locked in a heated stare. He wasn't going to chase her. He'd made that mistake before. He could run her down easy. He could give her a head start and still beat her, hands down, but he would end up losing.

He tucked his thumbs in the front pockets of his jeans and shrugged. "We can go swimming if you want. Like I said, the water's as warm right now as it ever gets, but I guarantee you won't last long."

"How about you?"

A smile tickled the corner of his mouth. "I can outlast you."

"You sure about that?"

"Try me."

She stared at him for a moment, as though she were trying to decide just how she might interpret his challenge to her advantage. Her sigh sounded like a concession to his staying power. "But no campfire?"

"I'll build you a fire." He looked into her eyes and touched the yellow-gold hair that swept her shoulder. "What else do you want?"

"I want to be exhausted." She closed her eyes. "I want to be able to sleep."

Gideon wasn't interested in doing any fishing once Raina had made her wishes crystal clear. Supper consisted of the meal packs supplied by the outfitter. Over campfire coffee they watched the setting sun spill a purple wash across a tall cloud's lumpy belly. Above their heads a spray of pine needles made a dark etching against the salmon-pink sky.

He set up the yellow igloo-shaped tent, tossed the sleeping bags inside, then stripped down to his black briefs.

Raina took the hint, again wishing she'd thought to wear a swimsuit under her clothes. But her underwear would serve. Her bra and panties always matched, and neither was ever skimpy. By the time she had folded the rest of her clothes and set them on a rock, he was already in the water. Which was cold. Smooth and clear as glass, but *cold*.

She waded in, carefully negotiating the slick, round rocks as she splashed a handful of cold water over the back of her neck to, as her mother had always said, acclimate her "cold receptors." She was almost ready to submerge gracefully when a soggy mop of black hair sprang from the water, laughing like a distressed loon. The monster clamped cold hands on her warm arms and dragged her, yelping and flailing like a dog on an ice slick, into the depths.

Once the monstrous laughing and distressed shrieking toned down, they bobbed like two corks, face-to-face, chins skimming the water, circling each other, taunting and giggling like children. Below the surface they were locked together, hands to elbows, hands to waist, now drifting at arm's length, now easing closer, knee sliding against thigh, thigh against hip.

"Told you it was cold."

"You said it was as warm as it gets."

He pushed his hair back. She did the same.

He grinned. "Told you it was cold."

Her teeth chattered. "I'm not cold."

"Is that purple lipstick you're wearing?"

Eyes, charcoal brown and crystal blue, glistened in the half-light of evening. Lips drew back in tight, waterproof smiles. "You know what?"

"What?"

"I learned this at a cosmetics demonstration once. 'Always remember—warm water plumps, cold water shrivels.'"

"Shrivels what?"

"Skin."

"You're tellin' me."

"On the other hand, some movie stars soak theirs in ice water every day."

"Their what?"

"Skin."

"Hmm." He shot a mouthful of water at her. "You don't play fair. You know that, don't you?"

"It can become a permanent condition."

"What?"

She shot water back at him. "Shrivelment."

"At least it won't show." His return volley hit its mark. "Like those purple lips."

They splashed around until it was almost dark, but in the end the shivering got to her first, and she waded ashore. Gideon used his hands to sluice the water off his arms and legs as he hurried to retrieve his T-shirt, jeans and flannel shirt. Raina huddled next to the dying campfire, dripping and poking at the embers with a stick. He helped her efforts along by adding a few pinecones, which went up like Roman candles, torching the log he threw on for good measure.

"Don't stand too close to the fire." He rubbed her briskly with his T-shirt. "I outlasted you, didn't I?" She gave him a tight-lipped stare, but he persisted. "Didn't I?"

Shivering, she nodded. "It k-kind of felt okay until we g-got out."

"Here, put this on." He handed her his flannel shirt, which looked voluminous hanging from her small hand.

She slipped it on, buttoned it, then executed the bra-removal-under-the-shirt trick, right before his very eyes.

"Slick," he said, his voice replete with genuine admiration. He tossed a loosely folded sleeping bag on the ground close to the fire and, with a gracious gesture, offered her a seat. Then he stepped away from the firelight. He kept his back to her while he peeled off the wet briefs.

Raina was soon mesmerized by the play of shadows over his perfectly taut buttocks. She was fascinated by the smooth, easy way he stepped into his jeans, pulled them up powerful legs and settled them at the base of his long, tapered back. He zipped them as he returned to the fire.

And he caught the look in her eye, just before she glanced away.

She could hear the smile in his voice. "You didn't peek, did you?"

She lifted her hair off the back of her neck and gave her head a little shake. "I didn't mean to."

"Right." He chuckled, thoroughly gratified. "I don't have your finesse at stripping off wet underwear."

"You don't need it. Doing what comes naturally is easy for you." She used her fingers as a comb. "For me, there are so many ifs, ands and buts. They're all in my head, I know. But—" She smiled wistfully. "See, there it is. That pesky old 'but.'"

"The hell, you say." He sat beside her, cross-legged on the sleeping bag, and extended his hands toward the fire. "You knew there would only be one tent. Which means we're going to sleep close to each other, unless you want to kick me outside in the cold."

"Oh, no, of course not. We're roughing it."

"You know what?" He turned to her and plunged his fingers into her hair, lifting it toward the heat of the fire. "All roughing it aside, I could make love to you so easy. If I started kissing you and touching you, it would come naturally. And I could make you forget all the ifs, ands and pesky buts." He looked into her eyes and smiled confidently. "But I won't."

"You won't?"

"No." He scooted closer, his knees touching hers as he ruffled her hair. "I've thought about it, and I've decided not to."

"Really." She stared, partly amused, partly incredulous. "Just like that, *you've* decided—"

"Not to." He watched her hair slide through his fingers, smiling complacently as though he had given it some style. "There, now, isn't that a relief? You can just put it out of your head."

"It wasn't *in* my head. It was in *your* head."

"Well—" his bare shoulders rolled in a shrug "—now it's not. Are you exhausted yet?"

"Exhausted?"

"We could take a run through the woods, and you could pretend I'm chasing you."

"Gideon!" Her quick laugh betrayed barely curbed

anticipation warring with inbred hesitancy. She laid a finger against his chin. "You're teasing me, aren't you?"

"It's up to you to figure that out." He tucked his chin and caught her finger with his lips for an impetuous nibble, grazing the tip with his teeth. He smiled, satisfied. "While I'm trying to figure out whether you're teasing me."

"I'm not sure I like this game."

"I'm not sure I do, either, but we seem to be playing it." With a forefinger he traced the arrowing neckline of his shirt until he hit the buttoned juncture in the shallow valley between her breasts. "How 'bout if we just sit by this fire you wanted me to build for you and swap hungry looks?"

"You're being difficult."

His deep chuckle sounded ominous with the darkness so close about them. "It comes naturally."

She mirrored his move, tracing the thong he wore around his neck until her finger reached the small leather pouch that hung to the middle of his chest. "What's this?"

"Just a…" He glanced down, as if he'd forgotten. "It's my medicine bundle."

"Is the contents a secret?"

"The contents is personal." He slid his hand over hers as he raised his brow. "Can I ask a favor? How good are you at massaging away an awful ache?" He ignored her wide-eyed double-take. "Do you know how long it's been since I did this much paddling? If you plan to go back the way you came, you need to give your workhorse a good rubdown."

"Oh. Oh, certainly. Why didn't I think of that?" She scooted around behind him and started thumping his shoulders with tension-busting karate chops. "Actually, I'm quite good at this. I took a course. Would you rather lie down?"

"I think it's better if I stay semivertical." His chin dropped to his chest. He closed his eyes and briskly ruffled his own wet hair. "If I fall asleep, there's no tellin' what I might miss out on."

"Try to relax, then, and give me the high sign when I hit on something that needs extra attention."

"The high sign it is," he said with a chuckle.

Her hands were more skilled than he'd anticipated. Her ministrations lulled him into total witlessness, and the sounds he made as the tension drained out of his neck, his shoulders, then his back, were unintelligible groans of pleasure. When she was done, she let him drift euphorically, his forehead pillowed on his knees. After a while he turned his head to the side and watched the mesmerizing dance of the remaining gold flames, listening to the pine wood crackle and the crickets chirp.

A sudden, long, drawn-out canine call brought his head up slowly. Even in the North Woods, this was a rare treat.

"Coyote?" she asked.

He inclined his head toward the sound, then shook it only slightly. "Timber wolf. Listen." The lone howl started low and rose slowly, stretching skyward. Then others joined in, and the distant darkness came alive with the woeful chorus.

"Are they far away?" she whispered, peering into the blackness beyond the orange flames.

"Can't tell." He bounced a playful fist against her flannel-covered thigh. "What, do you think I'm a bat?"

"No, but..." The wolf song filled the night. "There must be dozens of them."

"Half a dozen, tops. No two hitting the same note." He listened for a moment, letting the performers demonstrate. "See? If they do, one changes to a different pitch, so they sound like a huge pack."

"But they do sort of harmonize." She let the sound have its

way with her body, and her shoulders did the hoochie-coochie. "It sends shivers up my spine."

"Damn. I wanted to do that." His hands claimed her shoulders, and he turned her away from him. "Let me give it a try. You did a little paddling. I'll give you a little massage."

"I guess I am a *little* sore."

He leaned close to her ear and whispered, "You were great, by the way."

"Really?" She rolled her head from side to side in response to the muscle-kneading he was doing at the base of her neck. "It was good for me, too."

They hardly spoke as they arranged their sleeping bags side by side in the little tent. The slow, easy way they'd approached each other in the warm glow of the fire had been good and right, and now she wondered when and how he would make his move. For, of course, it *was* his move. He'd planned it. She hadn't. It would take her *almost* by surprise, and she would find it impossible to resist.

The sound of a zipper brought her head up quickly. He was opening the rain flaps, admitting the moonlight through the tent's mesh screens.

"Too much air?" he wondered.

"Oh, no," she said quickly.

"Your hair's dry, isn't it?"

She nodded.

He undid another zipper. "I get claustrophobic in these things. I hate it when it rains and you have to close them up."

"Me too." Actually, she'd never given it a thought.

He went to his bed. She slipped her legs into hers. He turned to her, slid his fingers into her hair and touched his forehead to hers. "Nice and dry," he muttered. "Still warm from the fire."

She returned the gesture. "Yours, too." Warm, long, thick and wonderful, she thought.

"You've got 'Sounds of Nature' all around you tonight." He turned his head slightly, rubbing the high part of his cheek up and down, over her temple, her eyelid, her cheek. He drew a deep breath, full of her scent. "Live, not recorded."

"Mmm, yes."

"You'll sleep like a baby," he promised, his voice deliciously husky. "Good night, Raina."

Unreasonably miffed, baffled by her own disappointment, she followed her sinking heart into the pocket of her bed, tossing him a whispered "Good night." She closed her eyes and listened to the night sounds. They were better than a tape, of course. The crickets, the owl, the loon, all blended their clear, soft calls, bidding her to rest. She felt peaceful. The intimate sound of Gideon's slow, shallow breathing made her feel safe. And warm. And more. Waiting for sleep, she inadvertently kept it at bay.

Gideon lay on top of his sleeping bag, slumbering blissfully. Then something in his dreams must have disturbed him, for he groaned and flung one arm above his head, nestling his face in the crook of his elbow. His hair looked longer now. It spilled away from his face and neck like a pool of black ink. Moonlight skated over the contours of his muscular chest and puddled in the shallow saucer of his belly. His jeans rode low on his hips, the waistband slack, the snap undone.

Raina closed her eyes. She could almost feel his warm, satiny skin against her palms again. She flexed her fingers and recalled the firm flesh, the hard muscle. So close. Close enough to hear the change in the tempo of his breathing. He groaned again, almost painfully. What was he dreaming about? she wondered. Or whom? She imagined him calling to her, saying her name in his sleep. It was a fanciful notion, of course, but it excited her. Almost as much as the bulge that had risen beneath the fly of his jeans.

Dear Gideon, in sleep your body betrays you. Your "high sign" refuses to lie dormant.

Her thighs tingled. A wicked urge sprouted deep within her and grew undeniably strong. Lying on her side, she scooted closer, braced herself on her elbow and slid her hand over his belly. It felt wonderfully hard and warm. Pleasure, she thought. It pleasured her simply to touch him, and it was a pleasure she longed to share.

Perhaps her touch alone would bring more pleasure to his secret dream. She found herself coveting his secrets, determined to become part of them, to insinuate herself into his dream. The contents of the pouch that lay against his chest was personal. The contents of the pouch in his jeans was personal, too. But while he slept, it revealed itself to her, beckoning, entreating. She told herself that she might do him another service. She might relieve this intensely personal tension, as she had relieved his other tension earlier.

Ah, he looked so beautiful, stretched out so that he filled the tent. Even in repose his body teemed with dangerous, alluring potential. Her hand stirred, her fingertips inched toward the unsnapped tab, searching first for the dimple in his belly. Her thumb found it, followed the rim, filled the depression, then moved on. The zipper gave way, a fraction of a fraction of an inch. Somehow his belly dipped away even farther, giving her hand more room to explore. What she sought was easy to find. The slick tip, the hard ridge, the oddly enticing thickness that filled her hand.

He held his breath for fear of scaring her away. He could understand the plight of a woman two years a widow, but did *she,* he wondered, understand his? In dreams she had touched him, but never, in his most compelling fantasy, had he been gloved this tightly in her small hand. He felt the light touch of her lips on his shoulder, and then her hand slid away. His whole body followed its retreat, turning to her, reaching for her, pulling her into his arms.

Her eyes were filled with moonlight and awkward surprise. His eyes demanded an explanation. Not why she'd touched him—he wasn't one to question such bittersweet serendipity—but why she'd stopped.

"You looked so…so beautiful. I…" Her breathy excuse got caught in her throat.

"Me?" He would indulge himself no further than a smile. "You've gone without too long."

"It's not that. It's…" *It's you.*

He didn't need to know what it was. Didn't even want to know. It was bound to make everything more complicated when he was doing his damnedest to keep from jumping the gun with her. But those eyes, those big blue eyes, were brimming with complications.

His hand skimmed the length of his flannel shirt, following the S-curve that filled it out. At the end of the road, her thigh emerged. He gripped it and drew it toward him. "Just tell me what you need, Raina."

"Gideon…"

"Gideon?" He nuzzled her neck and whispered into its hollows, "Gideon's what?"

"Gideon's everything."

With a throaty chuckle, he cradled her in one arm while his free hand slipped the shirt buttons loose, his moist lips marking her skin at each interval.

"What would you do with 'Gideon's everything'?" he muttered when he reached her belly.

"I would…I would…."

"Toy with it?" Reversing his direction, he nibbled a path to the soft underside of her breast, where he nuzzled and nose-butted, like a calf coaxing its mother to let the milk down. "The way you started to a minute ago?"

She started to reach for him again, but he stopped her and tucked her arm behind her back. His supporting arm lurked beneath her, and his hand was a ready clamp, putting her seeking hand out of action. Another time, he told himself as he lowered his mouth over her thrusting breast. He flicked his tongue over her erect nipple, then nibbled and suckled until she moaned, almost, but not quite, pitiably.

He slid his hand over her hip, rotating it away from him as he moved down the outside, then up the inside of her thigh. Her legs clamped together instinctively, despite her erratic breathing, despite her needy groan.

"Open your legs for me, sweetheart." He closed his eyes and rubbed his face in the vale between her breasts, tasting her salty-sweetness with the tip of his tongue. "Let me give you what you need."

"No, let me," she pleaded. "Let me show you…what I started to…what you want me to…"

"No, let *me*." His fingertips arrowed into the juncture he sought, gaining access, fingers spreading, prying reluctant thighs apart. He drew dizzying circles around her nipple with the tip of his nose, distracting her from the two fingers he slipped between moist folds. "Relax, baby," he whispered.

He suckled, and he stroked deeper, ever deeper. His tongue flicked, and his thumb did likewise, tuning her, then playing sweet, excruciatingly sweet notes. High notes. High, higher notes until there was only one note left, and she hit it like a bottle rocket.

Morning came veiled in blue-gray mist. Gideon had coffee ready. They sat side by side on a fallen log, scorching one another with stolen glances, scalding one another with every accidentally-on-purpose touch. Each had tried to relieve tension for the other. Both wondered why it was still there, thicker and heavier than ever.

"We should get a move on. This is the best time to be out on the water." Gideon heaved himself off the rustic sofa. He nodded toward the bright green head of a mallard gliding through the mist. "Everybody's out feeding."

Raina sighed as she followed his lead. "I hate to leave this place now."

"It wasn't easy to get you to come here." They looked at each other. She gave the first shy smile. He shook his head, then permitted himself to laugh. "I never know what to expect with you, Raina."

She walked away, dragging her feet against the grass. "It's just that it's so beautiful here."

She had called him beautiful, too. He remembered it clearly. He wondered if she'd meant it. Any of it. "You roused the sleeping dragon, Raina."

"I know."

"Did it help?" She stood still, her back to him. Gently, he rephrased the question. "Did you sleep better?"

"Did you?"

Questions, questions, questions. Why couldn't she just answer him? Tell him yes. Just say, *Yes, Gideon, you gave me what I wanted. Thank you very much.*

No, he had not slept better, partly because he didn't know where to go from here. He snatched his white T-shirt off the rock where he'd left it and pulled it over his head. It was damp and cold, and wearing it made him feel both good and miserable.

"It's beautiful out there, too," he told her gruffly. "We'll have our breakfast on the water."

He strapped the main camp pack to his back, hoisted the red canoe above his head and took the portage with determined stride. Raina followed in contemplative silence. Once they were out on the water, there was a certain freedom of motion that pulled their focus from each other, releasing mental suction in a way that produced an almost audible pop.

They slipped past a female moose feeding in the shallows. She lifted her shovel nose out of the water, grinding her dripping breakfast with powerful jaws as her eyes followed them with minimal interest. They both laughed when she shook her head, noisily flapping her big ears. Indifferent and absolutely unthreatened, she swung her head away, then dunked her nose for more juicy grazing.

As the morning wore on, low clouds kept the sun from burning the mist off the water. The fishing would have been great, Gideon thought. But he wasn't in the right mood. "I think we're in for some rain," he said absently as his paddle sliced the water. Slip-slide, slip-slide, slip-slide.

Raina looked straight up. "It's not supposed to do that." But an errant raindrop hit her nose. More drops pattered softly, scattering circles across the water in the pattern of a wedding-band quilt.

"Well, it's doing it anyway," Gideon said.

By the time they put in to shore it was coming down steadily. Thunder started rumbling as they set up the tent. Birch leaves rattled in the wind, and the water dripped from the pines, intensifying the evergreen scent. They tossed the packs into the tent and scrambled in after them.

"You're soaking wet." It was the only thing Gideon could think of to say. At least the stuff inside the packs was dry. He took out the two requisite towels, which, laid end-to-end, didn't add up to half a bath towel.

But at the prospect of spending a rainy afternoon inside the tent, he had it in his mind to be gallant. He tossed her a towel, which she used on her hair, while he did the same. Then their eyes met. She looked incredibly sexy with tousled hair and wet clothes.

He tried to clear the gravel from his throat. "Let me help you get dry."

It was an offer that entailed removing clothes. All it took was their shirts—skinning the cat with his, then peeling hers away with a bit more care and a thoughtful smoothing back of her hair after the shirt came away—and he was lost. He had the towel in his hand again, and he meant to use it, but his good intentions turned to mush at the mere sight of a drop of water on the swell of her breast. He dipped his head to claim it with his tongue.

The taste was pure ambrosia. He glanced up and saw the quick approval in her eyes. He unhooked the fastener between her breasts and stripped the wet fabric away. "So pretty," he murmured, but in daylight her pale breasts seemed to want covering. So he cupped them in his dark hands.

The thunder grumbled overhead. The rain pelted all around them. Gideon lifted his gaze slowly from the place between her breasts where his thumbs lay side by side, to the little hollow at the base of her throat where her pulse throbbed, to her lower lip as she quickly sucked it and left it moist for him.

The motion drew him like a hawk descending for prey. His lips claimed hers. His tongue darted in search of hers, and hers met him at the door. His hands slid to her waist and made short work of the fastenings on her pants.

"Would you say we're going to need a bed?"

She nodded.

His eyes never left hers as he reached for a sleeping bag, dragged it close, undid the bands and flipped it open, all with one hand. In another moment her wet clothes were gone. His were chafing him something fierce. He lowered her to the pallet and went hungering after her, pulling her hand down between the legs of his soggy jeans. He closed his eyes and caught his breath when she flexed her fingers, pressing, stroking.

He groaned. "It would be a damn shame if Gideon's everything caught a chill."

Her small laugh was sensuously deep. She helped him peel off the wet jeans. Then, in the gray light of a rainy afternoon, they admired one another with unabashed eyes and unrestrained hands, with openmouthed kisses and bold tongues. Dampness turned steamy as they rubbed skin against skin, driving one another to the brink again and again, just to see how close they could come. But close would not suffice this time.

"Tell me what you want," he exhorted gruffly as he rose above her, poised for a swift strike.

"This is what I want," she whispered, caressing him between his legs. "All of this inside me."

He prepared himself. All for her, he thought, properly gift-wrapped. But someday, maybe…

On that hope, he slipped himself inside her with long, strong, deep strokes. She gasped and cried out his name. He backed off only slightly as he slid his hands beneath her bottom. She locked her legs around his waist. His hips took the lead, tagging their tempo to the steady tapping of the rain, which picked up gradually until the heavens finally broke wide open and the deluge washed over them.

They dozed in each other's arms, reveling in timeless, weightless peace. The easy time. The afterglow. The distant thunder was a soothing sound, as was the soft rain. They drifted, awash in unspoken love words.

But the drifting eventually stopped, and the words slipped away, still unspoken. They were two separate entities again. And they found themselves purposely not looking at each other for fear of detecting something in a look—some kind of disappointment, some sign of rejection—that would make them feel chillingly naked.

It was she who broke the silence, because well enough wasn't well enough if it had to be left alone.

"This complicates things, doesn't it?"

"How so?" *Damn,* he *had* to ask. And then he couldn't help dipping the damn question in cold brass. "What do you want to make of it, Raina?"

"Nothing," she said tightly.

Nothing at all? Have it your way, then. "It's as simple or as complicated as you want it to be."

"What about you?"

He stared at the curve of the tent roof. "I'm flexible."

"Really." She covered herself with a corner of the sleeping bag. "Then I certainly appreciate the use of the condom."

"There's no other way these days, right?"

"Right." She turned her face toward the wall. Her throat felt scratchy, lined with sand. "Funny. I got used to thinking none of that pertained to me, but now…" She swallowed hard against the encroachment of awful heartache. "Now I guess it does."

"I guess so." He jammed his hands beneath his head and stared hard at the nylon ceiling. "Some women buy their own now. Dutch treat."

She shut her eyes tightly. "I'll keep that in mind."

Chapter 9

There was a part of Gideon's brain that was fully aware of the fact that sex was one of life's great wild cards. It was the great complicater. The gate to heaven, the road to hell. He didn't know how many times he had to prove that to the other part of his brain. One look at the woman sitting as far away from him as the pickup's bench seat would allow should have been all the proof necessary. If you wanted to get somewhere with a woman, leave sex out of it, at least until the trapdoor to hell was safely frozen over.

Things had changed between Raina and him, and the reason was clear. Raina had broken her own rules.

He'd never been quite sure what the rules were. He'd learned one or two hard lessons during his tougher years, and he'd taken those into account. Otherwise, he thought he'd read all the signals right. But, damn, for a while there she'd turned into a wounded bird. After the rain, they'd paddled back to Jim's place, with her in retreat and him walking on eggs. Her conversation had been soft and thready. She'd admired every bird, every bee, every bend in the waterway, like someone taking her last look at the world. When they got back to Pine Lake he half expected her to ask him to drop her off at a convent, or maybe a tomb, where she was ready to inscribe the epitaph herself: *Gideon Defender loved me to death*.

But she'd mended her own wings by the time they'd reached his house. The melancholy clouds disappeared from her eyes, replaced by distant, clear-day blue. *Distant* was the key word. Things had definitely changed.

Most women were hard to figure, but this one was a doozy.

When they pulled up to the house, Gideon was surprised to find his driveway blocked by a Jeep bearing the official seal of the Pine Lake Chippewa Band. This must have been a piece of the plan he'd forgotten.

"Wonder what Carl's doing here." He said it casually, but Raina's eyes turned anxious. "He's not a cop," Gideon hastened to assure her as he set the pickup's parking brake. "He's one of our game wardens. He gets out to the Skinner place pretty often, so I asked him to kinda discreetly make sure things were going okay with Peter."

She flung the pickup door open. "I knew it was a mistake to leave him with—"

"Hold on now." Gideon hurried up the driveway to catch up with her. "Let's not jump to any conclusions. Peter must be here, too. Otherwise Carl couldn't have gotten in the house."

They walked in on what appeared to be nothing more than a friendly card game, with Peter hosting his grandfather and Carl Earlie at the kitchen table. All three looked up when Gideon and Raina came in, but the greetings were ominously guarded.

"We figured we'd save you a trip out to Arlen's," Carl explained as he threw in his poker hand. "I'm gonna give Arlen a ride home."

Peter looked at his watch. "It's Sunday night. You said you'd be back Sunday afternoon. These guys have been waiting here for two hours for you to get back."

"We got caught in the rain." Gideon turned a chair away from the table and straddled it, bracing his forearms on the backrest. This was a switch. A kid watching the time on his parents.

Parent. Parent and guardian. Whatever. The damn complications came in battalions.

"Did you wear your grandfather out?" Raina asked as she stepped close behind her son's chair.

He looked up at her and shrugged. "We did a lot of stuff. Spent a lot of time at the powwow. I learned how to do a dance."

The chin jerk he made toward his grandfather was a new mannerism for Peter. It seemed perfectly natural to everyone in the room but Raina, who knew him better than he knew himself and noticed every change in him lately with a mother's mixed feelings. He was growing up. He was forging new connections. He was slipping away.

"What was that dance, *nimishoomis?*" Peter asked.

"Traditional grass dance." Arlen shared his nod of approval with Peter, then Gideon. "He did pretty good. We started making him a bustle."

"And the other thing I'm supposed to tell you is that I—" Peter cast a quick glance Carl's way, checking to see whether the man had changed his mind about the requirement. Clearly he hadn't. "Well, Tom and Oscar and me went out kinda late, and we had a couple beers."

Raina's response was automatic. "Oh, Peter, you *didn't.*"

"No big deal," Peter complained. "Nobody got drunk or anything."

"I was in bed sleepin'," Arlen reported. "I told him not to be sneakin' out. He didn't listen. Looks like he wants to learn some things the hard way."

"This isn't going to work, Peter." Raina laid her hands on Peter's wiry shoulders, while he hung his head, staring at the five cards he would never play.

Carl shoved his chair back from the table and rose to his feet. "Listen, I'm gonna get out of the way here and take Arlen on back." He turned to Gideon. "The other thing is, Rosie said to tell you that Judge Half wants to see everybody over at the court tomorrow afternoon."

The news hit Raina like a wrecking ball. "That hardly gives me time to get hold of my attorney." She wanted it over, but she wasn't ready. She noticed the ace in Peter's hand, and she wondered where hers was. She had no cards to play, in fact. Nothing but a mother's commitment to her child.

Gideon spoke quietly, avoiding her eyes. "All he'll be able to do is advise you, Raina."

"You mean I won't be represented?"

"You'll be heard," he said impatiently, as though she were speaking out of turn and in front of the wrong people.

But a rising sense of desperation kept her going. "I don't like the way that sounds."

"Call your attorney." His curt gesture smacked of resentment, even though his tone was utterly controlled. "You're right. You should have an expert around to advise you."

"There's something else," Carl announced officiously. He straightened his uniform, tucking his shirt into the back of his pants. "Arlen here says there's been some kind of secret meetings going on between the Strikes Manys and some of them big-shot sportsmen. They're all hot against the settlement, so they're talking about finding ways to defeat it so the treaty ends up in court."

"Where the sportsmen are betting we'll lose, and the Strikes Manys are betting we'll win. Makes for a strange alliance, doesn't it?" Gideon shook his head. "Why are you telling us this, Arlen? I thought you didn't approve of the settlement."

"I don't. But the Strikes Manys are fooling themselves real bad, talking with those guys about working together. We picked our leaders, even though some of us never voted for certain ones." He gave Gideon the loaded eye. "But they're who we've got, and they're Indians, at least."

"Those damn rednecks just wanna use the Strikes Manys to make it look like they're not against Indians," Carl said. With a sardonic chuckle, he added, "Hell, they *love* Indians. Some of their very favorite people are Indians. Like those guys who play for Cleveland and Atlanta."

The tension eased with the three men sharing in the bitter humor over one of their least favorite institutionalized insults to Natives.

"Dealing with those guys is gonna mean trouble for all of us. You need to read up on Red Cloud and Spotted Tail," Arlen told Gideon in passing as he angled toward the door.

"What for?" Gideon challenged kiddingly as he saw the guests out. "They were ornery Sioux."

"They were Indians. And they spent a lot of years trying to compromise with the white government." Arlen summed up his parting bit of wisdom with a solemn nod. "Some things change, some things don't."

After Arlen had left with Carl, Gideon figured it was time for a serious family-type powwow—the kind he'd rarely experienced, up until this summer. Raina and Peter were the ones who knew the ropes with this family business, but she was on edge, and he was sulking.

"How about some sandwiches?" Gideon suggested when he joined them in the kitchen.

"Not hungry," Peter mumbled, awaiting the inevitable cave-in with studied apathy.

"No, thank you." His mother folded her arms tightly under her bosom, her prestorm stance equally well rehearsed.

"All right, then, let's all—" Gideon glanced back and forth between them "—have a seat."

"Let's just get it over with," Peter suggested.

Gideon shook his head. "I don't know about your mom, but I'm not gonna lay into you over this sneaking out, Peter. Things are a little up in the air right now, and you took advantage of the situation. I don't feel real good about that, do you?"

"It was no big deal," the boy reiterated stubbornly. "If Carl hadn't come along, nobody woulda had to know."

"Listen, if this all goes okay tomorrow—and I really don't think we'll be looking at any big upsets—you and me are gonna have a little talk about some of the ruts along the road to manhood."

Peter rolled his eyes and sighed dramatically. "Not *this* again."

"Yeah, *this* again." Gideon's hand was allowed to rest on the boy's shoulder only briefly before Peter shrugged it away. "You don't need to be drinking now, Peter. You've got too much goin' for you. Booze can only get in the way."

"You got another false tooth to scare me with?" He indicated Gideon's lower half by way of the chin jerk he was quickly perfecting. "Maybe a wooden leg or something?"

"No, but I can bar the window and sleep outside your door, if that's what it takes."

"You'd be a fire hazard." Peter saw the chance to play both

ends against the middle and, like any normal kid, he used it readily. "Anyway, with any luck, we'll be goin' back home. Right, Mom?"

The question took Raina by surprise. Suddenly she had her little boy back. Her prodigal son was ready to be taken home. And, just for a moment, all that mattered was that he was ready, and that he had turned to her.

Tears scalded the back of her throat. If she spoke, they would surely surge upward and reduce her to an emotional wreck. She had no answers, anyway, but she gave a quick nod and opened her arms to him.

That he permitted a hug—even returned it—felt like something of a victory, particularly when Gideon's pat on the shoulder had been turned away. Oh, God, she was a poor excuse for a woman of character! But Raina was willing to take her small triumphs however they presented themselves these days.

The next morning Peter was up earlier than Gideon expected. He himself was up earlier than he wanted to be, after last night. He would have given anything to have been able to take Raina to bed and make the world—mostly *his* world—go away for her. But, of course, he was dreaming with his eyes wide open on that score.

Peter was helping himself to a bowl of the Lucky Charms he'd asked Gideon to stock for him. "Mom's downstairs, sleeping on the sofa in the den," he reported.

Gideon headed for the coffee fixings. "Let's try to be real quiet. She hasn't been sleeping very long. Couple of hours, tops."

"She's been up all night?"

Gideon nodded solemnly.

"Did she think I might run off or what?"

"She just wanted to stay close by." Gideon shoved the pot under the faucet and ran some water. "She's a strong woman, your mother. She's worried about how all this is affecting you. You need to give some thought to what it would be like to be in her shoes right now."

"And not cause any trouble."

"That would help." For a kid Peter's age, it was probably a lot to ask, considering the circumstances. "It's gonna work out."

"You think so?" It was a rhetorical question, quickly followed by the real concern. "Yeah, but how?"

"We'll know soon enough." Gideon turned the coffeepot on, then turned to watch Peter slurp spoonfuls of tiny pink and blue marshmallows into his mouth. "Your grandfather didn't have a chance to make a sweat with you?"

Cheeks puffed out like a foraging squirrel's, the boy grunted, "Uh-uh."

"That's maybe what we should've done this weekend. Might have kept us all out of trouble."

"You guys haff any twouble up in the Noth Wooz?" Two big gulps slid audibly down Peter's throat. "Run into any bears?"

"No bears."

"Too bad." The spoon clattered in Peter's bowl. "How come you don't have a beard?"

"What?" From bears to beards? Gideon rubbed his chin as if there had been some hair there just a minute ago, then pulled a dubious scowl.

"I was just thinking—my dad didn't have much of a beard, either." On his way to the sink, Peter stopped to check out the reflection of his profile in the toaster. "Do you think I'm ever gonna get a beard?"

"Why? You wanna be shavin' every day?"

"I was kinda wondering when I might start."

Gideon shrugged. "I maybe shave once a week."

"I noticed my grandfather doesn't have much of a beard, either." Peter gave his cereal bowl a hasty rinsing.

"Natives usually don't. It works out pretty good. We don't have to go around with little pieces of toilet paper stuck to our faces."

"Huh?"

Gideon chuckled. "I hear some of those muscle-bound pinup boys shave their chests, too. So if you ever wanna be a muscle-bound pinup boy, you've got the Chippewa advantage."

"I don't care about chests. It's just that some of my friends are starting to shave—" Peter did a double-take and let out a belated hoot. "You gotta be kidding. They *shave* their *chests?*"

"Strange world, isn't it?" Gideon smiled, pleased with the lead-in he'd inadvertently given himself. "A guy needs the old tried-and-true ways just to help him keep his head straight."

"We did smoke the pipe together."

"You and your grandfather?"

"He said I shouldn't smoke cigarettes, like he does, but that the pipe isn't like smoking. It's like a holy thing. I didn't understand all the prayers, but it felt…" A grunt conveyed his frustration with the puniness of mere words. "I liked the way it felt. Like someone was listening."

Gideon affirmed the feeling with a nod. "I know what you mean. You try to hang on to that, okay? Don't let anything make you forget."

That goes without saying, Peter's big, brown, twelve-year-old eyes said. The look was all innocence, total trust.

Gideon suddenly felt like a very old man.

"I want you to know something, Peter. You and your mother are both very important to me. You're family, and that means everything." He stood next to the boy, their backsides resting against the counter, arms identically folded, one ankle crossed over the other, each contemplating his own bare toes. "I know we haven't been close, but if you're willing, I'd like to see that change."

Raina appeared in the doorway, her sleepy eyes underscored by gray smudges of fatigue. By the look she gave him, Gideon knew she'd heard what he'd said. He saw no sign of approval, and none of disapproval. Only weariness.

"You look like you could use some coffee," he said, straightening as though somebody had said, *Hop to it.*

"I could, thanks."

"I could make you some toast, Mom," Peter offered, following Gideon's swift lead. "We've got English muffins, too, and raspberry jam."

"Just…"

Gideon looked up from the coffeepot. Peter turned from the refrigerator. Both pairs of beautiful brown eyes anxiously awaited her command.

She smiled. "Actually, I think I could go for an English muffin, too."

Peter smiled, too. "I'll make it for you."

Despite Gideon's efforts to pave the way for a friendly, open-and-shut hearing, the group that gathered in the lobby outside Judge Half's chambers could well have been an assembly of strangers from different parts of the globe. And they might well have been gathered for a wake, unhappily scheduled for a still, sticky, sluggish summer afternoon. The air was cloying, the silence deafening, the eyes politely blind.

In reality, the only new face belonged to Raina's attorney, Jeffrey Metz, who met her at the courthouse. He shook hands all around, then sidled up to Raina and quietly assured her that he had done his research and that he was "on top of the issues." The judge had acted in accordance with state and federal law so far. "But we'll see," he concluded as the judge opened his office door and announced that he was ready to discuss the Defender case.

They flowed toward the voice like molasses. First Arlen, then Metz, then Peter filed in. "Sorry about the air-conditioning," the man who was waiting for them was saying. "It broke down yesterday."

The judge's voice sounded prophetic. Gideon dragged his feet, reluctant to heed the call. And so did Raina. Just before they reached the office door, she tugged on his arm, suddenly desperate to draw him away from the others for a quick word. She looked up at him plaintively, as though ultimately he were the one she trusted.

"Gideon, I'm scared."

He wanted to hold her in his arms, then and there. He glanced at the plain round clock that hung on the wall just above her head, but he didn't see the time. What he saw was two people holding on to each other for dear life. What he felt was her silky hair against his cheek, and what he heard was his voice promising her that she had nothing to worry about because he would take care of everything, and the hell with Mr. Jeffrey Metz.

He looked down at her again and smiled. In her long-sleeved blouse and navy skirt, she looked the perfect image of the fourth-grade teacher of every nine-year-old boy's dreams. Bad things should never happen to a woman like this, he told himself. He cast about for some magic words, but he drew a blank.

"You're doin' fine, Raina." *Yeah, right. Some pitiful imitation of a hero you turn out to be, Defender.*

Raina closed her eyes and shook her head. Her lips were

so pale they were almost translucent. "No, I'm not. They're going to take my son away."

He put his hand on her shoulder and slid it slowly down the back of her arm. "I don't think so."

"What if they do?" She glanced at the office door, which stood open, waiting. Her chest heaved on a quick, panicky breath. "There must be something I can do. Something *you* can do. Isn't there?"

"Arlen's not going to press this thing much further, Raina. After what happened this past weekend?" With a cluck of his tongue he shook his head. "It's not gonna happen."

"What if it does?"

He squeezed her hand, her frantic question echoing in his head. As far as he was concerned, there was only one ultimate answer. "You're his mother. Nothing's ever gonna change that."

The judge's voice shot through their circuits like a power surge.

"You two coming?"

Judge Half made the session feel more like a meeting than a hearing. Everyone sat around in a circle. Each face in the room glowed with its own sweaty sheen. Arlen sat near the window, fingering his pack of cigarettes. Gideon rested his ankle on his knee and waggled his booted foot. Peter had his knees going up and down like pistons as he bounced his heels on the floor. Raina's hands were knotted in her lap.

But everyone had a say. As promised, Judge Half was interested in hearing from almost everyone present. Jeffrey Metz simply took notes. The judge said he'd heard a rumor that Raina had inquired about a teaching position with the Pine Lake School.

"We're getting a new facility pretty soon, right, Chairman? Casino profits are goin' for a good cause." At Gideon's affirming nod, the judge turned to Raina. "If you really want to teach here again, I hope you get the job."

"I enjoyed teaching here before," she said.

Playing his role like an orchestra leader, the judge swung his seat toward Peter. "I see you're getting along with your grandfather pretty good."

"We spent the weekend together." Peter gripped his knees, trying to force them to be still for a moment, but they kept popping up at odd intervals, as though they had a mind of their own. "We went to the powwow and stuff."

"That's good." The judge cued Arlen. "How did that go, then?"

"Good, good."

"I did sorta screw up on curfew times and stuff," Peter admitted. "But, you know, if *nimishoomis* is still willing to let me come and visit once in a while, I'll behave myself a lot better."

"*Nimishoomis*, huh? That's very good." Judge Half reflected for a moment. "What would 'once in a while' be, do you think?"

"I don't know." The knees started bouncing furiously again. "I get pretty busy once school starts. But we can come back next summer." Peter lifted one shoulder. "Or spring. I'd like to learn how to spear fish when Uncle Gideon gets us our treaty settlement."

"You've been getting to know your uncle pretty well, too, I see. These are interesting times for all of us, Peter." Without missing a beat in his lecture, Judge Half swept a handful of papers off the desk top just behind him. "It's good to be Chippewa. We are a small minority in this big American country, but we have much to be proud of. And these are interesting times for us. We know who we are, and we will let our neighbors learn who we are. And learn *from* us, if they will." He eyed Peter pointedly. "But we need every Chippewa we have."

"Well, I'm Chippewa, Judge. I know that. I've always known that."

"Good, good. Mrs. Defender has done well by you." He spared Raina a deferential nod. "I encourage you to follow up on the teaching job. We need teachers. Don't we, Gideon?"

"We do."

"So I just want to encourage that." Turning to his papers, the judge gave the top one a cursory glance, then set it aside and scanned the next as he spoke.

"Now, I've gone over all the records. There is one glaring piece of information that is missing, and that, of course, is the identity of Peter's biological father. In fact, the court records contain an affidavit requesting his mother's anonymity, so that information was not available to the social worker, or to Mrs. Defender. But Arlen knew, because his daughter told him. And Jared Defender knew, because he had contact with her. According to the records, Jared made all the legal arrangements." When he finally looked up, he directed his attention to Raina. "I found that interesting."

"Jared was able to make the arrangements because he was a lawyer," Raina explained quickly. "And Gideon told him that he knew—" she glanced at Arlen and said the next words softly, gently, seemingly for his benefit "—a woman who was looking for…adoptive parents for…"

It was as though another piece of the puzzle had dropped into the judge's handful of papers. He looked up at Gideon. "You knew."

"Yes."

"I see." Ostensibly deep in thought, the judge set aside another page. "You realize that since Arlen is Peter's closest blood relative, and since every case of this kind affects not only a child and a family, but also the interests and the future of the Pine Lake Band of Chippewa, I'm inclined to declare that the boy's biological grandfather—"

Gideon leaned forward. "Judge, my brother was an enrolled member of this band, and he was legally—"

"You're interrupting me, Mr. Chairman. And I am presiding here."

There was a brief stare-down. Eyes smoldering, Gideon glanced away.

Having made his point, the judge continued, his imperious tone never wavering. "Now, I'm willing to recognize Mrs. Defender as Peter's mother in every sense but the biological sense. And the biological sense is what establishes Peter's degree of Chippewa blood, his right to tribal enrollment, and his right to call himself Pine Lake Chippewa. So I hope that Mrs. Defender will continue to take part in Peter's upbringing—in fact, I intend to stipulate with Mr. Skinner, who, as primary custodial—"

"No!" Gideon shot out of his chair, instinctively putting himself between Peter and the judge.

The move stunned everyone. Gideon could feel the eyes boring holes in him from all sides. He had but one ace, and it took him a moment to drag it up from its deep, dark, well-guarded hole.

With it came an icy exterior and a calm, steady voice. "Excuse me, Judge Half, I meant to say no, Arlen is not Peter's closest blood relative. I am."

The judge didn't look too surprised. "I guess a simple blood test is all it will take to clear up this whole thing—"

"What are you talkin' about?" Peter demanded.

Gideon steeled himself against the voice until it came pounding on his ear. The boy's rising confusion speared Gideon right between the shoulder blades.

"Uncle…*Uncle* Gideon, what the *hell* are you talkin' about?"

Turning slowly, Gideon struggled with a thick tongue and a dearth of words. "Jared raised you, Peter. He was your father. I've got no right to make that claim." He forced himself to look the boy in the eye. "But I…"

"Gave me away?"

Gideon rubbed his forehead with unsteady fingertips, then muttered an expletive into his palm. The room seemed to be tipping and swaying like the deck of a big fishing boat, and somewhere on the periphery, seesawing at odds with him right now, sat Tomasina's father and Peter's mother. He wished one of them would just blast him and get it over with.

But it was Peter who demanded, "Why?"

"All I can tell you right here and right now is that it wasn't because I didn't want to be your father." Gideon turned unseeing eyes on Judge Half. "In a million years, I never thought you'd take the boy from the mother who raised him and give primary custody to…"

"An old man?" Arlen put in. "At least I know my duty to the boy."

"You see it differently is all."

Judge Half sat back in his chair. "Gideon, I guess you and me should have had a little heart-to-heart before we got everybody together for this. You know what's at stake here. We suffered the wholesale removal of Indian children from their tribes and families for longer than either one of us can remember, longer than Arlen can remember, and he's older than both of us put together."

When his nickel's worth of humor fell flat, the judge turned his lecture back on Gideon. "We've been through this before, in this court. And you stood with the tribe. If you hadn't been personally involved this time—"

"Yeah, well, I *am* personally involved. And I thought some kind of a compromise could be worked out, so that Peter could have his grandfather as a *grandfather*. And his mother…and his father, Jared was his…" Suddenly the words wouldn't go together in the right order. Jared was his real, legal, undisputed… "Hell, I've been Peter's uncle all these years. I'm not… I promised—" He closed his eyes, and his voice drifted in frustration. "I promised not to interfere."

"I'll order the blood tests. Soon as we have some results, we'll be able to make a decision." For Gideon's benefit, Judge Half added a footnote. "I don't know who you made this promise to, but I suspect he's dead."

He motioned Peter closer. "I'd like to talk with you just a little bit more, son, but the rest of them can listen in if they want. I have a feeling there's going to be some heated discussion after this little set-to breaks up, and I just want to give you a little background." He glanced at each of the adults as he expounded. "'Cause I get 'em in here every day. Domestic entanglements. I deal with 'em every day. It's hard for people to get along. Gettin' harder all the time, seems like.

"See, the old way, we didn't have judges. We had people who were a little older, a little wiser, who tried to mediate disputes. And the old way, if something happened that made it impossible for parents to raise a child—say, some kind of trouble—"

"I could see if somebody died or got killed," Peter said bitterly.

"Well, there's all kinds of bad trouble, son. Anyway, something happened, like, okay, maybe the baby's mother died."

"Yeah, but she didn't die until way later," the boy reminded him.

"I'm talking about an example here." Judge Half's reproach was followed by a pregnant pause, a silencing look. "If the baby's mother died, then it would have been a natural thing for a man to give his son to his married brother to raise, it being pretty hard for a man to raise a baby alone. Now, none of this probably would've been kept a big secret. In fact, the old way, a child's uncles were like his father, too. And his aunties were like his mother. No questions, no problems."

He shrugged, backed off on the romanticism and opted for honesty. "Well, that's not true. People are people, and they bicker and complain and make problems for themselves, but they work it out if they can. Maybe sooner, maybe later, but they do the best they can.

"And that's what we're gonna do here. We're gonna work this out. You've got people here who love you. You're probably a little mad at 'em right now, so I just wanted to point that out. I heard a lot of good things you had going amongst you when you all first came in and sat down. Things were a little strained, but everybody's been willing, deep down."

The judge wagged a finger. "So you go ahead and be mad, but don't be too hard on these people, son. They're all family. *Your* family."

"That's easy for *you* to say, Judge."

"You think my job's easy?" He snorted. "Maybe I'll turn it over to you one day."

"Don't bet on it." Peter scowled briefly at Gideon, then at the judge. "Do I have to stay with *him?*"

"Where do you want to stay?" the judge asked.

"He can stay with me." Arlen, too, glanced at Gideon. But there was no judgment in his eyes, and he spoke kindly. "We'll make a sweat tomorrow night. Maybe you'd wanna come."

"You think you're gonna make me get into some little tent with *him* and—"

Arlen rose from his chair slowly, his old knees cracking into place. "No one is ever forced into a sweat. You can try it out first with me if you want to. If you don't, that's up to you."

Raina was shell-shocked. Her heart hammered wildly, her pulse rang in her ears, but her senses were as dull as mud. She wasn't sure she had form or substance. Maybe she'd become invisible. When she turned to her attorney, she was surprised to find she still had a voice.

"Isn't *anything* up to *me?*"

"Well, the state's jurisdiction is limited where the child is an enrolled tribal member, but I intend to pursue some research along several possible lines." Metz scanned his notes. "Maybe there's some kind of a damage suit here against somebody. I mean, mental, emotional—"

"Damage suit?" The words sounded absurd. Dazed, Raina shook her head. "I want my son."

"Well, we don't have a ruling yet, but I'm just trying to get one jump ahead—"

Tell him to jump off a bridge, Gideon thought, his heart breaking as he stood there, angrily watching her seek out an ally other than himself.

"I want to know exactly where I stand," she said.

"In my opinion—" Metz edged her toward the door "—no matter what those blood tests show, your prospects are rather dismal. Except, as I said, if we can find an angle for a civil suit."

"Thank you." Miraculously the starch had returned to Raina's voice. "You've been no help whatsoever, but thank you for making the drive up here, Jeff."

She finally turned to Gideon. "I want to talk to you."

He was glad *somebody* did.

Chapter 10

She waited until they were alone, and then she didn't know where to start. Let *him* start, she decided. The ball was in his court. Unbeknownst to her, it had actually been there all along. So let him finally put it into play. Let him put forth some combination of words that didn't add up to craziness. She was all ears, which was appropriate. It surely made her look as foolish as she felt.

But they went to his house, ate his ham-and-cheese sandwiches, drank his coffee and sat on his porch, all without speaking more than a dozen words.

So it was up to her, and she went right to the sore spot. "Why didn't you tell me?"

"That I was Peter's biological father?" His voice was quietly strained, as though he had to pull it back through the sieve of his memories. "I didn't see how it would do anybody any good. I figured somewhere down the road, when Peter was older—after he'd gotten to know me a little better—I'd tell him about some of my past mistakes." He stared into the mug of coffee he held cradled in both hands. "And I'd tell him how he was the only good thing that ever came of those mistakes."

"What I'm asking you is…" She waited until he looked up. "Why didn't you tell *me?*"

"God, Raina. Tell *you?*" He glanced at the plank ceiling, shaking his head over a mirthless chuckle. "When do you think would have been the best time?"

"In the very beginning."

"Jared figured total anonymity was the best way to go."

"He did, did he? Except that *he* knew, so I don't see how the term *total* applies."

"Jared agreed to be Peter's father. That made me his uncle. The more people who knew otherwise, the harder it would have been to keep it that cut-and-dried." Gideon offered a wistful, self-conscious smile. "I knew I'd done wrong. I wanted to find a way to make it right, and I went to Jared. We were just trying to keep it simple, I guess."

"You could have told me."

"Jared thought—"

"Jared thought, Jared thought, Jared thought." She'd fallen back on the same crutch enough times herself, but she wasn't about to let him borrow it. Not now. "As the judge rightly pointed out, Jared is dead. *You* could have told me."

"I thought about it once or twice, but, hell, as little contact as we've had?" He avoided her eyes. "What would be the point? After all this time, it seemed like it would create more problems we didn't need."

She wanted to shake him and shout right in his ear. *We've had some pretty big contact in the last few days, Gideon. Am I the only one who's noticed?*

But, of course, she didn't. Instead, she calmly quizzed

him about things that touched her only indirectly. It seemed important to make him turn over everything that had been hidden from her, as though her knowing every detail might somehow undo the damage.

"Why did you give him… I mean, why didn't you and Tomasina—"

"See, that's why." His rigid hand leveled a curt karate chop on her questions. "That's why I didn't want to tell you. Because then you'd start asking why, and none of the reasons are gonna sound very good to you. It's all over and done with. The whys don't matter anymore. What mattered then and what matters now is that Peter got a good home out of the deal."

"What about his mother?"

"What about…?" His eyes filled with a tenderness that transformed the tone of his voice. "What about her?"

"Did you love her?"

"Did I love…Tomasina?"

The intensity in his eyes turned her away.

"I'm sorry," she muttered. "I shouldn't have asked you that."

"Why? What answer did you hope to hear? That I did?" He paused, and her heartbeat stalled in the interim. "Or that I didn't?"

"It's none of my business."

Then why was she asking? And why was she still waiting for an answer, *the* answer?

And why did he feel a need to tell her in the bluntest way possible?

"We had sex, and I got her pregnant." He looked her straight in the eye, daring her to judge him more harshly than he judged himself. "That was what was between us. Neither one of us liked the idea of getting married—at least, not to each other. She didn't want a baby, didn't want an abortion, didn't especially like the idea of giving him up for adoption until after Jared talked to her. But ol' Jared was always pretty persuasive."

"Did he support her financially?"

"I supported her, mostly. We lived together in St. Paul for six months, which was why I was surprised to learn that Arlen knew anything about it. I didn't think she talked to him much. Hell, she didn't talk to *me* much."

"Didn't Arlen even know that you were the man she was seeing?"

"You never knew any more about that woman than she wanted you to know. Especially how she felt about anything. She never let anything show." He gave a dry laugh. "I guess *I* should talk, you know, thinking back on what I was like in those days. But, anyway, she said it was none of her father's damn business."

"But she told him she was pregnant."

"Yeah, I guess she did. And that was the kicker, wasn't it?" He sipped his coffee, offering her a sheepish glance over the rim of his cup. Then he shrugged. "Surprised the hell out of me. Maybe it was her way of thumbing her nose at the ol' man. She liked to let people know that she was gonna live her life exactly the way she damn well pleased.

"But at least she kept her word," he allowed. "She said she'd carry the baby to term if I'd help her get away from home. She'd always wanted to live in the Cities. And, hell, she took to city life like a pigeon. But me, I hated it. I worked a lot of different jobs—construction, assembly lines, fast food. Tommy took some classes, played bingo, did pretty much whatever she wanted."

It was the first time he'd used a nickname for the woman with whom he'd conceived a child. He'd schooled himself to manage his memories carefully, and the only other person who had heard the story was an uninvolved counselor. Now, here he was, telling the whole damn thing to Raina. Raina *was* involved. She was practically sitting on the edge of her chair, and the look in her eyes—her intense, vicarious involvement in the whole sordid mess—was killing him.

"Except party," he noted quickly, grasping for any uplifting straw he might offer. "We agreed on that much. We stayed out of the bars while she was pregnant. Hell of a long six months, but…" He turned to look out the window. His voice drifted as the memories turned from bad to worse. "After Peter was born, she split. And I told myself I was nursing a big heartache. Aching for what, I didn't know, but it served as a nice, slick slide to the edge of nowhere. I ended up in detox."

"Which was not an alcohol treatment center," Raina recalled.

"No. It's a place where—" A place her experience wouldn't allow her to imagine, which was just fine, because he didn't want her be able to imagine what it had been like for him there. Four days in hell had convinced him he wasn't going any lower. "It was a place where they were putting too many Indians. Later on, I was part of the group of community activists and Native leaders that got the Health and Human Services Department to take a look at what was going on there. We forced them to shut the place down."

Her eyes brightened. "I remember. It was in the news. But I didn't know you were part of—"

"There were quite a few of us," he said, minimizing his contribution with a dismissive gesture. "But that came a whole lot later. After I dried out, I asked Jared to help get me into a treatment center. He did. And I'm grateful to him for that."

"Do you need connections to get into treatment?"

"Depends." He smiled indulgently. "You need a health insurance card, a bank account, a social worker…*something.*

I had a brother who was embarrassed to be related to me." He anticipated her objections and waved them away with an easy smile. "Anyway, I met this old guy who was working as a janitor there. He'd been a tribal councilman for his band. He'd also been through the program. I'd never thought about getting into politics, but I sure liked ol' Everett. I learned a lot from him. And I actually talked to him, told him things I never told anyone else."

He remembered telling Everett about Raina and about Peter. Everett had suggested that Gideon trusted his brother with what he loved most because somewhere along the line he'd decided he couldn't trust himself. He'd always thought it a strange observation, since he knew damn well he'd resented Jared, and for no good reason. Jared had always done everything right, for God's sake. Where was the crime in that?

"Everett must have been almost like a father to you," she said. "I've never heard much about your father. Not from Jared, and not from you."

Gideon shrugged. "My ol' man never had the time of day for us. But Everett told me that he'd missed out with his own kids, too. He said that's what drunks usually do." And when the time had come, Gideon told himself, he had done the same. Like father, like son.

Damn, it had been so much easier being an uncle.

"I knew Jared would make a good father. I knew you'd be the best mother a kid could—" Elbows braced on his knees, he spread his hands wide. "When do you think I should have told you, Raina?"

"I guess it doesn't matter now. I can see how it became more difficult, the more time that passed and the more distant we became."

"You were always the one who sent the Christmas cards

with all your family news and the school pictures." He thanked her now with a wistful smile. "God, he's growing up so fast."

She glanced away, then swallowed hard. He could see her putting words together in her head and gathering the courage to say them. Her breast quivered with her next long, deep breath.

She looked him in the eye. "Are you going to take him from me, Gideon?"

"No." He shook his head. "No, I can't—"

"You don't want him, and I can't have him—is that—"

"Don't want him!" The accusation drove him to his feet. "You think I don't want—" Old memories and new emotions swirled around them as she stood up to him. He grabbed her shoulders. "I want, Raina. I've wanted—" he closed his eyes and savored a quick, deep dose of her delicate scent "—so bad sometimes I could hardly…" He dropped his hands to his sides and turned away. "That's what happens when you stop anesthetizing yourself. The feelings catch up to you." And speaking of bad, God help him, he had it bad.

"Peter has feelings, too."

"Once he cools off, you're the one he'll talk feelings with. You're his mother." He glanced at her quickly, then away. "And obviously he'll still see Jared as his father."

"My parental rights have been stripped away. Abruptly. Unexpectedly." She grabbed his arm and made him look at her. *"Unfairly,"* she insisted, as though she thought she would get an argument out of him on that score.

When she didn't, she sighed. "And the most frustrating part is that I can't do anything about it. Peter's always been able to count on me." Her grip on his arm tightened for a moment, then fell away. The vigor in her voice withered. "I feel powerless, and I hate it."

"You've already taken steps. You've said you're willing to move back up here." He shoved his hands into the pockets of his jeans and stood for a moment like a diver mentally setting himself up to spring. "You know, there's an obvious solution to this," he said finally.

"What?"

Their eyes met, hers guileless, his guarded. "We could get married."

"Married?"

She said it as though she were unfamiliar with the concept. He felt like a guy who had somehow managed to get clobbered by the ton of bricks he had just dropped. It wasn't easy to shove the damn things off, but with a cavalier shrug he gave it a try. "Why not?"

"Surely," she said, sounding a little dazed herself, "the real question is *why?*"

"Because…" *I want you to be my wife* probably wouldn't cut it. "Because I want to marry my son's mother. Isn't that a good enough reason?"

She glared at him. "It may well be that the last person Peter wants his mother to marry is his father."

"Well, it's not up to him. We're his…" When he realized he'd placed his hand on his chest, he smiled ruefully and included her with an openhanded gesture. "We're the adults. It's up to us."

"This is absolutely ridiculous." She backed away, as though his outstretched hand threatened her somehow. "No, this is *outrageous*. I can't…. We stayed together out there in a beautiful, beautiful…and we…" She waved her hand vaguely toward the outdoors, and her voice suddenly teetered on a hurt-filled pitch. The misty glimmer in her eyes accused him of some cryptic crime. "But you didn't even…because it meant absolutely nothing. Nothing but…but what you said about…"

She made a cutoff gesture with two very shaky hands. "I have to go now."

Still stinging, he was a little slow on the uptake, but the sound of her heels on the wood floor incited his whoa-there reflex. He caught up to her before she got to the front door.

"Raina—" Now that he had her by the arm, he didn't know what to say. She'd called his proposal absurd, but she was hardly laughing.

"No. Don't touch me, Gideon." She shook him off and plowed her fingers through her hair, squaring herself up for a revised, more composed exit. "I guess I need to cool off, too. Peter and I both. We don't understand—"

"Let me drive you," he said gently, working hard to keep his twice-rejected hand from reaching for a third rebuff.

"No. I'll be fine." She took a deep breath. "There. I'm fine. It's important never never to lose your head, you see." She smiled weakly. "I'll be fine."

"I'm not letting you go like this."

"How *will* you let me go, then? The last time it was to your brother."

"He turned out to be the right man for you."

"And when did you decide that?" She wrapped her arms around her middle, steadying herself, setting her chin.

She was winding up to tell him off, he thought. He could feel it coming.

"You found a wife for your brother, and then you gave us a child," she clipped. "Quite a remarkable piece of work, Gideon. And now that you're a tribal leader, you're making big changes around here. If you can get this treaty thing through, I think a movie would be in order." Bolstered by an infusion of flippancy, she managed a stiff-lipped smile. "With somebody like Charlton Heston playing you. Gideon Defender, the leader, the prophet, the right hand of God."

"Cut it out, Raina." His befuddled gaze sharpened. "I'm just trying to get by, that's all. To work things out the best way I—"

"*Your* way. Which is to avoid making commitments."

"That's a damn lie!"

"You 'work things out' for everyone around you, while you manage to—"

"What do you mean, avoid commitments?" He grabbed her shoulders. "I just asked you to marry me, for God's sake."

She lifted her pretty, aristocratic chin. "You proposed an *arrangement,* not a marriage."

"I offered a solution to a problem. I knew damn well what kind of a response I'd get." Gradually he drew her closer, noting an unmistakable flicker in her eyes as he slid first one arm around her, then the other. His lips were a scant inch from hers, and his eyes glowed with a complacent smile. "But I know how to get a different kind of response from you, don't I?"

"Gideon, this isn't—" She closed her eyes. He splayed his hands over the swell of her hips and pressed her firmly against him. Her complaint turned soft, and he used it, molded her to his hardness. "It isn't fair."

"It isn't a game. There are no referees to decide what's fair—"

"And what's foul?" she challenged breathlessly, her chest heaving involuntarily against him.

He nuzzled her hair back from her temple and whispered, "It's up to us."

"We have to be sensible." It sounded like the hazy echo of some old, dusty advice.

"Why?" he breathed against the side of her neck. "I got a

lousy response to my proposal, but how about this?" He took her earlobe between his teeth, gently sawing on it, tormenting her with his flickering tongue as he deftly unzipped the back of her skirt. He tucked his hand into her cotton panties and stroked her bottom, drawing her up to him and holding her tight against his hard member. "How will you respond to this, hmm?"

She whispered his name so softly that it felt like a caress, and he hungered after her mouth, demanding more of the same. Her lips parted on a jagged sigh, welcoming his questing tongue. It was a hot, wet, seductive kiss, at once promising and postulating. His lips nipped, then sipped, then devoured, while his tongue made love to her mouth. He rubbed his hands teasingly over the warm curve of her hips, pushing her clothing down, but just a little.

"Yes or no?" He licked her lower lip, then nipped it as he rocked his hips against hers, whispering hotly, "Yes or no, Raina?"

"Yes." Her body listed, yearning for his. She gripped his shoulders. "Yes, yes."

"Yes, what?"

She loosened the first two buttons on her blouse, then looked up at him shyly. "Yes, make love to me."

"Yes, who?" he demanded, finishing the job she'd started as he lowered one knee to the floor. "Who do you want to—"

He tasted her nipple, tonguing and suckling until it hardened. She slid her fingers into his hair and cuddled him at her breast, whispering, "Gideon. I want you, Gideon."

The magic words. The words that turned him from mere man into hunter, warrior, prince, king. Words that compelled him to sweep her into his arms and carry her to his bed, to finish undressing her and to worship every sensitive part of her body with coddling hands and adoring lips. She pulled his shirt open and lifted her head, straining to touch the small nubbin of his nipple with the tip of her tongue. He played a little keep-away, enjoying the sweet shiver it gave him to let her touch and glide away.

Her teeth grazed him as she fumbled with his belt buckle, and he groaned. "How long will you respond this way, Raina?" He eased his thigh between hers, prodding her to ride it. When she did, he whispered, "Is this a yes?"

The buckle came loose with a soft clink. She tore at the snap on his jeans. "Yessss…"

He lowered his pants, lowered his hips, applied his rigid, needy probe to the private entrance to her body. He found her moist and ready for him. "And this? Is this a yes?"

"Yes, Gideon, yes."

He took pains to protect her, just as he took care to prepare her. She filled her hands with his hard, warm buttocks and urged him to come to her, arched to receive the full measure of his initial thrust and draw him deep, deep down into her inner self. He drew back slowly, like a bowman taking scrupulous aim at a very small target. But he was loath to let fly his arrow now that it was so sweetly notched. He set a slow, undulating rhythm, reaching ever closer to the target, attuning himself to her gradual need for a quicker pace.

"How long?" he whispered, then flicked his tongue over her temple, sipping her saltiness. "How long can you stay with me? I can keep this up all night."

"Then do it!" She pressed her cheek against his shoulder and wrapped him with arms and legs and earnest desire. "Oh, Gideon, yes, do it…do it."

He had no choice but to oblige with all his considerable skill, not to mention his heart and soul.

And later, when again she said, "Oh, Gideon," he knew he'd done it right. Her soft sigh poured over him like warm, cleansing water, and her intimate touch convinced him that he belonged to her and always would, whether she stayed or left him.

"You'll have to play yourself in the movie," she decided out of the clear blue.

"Why?"

"Because there's no one else like you." She propped herself up on her elbows and looked down at him. The shift gave him a nice view of her lovely bare breasts, but it took her hand away from him. "You're beautiful," she said, her voice filled with wonder.

"Don't stop touching me, Raina." He drew her back into the cradle of his arm, in one fluid move reclaiming her hand and placing it low on his flat belly. "Please. I've never…"

"Never what?"

"Felt this good." He'd dreamed of making love to her, and the dream was always good. But he'd never dreamed that she would come willingly to his bed. He closed his eyes, turned his lips to her hair and whispered, "I always knew we'd be good together."

She sighed. For a long, quiet moment neither of them moved. But when he nuzzled the fine wisp of hair at her temple, something cool and wet slid over the tip of his nose. It felt suspiciously like a tear—a tender, frightening, feminine thing with which he had precious little experience.

He whispered her name.

She stiffened. "I have to go."

"Go where?" He caught her and held her, searching her eyes for some explanation. All he found was a troubling semblance of the evening shadows that surrounded them. "This is the only place you need to be right now," he told her solemnly. "Stay with me."

"Gideon, I can't think." She took a quick swipe at the corner of her eye with the heel of her hand. "I have to go back to my room and try to sort things out. Try to—"

"You need sleep, Raina."

She closed her eyes, but she said, "I can't sleep."

"What is it?" He caught her face in his hands. "Tell me what's wrong."

She was trying, albeit feebly, to push herself away from him, but he was having none of it. He massaged her temples with his thumbs until, muscle by muscle, she relaxed her body against his, giving in, letting him take the pressure away. "Even when I'm exhausted, it's very hard for me to fall asleep."

"That's because you're trying too hard. You think too much. You always did." He stuffed an extra pillow behind his neck and settled her in his arms, pressing her head into the pocket of his shoulder. "I can help you sleep."

"Gideon—"

"Shhh, Raina. Which sounds of nature would you like to hear? I can do loons if you like. Or wolves, or…"

He started humming. She tipped her chin up, and he saw the surprise in her eyes. He touched his finger to his lips, then with one hand stroked her brow, gently coaxing her eyelids closed as he sang to her softly in Chippewa, words he remembered from his boyhood when *nookomis,* his grandmother, had sung them to him. Shortest boyhood on record, as he recalled. And it had been such a long, long time ago.

She slept well in Gideon's arms that night. She slept soundly, even when he slipped away early in the morning. It was when he phoned from the office that she finally woke. He told her that he'd checked on the status of her application for a teaching position, and she was in. Despite the bright lilt in the voice that delivered the news, and even though it was the answer she'd hoped for, the news was somehow disquieting.

It was decided, then. All the staid, comfortable, routine aspects of her life were about to change. It occurred to her that if she examined the great changes in her life too closely, she would find that one man had somehow played a major role in many of them. And she was lying in his bed right now, between sheets that smelled deliciously of his body. In bed, *where he'd always known they would be good together.* And that was not enough.

"Why so quiet?" asked the voice on the phone. The same voice she'd heard in the dark last night. The same voice that had sent shivers scurrying down her spine. "Isn't that what you wanted to hear?"

"Yes," she said, but her tone was flat. "It really is. I'll need a place to live. Any suggestions?"

"How fancy?"

"Two bedrooms. Beyond that, the basics would be nice."

Seated at his desk, Gideon tapped the eraser end of a pencil on a pile of letters, many of them written essentially to curse him and all his ancestors. He shoved the tedious rancor aside.

Two bedrooms, plus the basics. Hell, he could offer her that much. In fact, he had offered her that and more. But he wasn't going to beg.

"What are you going to do with your house?" he asked.

"Sell it. It's too much house for the two of us, anyway. It's time I unloaded it. I have a friend who sells real estate. I'll call her today." She paused, then added quietly, "It's time I made some changes."

"Right." *Choose your own time, choose your own brand, sweetheart.* "Well, you don't qualify for tribal housing, but there are always a few winterized lake cabins available for rent in the off-season."

"I'll start looking into that today." She sighed. "This is going to be so hard for Peter."

"We're remodeling the high school," he reported buoyantly. "Adding a swimming pool and a bunch of space for new programs. Putting the casino profits to good use, just like the judge said. And if things keep going the way they are, we'll be able to pay for college for any of our kids who want to go."

"*Our* kids?"

"Pine Lake Chippewa kids." Elbow propped on the desk, he rested his brow in one large hand and rubbed his temples. "Raina…somehow I think Peter's going to be our kid—yours and mine. Maybe if you'd try to look at it that way…"

"Like joint custody? Isn't that the usual fallout from a divorce?" She gave a little tsk. "The pain of a divorce without the legalities. How ironic."

"Yeah." He lifted his face to the morning sun and the breeze wafting through an open window. "Ironic as hell."

"It's going to be hard for Peter to look at it the way you're suggesting."

"I have a feeling Arlen's going to help us out with that. I mean, I think he's willing to let me, uh…"

"Take your rightful place?"

"They're concerned about Peter's place, not mine. They want him to be part of the tribe."

Absently he moved an official-looking piece of paper from one side of his desk to the other. "I was served with a court order for a paternity test this morning. The judge walked across the street and handed it to me personally." He gave a dry chuckle as he snatched a pencil from the howling coyote mug that Rosie had given him in honor of some holiday he'd hardly known existed. "As if he thought I might try to duck out on it or something. So I'm going over to the clinic before I head up to Arlen's this afternoon. I want the three of us to do a sweat, like Arlen said."

"What about me?"

"You're his mooring, Raina. He was already straining against the bonds before any of this other stuff cropped up. Now he's got a whole new cause, but he was gonna test out the big waters, anyway."

"He's too young."

"No, he's not." With one hand he snapped the pencil in half. "Look, he thinks he hates my guts right now. That's something we need to deal with."

"Thinks?"

"Okay, so maybe he does," he admitted, his exasperation level rising. "Maybe he always will. Maybe he'll let it fester and eat away at his insides until—"

"Gideon, please." Her voice sounded thready and distant. "It's just that I'm feeling rather shut out of all this."

"All his life you've been his safe harbor." *And I've been shut out. I shut myself out.* "Don't worry, Raina. He'll come back to you. It's part of the circle. Don't you see that?"

"Bring him home—*here*—as soon as you can. Will you do that, Gideon?"

"I will." He closed his eyes and swallowed back the sand in his throat. "Will you be there? At home, when I get back?"

"I can't stay here like this, like… Gideon, I feel so—" The space between them sounded long, hollow and empty. "If I'm not here, I'll be at the lodge. I really have nowhere else to go until…"

"I'll find you."

Chapter 11

Peter wasn't ready to go back to anyone. Far from it. Gideon found him sitting on the porch with his grandfather, both of them working on his dance bustle. Peter was preparing the vanes of the synthetic feathers that Arlen was working into a creation that would eventually become a dancer's fan-shaped tail feathers.

Gideon greeted Arlen with a handshake. Then grandfather reminded grandson of his manners, just as uncle had once done. The boy dutifully, if grudgingly, obliged Gideon with the requisite handshake.

"That cop came and got me again," Peter said as he went back to carving the end of a feather with his grandfather's penknife. "Took me to a clinic. I had to have a stupid blood test."

"I know." Gideon hiked one booted foot up to the porch and braced his hand on his knee. "I did, too."

"So, what if they don't match?"

Gideon hadn't given that possibility much thought. Maybe he was flattering himself, but he could see more of himself in Peter every day. "None of this changes anything as far as your mom and…and your dad are concerned."

"My dad?" Peter's dark eyes challenged Gideon to try to apply that designation to himself. Just *try*. But when Gideon wouldn't take the bait, the boy shrugged it off. "My dad's not concerned about anything anymore. He's dead. You can bet if *he* was here—"

"He's not." Gideon traded a hiked brow for Peter's glare. "So, you wanna do a sweat with your grandfather and me or not?"

The muscles in Peter's jaw were working just as vigorously as his hands. Gideon waited patiently for his answer. Finally the boy glanced up from his task. "I wouldn't have to be too mad at you if you wouldn't have to mention anything about being, you know…my father or anything."

"It's a deal." Gideon scraped the sole of his boot against the edge of the porch as he lowered his foot to the ground. "We go into the sweat simply as three men. Different generations, different experiences, all living in the same world."

Arlen flashed Gideon a glance that sparkled with approval. "Next time you go up for chairman, I might just vote for you."

In the close, dark heat of the sweat lodge, Peter learned new ways to pray. They were ways that were almost as old as the red-hot rocks that were used to make the steam, but they were new to him. He took the heat and the smoke in stride and contributed what prayerful thoughts he could come up with on the spot without giving too much of himself away. He'd already been given away once, and now that he knew who'd done it, he wasn't sure he could trust him again. After all, a guy had ideas, and then he had *thoughts*.

He'd told his uncle Gideon some stuff, but that was before he knew he wasn't really *Uncle* Gideon. Well, he was, but he wasn't. Either way, things could never again be the way they were. Which was okay. He wasn't a kid anymore, and he didn't like it when people treated him like one.

The trouble was, he felt like a kid sometimes. Not often, but *some*times. And when those times came, whose kid was he going to be?

Since nobody was anxious to force anything on him, he'd been spending a lot of time with his new friends. He talked about Tom and Oscar during the sweat, about how he was teaching them how to head a soccer ball and they were showing him how to do the men's fancy dance. He told his grandfather and Gideon that they were pretty cool dudes.

What Gideon didn't realize was that Tom Strikes Many had also given Peter a few political lectures. Tom had spent long hours listening to his father bemoan the prospect of limiting some of the treaty rights through what Marvin called "Defender's sellout." The Strikes Many clan had threatened to file a legal suit, claiming that the Pine Lake Tribal Council and its chairman couldn't speak for them. The federal court had denied their claim.

But there were new ideas being discussed now. Secret challenges were being issued by another group opposed to the settlement. Challenges like, *If you've got the guts to defend your so-called treaty rights in a real court of law, why not start out in criminal court? Why not do what you say you have the right to do—what the state says no one can do—and that's hunt and fish out of season or by illegal methods off the reservation in the ceded territory?*

It had been done, of course. But not blatantly. And now,

with the settlement in the works, the tribal fish and game wardens were guarding their jurisdiction closely. But there were other jurisdictions. And there were many ways to skin a cat.

The sweat had been good for Gideon. There had been no talk of politics, for such was not the purpose of a sweat. With their tangled relationships off-limits for discussion, they'd spoken of other things, and they'd spoken candidly, for in the dark, close, warm womb of the sweat, there was no other way to speak. They had shared cares and concerns for those close to them, for friends and family and the Native community. They had made prayers for wisdom and clear vision.

Gideon knew that Raina would not be happy to learn that Peter had not come home with him. The boy had said he'd made plans with his friends, and Gideon chose to respect that. But he hoped she would take what communication they'd had as a positive sign. Gideon certainly did.

Now if he could only figure out how to communicate with Raina. He called her at the lodge and asked her to have dinner with him. "Like a date," he said hopefully. "Like two people who just want to get to know each other."

"What's it going to take for us to get to know each other?"

"I don't know." Something like a sweat would have been good. Except traditionally, men and women didn't go in together. He could see why. Damn, it was hard to keep sex out of it. "I figured I'd get dressed up, though."

She laughed. "Oh, great. And me sitting here with nothing to wear."

"Wear the dress you had on the first time I saw you this summer. You looked all sunshine and flowers."

"That one isn't very dressy."

"Wear the hat, too. I loved the hat."

She was ready at the appointed time, and she was listening for the knock on the door. But when it came, her body had to jump up pretty fast to keep pace with her heart. Silly to be nervous, she told herself. Or overly eager. She'd just been with him in the most intimate way possible. For her, anyway. For him, well, maybe *that* was a date, and maybe conversation over dinner was an intimacy. Who could tell about men?

There would be none of *that* tonight. Nothing too personal. She'd already decided that she wasn't going to keep him waiting. She didn't want to have to invite him in, to have him sit on the bed and watch her comb her hair or put on her shoes. This was a date.

But the doorknob proved to be a tricky mechanism for an unsteady hand, and when she opened the door, the man who stood before her startled her even more than his quick knock. He was physically breathtaking. His hair seemed thicker and darker, more luxuriant, than ever, his eyes more penetrating, his lips fuller, his shoulders broader. And when had she ever seen him dressed in a sport jacket?

"Hi."

His smile lit a matching spark in his eyes. "Hi, yourself."

She smiled, too. She couldn't help it. Her senses were instantly, giddily glutted with all things Gideon.

"This is as fancy as I get," he said, sounding almost apologetic. Along with the brown jacket, he wore a blue chambray shirt, blue jeans and a wide brown belt. Very understated. Very handsome. The dentalium choker added a touch of true distinction. She reached up to touch it, forgetting all about her plan to remain impersonal.

"The loon's necklace." Her smile turned wistful as she traced a row of tubular shells with an admiring forefinger. "The sign of a chief."

"Sign of leadership," he corrected. "And the loon would have to fight me for it. I might as well admit right off, I wore it to impress you."

"I'm impressed."

"So am I." He braced his shoulder against the doorframe and gave her an appreciative head-to-toe appraisal. She'd worn the dress he'd said he liked, along with a silver bracelet that Peter had given her for Mother's Day. She fanned her skirt demurely, fluttering the soft cotton like a little girl with a brand-new full-circle skirt.

"You look great. Do I get a kiss?" He pushed himself away from the door and took her shoulders in his hands. "Isn't that what people do on dates? Give each other a kiss at the door?"

"That comes at the end," she said, smiling. Lord, he looked good enough to eat. "Like dessert."

"I like to start with dessert." He lowered his head, and her lips sank into his for a long, slow, wet, glad-to-be-together kiss. Their mouths parted reluctantly, their lower lips lingering to touch a little longer, tongues reaching for one more tiny taste. And their eyes held court together beyond that, acclaiming the dessert cum appetizer with a silent *mmm*.

Finally Gideon glanced at the top of her head and gave a lopsided smile. "Where's the hat?"

"It's kind of a *sun* hat."

"I'm kind of a sucker for sun hats."

With a light, feminine laugh she took the hat down from the closet shelf and let him put it on for her. It was just a hat, she told herself. Nothing too personal. Neither was the way he winked at her and flipped the petals on the big sunflower that was tacked to the hat band.

He'd made reservations at the most exclusive restaurant on the lake, one that was not on tribal land. They were seated at a table near the fireplace. Not far away, the dining room's huge windows overlooked the lake, its blue waters glistening in the summer's evening sunlight.

They talked about the day each of them had had in the comfortable conversational tones of two people who were more than friends, who shared more than a backyard fence or acquaintances in common. She was pleased to hear about the reception he'd gotten at Arlen's. Even though he couldn't tell her what was said in the sweat, he was able to convey the sense of renewal that had pervaded. He knew he had a long way to go with Peter and that it would take time to regain the boy's trust. But he believed he'd made a start.

Then he learned that in a single day she had been promised a teaching contract, put her house on the market and looked at several houses that would be available for rent when school started.

"Nothing I'm crazy about," she said with a shrug. "But who knows? Once the house sells, I might just decide to buy something here and fix it up to my liking."

"That's what I did. 'Course, I don't know much about stuff like decorating."

She planted her elbow at the edge of the table, rested her chin on the back of her hand and smiled warmly. "Your house is very comfortable. It suits you perfectly."

"What would you do to it, if you were going to, say, fix it up to your liking?"

"I might add on so I could open up the kitchen more. Do that whole great-room thing. The fireplace would be a real focal point. I like the woodwork and the stone. I like the North Woods feel." She glanced at the rafters and considered more possibilities as she reached for her water glass. "I'd put some flower beds in, maybe a deck. I love the porch."

He caught her hand in his and turned her wrist slowly,

inspecting her bracelet. It had a single silver charm attached. "What does this say?" He tilted the small, shiny cutout toward the flame that flickered within the amber votive cup in the middle of the table. It took a moment to decipher the words in the dim light, but finally he looked up, smiling. "So you're 'Number One Mom.'"

"My last Mother's Day present." She glanced away, her cheeks flushing. "I mean, most recent."

"There'll be more." He pressed her hand between his, massaging palm to palm. "I've never thanked you, Raina. Seeing him now, seeing the fine, healthy young man you're raising…I want to thank you."

"I'm his mother." Her tone was as level as the look she gave him. "I think… I hope I've done what good mothers do. Thanks aren't—"

"Necessary, I know." He rubbed his thumb over the links of the bracelet. "He thanked you with this. And I'm thanking you." He shook his head, chuckling as he tore his eyes from the bracelet. "I gotta tell you, you know what I thought?"

"What?"

"I thought this was probably something Jared had given you, and maybe it said 'I love you' or something, and I thought…" He looked into her eyes, lingering uncertainty muting his voice. "I thought, this woman's trying to tell me something."

"I do have gifts from Jared. Keepsakes and memories." But it was Gideon's hands that warmed hers now, his thumb caressing the soft side of her wrist. "He did love me, you know."

"I know."

"And I loved him."

"I know that, too."

"So did Peter."

Gideon nodded. They sat there for a long, quiet moment, holding hands across the table. There was such an aura about them that the waiter bypassed them twice, reluctant to offer menus until the mood at the table changed.

"Raina," Gideon began finally. "What you said about the way this is shaping up to be like a custody battle in a divorce…" He lifted his eyes to hers, probing deeply, earnestly. "It shouldn't be like that. I mean, why should Peter be part of that kind of tug-of-war when there's been no divorce?" With gentle urgency he squeezed her hand. "You know, we…when we put ourselves into it, we really get along fine. What I mean to say is, if we—"

A restive murmur spreading from table to table drew their attention from their own little world. Around the room other curious heads were popping up the same way. One of the waiters was hastily drawing the drapes, while a couple of people stood half out of their chairs, trying to get a peek before the view was cut off. A tide of noise seemed to be building outside. The buzz level in the dining room was also on the rise, along with growing disquiet.

Gideon signaled the waiter who had been patiently waiting for a break in their tête-à-tête. "What's going on?"

The young man handed Raina an open menu. "Just a little commotion at the boat landing."

Distracted, Gideon ignored the menu he was offered. "What kind of commotion?"

The dining room supervisor paused on his way back from the window. "We'll do our best to see that the disturbance doesn't interfere with your dinner, sir."

Gideon rose from his chair as the white-haired man in charge hurried away. He turned to the young waiter, who had already assumed the proper pose—hands clasped behind his back—for his presentation of the evening specials. "What's going on out there?"

The waiter chafed at the question. "I don't exactly know how to say this without, uh… What it looks like is some kind of a protest or something. Some Indians and, you know, some…other guys sort of yelling—"

"Don't go away," Gideon told Raina. He dropped his cloth napkin on top of the silverware next to his plate. "I'll check it out, and I'll be right back."

Raina tried to wait. She knew the best course was to stay out of the way. The voices sounded angry, and they were getting angrier by the second. She heard one of the waiters say that the police had been called. Then she heard another one mention that there were teenagers involved. "Just a bunch of Indian kids, got caught using spears." Someone else laughed and added, "They probably didn't even catch anything."

Raina was out the door in a heartbeat. She walked quickly, homing in on the shouting.

At first all she saw was a crowd of fuming people, mostly men wearing baseball caps, some carrying placards, and some brandishing what looked like bumper stickers. She saw a few red-slashed circles containing images of nets and spears. Great form of expression, she thought. What happened to the peace sign? She didn't see any "I-heart-Indians."

The bend in the shoreline suddenly afforded her a view of the far end of the boat landing. Her stride went from a walk to a trot when she got her first glimpse of the little group the protestors had surrounded. It wasn't just teenagers. Marvin Strikes Many and four other men had landed at the big public dock in two boats. But among the younger faces Raina recognized were Peter and his friends, Oscar and Tom.

The confrontation was quickly escalating toward violence.

Each side was doing its best to shout the other down, and Gideon was trying to muscle his way into the center of it all.

"Get back on the boats," Gideon shouted. Then, to the sign-carriers, "Listen, you people, the police have been called. Why don't you just back off and—"

The answers came from the crowd, which had become a single entity, a mindless animal with numerous mouths.

"We're staying right here until somebody gets here to investigate."

"Nobody gets off this dock now!"

"Did somebody call the game wardens, too? Tell 'em to come see for themselves what these people are up to."

"We got a treaty that says your state wardens got no say," Marvin Strikes Many shouted.

"And we've also got a right to use the public landing," his son put in.

Gideon waved his arm as he pushed his way to the fore. "Would you guys just settle down—"

"We got a right to see what you *think* you got a right to take out of this lake," one of the bumper-sticker wavers said.

"Yeah, and what methods you're using." The crowd surged like an inchworm, its body gaining a few planks' worth of dock space. "Look, they've got spears!"

"They got spears, and they got nets!"

"Where's the media when they could do some good?"

"They'll be here."

"This isn't Wisconsin. Damn Indians took over on the fishing there, but nobody's gettin' away with that here."

"Hell, you know what they say over there," one of the mouths shouted. "Save a walleye, spear a squaw!"

"Hey, spear a pregnant squaw, save two walleye!"

The threat stabbed Raina in the stomach. Real, physical pain. She felt sick. She was close enough now to see the fear in Peter's eyes. He'd suffered some stares, some thoughtless, ignorant remarks in his young life, but nothing like this. And Raina had felt a mother's pain at cruelties perpetrated on her child, but this, *this* was insufferable. Her rage was bigger than she was, and she about to leave some claw marks on somebody.

All she could see was Peter, and all she sought was a way to get to him. He was scared, but he wasn't cowed by the threats. And when he saw her running up the wooden steps, he was afraid only for his mother.

"Mom! Stay back! I'll be okay, we're just—"

"Mom?" The animal's myriad eyes shifted her way, and one of its mouths laughed. "How'd you whelp anything that dark, lady? You oughta be—"

The anger welled deep in her throat as she clawed her way through the belly of the animal. She saw no faces. She had no interest in names. She had blood in her eye and bile in her throat. She was going to reach her son, and the hairy arms and knobby knees were *going* to get out of her way.

The calm summer evening was no more. The clear sky was ugly with murky bedlam. The air crackled with explosive charges. Raina had no sense of herself anymore. She was a she-wolf, and her pup was behind a wall of cruel, sweaty bodies. The shouts came fast and furious now, but only a few penetrated her red rage.

"Raina, don't!"

"Mom!"

"That kid's got some kind of spear!"

The violence erupted so suddenly that it was hard to recount the incident later. No one was supposed to be armed. There was not supposed to be any physical contact. The protesters had all agreed. Even the man who drew the pistol claimed later that he didn't even realize it was in his hand. There was a lot of pushing and shoving, a boy with a weapon, and everybody was mad. Everybody was just plain damn mad.

And madness reigned.

Raina saw it all in bleary, smeary slow motion. Peter was on one side. A gun appeared on the other. The din turned into background noise for her scream when Gideon lunged for the gun. It sounded like a car backfiring, startling but unremarkable until Gideon's big body fell across the gunman, like a defensive tackle flattening the opposing quarterback. Both sides shrank back as the two men came thudding down on the wooden planking.

Shouts of "Look out! They're shooting!" and "Somebody's shot!" threw the mob into a panic. Raina's wrath and fear injected her with the physical strength to push her way past the jostling bodies.

"Somebody call the police!"

"Somebody call an ambulance!"

"Somebody call 911!"

But the shriek of sirens already filled the air.

Raina reached Gideon just as Marvin Strikes Many went down on his knees next to him, calling his name.

Pinned beneath his victim, the gunman was wild-eyed, blood vessels bulging in his forehead. "Get him up! The gun went off! The gun just went off on me!"

Marvin helped Raina pull Gideon onto her lap. His eyes were closed, but she could feel the pulse in his neck. His arm slid away from his body, pulling his jacket open. The front of his shirt was soaked with blood.

"Oh, God, get some help! Please!"

"Open his shirt up," Marvin ordered. He pulled his own T-shirt over his head and wadded it into a compress.

Raina tore at the front of Gideon's shirt, crooning to him

as her fingers flew about their task. "Gideon, can you hear me? It's going to be all right."

Her eyes met Marvin's as he pressed the cloth against Gideon's side. The eyes of an ally. The caring hands of a friend. "Hold it tight," she pleaded.

"You hold *him* tight," Marvin advised hoarsely. "He saved that boy. Don't you let him go."

She leaned over him protectively, cradling his head in her arm, rubbing her lips over his forehead. "I won't," she whispered. "I'm staying with you, Gideon. I'm holding on. You hold on, too, okay?"

The gunman scrambled away, but he was met by a policeman before he reached the end of the dock. The gun lay close by. Raina's peripheral vision clouded. Shock dimmed her awareness of people milling around, closing in, moving away. Shock permeated the crowd. It was tangible, heavy, stupefying. The hot scene had suddenly shattered, and the mob had broken into jagged shards. The people who came with the sirens seemed to flow into the cracks, rounding up the pieces.

"Mom! He's not gonna die, is he?"

Raina blinked back the tears as she reached for her son's arm. "Peter, are you all right?"

"That guy was gonna shoot me. We'd been praying on our way over with… All I had was this." Peter knelt near Gideon's head. The object in his outstretched hand was a small ceremonial pipe. "Oh, God, there wasn't supposed to be any fighting," he said as he touched Gideon's cheek. "Mom, that gun was aimed at me. He saved my life, and now he's hurt bad."

Raina understood the plea in her son's voice. *Do something, Mom.* And because her hands were busy doing what they could, she leaned across Gideon's face, touched her forehead to Peter's and whispered, "I'm praying for him. How about you?" She felt his nod.

"Who is he?" a bystander asked.

"Is that Gideon Defender?"

"Defender? Isn't he the tribal chief?"

The white dentalium shells lay against the ridge of his collar bone in stark contrast with his skin.

"The ambulance is here." A uniformed policeman knelt beside Marvin. "The paramedics will be able to help him."

"I'm staying with him," Raina told the next pair of shoes. They were black. Her eyes traveled up the black pants, over the paramedic's sleeve patch, to a woman's sympathetic eyes. "He needs me," Raina said. "I have to be with him."

"That's fine." The paramedic started checking vital signs. "You did fine. You slowed the bleeding. We'll help him now."

A stretcher appeared, along with more uniforms and the hands of people trying to take Gideon from her.

"You can ride with him," one of them told her. "Are you his—"

"Peter!" He was gone. Raina turned to the woman with the kind eyes. "Get my son. Please. I can't leave my son."

"The police are taking care of—"

"No, you don't understand. He's only twelve. He—"

"I'll look after Peter," Marvin promised. He stepped back as Gideon's large, limp body was moved to the stretcher. "You go with the chairman. You see they take care of him."

Chapter 12

Raina climbed into the ambulance behind the stretcher. Someone told her to keep talking to him, which she did. He was going to be all right, she promised quietly. The doctors would take care of him. She stroked his hair. The sirens, the flashing lights and the measures taken by the paramedics all dimmed for her when he turned his head toward the sound of her voice.

"Raina?" He struggled against the strap that immobilized his arm. "Where's Peter? Is he okay?"

"Peter's fine." She ran her hand along the length of his arm, found his hand and held it tight. "You took the bullet that was meant for him."

"*Chimau…ni…do,*" he muttered, drifting. "Thank God."

"We're going to have to get that necklace off him," one of the paramedics said. "Does it matter if we cut it?"

"Yes, it matters," Raina said. She slid her hand under the

back of his neck, found the leather tie and pulled it loose. "I'll take care of this for you, Gideon. Okay?"

He groaned.

She closed her eyes and brushed her lips against his temple, whispering, "Can you hear me, darling?" No response. "Please know that I love you."

At the local clinic a yawning garage door admitted the ambulance, and several people dressed in white were there to meet them. Gideon's stretcher soon disappeared behind double doors. Carl Earlie came running down the hall just as the doors swung shut.

"How is he?"

"He's been shot."

"I heard."

"He's terribly hurt. His side—" Raina gripped her own side and noticed the blood on her skirt for the first time. Gideon's precious blood, spilled in such large drops over the yards of soft pastel field flowers he'd asked her to wear for him. She looked up at his friend, whose eyes matched hers for near panic. "I don't know."

"Is he conscious?"

"He was for a minute. He asked about Peter."

"I got there when they were rounding people up. I took charge of the boy."

"Rounding people up? You mean the man with the gun?"

"They got him, yeah. And some other arrests were made."

"Peter?"

"Marvin and some other guys, but I've got Peter. And I sent somebody out to Arlen's place to get the old man. He's family."

One of the women in white came barreling through the doors again. "Mrs. Defender?"

"Yes." She glanced meaningfully at Carl. "I'm Raina Defender."

"He needs surgery, and we don't have the facilities. We've got him stabilized, but something's still bleeding. The bus leaves *right now*," the woman recited, as though she anticipated some dawdling. "We'll take next of kin, but we're moving fast."

So was Raina. She clutched the shell necklace to her breast. It was all she carried. "My purse is at the restaurant, but Peter has a key to Gideon's house. I should—"

"You should be with the chief. We'll be along, too, but you—" He lifted his hand beseechingly. "You stay right with him."

"Bring Peter," she said over her shoulder, and she followed the woman in white.

Gideon's condition was critical. He was flown by helicopter to the nearest hospital of any size, which was in Duluth. Raina waited, taking the calls that came from Gideon's secretary, Judge Half and others. No word yet. She would let them know. Tell everyone to stay calm.

Carl called from Gideon's house. Before he put Peter on the phone, he told her that Arlen had just gotten there, and they would be on their way soon. Peter said he could just see the sun coming up, and it made him think everything would be okay. Raina permitted herself a hopeful smile. She'd lost all track of time. She wasn't even sure how far Duluth was from Pine Lake, or how long it might take anyone to drive there. But it was good to hear her son's voice telling her that he believed in the sunrise.

When Gideon was brought from the recovery room to ICU, Raina was waiting for him. She was determined to be there when he woke up. There were moments when she thought he was lucid—when he looked at her and called her by name—but he was just as likely to call her Rosie and ask her to get someone on the phone. The someone's name was usually garbled. Raina had to give him credit for some kind of subconscious control, for he never called her Tomasina. At least, not in English. She didn't know what he was saying in Ojibwa.

But there were other things that he could not control, mainly his rebellious stomach. The nurses assured Raina that it was all part of the normal response to the anesthesia. But for a while he was a very sick man, and she was glad he was oblivious to it all.

She was also glad when Arlen and Carl finally brought Peter to the hospital. He was only allowed to see Gideon for a few minutes, which was just as well. The monitors, the tubes and bottles, and the sight of one so strong and vigorous now lying helpless, were distressing to a twelve-year-old boy. Especially when, as he said, "It could have been me."

Arlen was given permission to perform a pipe ceremony and burn sweet grass for purification. Raina found the scent a bit cloying, but it definitely had a soothing effect on Gideon. While he rested and Carl kept vigil outside ICU, Raina had supper with Peter and Arlen in the hospital cafeteria. She couldn't remember what she'd eaten in the last twenty-four hours. Not much. The last normal, sensible moment she remembered seemed part of a distant past, another life. She and Gideon had gone out for dinner together. But they'd never gotten around to ordering any food.

"I guess I screwed up, Mom." Peter's hamburger was fast disappearing into his stomach without being chewed. "I couldn't hit anything with a spear, but we did use a net, and we did catch some fish. And that's what those guys are angry about. But it's a Chippewa treaty right."

Raina nodded, then quietly asked, "Why did you let him go with them, Arlen?"

Peter was quick to defend his grandfather. "*Nimishoomis* didn't know. I didn't ask. See, it was kind of a civil disobedience thing, like Martin Luther King, you know? It was, like, to make a statement about our rights and stuff." The boy shook his head. "Nobody thought it would turn out the way it did."

"Strikes Manys were talking to the wrong people." Arlen stirred two teaspoons of sugar into his coffee. "That anglers' club, or whatever they call themselves. They have no respect. It's no good to listen to people who don't know the meaning of respect."

"Respect for what?" Peter asked.

"Respect for any way that isn't *their* way. They see only this much of the world." The old man bracketed his eyes with leathery hands, demonstrating blinders. "They see only their own straight line. The rest of the circle is invisible to them."

"But Marvin says that we have to stand up for our rights in court."

"And maybe we do." Arlen glanced at a fluorescent ceiling light. "But the man who's lying up in that room, bad hurt, that's the man who was chosen to speak for us. To go behind his back and make plans with people who shout in our faces and call our women 'squaws' and threaten to spear them—"

Raina grimaced. "You don't think they *mean* that, do you?"

"Is it supposed to be a joke? Is that what makes them laugh?" The old man shook his head in amazement. "No wonder they don't understand Indian humor." Then he tested her with, "Do you think they *meant* to shoot the chairman?"

"I think that guy meant to shoot *me*," Peter said around a mouthful of sesame-seed bun.

Raina recalled the scene on the boat dock—the rising heat, the growing tension, the words shooting like missiles. "It was a mob. It was terrible, totally irrational. It felt like…something inhuman. Evil, maybe." And she remembered Gideon's mission. "This is what the attempt to reach a settlement is all about. This is what Gideon hoped to avoid by offering to compromise."

Arlen ignored her observation. "What do the doctors say?"

"That he's a very strong man. That 'barring any unforeseen complications,' he should pull through." Raina touched Peter's arm. "He's going to be all right. I'm sure of it."

"That bossy secretary of his wants you to call her as soon as he's well enough to talk about tribal business," Arlen said. "She seems to think the Pine Lake Chippewa will be on hold until their chairman speaks. Since they don't want us in his room too much, I'm going to stay with my grandson at Pine Lake, if that's all right with you. There's a telephone at his… at Gideon's house."

"Of course."

Arlen smiled gently. "When he speaks, you must call us, too."

Raina nodded, as she struggled to recall the right phrase. "My brain's turned to mush. How do you say 'thank you' in Ojibwa?"

With a nod Arlen deferred to Peter.

"Mii gwech," the boy told his mother. She repeated the words to Arlen.

She lowered the guard rail and rested her head in her arms on the side of Gideon's bed, her face near his hand. It was the familiar heads-down-on-your-desks posture. She had given the command many times, but it had been a long time since she'd assumed the position herself. She only wanted to close her eyes for a few minutes, and this was as good a way as any. The IV was stuck in his other arm. This arm was free. She could stay close to it. If it moved the slightest bit, she would know.

But when it did, she was dozing, drifting on a cloud-white sheet draped over a wooden lift-top desk in her first-grade classroom. She was only half listening to Mrs. Wrist's reading of a story called "The Loon's Necklace." Oddly, her teacher called the loon *mahng.* She could feel Mrs. Wrist's fingers combing through her hair, and she could hear her watch going beep-beep-beep. But she wanted to keep her eyes closed. She really didn't want to answer when her name was called.

"Raina?"

The voice was deep and painfully raspy. It hardly sounded like the voice of Mrs.…

Her hair sifted through his fingers as she raised her head. He couldn't seem to lift his own head off the pillow, but he knew she was there. He knew her by touch and by smell. He knew he was alive, and he knew she was there. Somewhere. He heard her call his name, felt her lips pressed against the backs of his fingers. He was alive, and she was there beside him.

Her face rose over him like a sleepy morning sun. She smiled and brushed her hair back after he'd mussed it up, waking her. He had news for her. She'd never looked more beautiful. In fact, he would have done some more mussing if his arm hadn't felt so heavy.

So did his tongue. Thick and heavy. He started small. "Hi."

"Hi, yourself, sleepyhead."

"You're the one—" Muzzy-headed, he didn't have much voice, wasn't sure where he was except that he was down, and she was up. "You must be the one…sleeping on my bed, Goldilocks."

She smiled at him exultantly, as though he'd just said something remarkable. "Sorry."

"You're welcome to my bed…anytime." He needed to do something about the needles in his throat, but swallowing didn't seem to be one of his options. "Could use a shot of water."

"I'll have to ask. You've really been sick to your stomach." She laid her hand there comfortingly. He could almost feel her rubbing his abdomen, sort of off to one side. "I'll bet you're sore from it."

He felt as though he were probably on the verge of a lot of pain all over. But mostly he felt mummified. "Feel like I've been on a six-day binge. How many has it been?"

"Not to worry. Less than two."

"Where's Peter?"

"He's safe, thanks to you. He's with Arlen." She closed her eyes, leaned down and snuggled her face against the side of his neck. "He's fine, darling. He's fine, he's fine."

"Darling? That's a…first." Articulating his elbow was a matter of foggy mind over heavy matter, but he managed to bring his hand up to her face. He found a damp cheek. "Hey, what's this?" He felt a shudder slide through her. "Hmm? What's this? Am I in for some bad—" His words kept getting sanded off at the end. "Throat's killing me, honey. Please. A little water."

"It's probably from the tubes." She sat up and stroked his hair back from his face. "You've had tubes everywhere. Mouth, nose—" He started to test out his other arm—to see if he could do something about sitting up—but she stopped him. "Careful. You've still got one in your arm. And, um... other places."

"Question is, am I—" The details were fuzzy, but he remembered hearing gunfire, then feeling a flash of fire somewhere in his gut. "Am I missing any parts?" He meant to be funny. Sort of. But she wasn't smiling. "What?"

"Your right kidney."

"My—"

"It'll be fine," she told him quickly, but the way her voice was trembling, he wasn't so sure she was giving it to him straight. "The doctor says you'll be perfectly, perfectly fine. People donate kidneys every day. They wouldn't take a kidney from a healthy person and put it into someone else if a person couldn't live a normal, healthy life with just—"

He lifted the arm that seemed to be the only part of him he could get working and tried to touch her chin. The back of his hand slid over her breast. She grabbed it before it retreated ignominiously back to the bed and held it close to her heart. Her dress felt smooth and soft. The same one she'd worn to the restaurant. Two days, he was thinking, same dress? How un-Raina of her.

But he asked, "What else?"

"That's all. That's enough." She squeezed his hand tight and tucked it possessively between her breasts. Just where it wanted to be. "We almost lost you."

"We?" *You almost lost me?* You and... "We almost lost... Peter." Now he remembered where the gun had been pointed. He remembered his own insides freezing up in that horrifying, endless moment before the gun had been fired.

"He was here earlier. They wouldn't let him stay long, and anyway, kids... You know? He got a little..." She scanned the small room, which was crammed with equipment. "All this is a little scary. Especially after he saw you get…" She pressed her lips together tightly and blinked furiously.

"He's not hurt?"

She shook her head.

"Then what's to cry about?" He managed a wan smile. "You haven't been cryin' like this ever since—"

She shook her head even more vigorously, half laughing as she lifted her hand to her face. But his, energized by her emotion, got there first. His weary eyes held hers as he caught a tear, then licked it like cake frosting from his finger.

"Thirstier 'n hell," he said in his hoarse voice, and she gave a teary laugh. "Sure nothing important's missing?" Lips pressed together, she nodded, her eyes glistening merrily through her tears.

"Did you check?"

"Not yet," she whispered.

"Later, then." He closed his eyes. "They got me on some kind of fairy dust, don't they?"

"Mmm-hmm." Her soft, sweet voice came closer. "So you don't hurt so much."

"Don't feel much except tired."

"Sleep, then."

"Don't want to. Not while you're…still here."

"I'll be here when you wake up." She was toying with his hair again. He liked it when she did that. "Before you go back to sleep, I have one more thing to say."

"Better…hurry."

"*Mii gwech,* Gideon Defender."

Eyes still closed, he did his best to smile.

She felt as though he were slipping away again, and it scared her. *Stay with me another moment, just to make sure.* "Did I say it right?"

"Not quite." His lips hardly moved. "Supposed to end with a kiss."

She licked her lips, then used them to moisten his in a tender, loving way.

"Mii gwech," he said.

In the next two days there were a flood of flowers and a barrage of phone calls. The governor, legislators, congressmen—Gideon had no shortage of well-wishers. His doctor told him that the less he rested, the longer it would take him to recover, so he agreed to keep the visitors to a minimum. But he had to let his people know that he was going to be all right. He asked to see Carl, Arlen and Rosie as soon as he was able to sit up.

"One TV camera, one reporter, one microphone," he told Rosie. "I want to let people see that I'm still kickin'."

"We've got some guys who are all set to go on the warpath, Gideon. They're fightin' mad."

"What guys? Anybody starts talking like that, you tell them to keep a lid on it. We can have our day in court without taking any of our kids spearfishing just to see if we can get somebody to take a potshot at one of them." He knew he didn't have to tell that to Carl or Rosie, but he wanted them to relay his message to anyone who would listen. "I know, I know. It wasn't supposed to be like that. Hell, it's *never* supposed to be like that. But it doesn't take much of a spark to light a fuse."

He turned to the old man, whose approval he had recently come to covet. "I've done my reading, Arlen. I know all about Red Cloud's compromises to try to save the Great Sioux Reserve and the Black Hills. And I know the Sioux went to court over it. They wanted their land. And that's what we're trying to get. Some of the land back. A part of the lake where we can take the fish our own way. The way our more traditional people still remember."

"The treaty promises more than that. But either way, there's going to be a fight. Promises are like river water for them. An endless flow." Arlen eyed Gideon and gave him that mischievous look that put a youthful sparkle in his eye. "Do like the beaver. Find a way to build a dam."

"Not like the other night. I don't make a very good dam." Gideon touched his side, which was bandaged beneath the cotton hospital robe. "They put a hole in me real easy."

"And like Judge Half says, there are too few Natives left. We can't spare any more." With a nod Arlen urged, "Use the courts. See what they mean by 'justice for all.'"

"We will if we have to, Arlen. We know who we are, don't we?" He sought confirmation in each face. "We've been around for a hell of a long time. Against some pretty big odds, we're still hangin' in there. Main thing is, we remember who we are."

"And we teach the children, so they know who they are," Arlen said.

"Cool heads. Sharp minds. That's what we need." Gideon shifted uncomfortably. He hated calling for painkillers, but it felt like something was starting to eat at his raw insides again. "If this settlement fails, we go to court. The law's on our side. You hear anybody talkin' up the cracking-heads warpath, you bring 'em to me."

"What about the guy who did this?" Carl asked.

Gideon made a cutoff gesture. "They arrested him."

"You know they won't do nothin' but—"

"That's for the court to decide, too." He managed a fleeting smile. "We gotta work the program, Carl. Right? Do the best we can."

Peter's turn came that afternoon, after Raina had been ordered to "go across the street to the hotel and sleep off those raccoon eyes." He'd brought his mother some clothes, but he wasn't staying at the hotel with her. Now that Gideon was out of ICU *and* out of the woods, Peter didn't mind saying that he wasn't crazy about hospitals.

"I'm with you," Gideon assured him. "I can't wait to blow this pop stand." Then he added, "Sure has been one hell of a summer vacation for your mom, hasn't it?"

Peter avoided Gideon's eyes. "I know you saved my life. You took that bullet for me."

"I was going after the gun, not the bullet." Gideon chuckled. "I was bigger than he was. I thought I could take the gun." When Peter looked at him as though he were some kind of miracle worker, he protested with, "You think I'm crazy, or what?"

The boy shook his head. "I think you're pretty brave."

"I wasn't thinking about being brave. I wasn't thinking at all. I wasn't going to let anyone hurt you, was all."

"You weren't even scared," Peter insisted. "You didn't look scared."

"It all happened very fast." Gideon thought back, then shook his head. "No, when I saw that gun I was scared. I hope you were, too."

"Why?"

"Because guns kill people. You take the gun away from that scene the other night, probably nobody would've gotten hurt. At least, nobody would have gotten shot." He reached for the water bottle on the bed table, and Peter fairly leapt to put it in his hand. Gideon nodded, gave a quick wink and offered a teasing aside. "I'm supposed to move around a little."

He was also supposed to drink plenty of water, and he was damn well determined to do whatever the doctor ordered so he could be on his way. He downed half the bottle before he continued. "People get mad, they get a little crazy, too. You put a gun in some hothead's hand—" He snapped his fingers. "That quick, somebody can be dead. It's too easy. Too damned easy."

"It wasn't supposed to be like that. It was supposed to be like we were standing up for our rights."

"We have to do that, too. And that can be risky." Gideon shoved the plastic bottle aside. "You have to be careful who you follow, Peter. You have to listen to what they say and really think it over. Maybe talk to some other people."

"Like you?"

"Your grandfather, your mom. People who show you how much they care about you by treating you right."

"What about you?"

"Just say the word," Gideon offered lightly, but his eyes said, *I'd lay down my life for you, son.*

"I…" Peter polished his knees with his palms. "I don't know what to call you."

"How about just plain Gideon?" The boy looked up, dubious. "We'll take it one day at a time, okay? You take your time figuring out who I am."

"I miss my…my dad a lot."

"So do I."

"So that's okay, huh?"

"It better be."

Paddling with his heels, Peter scooted his chair across the floor until his knees touched the side of the bed. Then, awkwardly, he flopped one arm around Gideon's middle, pressing his cheek to Gideon's shoulder. "I'm glad you're gonna be okay."

"Mii gwech." Gideon was unaccustomed to the way his throat prickled as he ruffled Peter's hair. He had to swallow more than once before he could come up with a breezy "Careful, *ningozis,* I'm a wounded man."

"What does that mean? *Ningozis?*"

It meant that his shoulders, his hands, his tender side, would always be at Peter's disposal. "It means I've already figured out who you are."

When Raina came to the room that evening, she found him dressed in jeans and a T-shirt and sitting in a chair with a bed pillow at his back.

"You're up!"

"Dream on, honey. They just took out the last of the tubes, and I am one wilted puppy. Oh, you mean up out of *bed*." He gave her a cocky smile, just to show her how really good he was feeling about his accomplishment. "Since you're looking so damn sexy today, I thought maybe you were out to seduce me, and I was gonna say…" He eyed her up and down. She'd bought herself a new flowered dress, similar to the other one, but maybe just a little clingier. "Mmm, I think I'm getting my, uh…strength back."

"That's good news." She glanced up at the TV as she pulled a chair close to his.

"Yeah, well, *that* isn't." He aimed the remote at the local news, clicking it off with a vengeance. "Some damn retired football coach just held court at a screw-the-Indians rally today. What gives him any authority to speak on Native issues? Who appointed him lord of the walleye? What in hell is he talking about, special privileges? The man owns a million-dollar house, for…"

"Arlen was there, quoting chapter and verse from the treaties. Damn, that old man's got spunk." Gideon jabbed a finger at the dark TV screen. "And that jerk's answer is that Arlen's 'under the influence.' Under the influence of what? Time-honored traditional ways, that's what." He tossed the remote aside. "Damn pigskin-for-brains wouldn't know

American culture if it kicked him in the butt. And Arlen doesn't drink."

"I'll say you're getting your strength back." She sat next to him, the way they used to on his porch.

"*Native* American culture," he reiterated, carefully enunciating each syllable.

"But you *do* know," she said. "And you're absolutely right. The man is making a fool of himself, casting bigoted aspersions like that, so I'm sure no one will listen to him."

"You kidding? Every damn sports nut in this state will listen to him." He scowled. "What am I talking about. *I'm* a sports nut. I'm a Timberwolves fan even when they're in the sub-basement, and I can fish the pants off that pinhead." He turned a sly smile Raina's way. "Without him even noticing his fly's slipped."

She laughed, and because humor always helped his people through the bad times, so did he.

"I have a buyer for the house," she told him. He raised his brow appreciatively. The warmth in his dark eyes was all for her, but it made her dance away from the subject she had intended to lead up to. Evasively, she wondered, "Do the nurses know that you're going around here barefooted?"

He glanced down at his toes and shrugged. "You wanna make a note on my chart?"

"Didn't they help you get dressed?" She could think of one in particular who probably would have jumped at the chance. The little brunette who jumped to do his every other bidding.

"Did it all by my lonesome," he said, his tone irresistibly cute. "You should'a been here."

Now that he was in a good mood again, she had to avoid his eyes and charge ahead if she was going to get this out. "Arlen says that since we're moving to Pine Lake, he's not going to ask for custody of Peter. You're the only other person who can…press the issue."

"Peter's almost thirteen years old. It's up to him to decide whether he'll let me be his father after all this time. Not the judge." Suddenly all anger and all frivolity had disappeared from his quiet, steady voice. "I told you I wasn't going to take him from you. I meant that."

"So he can live with me?"

"You're his mother. There's never been any question about that as far as I was concerned." His eyes held hers. "But there is one question you haven't answered, Raina. My offer still stands. You can both live with me."

"You offered that as the solution to a problem," she reminded him. "But the problem no longer exists."

"So that's it, then?" he asked tightly. A frosty glaze slid across his eyes. "You can sleep with me, but you can't be my wife? You won't marry me?"

"Why are you asking, Gideon? You wanted sex—" she glanced away "—and we've had sex. You don't have to…" No, that was silly. She knew very well that that wasn't the reason he was asking. "Why did you pull away from me sixteen years ago? Was it because I wasn't ready to—"

"*I* wasn't ready," he told her calmly. "I didn't have much to offer you, Raina. Except a good time. I wanted you. And, God, how I wanted you to want me. But for what? What would you want from me?"

She looked up, puzzling.

He chuckled, remembering. "I couldn't let you know how bad I had it for you. A case of the hots, I figured, so I tried to be cool. Suave, you know. Figured if you'd go to bed with me, just once, you'd be mine."

He touched the back of her hand, hoping to loosen her tense grip on the arm of the chair. "But I scared you off, didn't I? I rushed you. And the hell of it is, I *know* better than to move too quick. I can wait out in the brush for hours, never move a muscle. Hell, I can stalk a deer all day long." He looked into her eyes. "You needed more time. Among other things."

"What other things?"

"The kinds of things I didn't have going for me back then."

"But Jared did," she surmised.

"Yeah. Jared did." He smiled wistfully. He'd loved his brother almost as much as… "I knew you'd like him. I knew he'd be just your type." He laughed and shook his head. "But, damn my eyes, I introduced you to him, anyway. Beauty, meet Prince Charming."

"And then you rode off into the sunset, as I remember."

"No way," he averred dramatically. "Can't do that scene without a horse. I just sort of politely bowed out. Exit Beast."

"I never thought…." She turned her palm to his. "I never knew what to think, Gideon."

"About me? Come on, Raina."

"Listen, Gideon, you pulled away from me, and you pulled away from Peter. You say you weren't ready." Her eyes narrowed, challenging him. "But now you've been to hell and back, and I have to know why you want to marry me. It's not for sex, and it's not for Peter." He tried to pull away again, but she held his hand fast. "What are you afraid of, Gideon?"

It took him a while to answer, but at last, at *long* last, he put it into words that almost surprised him. "Not being good enough, I guess."

With some difficulty he turned his wounded body in her direction and affected a lighter tone. "What you see is what you get. This is it. A little banged up at the moment, but I'll heal. I always do."

She extended her free hand toward his cheek, but he caught it midpath, kissed her fingertips and gave a jaunty smile.

No pity, Raina. Whether it's good enough for you now, I don't know, but what you see ain't half-bad.

"I've got plenty of muscle," he told her. "You wanna go somewhere? I can paddle you all the way to Tahiti. You want an addition on the house? I can cut the timber and raise the roof beams myself. I'd never let you go hungry. I'd protect you, defend you. Hell, I'd stop a bullet with my—"

She closed her eyes. "Oh, Gideon."

"You want a child? I gave you one. You want another one? I'll make as many babies with you as you want." He drew her closer, and his voice dropped to an intimate hush. "And I'll give you so much pleasure in the making that when the pain comes…" His head tipped toward her, forehead resting against forehead, and he closed his eyes against the wooziness he was beginning to feel. "But when it comes, I'll be there, just the way you stayed with me. Always. No matter what kind of pain it is. I want to be your husband so that I can be there for the good times and the bad."

The last confession pinched his heart—badly, this time, because everything else was out on the table, and his heart was completely, absolutely vulnerable. "What I'm afraid of is that all I can offer won't be good enough."

"Why wouldn't it be?" she asked, breathless from the beauty of his vows, praying for just one more. "If you love me."

He raised his head and searched her eyes, wondering whether his whole heartfelt speech had fallen on deaf ears. "That's what I just said, isn't it? That I love you?"

"*You* tell *me*. Why do you want to marry me?"

"Because I love you. Because I loved you when I had no business loving you, and now, here you are with…" He caught her face in his hands. "And now there's no reason in the world why I can't love you. And I'll be damn good at it, Raina."

She gave him a misty-eyed smile. "I think you already are."

"Then why are you making me jump through all these hoops?"

"Because I've already jumped through them for you." She took his hand from her face and placed it on her breast. She moved it over her racing heartbeat, slipped it over and under the neckline of her sundress and invited him to feel the hardness of her nipples. "To me, this means that I love you. You know that, don't you? There's no other way for me. And while my being in love with you was reason enough for making love…" Her hand sneaked into his lap, found his "wilted puppy" and gently caressed him. She smiled, for it was a puppy no more. "The recipe for marriage calls for *two* people in love."

"Two people making love?"

"Two people—one man, one woman—in love with each other. That's how you make a marriage."

"Looks like we've got the right ingredients, then." He figured he'd better get this hand thing under control before she had him howling. He enfolded both of hers within both of his. "Wanna make one with me?"

She laughed and cried, both at once. "I surely do."

Epilogue

The date was set for early October. Raina had gotten started in her new school, Peter in his. Some of the changes weren't easy to make, but, as Arlen had said, the sooner a person learned the lesson of the willow, the smoother life's road became. Flexibility. Learning when to stand firm and when to bend could keep a person from breaking.

Gideon's ears tuned in to such wisdom wherever he found it these days. The fate of the settlement rested with the state legislature now, for the Pine Lake Chippewa had made their offer. And the outcome of the vote, which would be taken a few months down the road, looked like a toss-up. The DNR and the attorney general's office were strongly in favor of the compromise, but those in opposition had financial clout. The sportsmen's groups, in particular, had powerful allies and vocal lobbyists working for them. In the end, the issue might very well be decided in federal court. Either way, Gideon realized that the fate of the Pine Lake Chippewa lay exactly where it always had—in the hands of the Chippewa people themselves and with *Chimaunido*.

For now, on this sunny October day, beside the sparkling blue waters of Pine Lake and with a blazing pink-and-yellow backdrop of sugar maples, there was a marriage to be made. During the feast, the people would launch the bride and groom in a red canoe, and he would paddle her across the water to their honeymoon bower—or as far as Tahiti, if that was her wish. His doctor had pronounced him fit to do anything he felt up to doing, and on this day he felt up to taking his bride to the paradise of her choice.

He was dressed for just such a journey. He wore jeans, along with moccasins and a buckskin jacket, both beaded in the traditional floral designs of the Chippewa. His hair was pulled back and tied at the nape. He had the ring. He was all set. Except that there was a knot in the dentalium shell necklace, and his hands were a little shaky. Must've had too much coffee this morning, he told himself.

There was a knock at the door of the room the lodge had provided him for dressing. Peter stuck his head inside. "Mom wants to know if there's a word in Ojibwa for two o'clock."

"Tell her the only word we've got for that is *Indian time*. When the time is right and the people are ready." Gideon motioned for the boy to come in and close the door. "And I'm ready, except for this damned knot."

Peter looked more than thirteen years' worth of sharp in his blue blazer and tan slacks. He smiled indulgently as he took over on the untying job. "You nervous?"

"Do I look nervous?"

"You look a little pale." He gave a quick shrug. It was the padded shoulders, Gideon thought, that made the boy look so much older today. "It kinda fits, though, because even in the sun, Mom's really… We used to call her 'pale face.'"

"We did?" Gideon chuckled. "Maybe we could come up with something more original."

"*You* can. 'Mom' works for me."

"Did anyone ever tell you that I knew her first?"

Peter glanced up from the slow-yielding knot. "*Knew* her?"

"Met her first. Went out with her first. And, no, don't ask any more than that, because a guy never discusses his private moments with his lady with anyone else." Gideon nodded instructively. It was becoming a habit. "You remember that."

"As far as I'm concerned, my mom's a virgin and always will be." Displaying his conquest over the knot, Peter's eyes twinkled as he imitated Gideon's instructive tone. "A guy's mom doesn't do that stuff. You remember that."

"I'll be good to her, Peter. I do love her, with all my heart."

"Siiick! Who turned on the oldies station?" Peter clapped a hand over the pocket of his blazer and crooned, "With aaaall my hearrrrt." Then he cut Gideon a meaningful look. "You'd better be good to her, with all your heart and whatever else you got."

"Gotcha. You wanna put that on for me?" Gideon asked, seating himself on the bed to make the job easier. "I seem to be all thumbs."

Peter draped the necklace in place. "I feel like the mother of the bride," he muttered, and they both laughed. Then an unsettled quiet fell over them. "You got a best man?"

Gideon shook his head, but damn, he was hoping.

Peter tucked the tied ends of the necklace under the back of Gideon's collar. "You want one?"

Gideon cleared his throat. "You available?"

"Somebody better make sure the ring gets there, nervous as you are."

Rising slowly from the bed, Gideon drew the gold band from his pocket and pressed it into the hollow of Peter's palm. He wasn't sure he could have said anything if he tried. His chest was full to bursting with love and pride. Maybe that sounded like the oldies station, too, but there was no other way to put it.

Peter looked up, his eyes filled with tears. "It's like I'm filling in for Dad. If he was here, this would be his job, because he was your brother."

Gideon nodded once. "If your father were here, this wedding wouldn't be taking place."

"You know what? I think my dad's here in spirit." He glanced away. "But I feel like my father's here in the flesh, too."

Gideon's arm went around the boy's shoulders. He closed his eyes and gripped a fistful of shoulder pad.

Peter pressed his cheek against the soft leather jacket. "It sounds confusing," he said, "but in my head, it works okay."

"Works great for me, too."

Then he saw Raina through the window, standing on the grass below. She was wearing a long-sleeved, soft white cotton dress, scattered with pastel field flowers. The gentle breeze lifted the long skirt and made it flutter as she walked. A broad-brimmed hat shaded her face. One of the girls from her class at school came running after her with a bouquet of wildflowers. She turned, took the flowers, then took the girl's hand.

"We're late," Peter warned.

"But not too late. God, she's beautiful."

And then they were on their way out the door. "One thing you gotta learn about Mom. She's always there when she says she will be."

Gideon smiled. "Then from now on, my time is her time."

* * * * *

Author's Note

Pine Lake Reservation and the Pine Lake Band of Chippewa are purely fictitious. The Anishinabe, or Chippewa bands (many of whom prefer the name Ojibwa or Ojibwe), are an indigenous people of the Upper Great Lakes Region. Even though I chose to create a fictitious band, many readers will recognize that the issues with regard to Native American treaty rights, especially as they apply to fishing rights, are genuine concerns. While many bands have negotiated settlements, the issues are still highly controversial and continue to be fought in the courts—and outside of them.

It should be noted that the vast majority of people who enjoy fishing as a sport have no interest in interfering with the relatively few Native Americans who seek to exercise their treaty rights. Typically, non-Indians who question the validity of treaty rights do so because they have limited knowledge of their historical background, along with limited understanding of and respect for Native American culture and its values.

Historically, movements to abrogate Native American treaties have been fueled for the most part by a common motive, and that has been greed.

BROOMSTICK COWBOY

For Judy Baer, Pamela Bauer,
Mary Bracho and Sandy Huseby.

Vive Prairie Writers' Guild!

Prologue

Tate Harrison cupped his big, callused hands around his face and peeked through the back door window into the Beckers' kitchen. Except for the two plates standing in the dish drainer along with two forks and a pair of tall tumblers, turned bottoms up, the place was as neat and tidy as the rows in a Kansas cornfield. It was Amy's kitchen, so naturally it would be. The only fingerprints would be those he was making on the glass right now, pressing his face to the window. The floor looked so clean he could almost smell the pine soap, and the stainless-steel sink was flooded with Indian summer sunshine, pouring through the ruffles of a yellow gingham curtain.

He shoved his hands in his jacket pockets and gave the rambler-style farmhouse a cursory inspection on the outside. The yellow trim was in pretty good shape, but the white clapboard siding sure needed a coat of paint. White sheers hung in the side window, but he would bet there were yellow curtains down the hall. Yellow was Amy's color. It looked great with her dark hair and dark eyes. Black-Eyed Susan, he'd called her, but that had been a long time ago.

He rapped on the glass a second time, put his hands back up and peered again. As always, Tate was on the outside looking in. He liked it that way, especially whenever he came home to Overo. The best part of Montana was definitely the outside. Plenty of elbow room. Plenty of scenery. Plenty of opportunity for a cowboy to move on to greener pastures whenever he felt like it. Moving on had become his stock in trade, taking him out of state, even out of the country, but whenever he was in town—and it had been a while—he always looked in on the Beckers.

He'd had mixed feelings this time about paying his more-or-less regular call. Up until a year ago Kenny Becker had been leasing the land Tate had inherited after his stepfather died. He felt a little funny about showing up now to talk business. Kenny was Tate's best friend, and Tate wanted to sell him the land eventually, whenever Kenny could swing the financing. At least, that had always been the plan.

When Kenny had dropped the lease last year, the only explanation had come in a note that said they were "cutting back on the horses." Kenny had assured him that there were plenty of neighbors interested in picking up the lease. But Tate wasn't interested in leasing his land to anyone else. He had called to wish the family a merry Christmas and to tell Kenny to go ahead and use the land, cut the hay on shares. He'd asked only a token percentage for himself, because he knew what Amy would say if she thought he was giving them something for nothing. But he and Kenny were friends, and if times were tough, he wanted to help out. He'd managed to keep his own financial obligations to a minimum.

"You sure you guys are okay?" Tate had asked over the phone. He couldn't imagine Kenny cutting his horse herd. He loved every useless broomtail he kept around the place, and year after year that sentiment had helped him run his operation into the red. But that was Kenny. "You know, if you need to, you can sell my share of the hay and use the cash to—"

"Hey, thanks, buddy, but we're doin' just fine. Amy's got us into this sideline that's…well, it's a long story, but next year things'll start lookin' up. You oughta get married and settle down, Tate. I tell you…"

"I'm doin' fine, too, Ken," Tate had said. "Come fall, we'll take a look at where things stand. If you want to pick up the lease again, fine. If you don't think you're gonna want to buy it like we planned, I'll probably just unload it. My banker tells me the mineral rights are worth more now than the grass."

Lately Tate had been thinking he wouldn't mind selling the land and cutting the last of his ties. He'd left Overo when his stepfather died seven years ago, and hadn't been back in at least the last two, maybe longer. There were a thousand other places where he could be outside without feeling quite so much like an *outsider*. He shouldn't be feeling that way anymore, not when he was standing here on the back step of a house he'd spent as much time in as his own when he was growing up. Kenny Becker was his *best friend*. Always had been.

But Amy was his best friend's wife. And they'd never made a very good threesome.

Damn, he'd knocked three times now, and nothing seemed to be moving except a fat calico cat. She padded across the white linoleum, stopped by the back door and blinked a couple of times, then rounded the corner and ambled down the basement steps. It all made for a pretty disappointing homecoming. Tate had been looking forward to surprising them, earning a couple of smiles, maybe even a couple of hugs and a home-cooked meal. He tried to remember whether he'd still had his beard the last time he'd been back. They might not even recognize him since he'd started shaving regularly again. Well, fairly regularly. No, Kenny would, he amended. Fifty years from now, when they were both nearsighted ol' codgers, Ken would still know him right off.

Amy was another story. She wasn't interested in knowing Tate Harrison. She had no use for his good intentions or his excuses or his apologies. She tolerated him because she loved Kenny. He wasn't sure she was really interested in knowing Kenny, either, not the same Kenny he knew. But she loved him just as sure as she had no use for his best friend.

A mystery, that woman. The kind you could stay up all night reading and never figure out until you hit the very last page. She was a city girl turned country. One minute she could be as stiff-necked as an old schoolmarm, the next she'd be bubbling over like she'd just popped her cork. Smart and sexy both. Tate figured she'd outsmarted herself when she'd married Ken, thinking all she had to do to shape him up was change the company he kept. On her wedding day, Tate had sincerely wished her luck. From the looks of things, somebody's luck was stretched a little thin right about now.

Tate tried the door, but it was locked. That had to mean they'd gone into town together. Kenny never locked the door, because he never had a key. If there'd been anybody out in the barn, they would have peeked out when they heard the pickup, but just to make sure, Tate walked around back and gave a holler. The only response came from the two dogs that had been yappin' to beat hell when he drove up. A Border collie and a Catahoula Leopard, both trying to see who could jump the highest inside the chain-link kennel. Tate didn't remember the kennel being there, next to the clothesline. The dogs were new, too. He wondered what had happened to the old black

Lab he and Kenny used to take with them when they'd go fishing.

On the way to his pickup he turned the corner around the dilapidated yard fence and nearly tripped over a pint-size red-and-white bicycle lying on its side in the gravel. Their little boy couldn't be old enough to ride a bike. Last time Tate had seen the little squirt he'd barely been toddling around, pigeon-toed like his ol' man. His hair was curly like Kenny's, too, only lighter, but he had his mother's big brown eyes. Cute little tyke. Cute enough to make a guy think he might want one of his own someday.

Tate lit a cigarette and leaned his backside against the headlight of his pickup. The crisp October breeze felt good against his face. This was a pretty spot. Plenty of water and grass, and a fine view of the snow-capped mountains. Wouldn't be long before the lowlands would snuggle under a blanket of snow and sleep until springtime. The only time he ever got homesick was when he thought of the Becker place. He'd sold his own house right off the foundation, along with the pole barns, the grain bins, even the damn toolshed. All he'd kept was the land. If you wanted to make a go of it on the land, you had to sacrifice, and you never knew what kind of forfeiture the land might demand. It had taken all it would ever get from Tate. He'd been making a damn good living as a rodeo cowboy, truck driver, construction worker—whatever came along. He'd socked the lease payments away in the bank. He didn't need the land, and it damn sure wasn't claiming his best years.

Didn't look like it was claiming much of the sweat off ol' Kenny's brow, either. He hadn't brought in much hay. The half section west of the house hadn't been cut. Worse yet, somebody's mangy sheep were grazing on it. Just like Kenny to let a neighbor take advantage of his good nature. But from the looks of things, Kenny couldn't afford to be so damned good-natured. Other than the dogs and the trespassing sheep, Tate didn't see too many signs of life around the place. No horses in the corral out back. Not a cow in sight.

The more he thought about it, the less he liked what he was seeing. Tate dropped his cigarette on the gravel driveway and ground it under his boot heel. Fishing in his jacket for his keys, he jerked the pickup door open. Surely on his way to town he would see a supply of square bales, stacked up in a nice long wall close to the road, where it wouldn't be too hard to reach in the winter. Probably down on his land, near the old homesite, where the access would still be pretty good. Maybe on the alfalfa field, where Kenny should have been able to get a good two cuttings this year. He should have hauled the bales in closer, though, damn his lazy hide.

But, then, that was Kenny.

Chapter 1

"What do you mean, *ever since Kenny Becker kicked the bucket?*"

Tate was ready to pop bartender Ted Staples in the mouth for coming up with such a sick joke. But Ted wasn't smiling. In fact, Ted had stopped pouring drinks. He set the bottle of Jack Daniel's down on the bar as if it were a delicate piece of crystal, and he looked at Tate with about as much surprise as ever registered on the gaunt man's leathery face.

"I mean, ever since Kenny *died*," Ted said more carefully this time. "Is that better? Since Kenny died, the women around here have been drivin' me crazy with phone calls, checkin' up on their men."

"Checking up…" The hinges in Tate's jaw went rusty on him. He could even taste the rust in the back of his mouth. No, the word *died* wasn't any better. For an instant the letters on the neon Pabst sign above the bar swelled up and blurred clean out of focus. Hell, he was only on his first drink, and somehow he'd missed the part where he'd taken a boot in the gut. "What in hell are you talkin' about, Ted?"

"I usually tell 'em the man ain't here or he just left, but you hear that damn he's-been-gone-too-long tone in their voice, kinda scared and trembly, and you know what they're worried about."

"Kenny…"

"Well, you know—" Since they'd hit on a touchy subject, Ted splashed another shot in Tate's glass for good measure. "—it took us a while to find him. Surprised you didn't come back for the funeral, Tate. You two used to be close enough to use the same toothpick. Where you saw one, you saw the other."

"When…" It felt as though somebody had just pulled the walls in a few feet. Tate was suddenly short on air and voice. It took a long pull on his drink to sear the goop out of his pipes. He pressed his lips together and pushed his big black Stetson back so he could get a better look at Ted's face. He needed to make damn sure the old man wasn't putting him on. "When?"

"Why, late last winter." Ted turned to Gene Leslie, who occupied the bar stool on the inside corner. "Was it March?"

"Early March." Gene swept his quilted jacket back with arms akimbo, poking his gut out while he took a moment to puzzle all this out.

Tate was listening, waiting for some sense to be made here. He felt clammy under the back of his shirt, under his hatband. He wanted to shed his jacket, open the door, let some air in the place. But nobody took his jacket off in the Jackalope Bar, because there was no place to put it, and everybody wore a cowboy hat, because you didn't hang out at the Jackalope unless you were a cowboy.

"Take that back," Gene amended contemplatively. "Believe it might've been closer to the middle of the month. Them heifers started calving on the tenth, and I believe…" He squinted, focusing on Tate through a haze of blue smoke. "You didn't know about Kenny?"

Tate shook his head, trying to clear it of the flak and home in on some answers. "Know what? What the hell happened?"

"He was here that day." Ted wiped his hand on the white towel he'd tucked into the front of his belt for an apron, then wagged his finger at the center booth next to the far wall. Two cowboys looked up briefly, then went back to nursing their brews and puffing their smokes as soon as they realized the finger wasn't pointed at them. "Sittin' right over there at that table, horse tradin' with Ticker Thomas 'til late afternoon, early evening. When his wife called, I told her Kenny'd left before suppertime, and I thought sure he was sober."

"Turned out he was, which was too bad," Gene added. "He'd 'a had more alcohol in him, he'd 'a made it through the night. My uncle Amos lived for two days in the middle of November when he went in the ditch that time over by Roundup."

"Your uncle Amos is too ugly to live and too ornery to die," thick-tongued Charlie Dennison said. The story was coming at Tate from all sides now, with Charlie getting into it from his perch near the door.

"You're damn straight. He was tanked up pretty good and glad of it, even when they cut off his frostbit toes." Gene adjusted his hat in a gesture that allowed no two ways about the facts in either story. "Poor ol' Kenny should'a had a few more shots under his belt."

"Kenny only drank beer," Tate said. "I didn't see his old Ford pickup out at his place. Was it a—"

Gene shook his head. "Nah, he didn't wreck his pickup.

He got throwed. Ground was still froze hard as rock. Split his head open like a melon."

"Nobody's figured out yet what he was doin' out ridin' that horse that time of night," Ted put in. "Like I said, his ol' lady'd been callin' around to hell and back. Then she went out lookin' for him, so there was nobody home. He must'a drove his pickup out in the pasture, caught a horse and went off ridin' bareback, far as anybody can tell. Damnedest thing."

"Moon was bright as hell that night, and it was cold as a witch's tit," Charlie recalled.

"We used to go out together on nights like that," Tate said. He could picture the moonlight flooding the snow-covered hillsides. Kenny loved those nights, when the big black velvet sky was filled with stars and their voices cracked the cold hush with pithy adolescent wisdom. "Bareback, too, so you'd keep your butt warm. Twice as warm as a woman and half the trouble," he remembered with a melancholy smile.

"Women don't usually buck as hard," Gene said.

"Tell you what, Leslie," Charlie grumbled. "Any woman does any buckin' with *you* has got be three ax handles wide in the hip and horse-faced as hell," Charlie said.

Ted let the perpetual banter go in one ear and out the other, but Tate's difficulty drew rare concern. "They must not've been able to track you down, Tate."

"Maybe they didn't try." Amy, he thought. Maybe Amy hadn't wanted him around when she'd buried her husband.

"That little girl was pretty damn broke up, but I'd be willing to bet she tried to call you or something."

Tate wasn't going to argue. "Who found him?"

"She did."

"Amy?"

"The pickup wasn't back, see, so that kinda throwed 'em off for a while. But when they found Kenny's pickup, and then they found the horse still wearin' a hackamore, well, they sent out a helicopter. A bunch of us went out on horseback. But his wife took those dogs of hers, and she went out on foot. She found him."

"He'd slid down into a ravine. Don't know what all he ran into. Head split open like a damn melon." Gene was stuck on the melon image.

It was all a dream. A bad one. The kind that wouldn't go away when he woke up. Tate knew it well; he'd had it before. He cast his gaze at the sooty ceiling and whispered, "Jesus."

Jesus, get me out of here.

Jesus, make it not be true.

Jesus, give him back.

He sighed heavily and dug into his shirt pocket for a cigarette. "Hope she got a decent price for her stock."

"She ain't sold much yet," Ted reported. "She says she's gonna run the place herself, her and the boy."

Tate glanced up from the match he'd struck on his thumbnail. "The kid's only, what? Three or four?"

"Hell, I was feedin' stock when I was four years old," Charlie claimed.

Gene laughed. "The hell you were, Dennison. Even at *forty*-four you wouldn't know which end to feed."

Tate dragged deeply on his cigarette, hoping the smoke would do better than whiskey at calming his innards. One of the cowboys had gotten up from the booth and chucked some change into the jukebox. It rattled its way down the hollow tube and clunked when it hit bottom. If they'd pitched it down Tate's throat, it would have made the same damn sound.

"She hired any help?" he asked. The cowboy punched his numbers, and up came the steel guitars.

"Well, she tried," Ted said. "She run one scarecrow-lookin'

guy off with a shotgun after about a week last summer. Said he'd tried to make a pass at her."

"My uncle Amos used to say some widows are just like cask-aged wine, and some are pure vinegar," Gene said.

"Your uncle Amos oughta take another drive out to Roundup," Charlie said. He was listening to Ted's story with increasing interest. "None of her family came to help her out? You woulda thought…"

"Her mother lives in Florida somewhere. She was here for a little while after Kenny died, but she went back." In response to Gene's signal, Ted slid another bottle of Blue Ribbon his way. "Mrs. Becker's got spunk—I'll say that for her. Winter's a bad time to sell, anyway. If she can hold out a few months, I'd say she'll get a good price for the place."

"She's over to the sale barn now," Charlie said. "I was just there. Looks like she's gonna run some horses through."

"Horseflesh is goin' pretty cheap," Gene said as he raised the bottle to his thin lips.

Tate was tempted to stay right where he was and get himself blind drunk, fight absurdity with absurdity. These people were talking about Kenny like it made perfect sense that he was dead. Like it was not possible for Kenny to be the next man to park his old green pickup out front. Like the next guy that flung that creaky front door open and let in a blast of cold air couldn't be Kenny.

It couldn't be true. It was inconceivable that Tate couldn't come home to Overo and buy Kenny a drink, listen to his tall tales and hear that bizarre, high-pitched laugh of his. Kenny was only thirty years old, for God's sake. He couldn't be lying stone cold and silent in a box six feet deep in the ground. That was the meaning of *dead*. His best friend couldn't really be dead.

Blind drunk was one thing, but Tate didn't know if he could

pull off a *deaf* drunk, and he didn't think he could handle any more of Hank Williams's "Cold Cold Heart" without getting awkwardly choked up. He tossed the rest of his drink down and stubbed his cigarette in the plastic ashtray. After he slid off the stool he slapped a twenty on the bar.

Ted pushed the cash back across the polished wood. "It's on the house, Tate. I'm real sorry you had to find out this way."

"Good a way as any," Tate answered as he backed away from the bar. "You give these guys another round on me. For Kenny. There were no flowers at his funeral with my name on 'em, so—" his gesture was all-inclusive "—you guys remember Kenny kindly over the next round. He always gave the best he had."

The words tasted a little saccharine in Tate's mouth, but everybody readily agreed with his assessment. Hell, yes, drink up, boys; Kenny Becker was a damn good friend.

"You say she's over at the sale barn?" Out of habit he flipped up the collar of his sheepskin jacket, even though he left it hanging open in front.

"Last I saw."

"Think I'll pay my respects."

Tate didn't feel like pretending to be glad to see people, but it was like old home week the minute he walked into the Overo Livestock Auction. Not too many of his own friends, but several of his stepdad's old cronies recognized him and made a fuss over seeing his picture in *Rodeo Sports News*. It was no big deal, he told them. He'd made a few good rides this summer, but he hadn't made the National Finals yet.

Bill Walker insisted that Tate had "done real good" and his ol' man would be proud of him. To this day Tate couldn't think of Oakie Bain as *his ol' man,* even though he knew his real father only from pictures. But it would have been rude to take exception to the claim aloud. And something in the back of his mind regularly put the skids to downright rudeness.

He stepped around the boxes of baby rabbits and mewling kittens the country kids had for sale near the front door and shook hands with longtime neighbor Myron Olson. Myron wouldn't let go until he'd figured out how long it had been, so Tate had to guess six or seven years before he could slap the old man on the back and head up the steps to the gallery. He didn't look for a seat. Instead he lit a cigarette and leaned against a post near the doorway, where he could observe without being seen.

It didn't take long to spot her. He couldn't see much more than the top of her head, which stood out from all the cowboy hats and straw-hued mops like a fur coat in a dime store. Her hair was the color of a dark bay mare he'd had when he was a kid. You could only see the red tones when she stood out in the sun. Indoors, it was a rich shade of ranch mink. She'd kept it long. Today she had it done up in a braided ponytail. She was sitting way over to the side, down close to the activity, but the crowd was pretty sparse. She was all alone.

She seemed intent on the proceedings in the ring, but maybe she was staring hard because her thoughts were somewhere else. He wondered where. She looked like a high school girl, sitting in class and paying close attention to the teacher. Could have been a foreign-language class the way the auctioneer was rattling off numbers a mile a minute. No problem for Amy. He hadn't known her when she was in school, but she was the type who had probably aced every class. Poor Kenny had nearly bombed out, but Tate had loaned him enough of his homework to see Kenny through to graduation.

He wondered if she knew that. She'd pegged Tate for a troublemaker. He'd always been the one getting poor ol' Kenny into hot water. He wondered if she knew he'd also gotten Kenny through school. Didn't matter, Tate told himself. By and large, she had his number.

He watched the numbers flash on the electronic sign. Good saddle horses were going for killer prices. He took a long slow drag on his cigarette as he listened to the auctioneer describe the merits of the next lot. Chief among them, the next four horses had belonged to the late Kenny Becker, who'd raised some of the best quarter horses in the state. According to reliable reports, these were the best of his herd.

Tate figured that auctioneer Cal Swick was likely stretching the truth pretty thin. These were probably the only ones Kenny'd ever managed to break out, despite all his big-scale horse-breeding plans. Kenny was a dreamer, but maybe Cal believed the reliable reports himself.

Saddle horses always sold better if somebody showed them under saddle, so Tate was glad to see that Amy had hired one of the kids who hung around the stock pens to ride her horses through for her. He remembered when he and Kenny used to compete for the same kind of job. They'd bet each other who could get his Saturday chores done first and beat the other one to the sale barn for the chance to earn a few bucks. People usually picked Tate over Kenny if they needed a rider. He'd been born looking the part.

The bidding wasn't going anywhere, so Tate decided to jump in and run the sorrel gelding up a few dollars. He pushed his hat back, gave a subtle nod and a hand signal, skipping over a few increments to make people take a second look. It worked the first time around, but by the time all four horses had gone through, the buyers had dropped the bid on him twice. He was satisfied. Five hundred was a damn good batting average. The only catch would be settling up in the sales office without letting Amy catch him. Then he would go out to the pens and figure out what to do with two horses he didn't need.

He'd bought himself a bald-faced sorrel mare and a buckskin gelding. A five- and a six-year-old, from the looks of their teeth. Well fed, sound legs. He was checking the buckskin's hooves when the woman of the hour caught him red-handed.

"You paid way too much for that one."

Her voice always got to him. Smooth and low for a woman's, it had a seductively smoky quality. He glanced up and connected immediately with earth-mother eyes peering at him between the fence rails. He straightened slowly.

"Hello, Amy."

"It's not like you to wait until after you've paid your money to inspect the goods, Tate Harrison. That was always one of the differences between you and Ken."

"I got here late." He brushed his hands off on his denim-covered thighs, choosing to take the remark the way he took his whiskey. Perfectly straight. "But I can usually spot a good saddle horse in the ring pretty easy."

"So I've heard. Ken swore by your horse sense." She spoke the name so easily that she nearly put him at ease, too. But then she added, "Unfortunately, you took it with you when you left."

He half expected her to take the high ground by climbing the fence and letting him know with another perfectly aimed barb just what the first one was supposed to mean. She didn't. She had all the advantages she needed right now. He was going to have to go to her and find out. "My leavin' didn't disappoint anybody around here too much," he reminded her as he scaled the fence. "People are glad to see me 'bout every two, three years, and for a week or so I'm glad to see them."

He swung one leg over the top rail and paused while she

turned her face up to him. He wasn't sure he wanted to get down. Kenny was dead, and, damn, she scared him. He was afraid he would say something stupid, maybe make her cry. The cold autumn air had brought color to her face, but the dark shadows under her eyes canceled out the illusion of rosy-cheeked vitality. It struck him that her black down-filled jacket looked big enough to go around her twice. Then he realized it was Kenny's jacket. Brand-new the last time he'd seen him.

Her eyes held his fast as he lowered his foothold halfway down the fence, then dropped to the ground. His arms hung awkwardly at his sides. He imagined putting them around her, the way he wanted to, but her eyes offered no hint of permission. He flexed his fingers. They were stiff from the cold.

"Why did you buy those horses?" she asked quietly. "You didn't really want them."

"Why didn't you call me, Amy?" She glanced away. "Ed Shaeffer over at the bank always knows how to get hold of me in an emergency. He would have tracked me down if you'd just—"

"There was so much to do. There were so many details, so many—" She hugged herself, clutching the voluminous jacket around her. "There were many things I didn't handle as well as I should have. I was…" A faintly apologetic smile curved her mouth as she lifted her gaze to meet his again. "…quite unprepared."

"I stopped in at the house on my way into town." If he told her what he'd been through, maybe she would give him an answer that had something to do with *him*. "Stopped at the Jackalope. They talked about it like I already knew."

"I'm sorry." He looked away. "Really, Tate, I'm sorry. I thought about—" She laid her hand on his sleeve. "Many times I thought about writing, but I kept putting it off, thinking someone must have told you by now."

"I would have been back, soon as I heard. You would have seen me the same damn day." He stared at her hand. "That's why you kept puttin' it off, isn't it?"

"Oh, no. Ken would have wanted you to be…" He looked at her expectantly, waiting for the charge of a dead man. "To take part in the service."

"To help carry him to his grave? Damn right he would have. But I haven't been in touch since Christmas, and ol' Kenny, he usually—" The guilt was his. Always, it was his. "I should've known something was wrong."

"Tate." She slid her hand down his sleeve and slipped it in his. It felt good—warmer than his, and small but capable. "You come up with a list of regrets, and mine'll double yours. That's just the way it is. It was all over so quickly. So quickly, it left my head spinning."

A fleet, flighty gesture parted the front of her jacket. Her pink shirt was too tight. Her belly was too big. He felt as though he'd just walked up to her bedroom window and seen her naked.

"You're…" He was about to say something totally inane, and there wasn't a damn thing he could do about it. Gates were clattering inside the stock barn, and some guy was calling for lot forty-two. Tate glanced over his shoulder, unconsciously looking for somebody to tell him his eyes weren't lying. "Amy, you're pregnant."

"You're very observant."

"But they were saying over at—" He motioned westward, because suddenly he couldn't get the name of the bar out, or any other word that might offend her. The hand he held in his felt even slighter than it had at first, and he flexed his fingers around it, gently reasserting his hold. "I mean, I heard that you were running the place yourself."

"I'm not letting it go, Tate." And she squeezed back, a secret gesture between two people who shared a loss, letting him know that she was worried about losing still more. "It's my home. Mine and Jody's and…"

"You can't—"

"I'm having a baby, not open-heart surgery."

He allowed himself to get lost in the depths of her eyes, her brave words, her sturdiness. "You got any help?"

"I might be able to hire someone now, maybe part-time—" she smiled and gave a little nod toward the pen "—since I got a good price for those hay-burners."

"How's the little guy doin'? Jody?" She nodded to confirm the name he remembered full well. Kenny had once confided that Tate had been his choice for the boy's godfather, but with him on the rodeo circuit and Amy insisting on having the ceremony "before the little guy went to college," Tate had missed out on the honor.

Amy withdrew her hand, as though the mention of the boy's name had introduced a constraint against hand-holding. She stepped close to the pen and peeked between the rails again.

Tate followed her lead. "Must be tough for such a little fella," he said quietly. "Old enough to know the difference, but not to really…" *Understand?* Who *was* old enough to understand?

"He was pretty mad at me today. He used to love to come to the horse sales with his dad. This is the first one I've been to since…since it happened." She leaned her shoulder against the fence and hid her memories beneath lowered lashes. "I wouldn't let Jody come. He wouldn't understand."

Tate stared into the pen. The mare was standing hipshot,

neck drooping, eyelids dropping to half-mast. The buckskin's perked ears rotated like radar as he blew thick clouds of mist through flaring nostrils. Whatever was up, the buckskin would be the first to know about it.

"The boy'll know they're gone," Tate said.

"Not right away." Amy sighed. "I didn't want him to watch them go through the ring."

"That must've been hard for you, too."

"Not at all. I'm glad to be rid of them." He glanced at her for an explanation. None was forthcoming. "What will you do with those two?" she wondered.

"Haven't given it much thought," he admitted. Then he smiled. "Just knew I couldn't pass 'em up."

"That's what Ken Becker would've said. Not Tate Harrison." He shrugged. She'd always thought she had them both pegged. "He missed you a lot, Tate," she added gently. "You were the brother he never had."

"He was—" He couldn't say that. He'd had a brother once, a long time ago. Jesse. But he'd grown up with Kenny. That, too, was beginning to seem like a long time ago. "He was the best friend I ever had. Guess I should've missed him more than I did." He turned, leaned his back against the fence and looked up at the distant white clouds. "Guess I'm gonna start now."

"Well…" She wrapped her arms around herself again and they stood there for a long moment of silence, together but apart. One of the stockboys ran by, hollering at someone in the parking lot to wait up.

"How long will you be in town?" she finally asked. "You're welcome to come for supper, if you can find some time. You should see Jody now. He's…"

There it was, he thought. The obligatory invitation. "I'd wanna know more about what happened to Kenny," Tate warned her. "Would you be up to—" She hung her head. "That's okay. I understand. It's just that it's so hard for me to believe he's…gone."

"Dead. There's no way to change that, and that's all there is to know." She looked up, more fire in her eyes than he'd seen so far. "He's dead, Tate. It helps if you just say the word. It happened—" she snapped her fingers "—just like that. You can't believe how fast it happened, and you can't believe it happened until you've said the word. Until you've sold his horses. Until you've given most of his clothes away, and until you've slept…" She sighed, as if the sudden burst of emotion had worn her out. "I have to pick up Jody."

No, he didn't want her to go. He laid a hand on her shoulder. "What can I do?"

"Do?"

"For you and Jody. What—"

"You've already done more than you needed to do." She nodded toward the pen. "You've bought yourself one docile saddle horse and one mean outlaw. You'll have to figure out what you're going to do with *them*."

She kissed his cheek before she walked away. Made him feel like a little boy. Like she'd already come through the fires of hell, and he was too green to notice there was any heat. Even so, he felt favored somehow. Excused. Blessed. Knighted. Kissed by the princess. It was his cue to rise to the occasion.

He would do it if he knew how.

He decided he would run the mare back through the ring and keep the high-lifed buckskin gelding. The buckskin was obviously the outlaw, which made them two of a kind.

Jody was still mad when Amy picked him up at his aunt Marianne's. Cousin Kitty had slammed his finger in the car door, for one thing, and then Bill, Jr., had jerked the cherry sucker out of his mouth and made him bite his tongue. Marianne assured Amy that she'd checked him over both times and Jody wasn't really hurt. His tongue had hardly bled at all.

Then she'd asked Amy for the two-hundredth time about the possibility of having core samples taken on her land, "Just to see if it's worth pursuing."

Amy wasn't interested in Ken's sister's latest scheme. The land Ken's father had left him belonged to her and Jody now. Marianne owned fifty percent of the mineral rights, which the attorney had explained was a technicality that would only become an issue if Amy decided either to sell the land or let people poke holes in it looking for something to mine. Neither proposition interested her, even though she knew one of Overo's poker clubs had a couple of betting pools going— one on her second child's birth date, and the other on the month in which she would file bankruptcy.

But Amy was not giving up. She was tired, and she was nearly broke, but she wouldn't be broken. Nobody was going to poke holes in Becker land or Becker dreams. Even if Ken's plans had frequently been farfetched, he'd been fond of saying that he could depend on Amy to get him turned around. Once he was headed in the right direction, he could make things happen. He could be hell on wheels, he would say. He'd spent much of their marriage spinning his wheels, but she'd known how and when to wedge her small shoulder under his axle and give him a push. He was a good man, a kind-hearted man and he had wonderful intentions. Amy's job was to find a kernel of feasibility in them and build on that.

So at least they had a ranch. It might not have been the kind of ranch Ken had envisioned, but they were raising livestock. They had a home. They had a family. Despite a few impulsive choices, a few setbacks, a few fits and starts, they had come *this* far. Now it was up to her. It hadn't been easy without Ken, but there had been times when it hadn't been easy *with* him, either. Amy would manage, just as she had always managed. She would just have to work harder.

But she did need a little help. Now that she had some money, she needed manpower. A couple of months' worth, she figured. She could have given birth to a new baby, looked after a four-year-old and tended to her business in the summer, no sweat. But winter in Montana could throw a fast-frozen kink into anybody's works.

She wouldn't let herself think about where the money had come from until after she had put Jody to bed and her feet up on two feather pillows and a hassock. It wouldn't have been so hard to sell Ken's saddle horse—especially that outlaw that had been the death of him—if the buyer hadn't turned out to be Tate Harrison. But there was probably some kind of poetic justice in it all. She'd never doubted that she would have to face Tate sooner or later.

In that first rush of confusion, the initial daze and the onslaught of questions and decisions, her first impulse had been to find Tate. It had been a foolish idea, and she'd rebuked whatever infirm hormone it was that had bombarded her brain with such a weak-kneed notion. She'd breathed the biggest sigh of relief of her life the day Tate Harrison had left Overo and all but removed his freewheeling influence from her husband's life. She didn't really know how to get hold of him, not easily, not on such short notice, and he probably wouldn't have been free to come. He would come home for a party, but for a funeral? She doubted it. Or rather, she elected to doubt it. It was simpler that way.

But, as fate would have it, she'd had to face him with her excuses right after he'd done his good deed. As if that weren't bad enough, she'd had to deal with those *stupid* feelings again. Tate Harrison always made her feel a little unsteady, slightly unsafe, as though she'd pitched camp on a geological fault. He made her want to do things she shouldn't do, just the way he had Ken. There was a look in his eyes, a challenge to be as bold and as rash as he was.

Even in sorrow, he challenged her. It would have been easy to let herself go, to break down in his arms. That was probably exactly what he expected—what everyone expected. It was also exactly the kind of behavior in which Amy could ill afford to indulge herself. She had responsibilities.

It was late when she heard the pickup drive up. She turned in her chair just as the headlights played over the sheers in the front window. Someone was probably stopping to tell her that that damned west gate was open again. She sighed and hauled herself to her feet. The dogs were going nuts outside. She would show them; she'd put them to work. Thank God she had the dogs.

Amy turned the porch light on, then peeked out the window. The face that peered back was disturbingly familiar. The angles softened earlier by daylight looked harder in the shadows, the bristly stubble darker, the black eyes less forgiving and the full, firm lips less patient. It was not the kind of face one welcomed late at night. But she unlocked the door.

Tate felt like the third guy from the left in a police lineup as he stood there waiting. Frost was nipping at his nose while she was looking him over, being none too quick about opening the damn door.

"Oh, Tate." She made his name sound like a protest against any and all surprises. "Come in. We've already eaten, and Jody's—" She shrank back, as though he were muscling his way into her cozy nest.

Feeling awkward and a bit oversize for the small entryway,

he stepped over the threshold, tucking his chin as he removed his hat.

"But I can heat something up for you," she added tentatively.

"I didn't come for supper, exactly." He fingered his Stetson's broad black brim. "I'm lookin' for a job."

"A job?" She laughed nervously. Standing there in her dimly-lit kitchen, he looked for all the world like a hulking, humble cowboy. "Did you blow all your money on those horses?" She knew all about that little routine from Kenny. Tate had his foolish habits, but burdening himself with useless horses was not one of them.

"I've got money," he assured her. "What I need is a place to stay for a while."

"Try the motel." She didn't mean to sound sarcastic, but the wounded expression on his face told her that it had come out that way.

"I've had a bellyful of motels." He squared his shoulders and nodded toward the door that led to the basement. "You've got a room downstairs. You need a hired man."

"I don't need—" she took a deep breath while his eyes dared her to effect a complete rejection "—a favor quite that big."

"It won't be a favor. I'm not an easy keeper. I eat a lot and I, uh—" he glanced past her, surveying the homey kitchen "—use a lot of hot water."

"I can't pay you much more than that."

"All I'm askin' for is room and board." He shoved his hands in the front pockets of his jeans and offered a lopsided grin. "And all the shells to the shotgun."

"You heard about that." With few exceptions, she'd always been good at setting people straight. Tate Harrison was one of the few she'd had trouble with. "That happened back in June.

I'm a little slower now, but you still won't get any further than he did, so don't—"

"You've got a belly sittin' out there as big as a four-way stop sign." The amusement in his eyes faded. "That's all you need, Amy. A big red stop sign."

Ah, so he remembered. Well, so did she. She'd never told Ken about the time Tate had made his move on her, partly because it had happened before they were married and mostly because she had handled it. There had never been a need to discuss the incident. It would have served no purpose other than to prove that she had been right about Tate. He, of course, had been wrong about her, and he'd admitted it. So maybe it wouldn't hurt to let him help out for a while. Nobody had ever suggested that Tate Harrison wasn't a hard worker when he wanted to be.

And from the spark that flashed in his eyes when she relented with a reluctant nod, he wanted to be.

"You're right. I need a hand," she said. "One I can trust. As long as you have some free time…"

He read the question in her eyes. "I can spare as much as you need."

"I promise you, Tate, I bounce back fast. I did with Jody."

"Every time I laid over with you guys, even for a day or two, I felt like you were in a rush to kick me out." It was an observation, not a complaint. "I'd try to get you both out of the house, take you out to supper or just honky-tonkin', and you always acted like I was—"

"Ken had responsibilities," she reminded him, although it wasn't something she expected a confirmed bachelor like Tate to understand. She smiled. "If it's any comfort, it was nothing personal. You weren't the only rowdy sidekick I ever bitched out royally."

"Admit it." He gave her a sly wink. "I always got your best shot."

"You earned it."

"I'll get my gear." He stepped back and put his hat back on. "First thing tomorrow morning, it'll give me a world of pleasure to run those flea-bitten bleaters off your land."

"You mean the sheep?"

"Must be a hole in the fence somewhere," he judged. "Either that or—"

"Oh, Tate." There it was again. *Oh, Tate.* This time the coolness was missing. In fact, he'd apparently said something delightfully funny, which was fine with him. He liked the rich sound of her laughter and the way her belly bounced with it.

She touched her hand to her lips, then to his leather sleeve. "Those are *our* sheep, cowboy. You just hired on as a sheepherder."

Chapter 2

Long before Amy had become Ken's wife, Tate Harrison had been his best friend. She remembered the earlier days well, but not, she had to admit, without a certain small niggling of dissatisfaction with herself, a sense that she had been tested and found wanting. It was not the only time in her life that her behavior had come up short, of course, and it would surely not be the last. She was only human.

More irritating, though, was that little voice inside her head that always had the last say when she thought about those old bygones. Same voice, same taunting tone, always suggesting that she had also been *left* wanting. But the idea was perfectly foolish, absolutely irrational. Amy Becker was nothing if not prudent. She always had been, even back then….

From Glendive to Missoula, Tate's reputation as a heartbreaking hell-raiser had been legend. Amy had never been interested in men like Tate. She much preferred his friend

Ken Becker, whom she'd met when she'd worked at a bank in Billings. When she'd become the head bookkeeper at the small branch in Overo, Ken had come courting. He'd seemed to think his role as bronc rider Tate Harrison's shadow was his best calling card. "We're gonna watch ol' Tate buck one out, and then we'll party," he would say.

It was hard to convince Ken that the best date he could plan with her was a picnic atop one of the beautiful red clay bluffs on his ranch east of the Absaroka foothills. He hadn't been running the place very long, and his goals for his ranching business seemed a bit scattered. But he'd been born to the business, she thought almost enviously. He was the third generation of Becker cattlemen on Becker land. He had the kind of roots Amy craved, and he needed her. She liked that. He was as impressed with her good sense as he was with her good figure. She liked that, too.

Tate Harrison, on the other hand, never seemed to meet a woman who didn't impress him somehow. But it never lasted long. Too often, Amy's dates with Ken would start out as a threesome, and then Tate would pick up a fourth somewhere along the way. Usually it was some empty-headed buckle bunny who couldn't smile prettily and carry on a conversation at the same time, so she would quickly give up on the latter.

The worst of that ilk was Patsy Johnson. Unfortunately, she lasted the longest. She loved to play with the buttons on his shirt and sip on his beer. She never wanted a cigarette of her own, but she was always taking a puff off Tate's. Whenever she did it, she always glanced at Amy, as if to say, *What's his is mine.* As if Amy cared. Amy wasn't interested in Tate's buttons. She didn't like beer. She didn't smoke. Ken had virtually quit, too, except when he was around Tate. In fact, the whole two-stepping, partner-swinging honky-tonk scene seemed to revolve around Tate, and Amy's little bottom simply wasn't comfortable on a bar stool.

One night she decided she'd had it with the rowdy cowboy-bar scene, where the soft drinks were too expensive, the music too loud and the women too cute. Ken and his friends were absolutely right; she did not know how to have a good time, and she didn't want to interfere with theirs. She made a trip to the ladies' room, then put in a phone call to solve her transportation problem. Enough of this noise, she told herself as she hung up the phone.

"Did you just call for a ride?"

Tate's voice startled her. Her heartbeat skipped into overdrive, and she had to remind herself that he wasn't catching her doing anything underhanded, which was almost the way she felt.

"Yes, I did," she said calmly as she turned to find him standing too close for comfort in the narrow hallway. The bare overhead light bulb cast his face in sharp light and deep shadows, playing up its chiseled angles. The knowing look in his eyes was unsettling. She was glad she had genuine justification, even if she didn't owe him any. "I have a headache."

"Does Kenny know?"

"He seems to be having an especially good time." Ken knew how to enjoy himself, which was part of what made him so likable, and when he was drinking, he enjoyed himself beyond Amy's ability to keep up. "And we came with you tonight, so I called—"

"Did he do something?" Amy shook her head quickly, and Tate laid his hand on his own chest. "Did *I* do something? I said something wrong," he supposed in all sincerity. "If it was that little joke about women in tight pants, I'm sorry. It didn't apply to you. I've never seen you wear—"

"It has nothing to do with anything you said. I just can't…" It seemed strange, but she felt as though she could level with him, now that it was just the two of them. He was looking at her intently, as though he were concerned about the fact that she felt so out of place sitting at a table with ashtrays overflowing with cigarette butts and an accumulation of empty beer bottles. "I'm not very good at this kind of thing." She gave a helpless gesture, the kind she generally scorned. "The loud music, the smoke…sometimes it gives me a headache, that's all."

"All you have to do is say something, and we'll—"

"No, just let me—" She touched her fingertips to her throbbing temple. "I don't want to break up the party. I just want to go home."

"Come on." He put one hand on her shoulder, guiding her toward the side door as he shoved his other hand in his pocket. She shook her head, trying to demur, but he cut her off. "No, I'll take you. It's no trouble."

"But I've already called—"

"I'll take care of it. Kenny's sister, right?" She nodded.

Reassuring her with a light squeeze of his hand, he signaled the woman who'd been waiting on their table. "Jeri, honey, call Marianne and tell her Amy found another ride. And tell Kenny I'll be back in half an hour, that Amy's okay, but she needs to get home right away." He glanced at their empty table as he tucked some money into Jeri's hand. Kenny and Patsy had taken to the dance floor.

Tate put Amy in his pickup and headed across town to the small house she'd rented. It was tiny, but it was the first real house she'd ever lived in. She'd had her own apartment in Billings, and before that she'd lived in apartments and trailer homes with her family. She'd always wanted a real house.

"It's a relief to breathe fresh air," she told Tate. It was

also a surprise to her to hear herself confiding, "I feel like a fifth wheel sometimes, especially when Ken has too much to drink." Too quickly she added, "Which he doesn't, usually."

"Well, I'm driving tonight, so Ken doesn't have to worry about having himself a good time."

She didn't understand their definition of having a good time, especially when it was bound to turn into a hangover by morning. "He's beyond the point where it would do any good to ask him to call it a night."

"Did you try?"

"'Just one more,' he said."

"Kenny's crazy about you, you know." He seemed to think he'd offered some great revelation, and he paused to let it sink in before he added, "He's making a lot of big plans. Not that it's any of my business."

"It is your business." Her tone betrayed her resentment. "Whatever his plans are, you'll know all about them before I do."

"We go back a long way, Kenny and me. A guy's gotta talk things out with a close buddy sometimes, especially when he's not too sure what's gonna happen." He dropped his hand and downshifted for a right turn. "He's afraid you'll turn him down." He kept his eyes on the road ahead, shifted again and surprised her by adding, "I'm afraid you won't."

"You think I'd spoil all the fun?" she asked scornfully, but Tate said nothing as he pulled over in front of her house. "There's more to life than rodeos and smoke-filled bars. If that's all you want, then fine, but I think Ken needs—"

"You're probably just what Kenny needs." Tate shut off the ignition, draped his left arm over the steering wheel and turned to her. "But he's not the kind of man you need. Deep down, I think you know that."

"He's a wonderful man," Amy insisted, reflexively bristling

in Ken's defense. "He has a good sense of humor and the kindest heart and the gentlest nature of any man I've ever—" she paused and lifted her chin, defying the smile that tugged at the corner of Tate's mouth, for her concluding word came all too quietly "—met."

"You're right about that. Kenny's a nice guy." He laid his right arm along the top of the seat and touched her shoulder lightly. "You'll walk all over him. And he'll let you do it, because when you're done, he'll just pick himself up and do as he pleases. He'll do all that nice-guy stuff he likes to do, the stuff that never amounts to anything and never gets him anywhere. And you'll cover for him, which means he'll be walkin' all over you in his nice-guy way." In the dim light his eyes were completely overshadowed by the brim of his black cowboy hat, but she could feel them studying her. "Is that what you want?" he asked.

She answered tightly. "That's not the way it would be."

"Like I said, Kenny and me…" He shoved his hat back with his thumb and stretched lazily. "We go back a long, long way."

"You said you thought he was crazy about me."

"I *know* he's crazy about you. I know what Kenny thinks long before *he* does." He chuckled. "It won't take you very long to achieve that skill. You're probably halfway there already."

"With friends like you, he certainly doesn't need any enemies."

"I am his friend. I'd back him in the devil's own ambush, and he'd do the same for me." He glanced past the windshield at a pair of oncoming headlights. The car cruised by, and Tate shook his head, smiling wistfully. "But if I was a woman, I sure as hell wouldn't wanna be married to him."

"You wouldn't want to be married to anyone. That's why

you go out with women like Patsy Johnson, who'll sit there and rub your thigh while she giggles at every word you say, whether it's supposed to be funny or not. She doesn't expect you to marry her."

"What does she expect?"

"You know what she expects," Amy snapped.

Tate chuckled. "Which part bothers you most? I don't like to be laughed at when I'm not joking, and when I am, you usually laugh, too. So you've got no reason to be jealous there."

"Jealous!"

"But it's hard to resist a woman who's got her hand on your thigh." His amused tone rankled almost as much as his male complacency. "'Specially if you've got no good reason to." He slid closer. "If you wanted to, you could give me a good reason to resist Patsy or any other woman."

"Why would I want to do that?" She knew what a dumb question it was. Dumber still was her willingness to sit still for the answer.

"Because you wanna be the one rubbin' my thigh."

He was smiling, looking just about as irresistible as any man who'd ever donned a Stetson, and she was melting like ice cream in July. She imagined slapping her own cheek to wake herself up, but it was more fascinating to watch him take off his hat and balance it between the dashboard and the steering wheel.

"You know this for a fact?" she asked, fully realizing that this banter was part of the game and she was just taking her silly turn.

"Sure do." He took her shoulders in his hands and turned her to him. "And you want me to be the one takin' you home, because you know damn well you'd never have to ask me twice."

He slowly pulled her close, challenging her to deny the truth in his claim, refusing to let her gaze stray from his. He'd brought her home, hadn't he? The house was only a few yards away, and she was still sitting there. She wanted his kiss, didn't she? When he brushed his palm against the side of her face and slid his fingers into her hair, she knew he was giving her all the time she needed to say otherwise. She couldn't. She parted her lips, but no words would come.

He hooked one arm around her shoulders, lowered his head and kissed her, softly at first, then more insistently, pressing for her response. Her mouth yielded to his as her breath fluttered wildly in her chest. His tongue touched hers like a sportsman testing the direction of the wind. Ah, yes, he seemed to say, that's the way of it, and he turned his head to try another angle.

She liked the sweet whiskey taste of him and the woody scent of his after-shave. His slim waist seemed a good place to put her hand. Her touch was his signal to draw her closer and kiss her harder. He rubbed her back with the heels of his hands, relaxing her, melting her spine, vertebra by vertebra. Then he slipped his hand between their bodies, cupping one breast in his palm while he insinuated his fingertips past her V-neck blouse and stroked the soft swell of its twin. Both nipples tightened in response.

She leaned into his embrace and answered his tongue's probing with the flickerings of hers. She wanted to be closer still. She wanted to feel his hand inside her blouse, skin against warm skin. She wanted to let him guide her, let him show her the way to lose herself in her own senses. Slowly she slid her hand up his long, hard back, up to his shoulder, where she gripped him as though she were teetering and needed support. He groaned, and his kiss became more urgent, more hungry.

"Let's go inside," he whispered.

"Oh, Tate." She wanted to. But making a move required her to open her eyes and realize that she was in the arms of a man who was more than attractive, far beyond adequate and a notch past willing. He was ready to meet her demands, but he would have his own ideas, as well. And he was not Ken.

Ken. The man she was supposed to be with tonight.

"Oh my God. No, Tate, this is all wrong." And it suddenly scared the hell out of her.

Her reluctance didn't seem to surprise him. "It'll be all right once you get it straight in your mind what you really want," he said evenly.

"I want a home. I want a family." Pulling back from him wasn't easy, so she resorted to the kind of ammunition she knew would scare a man like Tate off. "I want love first and then…and *then* sex. Ken—"

It was the name that did it. Tate's shoulders sagged a little as his embrace slackened. Amy closed her eyes and fought the urge to close her hands around his retreating arms before they got away completely. She had to say it again quickly. She had to *hear* it again. "*Ken* and I don't…"

"That's not something we talk over, whether you do or you don't. I'm not interested in hearing any of that," he snapped as he closed his hand around her left wrist and lifted her hand in front of her own face. "You're not wearing his ring. That's all I need to know."

Six months later Tate had known all he'd needed to. He'd carried the small gold band to the altar in his breast pocket, then turned it over to his best friend. He'd witnessed their vows, stood by while they were sealed with a kiss, even put his signature on the official documents. Amy wondered if his participation was Tate's way of backing Ken in "the devil's own ambush." He had kissed the bride properly in his turn and waltzed her once around the Overo Community Hall dance floor. It was the one time Amy could remember that Tate had left the party early—and alone.

On the first morning after he'd talked himself into the lowest-paying job he'd ever had, Tate was lured up the basement stairs by the commingling aromas of bacon and coffee. It had been a long time since he'd been up before the roosters, but he wanted to get started on the right foot with his new boss. He took it as a good sign when she glanced up from the big iron skillet and greeted him with a bright smile, never missing a beat as she turned a row of flapjacks, golden brown side up. It pleased him that she remembered his breakfast preferences.

"Sheep, huh?" He smiled back as he poured himself a cup of strong black coffee.

"Sheep."

"How many head?"

"Three hundred. And they pay the bills." The metal spatula scraped lightly against the skillet as she started dishing out the pancakes. "I can handle sheep, whereas I wasn't much help with the cattle."

"And cattle were the best excuse Kenny could think of for keeping horses around." Tate took a seat at the kitchen table.

"He really just wanted to raise horses, which would have been fine if—"

"If they'd paid the bills."

"Exactly." She wasn't fussy. She intended to keep her home intact. She would raise earthworms if the price were right. "Ken and I made a deal two years ago when he was beginning to realize that my little herd of sheep was more profitable than his whole—"

"You're a better businessperson than Kenny was," Tate said, cutting to the crux of the matter. "Did he ever realize *that* somewhere along the line?"

"Yes, he did. We all have our talents. Anyway, I agreed to the horses, and he agreed to the sheep. We got out of the cattle business."

"Sheep." The traditional bane of the cattleman. Not that Tate was in a position to care all that much, since he didn't own any cattle anymore, just a parcel of land, and it didn't appear that she'd used it to graze sheep. The damn woollies could crop the grass down halfway to China if a stockman didn't use a good rotation plan.

But here he was, offering his personal services, which would mean personal contact. He preferred the smell of cattle over the stink of sheep any day. He thought about it as he sipped his coffee. Finally he shook his head. "Well, you can give my portion of mutton to the dogs and double my ration of hot water."

"I don't serve mutton."

She *did* serve a nice plate of flapjacks and bacon, though, and he took a deep whiff as she set it down in front of him.

"Thank God for small favors. I'm going to have to fix that shower stall before I use it." He tasted the crisp bacon, then elaborated. "It doesn't drain right."

"I usually just mop up the water." The resignation in her voice irritated him. She planted her knuckles against her hip as she turned back to the stove. Her little fist was dwarfed by the basketball of a belly that tested the limits of her pretty pink sweater. "Ken was going to fix that shower, but there were other repairs that were higher on the priority list."

Tate imagined her down on her hands and knees, wiping

the floor with a towel. "You give me the list," he ordered as he cut into the stack of flapjacks with his fork. "And a mop, if you don't want me to use your shower upstairs this morning." She wasn't mopping up *his* water.

"You're welcome to use the upstairs bathroom. Just let me check to make sure I've got clean soap and dry—"

"Clean soap?"

"You know, *fresh*. And towels, and Jody's bath toys out of the way."

"Does he have boats? Maybe I'll take a bath instead." He was chuckling happily. She wasn't. He could see her adding another chore to her mental list. "Amy, soap is soap, and I can find the towels. I don't need any special treatment, okay? I'm the hired hand, not a guest from out of town."

"Housekeeping hasn't been tops on my list of priorities lately, but ordinarily—"

"I don't see anything out of place," he assured her. And then, as if on cue, a sleepy-eyed blond moppet appeared in the kitchen doorway. "Hey, who's this big guy?" Tate laughed when his dubious greeting sent the boy scurrying to his mother's side. "Are you the same Jody who used to twist my ear half off when I gave him horseyback rides?"

The little boy looked up at his mother for some hint as to how he was supposed to answer.

"Do you remember Tate, sweetheart? Daddy's good friend?"

Tate, sweetheart. He smiled, enjoying the way it sounded. "You were a little squirt last time I was here, but you sure are getting big."

"I'm almost five," Jody announced bravely as he flashed splayed fingers Tate's way.

"Well, you must be big enough to ride a two-wheeler.

I almost tripped over one out by the yard fence. Is that yours?"

"It *was* Bill, Jr.'s." Jody ventured a few cautious steps from his mother's side. "I'm gonna give it back to him," he added, clearly for Amy's edification.

"You'll get the hang of it, Jody. Maybe we'll put it away until spring." Amy sighed. "By then it won't be quite so hard for me to get you going."

"You just learning?" Tate asked as Jody joined him at the table.

"I keep falling off when my mom lets go. I'd rather ride a horse."

"I'm with you there, partner. If your mom'll let me use the horse trailer, I'll head into town after I get some chores done around here and bring back your dad's—"

"Breakfast first." Amy cast Tate a warning glance as she plunked a glass of orange juice on the table for Jody.

"My dad's what?"

"Your dad's…"

"Tate is going to help us out for a while, Jody, and he needed a horse, so I sold him—"

"The buckskin," Tate supplied. "That's the one I—" wrong choice, obviously, the way she was rolling her eyes "—kept. He moves out spirited and stylish, and he's got a nice head on him, good chest. The mare was kinda goose-rumped and paunchy." He eyed Amy playfully. "Like mares get sometimes."

"Very funny." Both hands went to her hips as Jody slipped away from the table. "In other words, you weren't about to listen to me."

"I know good horseflesh," Tate pointed out quietly. He hoped Jody wasn't beating feet down the hallway because of something he'd said. He'd just wanted the boy to know that his dad's horse would still be around.

"The buckskin was Ken's favorite, too," Amy said.

"So you were down to the four?"

"No. There are eighteen registered quarter horses out there. The mares aren't bred. The geldings aren't broke. You might say we're horse-poor. I can't afford to keep them, can't afford to give them away." She shook her head sadly. "Not Ken's dream herd."

"Horse-poor, huh," Tate echoed reflectively.

Jody reappeared, carrying a broken stick horse with a missing ear.

"Whatcha got there, partner?" Tate asked. Jody handed over his steed. "Does this guy have a little better handle than that two-wheeler? Looks like he got hogged." Tate ran his hand over the remains of a yarn mane, which had obviously been cut short by an inexperienced groom.

"I buzzed him with the scissors. He's glass-eyed, see?" Jody pointed to the pony's eye, which was indeed made of glass, but a horseman would term him glass-eyed because it was blue. "But whoever heard of a horse with blue-and-white polka dots?"

"You've never seen a blue roan?"

"That's not a roan."

"Looks like a roan to me." Tate turned the stick in his hand as he examined what was clearly a well-loved toy. "I think I can fix him up for you. Do a little fancy blacksmithin'." He winked at the boy, who listened spellbound at his knee. "And we can probably get that bike of yours at least green-broke while I'm here. When you get throwed, best thing is to climb back into the saddle."

"Ready for pancakes, Jody?"

"Soon as I put Thunder back in his stall."

After the little boy had galloped out of earshot, Amy turned from the stove, plate in hand. "Don't make him any more promises, Tate. Two is enough. He's pretty confused as it is."

"I don't make empty promises." His look challenged her to disagree. When she didn't, he glanced away. "He looks a lot like his dad."

"Yes, he does. And now he reminds me of Peter Pan's shadow, sort of at loose ends." In another part of the house a closet door was opened, then shut. Amy set Jody's plate on the table and spoke softly. "Just be careful. I'm afraid he's looking for a man's boots to attach his little feet to."

"You think I'm gonna drag that little guy along behind me?" He reached for his coffee. "That's not my way, Amy."

"What is your way?"

"With kids?" Tate shrugged. "I don't know. I'm a little short on experience. Just be a friend and stick around while times are tough, I guess. Is that okay?" She nodded, and he smiled. "Good. So far his size doesn't scare me much. Long as I don't have to get on that two-wheeler myself, I'll be all right."

The autumn grass provided the sheep with plenty of roughage, but they needed supplemental feed. Amy laid out her instructions to the letter before turning the chore over to "the guys." Tate shoveled a load of grain into the pickup bed and took Jody along to show him where the feeders were. The sheep trotted across the pasture, bleating to beat hell when they saw the pickup coming.

Tate pulled up to one of the scattered feeders and set about filling the trough with grain. For an almost-five-year-old, Jody seemed pretty grown-up. He often mirrored what Tate recognized as Amy's instructive manner. "We have to spread it out in the trough so they won't climb all over each other," the boy said soberly as he put his small hands to the task.

"Who's been hauling this out to the sheep since the last man quit?" They'd probably been supplementing for a month or more, Tate figured. He stood back and watched the dingy white merino ewes jostle for position around the trough.

"Me and Mom." Jody squinted one eye against the glare of the morning sun. "We're not as strong as you, so it takes a long time. We put the feed in a lot of small things, like ice-cream buckets, load them up in the pickup and—" with a gesture he drew a beeline in the sky "—buzz on out here. Did you know we're gonna have a baby? That's why my mom has such a big tummy."

"You mean it's not always that big?"

"No, that's a baby inside her. A little baby about—" he held his little round hands inches apart "—I'd say this big. That's why Mom had to stop using the scoop shovel to load the grain. Her big tummy got in the way."

Tate forced a chuckle for Jody's benefit, but it pinched his throat. He thought about Amy wielding that big shovel, and he shook his head. "Brother or sister, do you know?"

"No, that's going to be a surprise. I'm hoping for a brother."

"But a sister would be nice, too. Right?"

"I don't know." Jody scowled, then thrust his hand up for Tate's inspection. "My cousin Kitty slammed the car door on my finger yesterday. See?"

Tate hunkered down behind the open tailgate and studied the purpling fingernail. "Does it still hurt? It looks like it must've hurt like a bit—" *Wrong choice of words.* "*Biddy.* Like an old biddy with a baseball bat, right? Boy, that can be murder."

"What's a biddy? Is it a girl, like my dumb ol' cousin Kitty?"

"Yeah. Only older and meaner." He smiled. This curly-haired little fellow was cuter than a spotted colt. "You might get a new fingernail out of this deal. Did your mom tell you that?"

"No." Incredulous, Jody took a closer look at his finger. "You mean my fingernail might fall off?"

"After a while. But it'll be okay, because you'll get a new one. It's happened to me a lot of times."

"By a biddy hittin' you with a bat?"

"By getting my hand caught in a door or stomped by a horse or banged with a hammer." He ruffled the boy's cotton-candy curls as he stood. "It's not always a girl's fault."

"I still want a brother," Jody insisted.

"Either way, you'll have a new baby." Tate tossed the shovel into the pickup bed.

"Do you know about babies?" Jody wondered.

"I know they don't play much for the first year or so, and then they start gettin' into things. Have you had pups around, or kittens?" Jody nodded vigorously. "Kinda like that. Brothers get to be more fun when they get a little age on 'em."

"But he plays around in my mom's tummy right now," Jody disclosed as he followed Tate to the driver's side.

Tate pictured an unborn child "playing around" in a warm, dark, cozy haven. He smiled as he hoisted Jody into the pickup. "What does he play?"

"He kicks." Jody scrambled over on the bench seat to make room for the driver. "Sometimes Mom says it feels like he's playing football. She lets me feel it, too. He kicked my nose once when I was just tryin' to talk to him in there."

Tate was still smiling as he buckled Jody's seat belt.

"Next time I'll let you feel, too," Jody offered magnanimously.

"Feel what?"

"The baby kicking."

"Oh, well, your mom might, uh…" Let him put his hand on her belly? Yeah, right. But he was *still* smiling. "She might have something to say about that."

"She'll let you. She always lets me."

When they got back to the barn, they found Amy raking out stalls. Her long, chestnut-colored hair was clipped back at the nape, but bits of it had strayed over her face as she worked. She'd tossed Kenny's black parka aside and pushed up the sleeves of her pink sweater. She looked up when she heard them coming, then leaned on the rake handle as she pressed her free hand against the small of her back.

"Whew, I'm working up a sweat here." She wiped her brow with the back of her hand. "Lately it doesn't take much and I'm all in a sweat."

"Go back in the house, Amy. I know where everything is, and I swear to you I've already got the hang of the routine down pat. Jody and me—" She wasn't listening. She'd slid her hand over her ripe, round belly and gotten a funny look on her face. "What's the matter?"

"Is he kickin' again, Mom?"

"*She*—" Amy put her hand under Jody's upturned chin and offered a motherly smile "—is going to be a Rockette. The little rascal is in top form today."

"Where, where, where?" Jody jumped up and down like a pogo-stick rider until Amy took hold of his hand and placed it against the lower left side of her stomach. "Yow! Mom, that baby kicked me again," Jody chirped. "Let Tate feel."

Bubbling with excitement, Jody was puzzled by the sudden stillness. He looked up at one face, then the other, and he wondered at his power. He'd just created two awkwardly flash-frozen big people, staring dumbly at each other. "Come on, Tate wants to feel, dontcha, Tate?"

"Jody, my hands are pretty—" Tate looked down at hands

that might have belonged to someone else, as awkward as they suddenly felt. He flexed his fingers as though he were working out some stiffness in the joints. "They're too dirty and…too cold."

"He won't know that," the boy assured him with exaggerated patience. "He's inside Mom's tummy." He claimed Tate's big, rugged, reluctant hand in his small but sure one. "Where do you feel it now, Mom?"

"Here," Amy said softly. She leaned back against a short stack of square bales as she reached for Tate's hand.

Her skin felt like a firebrick against his. He tipped his hat back with one finger as he sought and found her permission in her soulful, brown, earth-mother eyes. He swallowed convulsively. She directed his hand, pressing it against her as though she were showing him where to find her most personal, most intimate secret. Her belly was harder than he had thought it would be, and wondrously round, like a perfect piece of fruit. He wanted to slip his hand under the sweater—damn pesky wool—and touch taut, smooth skin, but not in an invasive way. More like reverent. It was sure corny, but that was the way he felt. He'd almost forgotten what he was supposed to be feeling *for* until the little critter he couldn't see actually *moved* beneath his hand.

"Ho-ly…" Without thinking, he went down on one knee. As though he were gazing into a crystal ball, he focused his whole attention on this precious part of Amy, the part that held her baby, the part that she permitted *him* to hold in his two hands.

"Hey, Mom, there's Cinnamon Toast." Jody pointed at the feline face peering down at them from the rafters. Neither Amy nor Tate flickered an eyelash. "C'mere, Cinnamon," Jody coaxed as he headed up the ladder to the loft.

"Is that a foot?" Tate asked quietly, afraid he might scare

whatever was in there, whatever, *whoever,* seemed to be responding to his touch.

"What does it feel like to you?"

"Like somebody tryin' to fight his way out of a—" He looked into her eyes and gave a teasing half smile. "A balloon?"

"Tactful choice."

"Does he do this all the time?"

"I think she's one of those children who loves to perform for an audience."

"Jeez, she's really—" he moved his hand, following the movement within Amy "—goin' to town here. How long before she's supposed to make her appearance?"

"Three weeks. But you can give or take two. Jody was late. But, then, I know when this one got her start, almost to the hour."

They shared a solemn look. Then an oppressive thought hit Tate like a cannonball. She was speaking of an hour he didn't want to think too much about, not just because it had been one of Kenny's last, but because…because he'd made himself stop thinking about the two of them in that way a long time ago, and he didn't want to start in again. He drew his hands away gradually as he rose from the straw-covered floor.

"Ken never knew," Amy said.

"He knows now."

"Do you believe that?"

"Sure." He sought to put some distance between himself and the bone-melting experience he'd just had by remembering his friend the way he ought to have been remembering him. "I can't see him wearin' a halo or any of that kind of stuff, but I believe he's in a good place, and I think he'll be with you in spirit." Her eyes took on a misty sheen, and her brave smile consecrated his amended efforts. Damn, he could talk nice when he saw a need. "Especially when the baby's born," he added. "I think he'll be there, come hell or high water." He laid a comforting hand on her shoulder. "So to speak."

"So to speak," she echoed softly.

He nodded, and his eyes strayed to her distended belly again. "That's pretty amazing. I mean, you don't realize how amazing until you actually..." He extended his hand impulsively, then arrested the presumptuous move to touch her stomach once more, turning it into an empty-handed gesture. "That's pretty amazing."

"You're blushing, Tate Harrison." He glanced at her, then glanced away, shaking his head. "Yes, you are. You are as pink as—"

Tate chuckled, genuinely embarrassed. *Damn.* Where had this big, dumb cowboy come from? Hadn't he just been doing the silver-tongued knight like a seasoned pro?

"You look like a newborn with a five o'clock shadow." She cupped his bristly cheek in her small hand. "*That* is pretty amazing."

Chapter 3

Tate's plan was to get in a few chores before breakfast, but Amy had already foiled it three days running. The woman didn't know how to sleep in. He could have sworn it was still the middle of the night, but she had him waking up to the smell of coffee. Her time was getting close. Surely she needed more rest. Each time he heard those early-morning footsteps overhead, his first thought was, *Maybe this is it.*

Nah, couldn't be. If anything serious had started, she wouldn't be fooling with the coffeepot at whatever the hell time it was. In order to see the time, he would have to turn the damn light on. He would find out soon enough. He dragged himself out of bed and felt his way to the bathroom door. Once he'd stood in the shower long enough to steam his eyes open, the smell of her coffee drew him up the steps to the kitchen table.

"Oh, did I wake you up?" Amy asked sweetly. "I'm sorry. I really was trying to be quiet."

"You wanna be sneakin' around, you need a different pair of shoes," he told her, his mood lightening gradually. Her hair hung over her shoulder in one thick braid. He liked her light floral, fresh-from-the-shower scent. He also liked the way their fingers touched when she handed him his coffee.

"Ken gave me these." She lifted her foot and glanced down at the plastic heel on her slipper. "They're noisy?"

"Like Mr. Bojangles found a linoleum cloud in heaven."

"I'm hardly that light on my feet," she said with a laugh as she set a plate in front of him. "But see if these scrambled eggs are light and fluffy enough for you. How are you getting along with the dogs?"

"We're on speaking terms." The eggs went down easy. With a wink and a nod, he told her so. "I tell 'em, 'Speak,' and they say, 'Grrr-ruff.' Kinda meanlike, so my guess is we're speaking about territory, and they're tellin' me this is theirs."

"Don't take it personally. They didn't like Ken, either. Do you think you could bring the herd in by yourself?"

"You're talkin' to a professional cowboy here, ma'am." He smiled as she joined him at the table. "Among other things. If I can work cows, I sure as hell don't need any help bringin' in the sheep."

"Good. You'll bring them in, the dogs and I will sort them and we'll take the rest of the lambs to the sale barn tomorrow."

"I can tell the big ones from the little ones, honey. *I'll* do the sorting."

"The dogs do all the work." She studied her coffee for a moment, and he waited for the second shoe to drop. "Tate, I know it's just an expression, but I think it would be better if you'd try not to use it, um…in this particular case."

"What expression?" He was truly at a loss. If he'd said

a cuss word, it had slipped right out without him even hearing it.

"Honey."

Honey was bad? "Just an expression," he agreed.

"Jody might hear it and get the wrong impression."

"Which is—" he gave her the opening, but she left it to him to fill in the blank "—that maybe I like you some?"

"Some?" Her indulgent smile rankled *some*. "Jody wouldn't understand that 'honey' just means 'female' to you."

"So I should use the word *female?*" He tried it out. "I can tell the ewes from the lambs, *female?* Or should I say, I can tell the females from the kids? But kids are goats," he amended with a boyish grin. Now that he was rolling, he had her rocking with laughter. "If I start calling the ewes 'honey,' I want you to get me to a shrink, right away. Sign the commitment papers and tell 'em I'm crazy as a sheepherder."

"Crazy as a pregnant *female* sheepherder?"

"Uh-uh." He shook his head slowly, enjoying the sparkle in her big brown eyes. "Just 'crazy as a sheepherder.' It's a cowboy expression. You've got a *cowboy* workin' for you, lady. You can boss his hands, but not his mouth."

"First *ma'am,* then *honey,* and now it's *lady.* I don't know." Her laughter dwindled into a sigh. "They say cowboys are just naturally fickle."

"Can't live with 'em, can't shoot 'em."

"Can't resist 'em, either," she mumbled, drowning the better part of the comment in her coffee cup.

"What was that?" Had he heard her right? With a quick shake of her head, she jumped up from the table, leaving him to guess whether his ears had lied to him.

He shrugged and let it go. "Anyway, what I was trying to say was, I've got a pretty good whistle on me. I can do the sorting. I don't want you out there in those pens until you've calved out."

She returned with the coffeepot and poured him a refill. "Wet your whistle with this, cowboy. You'll need it. It's hard to get the dogs to work for somebody they're not used to. They're my dogs, and they're my pens and I'm not a cripple. I'm just—"

"The mule-headedest woman I ever met. You can supervise, okay? Give orders." His fork clattered on the plate as he took a swipe at his mouth with a paper napkin. "To the dogs, not me. You can tell me what to do, but not how to do it. I might be herdin' your damn sheep, but I've still got some pride left."

"I never doubted that." She smiled complacently as she claimed his empty plate.

He sighed. "So how many head are we sellin'?"

"I sold half the crop as spring lambs back in July, but the price wasn't nearly what I needed to get, so I've been holding off on the balance to put more weight on them." She let her guard down and eyed him solemnly. "I'm running out of time, though."

"They're not spring lambs anymore."

"No, but they're still lambs. Nice ones. They're pretty and plump right now. I was betting on a friendlier fall market, but it hasn't improved much, and my bills need to be paid. I think I'll be able to meet them. I really think I will." She was working hard to convince somebody, but he didn't think it was him.

"Did Ken have any insurance?" Tate asked. Without looking him in the eye, she shook her head. It surprised him a little, but he didn't let it show, because it would have embarrassed her.

"Insurance premiums aren't at the top of the priority list

when you've got your whole life ahead of you, and your whole life is tied up in this place."

"Kenny inherited this place."

"And we mortgaged it to stock it and buy equipment. The land and the house. That was Ken's share. The rest was up to him." She slipped the plate into a sink full of soapy water. "When he married me, it was up to *us*."

Tate snagged a toothpick from the little red container that stood next to the pepper shaker. "But he's gone now, and *us* adds up to you and a little—*two* little kids." He slid his chair back from the table.

"It's the life I want for me and my two little kids. So I'm going to fight for it."

"Then I guess I'd better saddle up and move some sheep." He ambled over to the counter, thinking a toothpick was a poor substitute for a cigarette, but a guy had to make do. "Speaking of priority lists, I fixed the shower."

"Already?"

"Didn't take a lot of study, just a little muscle. You tell me what needs doing, and I'll figure out how to do it." He drained the last of his coffee before he handed her the mug. "But if you don't clue me in on the rest of your list, I'll have to come up with one on my own."

"See if you can get the dogs to go with you." She made it sound like a consolation of some kind. "Once you get them out in the pasture, they know what to do. Getting them to work the sheep in the pens takes a little more direction."

See if you can get the dogs to go with you. As if a sheepdog was going to be particular about keeping company with a cowboy. But when he let the two out of the kennel, they took off hell-bent-for-leather for the tall grass in the shelter belt. An explosive beating of pheasant wings promptly had them yapping their fool heads off as a ring-necked cock sailed majestically out of reach, his coppery feathers stealing a glint of sunrise.

"Nice move, bird," Tate said, turning a squint-eyed grin up to the sky. "To listen to *her* talk, you'd think these two sheepdogs had more brains than a cattleman." He plucked the toothpick from the corner of his mouth and tucked his tongue against his teeth, but then thought better of giving a whistle so close to little Jody's bedroom window. He used the toothpick as a pointer. "Come on, you two, we've got work to do."

All they did was play around. They chased each other around the shed while Tate gathered up his gear. They spooked the buckskin while Tate was trying to get him to take the bit. Damn horse was head-shy as it was. The rowels on Tate's spurs jingled as he gave a hop into the stirrup and swung into the saddle. The dogs ran circles around him as he trotted past the yard-light pole.

"If you two mutts are goin' with me, you can stop actin' like jackrabbits any time now."

"The collie's name is Duke, and the spotted bitch is Daisy," Amy called out. "She's a Catahoula Leopard."

Tate hadn't heard the door open, but there she was, waving to him from the back porch like he was some kind of explorer heading out to sea. "I can see that," he called back.

"She's won two blue ribbons."

"For what? Chasing cars?"

"They know their names." As showy as the pheasant's feathers, Amy's rich chestnut hair trapped a red glint of sunlight. She gave another jaunty wave. "Just call them."

He didn't need her advice on what to call them. "Come on, you fleabags. We're burnin' daylight."

When he topped the rise, he looked back. The dogs had

treed some varmint, and their tongues were lolling in apparent expectation that the thing would fall out of the branches and land at their feet. One more chance was all they were going to get.

Tate popped a crisp whistle. "Daisy! Duke! Get your carcasses up here!"

And they came a-running.

The dogs had pushed the sheep along the draws without much coaxing from Tate, but it was a wonder to watch them work the pens for Amy. She whistled like nine different kinds of bird and used hand signals to let the dogs know which animals to drive where. All Tate and Jody had to do was mind the gates.

He still didn't like the idea of letting her get near any livestock so close to her time. Sheep had legs. They could kick. She was already getting kicked pretty good on the inside. When she paused to rub the side of her belly, he whacked the gate shut on the pen where he was working and started to go to her, but then she smiled. Another one of those little kicks. He clenched his fists to stop himself from going to her anyway and putting his hand where hers was. He liked feeling the movement inside her. It was sort of like having a new foal trust him enough to come close and nuzzle his palm, then stand still for a little friendly petting.

"What time are they sending the truck?"

"Five," she told him. "I want to be at the sale barn when they're unloaded so that I can get them settled down and fed."

"You're staying right here." With a quick gesture he cut off her protest as he strode across the corral, closing in on her. "Look at you. You're all done in. If you wanna go to the sale tomorrow and have your remarkable business-lady wits about you, you'll let me…" He heard footsteps tagging along behind him, at least three steps to his one. Without missing a beat, he scooped Jody up in his arms and patted the back pockets of his pint-size blue-jeans. "You'll let *Jody and me* take care of the grunt work tonight. Right, partner? You think we can handle it?"

Jody nodded vigorously.

"I'm not a business *lady*. I'm a business…"

"Person. Female. Female person. Give me a break, Amy. I got the remarkable part right, didn't I? And I'm just trying to give *you* a break." As part of the effort, he held the gate open for her. "I suggest you take me up on it. It would be downright humiliating if you happened to collapse at the sale barn and I had to carry you out of there. I mean, what if I couldn't lift you?"

She laughed and shook her head as she headed for the house.

"Huh? What if I had to haul you out in a wheelbarrow?" Close on her heels, Tate gave Jody a male-conspiratory wink. "How much does a pregnant lady weigh, anyway? Pregnant *female,* pardon me."

"I *do* think of myself as a lady, but not like, 'Whoa, that's too much for you to handle, *little lady.* Better let a *man* take over for you.'"

"Did I say that? Hey, I've made my reputation as a top hand. You're a *sheep* rancher. You think I'd set my sights on takin' over for a sheep rancher? No, ma'am. Not this cowboy. I'll just be Miz Becker's hired hand, down on his luck and workin' for a dollar a day and board. Only way to hang on to my self-respect."

"A dollar a day?" At the top of the back steps she turned to him, hands on her hips, and flashed a saucy smile. "When did I give you a raise?"

* * *

Amy's lambs did better than most, but prices were depressed. So was Amy. She didn't say a word on the way home from the auction. There wasn't much supper conversation, either, and anything coming from Amy was directed quietly at Jody. Tate felt like an interloper. He helped Jody clear the table. When the boy was told it was his bath time, Tate figured he'd been dismissed from the domestic scene. He went downstairs, flopped back on his bunk and played a few tunes he'd taught himself over the years on the harmonica he'd gotten from his dad. His *real* dad. He thought of him as Carter Harrison, the black-and-white photo phantom. Carter had played the harmonica, too. Sad songs, his mother had told him. Songs to fit his mood, like, "I'm So Lonesome I Could Cry."

"Can you teach me to play that?"

Tate raised his head and smiled. Jody looked small and wide-eyed and shy, standing there in his blue pajamas with the plastic-soled feet. Eagerly awaiting his cue, he gripped the door frame, ready to pop in or vanish, depending on Tate's answer.

"I can try," Tate offered.

Jody fairly leapt across the threshold, skidding to a stop at Tate's knee.

"How much time do we have before you have to be in bed?" The boy managed to shrug his shoulders as high as his ears, but Tate detected a guilty look in his eyes, which probably meant he was supposed to be in bed already. He decided to risk it. "I'd say we've got some time."

The two sat side by side on the narrow bed. Tate tapped the harmonica in his palm a few times, then held it steady for Jody and directed him through a series of notes. "Now the same thing, only a little faster," Tate said, and Jody complied intently. "What song did you play?" Tate asked at the end.

Jody gave a big-eyed smile, his blond curls shimmering under the overhead light. "'Twinkle, Twinkle Little Star.'"

"That's right. Did you know that's a cowboy's song?" Jody shook his head. "Sure is. You're camped out under the stars, you got your saddle for a pillow, your ol' six-shooter handy in case you find a rattler in your bedroll."

Jody's eyes grew big as saucers as Tate animated his tale with broad gestures.

"You take out your mouth organ, and you serenade the stars. This is their theme song." He slid the instrument back and forth across his lips and played the familiar tune again. "They like that all over, and, man, do they twinkle in that big Montana sky."

"Let me do it again."

By the time Jody returned the instrument, Tate was ready to pay him to stop twinkling. They shared a pillow while Tate played every soft, soothing song he knew. Jody finally drifted off to sleep. Tate carried him upstairs and managed to sneak past Amy's room. The desk light was on, and her back was to the door. He figured she was going over the books, dividing the amount of the lamb check among the outstanding bills. She'd been at it awhile. Either she had an extremely long column of numbers, or the check just wasn't big enough.

He decided to take her a comfort offering, and he knew she liked tea. He wanted to let her know that he didn't have to be told what her problems were. He'd been around long enough to take account. He had some ideas, and when she rejected those out of hand, as she was bound to do, he would be prepared with some alternatives. She was a fighter with her back to the wall. She would probably take a swing at him out of frustration, but he was pretty good at ducking. He could also be pretty good at talking sense. And because she was basically a sensible woman, eventually she would hear him out.

But she'd fallen asleep over her books. He stood in the doorway, steaming cup in hand, trying to decide whether he should knock or just walk right in like he owned the place. He wasn't going to leave her slumped over the desk for the night.

She solved his problem by awakening with a start, as though someone had shouted in her ear. She gripped the edge of the little writing desk and turned on him abruptly, her chair swiveling like the lid of a mayonnaise jar. He was sure he hadn't made a sound. Impatiently she swept the mop of errant hair out of her face and, with an indignant look, challenged him to explain himself.

He lifted the cup. "Tea."

She gave him a blank stare.

He was tempted to turn on his heel and leave her to sleep sitting up if it pleased her, but he said, "I thought I could get you to take a break, but I see…"

"For me?"

"Well, yeah. If I'd made it for me, I'd 'a put a kick in it." He sniffed the steam. "Smells like virgin orange."

She smiled. Finally. "What is a *virgin* orange?"

"Pure." He circled the foot of the bed and offered her the cup. "I read the box. It's got some kind of natural sleeping potion in it, but you have to be in bed for it to work."

"It doesn't say you have to be in bed."

"*You* have to be in bed—" he checked his watch as he sat down on the bed "—by midnight, so put the books away. Can I sit here?"

"You've already made your wrinkles in my coverlet." Flustered, he started to get up again. "Just kidding," she said quickly. "I'm not *that* fussy." She sipped the hot tea, then puzzled over it. "I do have to wonder why you're being so nice to me."

"Why wouldn't I be?" he asked, then added with mock indignation, "What, I don't have it in me to be nice?"

"You have it in you to be…a lot of things, I'm sure."

"Versatility is my stock in trade. I like being a lot of things. Keeps life interesting." He sat spraddle-legged, hands braced on his knees. "But I'm between jobs right now. It's either hire on to push an eighteen-wheeler down the road for a while, or tend sheep. Never had much truck with sheep."

He chuckled at his own wit and caught the weary smile in her eyes, peering at him above the rim of her cup.

"Guess it's something different," he allowed. "Besides, I'll take the view from the back of a horse over a truck cab, any day. Even if it's a view of sheep rumps headin' home."

"I'd like to get rid of the horses. All of them. Especially that outlaw you brought back here."

"One thing I can tell you for sure, Amy. It wasn't ol' Outlaw's fault." He paused for her objection, but she only drank more tea. "I figure he must be the one Kenny was riding that night. He's high-lifed, but he's a good horse. If he got spooked or missed his footing…" She gave him a sharp look, and he added quietly, "Kenny would be the first to tell you not to blame the horse."

"You're saying he shouldn't have been out riding that night."

"I'm saying it happened, and there's no sense to it. It's the kind of thing that could happen to anyone. Kenny drew the wrong cards that night."

"He shouldn't have been playing cards," she said flatly. "Or drinking. Or riding out there by himself. Or—" Quiet anger rose in her voice, and there was only Tate to be angry with.

"That was Kenny." Her husband, his friend, but they'd both known the same man. "He was a good-hearted, easygoin' guy who didn't like to think too far ahead."

"Well, I *do* think ahead." She was staring so hard at the papers on her desk that he half expected to see the edges start curling up and smoking. "I plan things. I planned the way I was going to sell the lambs, and I planned on getting more for them. Now I'll have to sell breeding stock so I can buy feed."

"I've been giving that some thought," he said lazily as he folded his hands behind his head and leaned back against her brass headboard. "I know I'm not getting paid to do any thinkin', but, hell, it just happens sometimes. You didn't take any hay off my land this year."

"We hadn't paid the lease." Her eyes darted about the room, finding bits of her explanation in every corner of the room, anywhere except in his eyes. "I didn't have anyone to cut it, anyway. Not that I would have, without your… I know Kenny agreed to cut it on shares, and then… I should have let you know that wasn't happening, so you could have made a deal with someone else, but—" She resigned herself with a long sigh. "I'm sorry. That was irresponsible of me."

"Well, now that you've got that off your chest, you can forget about it, okay? I'm not hurtin' for crop money or lease money or any of that. Come spring, I'll see about selling the land." With a gesture he dismissed the whole issue. He was eager to put forth his plan. "I figure with a little supplement we can put the herd out there and graze them 'til it gets too cold. Meanwhile, I'll shop around for some hay."

"I can't buy hay," she informed him stiffly. "I don't have the money."

"What if I said that I do?" She didn't need to say anything, what with that granite look in her eyes. "Yeah, that's what I thought."

"I should just sell those worthless horses."

"Now, I wouldn't call them worthless. They've got

potential." He ignored her delicate sneer. "But if you sold them now, they'd go for killers. Butcher meat and dog food's about the only market for unbroke horses right now."

"They're registered quarter horses."

"And we both know that doesn't matter. Stock prices are low across the board. Nobody's got money for horses right now."

"Ken did." The resentment in her voice did battle with the guilt in her eyes. "He always had money for another great horse bargain."

"That's because he had you, makin' ends meet." Guilt gave way to a flash of gratitude. He understood. He smiled sympathetically. "So now you're done buying horses, and you've sold your lambs, and you're down to your ace-in-the-hole."

"Which is?"

"You've found yourself some cheap labor. You let him do what he can for you."

She looked at him, long and hard, and he could almost hear those gears clicking away inside her head, questioning, always trying to figure the odds and hedge her bets. In her position, he couldn't blame her.

"Why?" she asked finally.

"Because you're a smart woman, Amy. And you've run low on options."

"I mean, why are you willing to do this?"

"It's kinda out of character, isn't it?" He smiled knowingly. "I don't like being too predictable. Every once in a while I like to be nice. I like to be useful to somebody, just for a change."

"I never said you weren't nice…sometimes."

"Boy, that was a squeaker." He laughed and shook his head

as he got up to leave. "On that happy note and the strike of the eleventh hour, I'd better drag my tail downstairs."

"I know *I'm* not always nice," she admitted with another sigh. "I didn't even thank you for the tea." She took another drink, just to show him that she wasn't going to let it go to waste. He figured it had to be cold by now. "This is nice, and I thank you."

"My pleasure." He touched her shoulder as he passed. Her surprisingly unguarded look of appreciation made him want to hang around the bedroom a little longer. "I fed the ewes. Tomorrow morning I'll start moving some grain feeders out to my place. I'll be putting the rams out there with them." She raised one brow, but he detected the hint of a smile. "Won't I? I mean, is that your plan, boss lady?"

"We'll have to watch the weather closely if we're going to move them over to your place."

"This is Montana." He chuckled. "What else have we got to do in the winter?"

"Some of the grain feeders might need a little repair," she warned.

"I've already got that covered." He gave her a reassuring wink as he turned to leave.

"Tate?" He glanced over his shoulder, eyebrows raised. "I may not always be nice, either, but I *am* good. I try to be a good person, anyway. I do understand why you're doing all this. I know how you felt about Ken, and I don't want to take advantage of you, especially since I didn't make much of an effort to—"

"If you're seeing some advantage to be taken, I'm makin' progress."

It took him a good part of the morning to make the repairs on the free-standing grain feeders and put them in accessible locations. When he came back he found his lunch waiting for him, but the house was deserted. Jody was playing with a fleet of toy trucks outside the barn, and Amy was inside, sitting in a pile of straw with the shoulders of a one-hundred-and-seventy-pound ewe planted in her lap.

"What the hell do you think you're doing?"

"Poor baby had a nail in her hoof."

Hunkering down next to her, he pulled off one buckskin work glove, pushed her open coat aside and laid his hand protectively over her belly. "*This* is a baby," he corrected, and with a gloved finger he touched the ewe's foot. "This, as you know, is a hoof. This hoof might kick this baby."

"The hoof belongs to a sheep, not a horse or a cow. They have to be trimmed every fall," she explained as she continued to pare the cloven hoof. "And since we're going to move them, I have to get them all done."

"God-*bless,* woman!" The docile, flop-eared ewe sniffed at his jacket, but she was no more intimidated by his exasperated protests than Amy was. Ordinarily he wasn't one to expound much, but he figured a lesson was in order. "A hoof is a hoof." End of chapter one. He sat down on Amy's straw cushion. "Why don't you tell me about these things before you go and—"

"I *always* trim their hooves, twice a year, and I have never gotten hurt doing it. They're gentle animals, Tate."

"Tell that to the two rams I just separated."

"Well, the rams…" She inspected the inner hoof for debris, probing with her parer. "They do butt heads during breeding season. It's a man thing." She spared him a coy glance. "I'll let you take care of the rams."

"I'll tell you something else that's a man thing." He draped his forearms over his knees and removed his other glove. "You see a woman in your condition, you just wanna put her in a pumpkin shell and keep her very well until everything's—" he slapped his palm with the leather glove "—over with. Safe and sound."

"And a woman in my condition happens to have a good deal of energy, especially as the time draws closer. She wants to make sure everything is in order, and nature seems to provide her with the energy to do just that." She looked up at him. "I couldn't breathe in a pumpkin shell. You need your space, Tate. Let me have mine."

"I'll let you show me how to do this," he offered as he scooted the ewe from her lap to his. A hoof was a hoof, he'd said, and he'd trimmed his share. He held his hand out for the knife.

"Actually, I was going to need some help catching them. This one was limping, so she was slower than I was." She relinquished the tool to him. It was useless to argue, and she knew he didn't need much instruction. "I'm used to handling most of it myself, but Jody's helping out, too, now. He can bottle-feed a lamb. He can—"

"Jody's just a little guy." Too young to be given some of the jobs he kept asking for. Tate remembered how it felt to be given the kind of responsibility that made a boy feel like a man. Heady at first, but there was no turning back once you'd taken the step. At least there hadn't been for him.

"I heard you reading that nursery rhyme to him the other night, about the pumpkin shell," he said. It was the kind of kids' stuff he'd sailed right past on his shortcut to manhood. "What's that supposed to mean, 'had a wife but couldn't keep her'? You don't get married unless you've got some way to keep her."

"Keep her what?" Amy teased. "Happy? It's usually the woman's lament, that she had a husband but couldn't keep him."

"Keep him what?" he echoed.

They traded smiles while he switched to the other front hoof. Then he made short work of the back hooves and let the animal go.

"When are you going to settle down?" she wondered. "For longer than a few months, I mean."

"The word *when* supposes I will, sooner or later." The straw rustled beneath him as he shifted, raising his knee for an armrest. "Is that what you suppose? Every man oughta settle down, sooner or later?"

"They don't all want to. I know that. And some try to have it both ways." He looked up, wordlessly asking whether she meant him. "Ken wasn't like that." Missing Tate's message, she went on. "He had built-in roots. I like that. I found a sense of security in it. That's funny, isn't it?"

"Why?" He felt no urge to laugh now that she'd changed the subject to Kenny's attributes.

"Because he found a way to wander off after all, didn't he?" It wasn't the answer he was ready for, nor the one she'd expected to give. She glanced away quickly. "I don't know why I said that. It's a terrible thing to say."

"But it's true. He's gone, and you're still here."

"He didn't mean to," she said sadly as she picked a piece of straw off his thigh. "He never meant to leave us. He didn't even know he was leaving *two* children, and he didn't mean for things to be so—" Here it comes, he thought. He couldn't see her eyes, but her voice was weakening. "—damn hard."

"It's okay." She shook her head as he took her hands in his. "No, come on, Amy, it's okay to tell it like it is."

"It isn't like that. He's not to blame." She glanced at the open barn door, her eyes shining with the threat of tears. "That horse, that crazy horse."

"I'll get rid of the horse," he promised. Her bottom lip

trembled, but she said neither aye nor nay. Gently he squeezed her hands. "Will that help?"

"Yes!" She closed her eyes and shook her head again as he moved into position. "No, no, no, it won't do any good."

"Come here, honey." He reached out to her, ready to hold her, anticipating the feel of her weight against him. "It'll do you good to—"

"No," she said firmly, wiping her eyes with one hand and pushing him away with the other. Jody's truck-engine sound effects intruded from a distance. "I can't let Jody see me like this."

"Why not?"

"I'm all he's got." She scrambled to her feet so fast that he missed his chance to offer any gentlemanly assistance. "And I can't come apart now. I don't have time. I have too much to do. I have to—" Her hands were shaking as she struggled for control. "*We* have to get those hooves trimmed."

She'd streaked some dirt across her cheek with the tear she'd banished so quickly. He reached his hand out to her. "Amy, take it easy." He would clean her face if she would let him. He would kiss away her tears.

"Are you going to help me or not?"

Her lips were trembling, and her eyes were wild with an emotion he couldn't begin to name. He let his hand fall to his side. "I'm gonna do the work," he said gruffly. "You give the damn orders."

Chapter 4

In trade for hay, Tate agreed to break a couple of two-year-olds for Myron Olson. He knew Myron needed green-broke two-year-olds about as much as he needed a swimming pool in his backyard this winter, but Myron happened to have plenty of hay and welcomed the excuse to truck some over to the Becker place. Like some of the other neighbors, he'd offered to help the widow out with whatever she needed, but she always said she was doing just fine.

Just what she needed, Amy grumbled when he unloaded the new stock. More horses around the place. But Tate detected a glint of relief in her eyes when the first load of hay rolled into the yard. He wasn't going to let the horses interfere with his other chores, but he liked to work with them when he was minding Jody, who loved to watch. Tate found himself wishing Amy would come out to observe him in action, too, just to reassure herself that it was perfectly safe to keep horses around.

* * *

"Mama, Mama, Mama!"

Jody only called her "Mama" when he was excited or scared. The way his little legs were churning up the gravel, she could tell he was both. She flew out the door and met him at the foot of the back steps.

"Come quick! Tate got kicked!"

"Where!"

"In the head, by one of the—"

She took his hand, and together they trotted across the yard. "Show me where."

"It's nothing," Tate insisted as soon as Amy and Jody burst into the barn. He was sitting on a hay bale, hat in one hand, head in the other, looking like a guy who'd just lost round one. "I'm okay. Just grazed me. No blood spilled." But when he took his hand away from his forehead, he had a glove full of blood. "*Hardly* any blood spilled."

"You're bleeding all over the place!" Amy exclaimed as she knelt beside him, trying to catch her breath. "Can you walk?"

"Legs are fine." He scowled, arching the eyebrow that was catching most of the blood. "You been running?"

"Jody's been running. I've been waddling."

"You shouldn't be running." He took a swipe at the blood with the back of his wrist as he tried to duck away from her scrutiny.

"*You* shouldn't be—" She took his face in her hands and made him look at her. The light was dim, and his eyes were so dark that it was hard to tell anything about his pupils. "Can you walk?"

"You asked me that." He proved he could stand up. "Point me in the right direction."

"You okay, Tate?" Jody asked anxiously.

"If I start to go down, just holler 'Timber!' and get your mom out of the way."

"That's not funny," Amy insisted as she slipped her arm around him. He put his arm around her shoulders, and she gave his flat belly a motherly pat as they headed for the house. "You'll be okay."

"That's what I said. Just feelin' a little booze blind, which is no big deal." But he grabbed for the gatepost as they entered the yard, taking a moment to steady himself without leaning on her. "Except you'd like to start out with some fun before you get the headache."

"You mean you're not having fun yet, cowboy? You and your damned hardheaded horses."

"I'm the hardhead." He closed his eyes briefly, then forced a smile. "The horses are jugheads. There's a difference."

"I'm sure I don't know what that is."

"The difference is, I should have known better. I was sackin' her out, and I should've used a hobble."

"We don't need the hay this bad," she said as Jody scampered up the steps and held the door for them.

"Yes, we do." Neither of them had accented the word *we,* but it resounded in the look they exchanged. "And it's not bad," he assured her quietly. "I'd know if it was bad. I've been kicked before."

"I don't like taking charity."

"It's hardly charity when I'm…" He was looking for a place to sit before he collapsed. She provided a tall kitchen stool close to the sink, and he sank down on it gratefully. "I'm working for the damn hay, and I'm doing it on your time."

"Stop patronizing me. I'm not paying you, and even if I were, I wouldn't pay you to get kicked in the head by a horse."

"I'll get the doctoring stuff," Jody offered sensibly. He disappeared down the hall.

Amy grumbled as she set to work on Tate's head with a clean towel, soap and water. "I don't want anyone else getting hurt. Horses are dangerous, they're unpredictable, they're..." She worked gently around the cut, brushing his hair back with one hand and blotting the blood with the other. "Tate, this won't stop bleeding. You probably need stitches."

"If you say so." He almost lost himself in the sympathy he saw in her eyes, but Jody's return brought him back to reality. A bottle and two small boxes clattered on the counter. Tate rewarded the boy with a smile. "We'll go get us some stitches. Right, Jody?"

"You mean you can sew his head?"

"I can't," Amy said absently, still trying to staunch the blood. "A doctor can."

"Will it hurt?" Jody backed away slowly. Remembered fear crept into his question. "Is it like an operation? Will he die?"

"Jody, come here." Tate held out his hand. "It's not like an operation, and I'm going to be fine."

"You didn't fall off a horse, did you?" Jody asked anxiously, inching closer.

Tate shook his head as he hooked his hand around the boy's nape and drew him close.

"No," Jody reassured himself. He draped himself over Tate's thigh as though he were hitching a ride. "You got kicked, but you never fell off. That's different."

"I've fallen off lots of horses," Tate admitted, looking to Amy for approval. He was willing to admit to the risks. "Sometimes you get hurt, but most of the time you just dust off your jeans and climb back on."

"Or you get smart and stay away from them because they're

dangerous," she instructed as she peeled adhesive tape from a roll. "Jody knows that."

Tate ruffled Jody's soft curls. "I'm okay, Jody. In a week or so, this will just look like a scratch."

"And don't tell him it doesn't hurt, either, because it does." She sucked air between her teeth, grimacing as she considered the best way to cover the wound. Finally she bit the bullet and applied the bandage. Tate winced. "I'm sorry. Does that hurt?"

"It does hurt a little. You'd probably feel a lot better if I took some aspirin or something."

"We're taking you in for some stitches, and then I want those horses—" She swept them away with a quick gesture.

"Uh-uh." Tate wagged his index finger under her nose. "I took on a job, and I'll get it done. But I'll be more careful."

"You could sue me, and I don't have any liability insurance," she suggested too easily. His steely, dispassionate look set her back on her heels. "I guess you wouldn't sue me."

"I guess I hadn't thought of it."

"I did have insurance, but I didn't pay the premium this fall. That's the next thing on my list, but I haven't had…"

"Jody," Tate began, giving the boy a pat on the back. "Just between us, I don't feel much like driving the pickup. You wanna go look in your mom's sewing box and find me a needle and a piece of thread about—" he thrust his white shirtsleeve in front of Jody's face "—this shade of passin'-out pale?"

Amy threw in the towel. "I'm getting my coat."

A few hours of convalescing went a long way with Tate. And a little TLC was about all Amy had the time for. Otherwise, about the only progress he could say he'd made with her in the time that he'd worked for her was that she didn't seem to hate him. He wasn't sure what more he wanted from her. Not sex, obviously; she wasn't exactly in any shape for a real good roll in the sack. Maybe a little cuddling in the sack, where he could hold her close enough to feel the baby move again.

Hell, what was he thinking? It wasn't even his baby, and she damn sure wasn't his woman. He didn't know why he kept hanging around. She couldn't bring herself to admit she needed his help. If anybody asked, she was honest enough to admit she needed *some* help, but any damn drifter with a strong back would do, long as she kept her shotgun handy in case he had any ideas about…

In case he had the nerve to think about getting her in the sack, where she could put her hands on him the way she had when he'd been hurt. She was the kind of woman who might reject a man's appetite for the roving and rollicking life, but she could still touch him with forgiving, healing, caring hands. Maybe if she would once touch him in the dark, he thought. Maybe if they couldn't see into each other's eyes, they wouldn't be as likely to start the delicious drowning, start the lovely slipping under, then, bam! There was Kenny, floating above their heads like an avenging angel.

And Amy would end up feeling bad about spending any of her affection on Tate. She'd felt bad about it years ago, even before she'd married Kenny, and it would be worse for her now that he was dead. She was too damn hard on herself. She wouldn't think it was a good thing for a good woman to do, and she was good. She had certain standards she tried to live by. She'd made a point of reminding him of that. It wasn't just a matter of being good at what she did. Hell, *he* was good at what he did, not that what he did was any great shakes, but he was good at it. Still, he wasn't *good*.

And just to prove it, he was about to do Saturday night up right.

He started out at the Jackalope, but the atmosphere was too

dismal there. Charlie Dennison had gotten his butt in a sling at home. His ol' lady had thrown all his gear into a cardboard box and left it on the back porch. No question that ol' Charlie was completely misunderstood. That put Ticker Thomas in mind of the girl he should have married, damn sure *would* have married if she hadn't run off to Seattle. The music was downhearted, the drinking was solemn and the patrons were all male.

After one drink Tate moved on to the Turkey Track, where the dance floor was hopping. He met up with Kenny's sister, Marianne, who had managed to persuade husband Bill, Sr., Overo's staid, colorless grocer, to shock everybody by taking his wife out on a Saturday night. Marianne professed to be damn glad to see Tate and damn sorry she hadn't tried to get hold of him herself when Kenny died. She'd just assumed— well, everybody knew Tate was footloose.

"You remember Patsy Drexel. Used to be Johnson," Marianne shouted over the strains of "The Devil Went Down to Georgia." She shoved the voluptuous blonde into his arms, and he took a turn around the dance floor with her.

Sure, he remembered Patsy. Patsy was Marianne's friend. Three years ahead of him in school and light-years ahead of him in experience, at least to start out with. Experience had been one hell of a zealous teacher. They'd had some good times together back then, and once or twice in the intervening years, whenever he'd happened to be in town and Patsy had happened to be between husbands.

"Drexel," he said consideringly. That was a new one. "So you got married again, huh?" Before the conversation went the way it usually did with Patsy, he had to get a few things straight. "Where's your ol' man?"

"Which one? The last one ran off to Reno to play guitar in a band. He had the hots for the singer." She looked up and smiled. "It was an even shorter marriage than my first. You think I oughta take back my maiden name now that I'm unattached again?"

"I've still got you down as Johnson in my memory book. Is that your maiden name?" He charmed her with a wink. Here was opportunity tapping a bright red fingernail just above his shoulder blade.

But when he escorted her back to the table, she made the mistake of saying, "Thanks, honey." He wasn't sure where the prickly sensation had come from, but he told himself to ignore it.

"So you're working out to Becker's place for the winter?" Patsy claimed the chair next to Marianne's. "Haven't seen her around town for a while. Bet she's big as a hippo and twice as testy."

"She's all baby," Tate said tightly as he lit a cigarette. "She looks uncomfortable, but I don't hear her complaining."

He eyed Patsy pointedly as he blew a stream of smoke, hoping she'd gotten the message that bad-mouthing Amy wouldn't earn her any points with him, if that was what she was looking for. Patsy was in no position to talk, anyway. From what he could see, all her experience had put more age on her than any UV rays could account for.

"Well, it's real nice of you to help her out," Patsy allowed generously. "But it must be frustrating in a way, considering how you've always kinda carried a torch for her."

"What are you talking about? Amy's the vine-covered cottage type, and I've never been one to let any grass grow under my feet." There, he thought, that sounded definite. "Besides, she was a one-man woman, and that man was my best friend." For good measure he mentally toasted Kenny before he took a drink.

"You might've been hiding your torch under a bush, Tate, but everyone knew it was there. That's why you left Overo."

He smiled humorlessly as he aligned his glass with the water ring it had left on the table. "I had a lot of reasons for leaving Overo, and Amy Becker wasn't one of them."

"You walked away from your father's land," Marianne said. "That place was rightfully yours, not your stepfather's, from the day your mother died. It was always Harrison land."

"It still is." He glanced at Bill, who was busy people-watching, then at Marianne. Patsy was the woman after his body, but Marianne was a woman after his own heart. Calculating and practical. Cut to the payoff. He just needed to put his basic instincts to work for a change. "Until somebody makes me a good offer."

"Check with some of the oil companies," Marianne advised. "There are about half a dozen speculators looking to take core samples, but some of these old ranchers around here refuse to poke anything but a posthole through the sod. And you know damn well there's money down there somewhere."

Patsy leaned closer. "I can't see you as the sentimental type when it comes to poking holes wherever it suits you, Tate." Her smile was as suggestive as the beat of the music. "Whenever there's a need."

"Leave it to a woman to fancy she can see right through a man's skin," he said smoothly.

"It's in your eyes, sugar. You've got a need."

"Just a simple itch, honey." *Honey.* Damn. He adjusted the brim of his hat, which covered his bandage even while it punished him with a dull headache. He signaled the server for another round of drinks. "Alcohol works wonders."

"Where does it itch? I just had a manicure." Patsy ran her nails up and down his back. "How does that feel? Tell me when I hit on the spot that's bothering you, sugar." Smiling lasciviously, she discovered her favorite thigh. "Am I getting warm?"

"You aren't even close, Patsy." He couldn't believe he was actually moving her hand, patting it apologetically as he settled it in her own lap. Damn his eyes, maybe he *was* getting sentimental in his old age, but he didn't feel much like poking around Patsy or vice versa. "Even if you were, it'd be no use. The itch just keeps on coming back."

"That's because *you* keep coming back."

"So do you." He nodded across the table. "So do *you,* Marianne. Remember when you lit out with that bull rider? Kenny and me had to do some fancy talkin' to keep your dad from headin' into Billings with a shotgun."

"Those were my wilder days." Marianne turned to her husband, who was only half listening. "Can you believe I was ever that wild, honey?"

Bill, Sr., a dubious honey at best, responded with a grunt in the negative.

"We were all born to be wild," Patsy said, cheerfully resigning herself to Tate's rebuff. "That's how I look at it." Then she sang it, pounding on the table for added emphasis. "'Course, if *I* was born to be wild, what about my kids? God, I *dread* having teenagers."

"How many kids do you have?" Tate remembered hearing about one, but Patsy never talked about her children.

"Three. One for each of my two ex's, and one for this guy I used to work for. Thank God Sally's old enough to watch the other two once in a while."

"How old is she?" He was asking for the kind of details he'd always considered none of his business.

"Eleven," Patsy reported without the slightest show of emotion. "Almost twelve. Almost a teenager. Now *her* father was the one I should have kept around if I wanted to be married, but back then the grass looked greener in my boss's bed. Which it was for a while. Then I met the guitar player." She planted her elbow on the table and sank her chin into her hand. "One of these days I'm going to pack up and move to Denver."

"You think you'd like the grass down there better?"

"I don't know. I've just always wanted to live in Denver. Mile-high pie and all that."

"Denver's just like any other place," Tate said as the server appeared with a tray of drinks. "Take my word for it."

"The voice of experience," Patsy quipped sarcastically.

"That's right." Tate wanted to laugh, but he would be laughing *at* her, and he had no right. He was no better. In fact, she was his flip side. She had her experience, he had his.

"I suppose you've spent enough time there to really know."

"As much as I've spent anywhere." There was a dose of sympathy for each of them in his sad smile. "I really *do* know."

"Then you're lucky," Patsy insisted. "Do yourself a favor and don't settle down in any one spot for too long. Before you know it, things'll start to get sticky. You'll have all kinds of baggage and bills, ex-spouses and kids. That stickiness turns out to be glue, Tate. Before you know it—"

"For heaven's sake, Patsy, I try to fix you up with somebody, and you get morbid." Marianne's laughter lightened the mood. "If you can't have a good time with Tate Harrison, then you're over the hill, because, according to my brother, Tate always did know how to have a good time."

"I can vouch for Tate." Patsy gave him a wistful smile. "Even though it's been a long time."

"A long time for what?" Tate figured he could still party,

even if he wasn't interested in finding somebody to take him home. "We were dancing just a minute ago."

"You're a great dancer."

"Well, then, let's dance." With a gallant flourish he assisted Patsy with her chair. "Let's just bop 'til we drop, and the hell with all the bills and the baggage."

It didn't do him a damn bit of good to tear up the dance floor with Patsy Johnson Drexel. The way she kept crowding him made slow dancing impossible. He favored a heel-kicking "Cotton-Eyed Joe" or a twirling "Cowboy Two-Step." When his eyes started playing tricks on him and blue-eyed Patsy suddenly went brown-eyed on him, he knew he was beyond dance-dizzy. He decided it was time to quit going through the motions and call it a night.

He was looking forward to falling into bed and spinning himself to sleep, although he realized as he shut off the pickup's engine that there wasn't much night left.

He found Amy standing in the middle of the kitchen, barefoot and dressed only in a pink cotton nightgown. She didn't seem to want to let go of the edge of the sink as she turned to him. Backlit by the light above the kitchen window, the curves of her fecund body made a lovely silhouette beneath the opaque gown. In that instant, Tate knew for certain that God was a woman. A man-God wouldn't have tortured him this way, like making him stand outside a bakery window during Lent.

"Are you just getting up, or just going to bed?" He didn't like the wounded-animal look in her eyes. He wanted to see fiery judgment, so he could say, *Back at you, baby.* But she just stood there while he hung his sheepskin jacket and his hat on the hooks in the back entry. "You weren't waiting up for me, were you?"

"Oh, no," she said quickly. She turned away from him as she tightened her grip on the edge of the sink. "I wouldn't do a foo-fooooolish thinglikethat."

"What's going on?" He crossed the floor in two strides and took her slight shoulders in his hands. "You okay?"

"I could use a top hand." Her shoulders were shaking. She struggled with words and shallow breaths. "You know of one who's not too...too busy? Oh, dear..."

"It's not time yet, is it?" Her whole body went stiff as she nodded vigorously. He pried her hand away from the sink and draped her arm over his shoulder. "We gotta sit you down. You mean, now?"

She pressed her face against his neck and let him lower her into a chair. His mind was spinning. One thing at a time, he told himself. "You hold on. I'll get you some clothes. I'll get Jody."

"I'm hoping he'll sleep."

"Sleep?" This was no time to argue with her, but it was definitely time to take charge. "Amy, we can't leave him here alone."

"I don't know about you, but I'm not going—" she held on to the seat of the chair as though she were preparing for a bumpy ride "—anywhere. Especially not with you driving."

"I'm fine—wide-awake. I got home all right, didn't I?" Damn right, he was home. *Home,* where he was needed, where it was all up to him now. "I can get you to—"

Her shoulders started to shake again as she dropped her head back. Holy God in heaven, he couldn't take her out on the road like this. The thing was, he had to stay calm. He had to do something quick, and it had to be the right thing. He laid his hand on her shoulder, and the phone on the wall caught his eye.

"You're right, honey. We'll call someone to—Amy!" She

groaned softly and pressed the side of her face against his arm. He could feel her hurting. He felt like a powerless lump of male flesh, afraid to step away from her, scared to death not to.

"The first thing to do is get help." He took a step, reached for the phone, pointed a finger at the dial. "Who to call, who to call, who's close, nobody's close…"

"Tate." He hadn't heard her move, but she was leaning against his back now, her hands on his shoulders, just the way he had held her moments ago. "Tate, there's no one else right now. Just you."

"You mean it's coming right *now?* We have to tell them to come." He closed his eyes. His head was devoid of numbers. "Ambulance…police…"

"Right *here,* Tate." She laid her cheek against his back. He hung up the phone and turned to take her in his arms. "Having the baby…right here, right—"

"Not on the kitchen floor, honey, let's get you—" He lifted her easily as the answers started to come to him. Make her comfortable first, *then* call. "Okay, let's get you to bed, and I'll call—"

"I've called…the midwife…I've been seeing for prenatal exams. Left a message."

"Midwife? What is that, some sort of—"

"She'll be here." He laid her on her bed, which she'd apparently prepared in advance with a rubberized sheet. He wasn't sure what to make of all this, or of Amy's soft babbling. "Soon. She'll be here. It came on so f-fassst."

"What if…" A *midwife?* It sounded to him like something out of the Dark Ages. "I'm calling an ambulance."

"No," Amy insisted. She grabbed his arm and with amazing strength pulled him down close to her. "Now, listen to me,

Tate, there's no time, and women have been having babies since time began, and they don't…"

He shook his head and tried to pull away, but even as another contraction started, she was having none of his resistance. "I don't have any health insurance, and I don't want any more bills I can't p-p—" She held his arm while he looked on in terror, gripping her shoulders. When it was over, she smiled bravely. "That was a good one."

"It didn't look good."

"Think of it as pulling…as calving out a…no, *easier* than a first-calf heifer, Tate. I'm on my second." Her eyes pleaded with him as she fought to control her breathing. "Tate, I'm afraid you're going to have to do this for me."

"Not me, for God's sake, I'm just as—" Just as what? Scared? Stupid? Weak-kneed as a new foal was the way he felt, but he tried to return that brave smile of hers. He brushed her damp hair back from her forehead. "I don't know anything about this, honey. We need a doctor. Hell, if I make a mistake, you might sue me, like—"

"No, it's not funny. I have to be able to count on you. You have to deliver—"

"No, it's not safe. I might… Let me get you a doctor, honey. When the pain comes, let me just hold your hand until it—"

"Wash yours, damn it!" Then the pain seized her, along with all the anguish and frustration and anger that came with birthing. "Damn damn damn you, Tate! Look at me!"

"Hey, I wasn't anywhere near—" It didn't matter. The technicality wedged itself in his throat, and it occurred to him that there was no excuse for him. He was a man. Watching Amy suffer made him feel like a worm.

"I'm sorry, honey. I'm sorry." He smoothed her hair back again, kissed her hot temple and whispered, "Kenny's sorry, too."

"You smell like smoke—" She grabbed his hand and squeezed for all she was worth "—and beer, and you…and you…and you…"

"Shhhh, what can I do?"

"I don't wanna shhhh!"

"Yell, then, what can I do?"

"Oooh, oooh—" Pant. Pant. "I think you should wash your hands, and I put all the stuff Mrs.…midwife…" She waved her free hand toward the supplies she'd set out on a white towel on the dresser, then groaned. "Scissors and surgical thread… alcohol… Hurry, Tate, hurry—oooooh…"

Crossing the room in a single stride, Tate tore open his cuff and started rolling up his sleeve, but by the time he'd reached the bathroom sink, he'd stripped the shirt off entirely. He washed his hands and his arms up to his T-shirt sleeves. God help him, he was covered with germs and dirt and sin. He grabbed a bottle of rubbing alcohol and doused his hands in it. They seemed relatively steady, even though he felt like he'd swallowed a cement mixer.

"Tate!" Amy called, straining to control her voice. And then, "Taaaate!" She screamed his name as though things were coming apart and he was supposed to be able to put them back together. Like pulling a calf? *Pulling?* Oh, God, why did she have to say *that?* He took a deep breath and a big step.

"Tate!" Eyes wild with terror, Jody stood in the middle of the hallway. "Tate, my mama! Don't let my mama die, Tate!"

Chapter 5

"*My mom can't die of this, can she?*"

That had been Tate's question, too. Even in the best of times his stepfather had been a man of few words, but after his mother had gotten sick, no words had been forthcoming from Oakie Bain. No comfort. No counsel. Tate's questions went unanswered until the day Myron Olson's wife, Joan, had come to take him out of school. "Get your jacket," Joan had said, and he'd stared at the denim thing hanging on a coat hook in the hallway. It hadn't been washed since his mother had gone away to the hospital.

He remembered the sound of Joan's boots clopping down the hallway toward Jesse's classroom. There was his answer, in the sound of a woman's retreating footsteps. Never again would he hear the quiet voice that had willingly given him what answers she'd had. No more would he see the light of approval in his mother's eyes. The terrible reality had fallen over him like a weighted net. He'd felt hot-faced and sick to his stomach, and he'd barely made it to the boys' bathroom.

"Tate?" Jody's brown eyes were as big as basketballs.

Tate took a deep breath. "Your mom's having the baby. It's kinda like lambing. Have you seen a lamb get born?"

"Once," Jody said. "But Mama's screamin' a lot worse than a ewe."

"It hurts her pretty bad right now, but after the baby comes out, it'll stop hurting. It just takes a little while."

He knelt like a supplicant before the boy, holding his arms out awkwardly. "We're going to help her. I'm going to keep the door open, and you're going to sit right outside in the hallway and be ready to run and get me something if I need it, okay?"

Jody nodded hesitantly.

"We can't shake on it, because I have to keep my hands real clean, so put your arms around my neck and give me a hug." The little boy's arms gave him a shot of encouragement. His angel-hair curls clung to the stubble on Tate's jaw. "Thanks, partner."

Amy's breathy pain-ride suddenly sounded less threatening. Clear-eyed confidence took a firm grip on his insides. She needed him, and he was there. The rest would follow in due course.

She was between contractions.

"Do we need to anchor your legs somehow?"

She grimaced and shook her head.

He offered her a sympathetic smile. "Is this it, then? You gonna take this lyin' down, boss lady?"

She nodded again and lifted her chin, returning a tightly drawn, stiff-upper-lipped expression. "There's hardly any letup now." Her voice was stretched thin. "The pains are so bad… won't let me have an-nnnnunhhhh…"

She gripped the brass rails of the headboard as she gathered her forces at her middle. Her stamina amazed him. Unable to touch her, Tate stood watch over her labor.

Anxious eyes peered at him from the dim hallway. Jody was sitting there tight-lipped, clutching his knees, trusting Tate to do whatever needed to be done. Amy rolled her head to the side and saw him there. "Oh, Jody…" Her voice was weak, but her tone took exception to the child's presence.

"Jody's lookin' out for you, too," Tate said softly.

"But I don't want him to see me like thhhhhiii—"

Tate gave a nod. "Jody, I want you to stand guard right by the door, okay? Just like a soldier. And tell me if you hear anyone at the back door."

"Mama, are you gonna die?"

"No!" She turned her head away. "Oh no, oh no, oh no…"

Tate nodded again, and Jody scrambled for his assigned post on the other side of the doorjamb.

"He's scared, honey." He looked down into Amy's eyes, begging her indulgence. He knew she was up to it. He couldn't fathom the extent of her pain, but he could see how strong she was. "We can't shut him out. If you can just tell him you'll be okay…"

"I'm okay, Jody." She was getting hoarse. "I'm okay, I'mokayI'mokay—" She closed her eyes through the next contraction. A gush of water flooded the bed beneath her hips.

"Tate, I think it's time for you to—" Amy pulled her nightgown over her distended belly and spread her knees apart "—check…things…."

This was no time for modesty, and no time for him to back down from a woman's invitation to get personal. Not when a soggy thatch of baby hair was presenting itself at life's door. After the next contraction, Tate quickly swabbed Amy with rubbing alcohol. He'd barely managed to set the bottle aside when she gave a long, deep, terrible groan and pushed. Everything, including his eyes, widened. The tiny head was expelled.

"Good job, Amy!" He felt like a cheerleader in the playoffs—overstimulated and underuseful. "Can you do that again?"

"I can't *not* do it," she barked between gasps. "I can't— ohhhhh…"

"Mama?"

"She's doing fine," Tate said excitedly. His whole being was attuned to the sound of her doglike panting, the smell of life-producing blood and the sight of her body transforming itself in the most miraculous way. "You're doing great, honey. Just one more time."

"Jody, don't…"

"Jody, run get me some more towels," Tate ordered. Jody sprang from his post like a sprinter.

"Ohohohohoh…"

"And peek out the window to see if anyone's coming," Tate called out.

The baby's head turned to the side. Tate cleared its mouth with his big forefinger. Amy whimpered a little as she braced herself for the next onslaught. Tate braced himself against the sound of her pain, which erupted with a fury this time as the baby whooshed into Tate's waiting hands like a tot on a water slide. She bawled the minute he caught her.

"A little girl!"

She was all pink and petite and perfect, and he was actually holding her in his own two hands. A squirming, wrinkled female connected to her mother by a coiled cord, like the receiver on a telephone. Only *Tate* was the receiver. He bore the good news.

"Amy, she's here. Your little girl just made her debut."

"Is she okay?"

"Can't you hear her?" Grinning from ear to ear, he put the slippery prize on Amy's belly. Amy lifted her head, trying to get a peek. Her face was pale and slick with sweat. He took her cool hand in his slippery one and guided it to the baby's head. "She sounds just like you. All pretty and mad."

"Like me?" Chest heaving, Amy dropped her head back. "Not mad," she gasped. "Hardly pretty. But strong. I did it."

"Damn right, you did it. Hold on to her while I do the rest."

He hoped he was doing it right. In some ways it wasn't so different from the nonhuman births he'd attended. His hands were rock steady, and his heart was singing like a meadowlark as he snipped the cord between tiny tourniquets he'd made of surgical thread. "You're on your own now, little girl."

He was wrapping the baby in a white flannel blanket when Amy was seized by another contraction. All she had to do was point to the towels on the nightstand and he understood. They were a team now. He slid one towel in place beneath her, tucked the squalling bundle in the crook of his arm and massaged Amy's belly with the heel of his free hand. "You'll be all done in a New York minute, honey. Just one more good—"

"Awwwwfullll!"

"One more awful pain. God, I could never be a woman. You're amazing, Amy." In both will and body, he thought as she expelled the afterbirth. He rubbed hard. Her belly felt like rubber on the outside and rock underneath. "You made a miracle. I saw it with my own eyes."

The baby squawked angrily as Tate cradled her against his

chest. "That's right, little darlin'. Take charge, just like your mama."

But it was Tate who was in charge. He folded the towel around the afterbirth and set it aside. Then he tucked another towel between Amy's legs and covered her with a sheet. She needed a moment to catch her breath.

"Tate?"

He turned, and Jody offered up several towels. "Thanks, partner. Look what we've got." Jody lifted his chin for a peek. Tate chuckled, knowing the crinkled red face hardly met the little boy's expectations.

He sat on the bed and leaned close to Amy. "Soon as I get this little gal acquainted with her mother's face, maybe she won't be quite so…"

The bawling subsided to a whimper when Amy took the baby in her arms. Weary as she was, her pale face lit up like a firefly in a jar.

"That's better," he said. "She wasn't expecting to see my fuzzy face first thing."

"She's glad you were there," Amy said, her eyes smiling up at him. "So am I."

"I never thought I'd…" He shook his head as all words failed him. They looked so pretty together, triumphant mother and tiny daughter. Tate knew damn well he was blushing head to toe. "I'd better clean things up a little."

"Things?"

"You and her." He wasn't sure what to do for Amy now. He knew she might need stitches. The sooner he put in a call for medical help, the better. Then he was going to dispose of the contents of the towel….

"We have to save that," Amy said, reading his intentions. Baffled, he figured the pain had taken its toll on her senses.

"It goes in the freezer downstairs, and then into the ground next spring when I plant the baby's tree."

"Oh." He shrugged. "Whatever you say."

"Jody has a tree. Don't you, Jody?" Jody nodded, gratified to hear his name. "Come here and say hello to your new sister. I'm fine now, see? I'm just fine."

The back door opened, and a woman's voice called out, "Anybody home?"

"Mrs. Massey," Amy explained.

The bespectacled woman appeared in the bedroom doorway. Curiously, Tate heard no great flood of relief in Amy's greeting. "You just missed it, Mrs. Massey."

"I can see that." The stocky, middle-aged woman took account, acknowledging Tate with a nod as she removed her red quilted jacket. "My, my, my. Did you steal my job away?"

"I hope I didn't do anything…I mean, I hope I didn't make any mistakes."

"You didn't," Amy said happily. "You were wonderful. I don't know what I would have done if—"

"I should have been here earlier."

"I think that's my line," Mrs. Massey said. "But there are some little details I can attend to. I'm going to scrub up while you put that floor lamp right there next to the bed." She chucked Jody under the chin on her way back out the door. "What do you think, Jody? A brand-new baby. Isn't it fun?"

"Fun?" Hell of a way to spend Saturday night, Tate thought. Then he realized the sun had dawned somewhere along the line and it was actually Sunday morning. He shared a conspiratorial smile with Amy. "How are you feeling? Having fun yet? Can I bring you anything?"

"Mrs. Massey will tie up the loose ends, so to speak."

"I tied one up myself." He was grinning like a kid who'd hit a grand slam.

"Yes, you did. Thank you."

"You sure have a hell of a way of soberin' a guy up, lady." He couldn't understand how he could be steady as a rock and still feeling so high. "Both of you ladies. Look at her. She's sucking on her little hand."

Amy's hand went to the buttons on her nightgown. "Maybe I ought to—"

"Before you do that, let me do my little job," Mrs. Massey instructed as she swooped back into the room.

Tate leaned out of her way, but he was in no hurry to relinquish his post. He wasn't sure he liked the way the midwife took over on the baby, peeling the blanket back to scrutinize her.

"Oh, look at her color. Just what we like to see. Nothing old, nothing new, nothing borrowed, and especially nothing too blue."

Mrs. Massey gave the baby her first test and announced that her score was outstanding. Tate's suspicions fell away as he suppressed the urge to applaud. The woman recognized a perfect kid when she saw one. He was surprised when she bundled the baby back up in the flannel blanket and handed her to him.

"Now, if you and Jody would like to clean the little one up a bit while I tend to Amy…"

"She's so little." And she didn't want a bath. He could tell by the scrunched-up look in her face. "You mean just wash her with ordinary water?"

"Body temperature," Mrs. Massey instructed. "Water will comfort her. You can handle it. You've done fine so far."

He looked down at the tiny prunelike face nestled in the blanket, then glanced at Amy. She looked exhausted, but she nodded, her eyes bright with approval. Even now it amazed him to think she trusted him to take the precious bundle in his big, clumsy hands and leave the room. Instead of pleading incompetence he heard himself promise, "I'll be real careful."

"Jody knows where her clothes are," Amy said. "Jody, remember which drawer has the baby clothes?" Jody bobbed his head. "Will you pick out a little shirt like the one Tate's wearing and a little tiny sleeper like yours?"

"And a baby diaper?"

"Yes."

"And get the baby bath stuff?" He was out the door, sliding down the hallway on slick pajama feet. "I know where the baby bath stuff is, Tate. We have a baby towel, too."

Tate followed him to the third bedroom, which had been decorated in white and soft pastels for the long-awaited occupant. Jody opened the third bureau drawer and took out a white sleeper with a row of pink lambs marching across the yoke. "This brand-new one," he decided and held it up for Tate's review.

"Your mother will definitely approve."

"And here's the shirt, and these baby pants to keep her clothes dry and a—"

"What do you think, Jody? I say we turn the heat up a little and treat her just like a newborn calf that maybe took a chill, huh?"

"Uh-huh."

"You're just lucky there was an experienced cowhand in the house tonight, baby girl. And a little broomstick cowboy in training." He might have plopped a calf into the washtub downstairs, but he figured the kitchen sink would work better for this job. He closed the blind against the morning sunlight streaming through the window. Too much shock for a little person fresh out of the womb.

"We're a team, right, Jody?"

"Uh-huh." Jody climbed up on a chair and handed Tate a bottle of liquid baby soap and a soft hooded towel. "This is the stuff we have to use. She sure has messy hair."

"And a lot of it."

Mrs. Massey was right. The water seemed to soothe the infant. Tate ladled it over her with one hand as he cradled her head in his other palm. He didn't want to mess too much with her face, and he figured the white, waxy stuff was probably nature's cold cream, so he left it alone. But he knew a lady didn't like having sticky stuff in her hair. That had to go.

"Your next job is to find the hair dryer, partner."

"I know where it is!" And Jody was off like a shot.

"She's all cleaned up now," Tate announced as he lowered the fussy little one into her mother's arms. "She's just as pretty as a Thoroughbred filly, and she wants her mama right now."

"Oh, yes, come here, sweetie."

"Before I go, I have a few instructions for you menfolk," Mrs. Massey said. "Starting with taking care of Mom. After she rests, we want her to get up and walk a little, but we don't want her to overdo. It's up to you boys to do the cooking and the cleaning up for a few days, you got that? Because if you leave a mess in the kitchen, she's not going to rest until she gets it cleaned up."

"I'm not an invalid, Mrs. Massey."

"She's been using that line on me ever since I started to work for her," Tate said. "I'll snub her to the bedpost if I have to."

"You're the—" the older woman glanced at Amy, then back

to Tate "—hired hand?" He affirmed the title with a humble shrug, and she laughed. "Well, now you can *really* claim to be a jack-of-all-trades. I'll be stopping by daily for a while, but you call me if you need anything." She turned to Amy. "You know what kind of bleeding to expect. Anything heavy, any dizziness or fainting—" The finger was pointed Amy's way, but the final charge was given to Tate. "—she goes to the hospital."

"Got it."

"Don't let that baby keep her from getting her rest. Got a name for her yet?"

"Karen," Amy said—reverently, because it was the first time. "Karen Marie Becker."

It was a nice name, Tate thought. He had an aunt named Karen, but she lived in Texas. And his mother's name had been Mary. He liked it. Karen Marie…Becker.

Of course it was Becker. She was Kenny's daughter. He'd just helped to bring his best friend's daughter into the world, given her her first bath and dressed her for the first time. And now she had a name. Nothing wrong with Karen Marie Becker…except that when Amy had said that last part out loud, it had felt like a pinprick in his euphoric bubble.

Mrs. Massey gave him a colleague's pat on the back before she left, declaring that more duty called her. "The stork's having a field day in Overo. Now that you've got your feet wet, how about—"

"Not a chance," Tate demurred with palms raised in self-defense. "I don't care to press my luck."

"Luck, schmuck. The Lord doesn't always give us what we think we want, but most times He gives us what we need." She punctuated her homily with a nod and a smile. "He gave you stork wings last night, Mister Hired Hand."

Stork wings? Tate flexed the muscles in his back as he

watched Mrs. Massey back her Blazer down the driveway. He did feel a pinch right above the shoulder blades.

He stuck his head in the door of Amy's bedroom. "Can I get you anything? A glass of milk maybe—whoa!" A short-armed tackle pinned him around the knees. He looked down, and Jody looked up, pleading to be noticed.

"Jody…" Amy applied the universal mother's warning tone.

"You got a steer wrestler's grip, there, partner." Tate lifted the boy into his arms. "We got our instructions, and we're at your service, ma'am."

"Karen might take you up on that glass of milk. It's slim pickings until mine comes in."

The baby was asleep in her mother's arms. Tate and Jody looked on like shepherds in a crèche.

"Is there colostrum?" Tate asked absently. He glanced up and caught her eyes laughing at him. Hell, he didn't know. He was just curious.

"Like with cows and sheep? Yes, for the first few days. We mammal mamas are all the same."

"So, you want some kind of oat—" he winked at Jody and teased Amy with a grin "—meal?"

"I want you to sit with us. You and Jody." She nodded toward the wicker rocker next to the bed.

"C'mon, cowboy," Tate said. "Come take a ride on your partner's knee."

"We couldn't have managed this without you two." Amy touched the baby's cheek. "She came a lot quicker than Jody did. She didn't give me much warning at all."

"Women are like that. You never know what to expect." Tate jiggled his knee, and Jody bobbled happily. "You remember that, partner. Every woman's got her own timing, and there's no point in a man tryin' to set his watch by it."

"I can't think of a single comeback, so I guess we'll let that one stand." She smiled at the sleeping infant. "For now. Right, Karen? When they're good, they're very, very good. And today they were incredible."

"And whenever you're willin' to give in that easy, you have to be very, very tired," Tate observed. "We've already put in a big day, and there's still about sixteen hours to go. You're one of those bosses that doesn't give a guy time to sleep it off."

"I think we'll all be napping today." She couldn't take her eyes off the tiny, tranquil face. "One of us has already started."

"And one more is on her way." Time for the boys to take their leave. "That's you, so if you've got any other surprises, lay them on me before I head out to the barn to get started on the chores. I've got another load of hay coming today."

"No more surprises. Just gratitude."

"Just doin' my job, ma'am."

"You need rest, too," she told him.

"I'll get it eventually." Tate grinned. "Now, if I was a sheepherder, I could lie around on the hillsides all day and do all kinds of cloud-dreamin', but a cowboy's work is never done."

But it didn't matter. Today he had adrenaline to spare.

He'd never imagined himself holding a baby, much less delivering one. Thinking about it made him feel a little weak in the knees. When he told Myron Olson about it, he couldn't help grinning like a sailor on shore leave. Myron was so tickled, he offered to throw in another load of hay. Tate told him he could bring over another horse, too.

He climbed into the driver's seat of Amy's big John Deere 4020. He was beginning to feel the effects of lack of sleep.

Once he got Myron's flatbed unloaded and fed all his charges, he figured he would be ready to hit the hay himself.

He didn't know how the dogs had gotten out, but they were making fools of themselves again, chasing a damn tumbleweed. As he started backing the tractor he took a quick check over his shoulder. For a split second he saw Jody's face looking up at him just beyond the rolling ridges of one big black tire. Then it was just the tire.

The whole sky toppled over on him. He heard a piercing scream, and for a moment the world went black. His legs wouldn't work, nor would his arms, and his head wouldn't turn. He was surrounded by shouting, and the scream rose in terror, pitched so high it was beyond the reach of his ears. It was infinite, soundless, nameless and timeless.

When the scream plummeted back to the present, it was lodged in his own throat. He whirled and spat it out as he dropped to the ground. And there stood Jody, looking up at him, wide-eyed, trusting and innocent as always.

Trembling terror overrode reality as Tate towered over the child. He leaned down, his big hands laying claim to slight shoulders, making sure they were real. Sweet Lord, he hadn't been touched, had he? He was still in one—

"I damn near ran over you, boy!"

"I f-found my horse's ear." Shyly, Jody displayed a scrap of leather, as if such an offering might assuage the big man's anger.

"Jody, I just barely saw you. I almost…" Tate sputtered, his heart racing. He pointed a gloved finger and commanded with all the fervor of Moses, "You go in the house now. I'll look at that later. You go inside and stay out of the way."

He saw Jody's lip quiver, saw the tears welling in the little boy's eyes as he turned and ran toward the house. The same tears burned deep in his own brain. Remembered tears. God, it could happen all over again, so easily, in the blink of an eye. He turned and stared the damn tractor down, its bucket-loader lifted skyward as if to say, "Don't blame me. It's Tate Harrison again."

Damn, he hated operating farm equipment. He would rather buck out a horse any day. At least then the only neck he was likely to break was his own.

The house was quiet when he went back inside. He thought about looking for Jody first thing, but he felt so bad about the way he'd barked at him that he decided to make supper instead. He wondered what a person who'd just had a baby would feel like eating. He wondered whether a little person who'd just had his butt chewed out by a big person with a thick head would feel like eating anything at all. Down at the end of the hallway, behind the closed bedroom door, he could hear the baby, bleating like a hungry lamb. The crying ceased abruptly, and Tate wondered whether little Karen was getting real milk yet.

Too soon, he thought, but obviously Amy was able to give the baby what she needed. He wished he had something like that to give Jody right now. Something warm and nourishing, something that would flow easily, without worthless apologies or asinine explanations. Hell, Jody was just a little boy. Tate was the one who had a history of being careless. *Tate* was the one.

He stood awkwardly outside Amy's door, flexed his hand a couple of times before he rapped his knuckles on the wood and quietly announced himself. "Are you girls decent? Can I bring in some food?"

"Come in." Amy braced herself and slid up gingerly, reaching around to adjust her pillows. "Oh, my, we've just been sleeping and nursing, nursing and sleeping. Karen's sleeping again."

"Figured you'd fed her." He handed her a mug of chicken soup, then stuffed an extra pillow behind her. "Figured *I'd* feed *you*."

"Thank you." She smiled sleepily. "Just for today. You won't have to do this tomorrow."

"I want to." He sat on the edge of the bed. "I'm not real great at it, but I can open a can."

"Have you and Jody eaten?"

"We will in a minute. I wasn't sure where...I mean, I thought he might be in here with you. Guess he must be in his room." He glanced at the bassinet he'd brought in earlier and set next to the bed, within Amy's reach. It hadn't been too long since Jody had slept in that little straw bed. "Did he tell you...that I acted like a jerk a while ago?"

"What do you mean?"

"I didn't know he was outside. I was backing up the tractor. He was standing pretty close." He closed his eyes and gave his head a quick shake. "I...I made him go in the house."

"There's nothing wrong with that, Tate."

"Yeah, but I yelled at him. I haven't been around kids much. All I know is when a calf tries to get himself into a bad place, you put a scare into him, send him packing." He couldn't look at her, but he could feel her looking at him. He could feel her waiting. "I scared Jody. I scared him worse than—" he swallowed hard "—worse than he scared me."

"You yelled at him? Is that all?" she asked quietly, and he heard the fear in her voice.

"I grabbed him by the shoulders. I was so glad he was still standing there, I don't know if I held him too tight, but I shouted right in his face and I...I told him to stay out of the way. Like I was tellin' him it was his fault, when it was mine."

He turned to her, his voice as doleful as autumn rain. "I didn't hit him. I wouldn't do that, I swear."

"I didn't think you would, Tate." Wearily he rose to his feet. She caught his hand. "What are you going to do?"

"See if he's awake. Ask him if he's hungry." He squeezed her hand, then let it go as he stepped back from the bed.

"Tell him why you shouted at him."

"What difference does it make why?" Her eyes held his until he knew he needed the answer for himself. "I was scared stupid, that's why."

"Tell him that."

"What if he doesn't want me…" *Around him. Close to him. Breathing his air.* "…want to look at me or anything?"

"Give him the benefit of the doubt, Tate. He's a very mature four-year-old. He knows about safety and responsibility. I've taught him that." She nodded encouragingly. "Just ask him if he's hungry. That'll be a start."

He found Jody sprawled on his stomach, driving his toy cars down the parallel roads in the hardwood floor in his bedroom. He looked up, surprised, but he lowered his chin quickly and went back to his cars.

"Don't mean to interrupt, but I've got some supper ready."

"Not hungry."

"Your mom said you liked those little baby hot dogs in the can. I fixed you some with biscuits and soup." Jody looked up again. "And some chocolate milk," Tate added, encouraged. "You like chocolate milk?"

Jody rolled his toes against the wood and wagged his heels back and forth. But his belly seemed glued to the floor.

Tate noticed the broomstick horse lying on the bed, along with the detached leather ear. Moving like old molasses, he made himself walk over to the bed. He picked up the broken toy as he seated himself. He felt like a giant in a dollhouse sitting on the youth bed, which hadn't been made that day. The sheets were printed with teddy bear cowboys riding rocking horses and spinning perfect loops above their ten-gallon hats.

"I promised I'd fix this, didn't I?"

"I found the ear in my toy box," Jody reported as he lined two cars up side by side.

"And that was good finding." Tate watched him add a third car to the row, then a fourth. "I'm sorry I yelled at you before." A yellow car came into line, but this one drove up slowly. "I know I sounded like I was mad at you. I wasn't. Not really."

With his thumb on its roof Jody rocked the yellow car back and forth on its diminutive wheels. "I'm not supposed to get around the tractor when it's running," he confided quietly. "The tires are big, and the PTO can grab my hair or my shirt and really get me hurt."

"That's right." As formidable as the huge tires were, the tractor's power takeoff was an appalling threat, and the danger of lost limbs was one of the earliest warnings every ranch kid heard. "Your mom has told you all that, huh?"

"Oh, yeah. And my dad." He sat up, pivoted on his bottom and looked up at Tate. "I just forgot for a minute."

"I know. That can happen." Tate glanced at the yellow car as he laced his fingers together. "You know what happened to me when I looked down and saw you there?"

"No."

"I was scared I was gonna hit you. And I yelled at you because I was mad at myself for not seeing you sooner." His eyes darted back to the anxious little face. "The driver is responsible, Jody. Not you. When you're driving a vehicle, you have to make sure there's nothing behind you, nothing in front of you that you might hit…."

But Tate realized that there was only one thing the boy understood. The big man had been as threatening as the big tractor. "I'm sorry," Tate offered. "I didn't mean to yell at you. It wasn't your fault. It was mine." The boy hung his head. "I scared you, huh?"

Jody nodded. "I was a little bit scared."

"I was a lot scared." Tate lifted his hands and spread them in invitation, and Jody scrambled to his feet and came running. He threw his arms around Tate's neck with grateful abandon, and Tate closed his eyes and hugged him for all he was worth.

"It was a close call, Jody. You know what a close call is?"

"I could have got hit by the tractor?"

"After a close call is all over, it's too late to be scared, but it doesn't matter. It still haunts you for a while, kind of like a bad dream." He leaned back and looked Jody in the eye. "If I'd hurt you, I don't know what I would have done."

"You'd take me to the doctor, wouldn't you?"

"Yes, I would." He lifted the boy onto his lap. "I sure would. We're partners."

"We're partners."

"We birthed a baby together today, didn't we? You and me, we helped your little sister get born." Jody tested the prickliness of Tate's stubble against his palm, and Tate smiled. "'Course, your mom did most of the work. That's why she was making all that noise—because it's hard work pushing the baby out. That's why they call it *labor*. And now she needs rest, so we're gonna do all the work around here, 'cause she's done her share for a while."

"I can fix my own bed, and I can feed Daisy and Duke and Cinnamon Toast."

"And I can feed you," Tate said as he patted Jody's bottom. "You ready to eat?"

Not quite. Jody was still thinking. "It scared me more when *she* yelled," he mused. "I never heard her yell like that before."

"And then I yelled, and you must think all the grown-ups went crazy today. But we're okay now. It's been a crazy, terrible, fantastic day, and we made it through." He squeezed Jody's shoulder. "So let's have ourselves something to eat."

"Are you gonna shave?" Jody asked as they headed toward the kitchen.

"Prob'ly I should."

"Can I watch?"

Amy laid her head back against the pillow and closed her eyes. Tate Harrison was such a difficult man to figure out. One minute he was out boozing with Overo's hell-raisers, and the next he was bringing her daughter into the world with more levelheadedness and every bit as much tender concern as she might have expected from her child's own father. She'd never seen Tate more shaken than he'd been today, or more jubilant.

Vigilant as any brooding hen, she was glad she'd been able to eavesdrop on the conversation he'd had with Jody across the hall. She wasn't sure what to make of the terrible guilt she'd seen in Tate's eyes when he'd told her about the incident with Jody, but she knew he had not harmed her son. She breathed a long, gratified sigh. She was fundamentally independent, but she had trusted Tate with a most intimate and momentous task, and he had come through for her in spades. Thank God she could continue to trust him with her son.

She wasn't going to start relying on him, she reminded herself. The man's feet were made of sand. But he had more heart than she'd ever given him credit for, and she was hoping she could lean on that particular muscle and a few others until she could truly get back on her feet again. She wouldn't *depend* on his support. But as long as he was willing to stay, it wouldn't hurt to lean on it, just a little.

Chapter 6

When Amy's milk came in her breasts blew up like twin beach balls. Tate had never seen anything like it. He'd brought her a sandwich and discovered, once again, a changed woman. He tried not to stare, but she caught him at it. She laughed, he thought quite charitably. He stared at the toes of his boots, then tried to zoom back up to her face. But his damned eyes were drawn right back to the same amazing transformation in her otherwise almost-back-to-normal body.

He shook his head and gave up trying to be cool. "Are they gonna stay like that?"

Now she howled. "Lord have mercy, I have finally arrived. Voluptuous at last."

"Well, either way, I mean…I always thought you had a nice—" *Chest on you.* He tore his eyes away as he groped for an alternative. "*Shape.* Really nice. But, you know, this is… nice, too."

"They won't stay this way long." She accepted the proffered

plate and gave a quick shrug. "My milk just came in with a vengeance is all."

"Do they hurt?"

"Suck in a real deep breath." He complied. "Now suck in some more. Now a little more. Feel like you're gonna bust yet?" He nodded. She took up the sandwich. "Now hold it for a couple of days and see if it hurts."

He deflated quickly. "I gotta give up those cigarettes. Damn, that pinches."

"Exactly." Amy set her own lunch aside on the signal of soft baby murmurs. "Would you like to hand me my little milk drainer?"

Tate stepped over to the bassinet. Karen had kicked off her pink blanket, tiny legs churning involuntarily. He folded it around her and lifted her in his hands. She was cranking up to cry, but she changed her mind when he cuddled her against his chest. He liked the sweet little sounds she made, even though she was rooting around a dry well.

"Can't help you there, little girl. Your mama's got what you want and then some." He shifted Karen for the transfer as he came to the side of the bed. "You got a preference which side?"

"Ready on the right, ready on the left."

The buttons on Amy's nightgown already lay open between her bulging breasts. Tate swallowed hard. Amy pulled her white gown aside as he laid the baby in the crook of her left arm, positioning the little pink cheek near the source of mother's milk. The miniature mouth fit over the distended nipple like a trailer coupling. Tate felt a surge of excitement that had nothing to do with hunger and little to do with sex. Pride, maybe. He wasn't ogling, but he was having a hell of a time tearing his eyes away.

"Would you hand me a bath towel off the dresser?" Amy asked.

He snatched it up and returned to her, glanced in her eyes for permission, then admired the tranquil activity at her breast again. A wet spot was quickly growing over her right breast, and he understood the need for the towel. Impulsively he knelt beside the bed. She lifted her right elbow. He tucked the towel under her side and arranged it over her breast.

"I keep getting everything wet."

"I'll change the bed when you're done." The baby's contented little noises made him smile. "Seems like a waste of good produce."

"There's such an abundance to start with. If I were a ewe, I'd probably have twins. Two mouths to suckle."

Now it *did* have something to do with sex, something to do with a man's urge to kiss a woman at the damnedest times. His head was falling fast. He was drowning in her eyes, sinking like a stone, going under for the third time. When the authorities dredged up his corpse, it would be obvious where he carried the lead weight that had pulled him under. He hoped she would be able to explain it away in the eulogy.

Amy saw it coming, and she met it head-on with a warm, wet, open-mouthed kiss.

Just one kiss, but it was a real breath-stealer. When it was over, he couldn't quite draw away. Forehead to forehead they rested, their mouths sharing hot breath, their nostrils filled with the scent of sweet milk.

"I couldn't help myself," he whispered.

"It's all right." She drew a long, slow breath. "A woman needs a man's kiss when she's…" He lifted his head and looked expectantly into her eyes. She glanced away. "I heard you talking to Jody. I get scared, too, sometimes. When I realized I was in labor, and I knew I was alone, I really got scared."

She wasn't alone now. He wanted her to know that. He cupped his hand around her cheek and kissed her again, more gently this time. He couldn't remember when he'd ever gotten down on his knees to kiss a woman. He told himself that he just wanted to assure her that he was there, but her lips were remarkably responsive, and she tasted so damn good.

She took his hand, put it on her belly, then covered it with hers and pressed it tight. He felt a bulge in her stomach, but it was hard, like muscle.

"It hurts when the baby nurses," she explained quietly. "It's nature's way of making my uterus contract back down to size, but it…" Her fingers dug into the back of his hand. He took the hint and began kneading the knot in her belly. "I've had enough of pain," she said.

"Yes, you have." If he could take it away, he would thank her for the privilege. "It doesn't seem fair. It was hard to watch you suffer with it. It's no wonder you were scared."

"I was afraid for my baby. I was afraid I wasn't strong enough." She tipped her head back against the pillow, eyes closed as she remembered. "I was going to call someone else, the sheriff or someone, but I was afraid it was too late for anyone to…" She gave him her soft earth-mother smile. "Thank you for coming back in time, Tate."

"I shouldn't have left."

He never should have left Overo in the first place, not without her. He should have stayed and fought for her instead of letting Kenny…

Oh, hell, he'd been through all this before, beating himself up inside in a way that no other judge or critic could manage. It was pointless. Kenny was the family man, not Tate.

"I shouldn't have left at all *that night*," he clarified, still kneading her gently. "I knew your time was close. I shouldn't have left you alone."

"But you're not my husband, so you didn't owe me that kind of commitment."

"No." He knew she meant to absolve him. He wasn't sure why it felt like a rejection. "I'm not your husband. But I'm your husband's best friend. I'm, uh…" Reluctantly he drew his hand back and pushed himself to his feet. "Committed to him. His memory. To taking good care of his wife and his—"

"Tate, don't—"

"And his kids. Anything for Kenny's family. You need anything—food, sheets, towels…" He tossed her a cocky wink. "You need a man's kiss, honey, you just call on me anytime."

He brooded on that scene for the rest of the day. He would have gone into town and gotten himself good and drunk if it weren't for the fact that there was so damn much work to do around the place. That night he fixed Jody's broomstick horse. He gave it a new horsehair mane. He'd culled the black hair from a trimming he'd given the gelding he'd stopped thinking of as Kenny's horse and started calling Outlaw. He fixed the ears and the frayed rein, and he gave it a whole new broomstick.

Jody's response to the refurbished toy couldn't have been more rewarding for Tate if he'd bought the boy something grand and new and presented it all tied up with a big red bow. Jody announced that his horse's new name was Outlaw, Jr., and that he was going to ride him "up and down and all around the town." He was Amy's mounted escort when she went out to the barn "just to say hello" to a ewe that Tate had brought back from the pasture and treated for foot rot. And Tate was the baby-sitter.

"How's my little girl?" he whispered as he knelt beside the bassinet. Since nobody but Karen could hear him, he figured he could indulge himself in the possessive claim. The baby knew what he meant. She grabbed his forefinger, and they shook on it.

He liked the soft little baby sounds she made as she waved her fist and turned her head from side to side, trying to focus on his face. "What are you telling me, huh? What do you see? It's not your mama's face. Kinda bristly. Needs a shave, same as it did the first time you saw it. Remember how you bawled? Was I that scary?"

He picked her up, taking a yellow flannel blanket with her, and he held her high against his shoulder. "Not anymore, huh? Wanna go for a little walk and see some more stuff?" *Just you and me, kid. Nobody else hears me babbling like this.* "You know what? You're not scary anymore, either. I've gotten used to you being such a little tyke."

He rubbed her flannel-covered back as he carried her into the living room, just for a change of scene. "'Course, this is as little as you'll ever be. Next time I come to visit…" She rewarded his back rubbing with what seemed like a very big burp for one so small. Having unwittingly done her a service, he smiled as he went on talking. "Well, you'll be a lot bigger next time. You'll be walking tall and talking big, just like your brother, Jody." His smile faded as he stared out the window at the distant mountain peaks. "And you won't remember me."

Amy came through the back door with a mighty, "Whew! Feels like I just ran the marathon." Tate could hear "Outlaw, Jr." clopping at her side across the kitchen floor. Amy looked surprised when she saw him in the living room with the baby. "Is she already hungry again?"

"No, but she was awake, and she's wantin' to tell the world hello, too, just like her mama."

"I have to get active and get my strength back." Her cheeks were rosy. From where Tate stood she was looking pretty bright-eyed, bushy-tailed and back in charge as she took the baby from him. "I'll make supper," she said.

"Tired of my canned soup and cold meat sandwiches?"

"I know you guys are ready for a change. Chicken and dumplings?" A pint-size lasso loop landed over the back of a chair. "Jody, I asked you not to do that in the house. Maybe Tate could give you a bike-riding lesson while I make supper?"

"We could play with the baby while you cook," Tate suggested.

"She doesn't know how to play." She rocked the baby in the crook of her arm. "And anyway, she's almost asleep."

"C'mon, partner." Disgusted, Tate reached for his jacket. "We're gettin' kicked out of the kitchen."

"It'll be worth your while, I promise."

Yeah, right. Tate left the house feeling as peevish as a wet cat. Jody followed at his heels in the same mood. He kicked a tire on his bicycle as he passed it in the yard. Tate turned, one eyebrow cocked solicitously.

"I don't wanna ride that ol' bike." Jody pouted. "I like to ride horses. When I get big, I'm gonna have a real horse, but I won't fall off, and I won't get killed. I'm gonna be a cowboy, like you."

"What should we do with this?" Tate's nod indicated the bike.

"Put it in the shed."

"Good idea." He lifted the offending toy by its handlebars, and they headed for the shed together. "Out of your mother's sight, out of her mind, huh?"

"She just came out here and petted that ewe that's limping around, and then she went back to that baby."

"Uh-oh." Tate remembered what it was like to be upstaged by an attention-grabbing new baby. "How do you like the new baby, Jody?"

"She doesn't *do* nuthin'. She just cries and smells funny." Jody kicked at the gravel in his path. "I told you a brother would be better than a sister. I wanted a baby brother."

"And I told you, they're both the same at first. They don't do much. Karen couldn't go out to the corral with me and help me feed Outlaw."

"I could!"

"And since she can't even sit up yet, I couldn't put her up on Outlaw's back and lead her around."

"You could do that with me. I can sit up." His feet suddenly stopped dragging.

By the time they'd reached the shed, Tate wondered whether Jody had springs on the bottoms of his tennis shoes. "That's just what I was thinkin'. The thing is, we might not wanna mention it to your mom." He spared the boy a warning glance as he turned the handle on the door. "I mean, unless she asks. Then we'd have to 'fess up."

"What does *'fess up* mean?"

"Means a cowboy tells the truth when his mom puts a question to him. It's part of the code."

"What's a code?"

He didn't mind Jody's questions. He took a shot at answering every one. Too many of his own questions had been ignored when he was a kid, and he'd been looking for answers ever since. He'd found a few, but he was still looking for the big ones. Fortunately, either Jody hadn't thought up the big questions, or he'd decided to break Tate in easy. Baby girls were easily explained. Women were something else.

At bedtime Amy read Jody two extra stories, sticking with

it until he fell asleep. When she returned to her room, she was surprised to find Tate sitting on the bed with Karen. Wonder of wonders, he was putting on a clean diaper. Amy tried to remember the last time she'd seen a man voluntarily tend to that particular chore.

"I was eavesdropping on the stories again," he admitted. "Jody says he wants to be a cowboy, and when he follows me out to the pickup, he tries to take steps as big as mine." Intent on his job, he didn't look up until he'd finished carefully fastening the second pin. "But he's not quite done being your first baby."

"I'm afraid he's going to grow up faster than either of us really wants him to."

"Either of *us?*"

"Either him or me." She couldn't help smiling. "I never thought I'd see Tate Harrison change a baby's diaper."

"Nothin' to it. Right, Karen?" He slid both hands under the baby and lifted her to his shoulder. "Only one thing ol' Tate can't do for you, and that's feed you. That's up to Mom, whose—" his eyes danced mischievously as he glanced at Amy "—jugs appear to be getting smaller, so I'd say you'd better get while the gettin's still good."

"Jugs?" She postured, hands on hips. "You'd better watch it, cowboy."

"Hey, just because you domesticate me a little, it doesn't mean I'm show-ring material."

She glanced down at her chest. "There's no less milk, just a little less pouf. I'm not show-ring material, either."

"You did a lot today." He piled the pillows against the headboard to make a backrest for her as she joined him on the bed. "I read somewhere that having a baby's like having major surgery. Takes a while to get your strength back."

"Where did you read that?"

"One of the magazines in that pile downstairs." Reluctantly Tate handed the baby over to her mother.

"Wouldn't be Ken's old *Quarter Horse Journal*s. Must be one of my old *Parents* magazines."

"Yeah, well, I've already read all the horse stuff." He planted his hands on his knees. "I'll go check on—"

"Stay, Tate." She worked the buttons on her nightgown with one hand. "We haven't talked much since—" the soft look in her eyes personalized her invitation "—since the last time you watched me do this."

"You don't mind if I watch you take your—" That's not it, he told himself, and he gripped his knees a little tighter as the last button slid though its hole. "Watch you feed the baby?"

"You've seen all there is to see. More than my husband saw, in fact." The blue-flowered flannel slid away, baring her round, scarlet nipple. "I went to the hospital when I had Jody. Kenny wasn't there."

"Really?" Tate didn't want to know why. He didn't want to talk about Kenny at all right now. Not with Amy's breast bared for the baby and blessings bestowed on his voyeurism. He wondered whether her nipples were sore. "Do you need a towel?"

"I have one." She patted the bed, offering him the spot right next to her. "I promise not to squirt you."

"You could squirt me?" Mesmerized, he moved closer.

"On a good day I have a six-foot range."

"Does it taste like regular milk?" He glanced up and caught her smiling indulgently, the way he might look at Jody. Hell, he had his questions, too. He told himself to watch the baby suckle, think warm milk, and he would have the general idea. "I guess I've had it, but I don't..."

She uncovered her free breast.

He lifted his gaze to hers. "...remember."

She couldn't make the offer in words, but her eyes were willing, mainly because he'd always been so easy on them. He was a beautiful man. His dark eyes held her gaze as he dipped his head slightly. Then he glanced down at the blue-white liquid dribbling down the underside of her breast. His full, sensuous lips parted as he looked into her eyes one more time to make sure. She nodded almost imperceptibly. He touched her nipple with the tip of his tongue.

She held her breath as he passed his tongue back and forth. The flow increased, and he took the bud of her nipple gently between his lips and let the milk leak into his mouth. He was cautious, like a humble petitioner, asking only to glean the overflow, while the tiny mouth on the left side was all business, working her like a milkmaid.

"Is it awful?" Amy asked timidly.

He made a low, contented sound, brushing his nose against her, scarcely moving his head in demurral. She forgot about her soreness. She forgot about feeling a little shy around him because she had been extraordinarily vulnerable and exposed, and she'd had time to reflect on what he might have seen and thought and felt. But for the moment misgivings and discomfort took a backseat in the presence of pure and natural tenderness.

He put his hand over her belly and felt for the distended muscle he'd learned so much about in recent days. He found it and massaged slowly, testing her receptiveness. "Does it still hurt here?" His lips hovered close to their post.

"Not as much, but…" *Yes, do that. Oh, yes, Tate, help me heal*.

"Will it hurt if I…suck a little?"

"Not if you're gentle."

He was gentle. The man who was wildness personified now suckled her with exquisite gentleness. She could not think how wanton she must be to permit such a thing. She could only feel. Deeply touched by the potential of his power bridled by his own tight control, she relinquished her doubts and permitted herself a separation from anxiety, however brief.

"It's warm and sweet," he murmured appreciatively. "Am I taking candy from the…" A tear slipped silently from the corner of Amy's eye and slid down her cheek. His heart fell with it.

"She's fallen asleep," Amy said quickly. He drew back, and she covered herself with her open nightgown as she got up to put Karen to bed. "Does it taste like candy?"

Propped on one elbow, feeling foolish and deserted, he watched her bend over the bassinet, absently clutching her nightgown together in front. What kind of stupid, juvenile thing had he done, and what in hell was he going to do with the ache it had left him with?

She straightened slowly and laid her hand over her eyes. His problem was minor. She turned, her face full of desolate tears and confusion, and he knew that, no matter who she was looking for on her bed, Tate Harrison was all she had. She sat down next to him. His problem was major again.

"Would you hold me for a while?" she asked.

"Sure." He reached for her, and she buried her face against his neck. He knew better than to expect an outpouring of emotion. This was Amy. She was stingy with her tears, and she sure as hell didn't shed them over spilled milk. "You were thinking about…somebody besides me."

"No." She put her arms around his middle and sighed. "Ken would never have done what you just did."

"I was just curious," he claimed.

She looked up at him, smiling through unshed tears.

"Okay, so maybe *curious* isn't the right word. Maybe I was just flyin' by the seat of my pants." Maybe that was exactly what he'd been doing since he'd first heard about Kenny's death, telling himself he had nothing but good intentions. "I'm sorry if I embarrassed you or made you feel...guilty or something."

She closed her eyes and buried her face again. This time he could feel her trembling. "Don't cry, honey."

"I can't help it," she sobbed. "I have to cry. Isn't that stupid?"

"No stupider than what I did. I didn't mean to do anything bad, I just—"

"It wasn't bad," she insisted, sniffling. "You were trying to make me feel...to help me..." She hated it when she got like this. "There's no reason for this ridiculous crying, so I'm stopping right now. See?" She used her hand until he plucked a tissue from the box on the night table and handed it to her.

She glanced ruefully at his shirt as she wiped her nose. "I'm getting you wet."

"Don't worry about it. It's a release, like we all need from time to time." *If she only knew.* "It's a natural thing, honey. Perfectly natural."

"Yes, I suppose. I try to convince myself I'm above those things, but obviously..." She gestured in frustration, the pink tissue balled up in her hand. "I do know the only thing I have to be embarrassed about is the way I've always—" She glanced up, red-eyed and apologetic. "I've always sold you short."

"You mean I ain't as cheap as what you thought?" he drawled with half a smile.

"It didn't surprise me that you bid the horses up. It was the kind of grand gesture I would have expected, and, after all, it was *only* money." Still shaky, she took a deep, steadying breath. "But the Tate Harrison I *thought* I knew would have walked away after that, satisfied he'd done his duty to his old *compadre*."

He had come close to doing just that. "Honey, if I'd known you'd taken up sheepherdin'…"

"One favor," she entreated. "Try to remember not to call me 'honey.'"

"Is that what Kenny called you?"

"No." She smiled. "He called me 'Aims.' I don't want you to call me that, either." With a quick motion she erased the very idea. "I've heard you call at least a dozen other women 'honey.' It rolls off your tongue too easily, and it doesn't fit me."

"How about Bossy?"

She pressed her hand to her lactating breast and groaned.

"How about 'Black-Eyed Susan'?" he offered quietly, and the bittersweet reminder of "the road not taken" gave them both sober pause. He glanced away. "I'll come up with something better. Just give me a little time."

Her real question was, how much time would he give her?

His real question was, how much would she accept?

"Would you like me to fill the tub for you?" he asked.

"I guess you've noticed it's one of my favorite places to be lately."

"I can't imagine why." His smile faded as he searched her eyes. "Does everything…seem to be healing up the way it's supposed to? I asked Mrs. Massey if everything was okay when she checked you over the other day, and she said, 'Just fine, and how are you?' Like I was askin' after *her* health." He gave a quick shrug. "Which I could have been, for all the conversation I had with her. She probably thought that was all the hired hand needed to know."

"She's a woman of few words, and that was all the news.

But I have one more important thing to say." She took his hand in hers, and he lost himself in her eyes. "Thanks for asking."

He nodded. "Nice and warm, but not too hot, right?"

She nodded, too.

Half an hour later Amy emerged from the bathroom in her long white terry-cloth robe. Tate was watching TV in the living room when she came in to say good-night.

"Can I get you anything else?" he offered as he rose from the chair. He'd made himself some coffee. "Maybe some milk or some tea?"

"If you don't stop being so nice, I'm going to start crying again."

But she offered no objections when he took her in his arms again. Her hair was damp, and she smelled of strawberry soap. Hugging her felt right. Kissing her would feel even better. "Ask me to hold you through the night, Amy."

"Tate, I can't have—"

"I know that. It's just good to hold you. It made me feel good when you asked me to."

"I think maybe we're both kind of turned inside out right now, Tate. I know I am, and I know it would be a mistake for us to spend the night in the same bed." She leaned back and gripped his arms as she looked up at him. "A big, big mistake."

"Turned inside out" was a good way of putting it. He told himself to keep that in mind while he straightened up the kitchen and thumbed through a magazine. His damn ear had turned itself inside out. He wasn't sure when he'd started keeping it cocked for the baby's cry or for the sound of little pajama-covered feet shuffling down the hallway.

He heard the telltale squeak of Jody's bedroom door open. No footsteps. Amy was looking in on him. Maybe she was thinking about changing her mind about Tate. Maybe if Jody was sound asleep, and maybe if Amy was having second thoughts about her own empty bed, then *maybe* Tate wouldn't be spending another night tossing and turning on that wretched cot.

But the family slept upstairs. Their hired hand slept in the basement. Damn it all, it wasn't *his* family. She wasn't his wife and they weren't his kids. He was doing it all for the *late* Kenny Becker, his best friend. He heard her footsteps and the softer chirp Tate had learned to recognize as the hinges on her bedroom door. There was a pause.

"Good night, Tate."

"Good night."

By Thanksgiving there was snow, and it was time to bring the sheep closer to home. Tate wanted to leave Daisy and Duke at home, but Amy insisted that the dogs would save him time. They might have saved *Amy* time, but they were playing games with Tate this time out. When he dismounted and opened a gate, the dogs turned the herd and ran them down the fence line. Tate waved his arms and whistled and cussed to no avail. The sheep were scattered to hell and back, and all the dogs wanted to do was frolic in the wet snow.

By the time Tate had bunched the herd up again, the dogs were nowhere in sight, which was just fine by him. It was nightfall, and he was cold and hungry. He and Outlaw could push the herd without the help of any fancy dogs, just as soon as he figured out where the hell he was. The snow had thawed some during the day, but dropping temperatures had formed a crust that glistened by moonlight. The rolling hills all looked the same. But for the crunch of hooves breaking the snow crust and the creak of leather, the night was calm and quiet.

It was the kind of night that used to bring Kenny over to his place for a moonlight ride.

This was no time to let himself start thinking about Kenny. Tate's butt was getting numb. His face was stiff with the cold. If Amy was his friend, she would have a hot bath and a shot of whiskey waiting for him.

But Kenny was his friend, or had been, and Tate had an eerie feeling that he was surveying the same moonscape Kenny had been looking at that last night. He sensed that he was hearing the last sounds Kenny had heard. "Did you lose your bearings that night, buddy?" he asked the night breeze. "Did you get turned around the way we used to sometimes?"

Kenny had been out joyriding that night. Tate was doing a job. He was trying to bring Amy's herd in. Not that he was drawing any comparisons or thinking any critical thoughts concerning the dead.

"I never interfered with you, man, except that once. But she was your woman, 'til death do you part. And she misses you. Hell, *I* miss you. So I'm tryin' to do the right thing, here, helpin' her out." He tipped his hat in unconscious deference to the myriad stars. "She's one hell of a woman. She always was, even though it seemed like she was afraid to loosen up and just have fun."

Okay, so maybe his wits had left camp temporarily, but he figured he could count on the witnesses to keep his secret.

"I have a feeling you can hear me tonight, Kenny. Either that, or I'm talkin' to myself. Or a bunch of dumb sheep."

Amazing how close the big ewe's bleating resembled laughter.

"What's that, you big pile of wool? You're sayin' I'm the one who's lost? Hell, I know where I am. I'm back in Montana. Big Sky Country." He lifted his eyes to the diamond-studded, black velvet sky. "I hope. It damn sure ain't heaven if Tate Harrison's allowed in, right, buddy?"

Tate read his answer in the distant glow of Amy's yard light. He managed a stiff-lipped grin. "But it's likely as close as I'll ever come."

Chapter 7

"Mom, where's Tate?"

Amy turned from the window. "He's bringing the sheep in, Jody." But the pens were still empty, the west gate was still closed and there was nothing stirring on the snow-covered hill above it. "He's out in the pasture, rounding up the sheep."

Jody was satisfied with Amy's answer for all of ten minutes, which was the time it took her to cut up vegetables for the stew she was planning for supper.

"Mom, when's Tate coming back?"

"Soon, Jody. He'll be back soon now." She glanced out the window again, this time noting the rosy streaks in the western sky. Sundown had a way of sneaking up on a person this time of year.

Not five minutes later Jody's broomstick horse was dragging its tail on the kitchen floor again. "Mom, what's taking Tate so—"

"I don't know!"

The moment the words were out, Amy regretted her tone. Jody's big eyes displayed the same kind of worry she'd been trying so hard to disown. He came to her and put his little arms around her hips, not looking for a hug, but offering one. She dropped to his eye level and took him in her arms.

"Tate rides really good," Jody assured her. "He hardly ever gets bucked off when he rides saddle bronc."

"Did he tell you that?"

"He showed me one of his buckles. They're like prizes you get for winning in rodeos. Tate rides *real* good."

So did your father. Horses were his life.

"You don't have to worry, Mom."

"You don't, either." She raked her fingers through the polka-dot horse's new mane. "Daisy and Duke aren't used to Tate, so he probably can't get them to work for him as fast as they do for me." The explanation sounded good. It even made sense.

It even made Amy herself actually smile. "Tate may be good with horses, but your mom is the dog expert around here." She gave Jody another good squeeze. "Of course, if he had the common sense of a good sheepherder, he'd take them the long way, which would take him safely along the highway. We could drive out a little ways and take a look."

Taking a look was better than sitting around worrying, Amy decided. She bundled up the children and drove her pickup several miles down the two-lane road, but there was no sign of sheep, dogs or horseman. Still nothing to worry about, she told Jody. If Tate was trying to get back before dark, he had to cut across the pasture. In that case, they wouldn't have been able to see him from the highway. But it was getting dark. When the dogs came back on their own, Amy called the sheriff.

"Miz Becker, it ain't all that cold out yet, and it ain't all that late," Sheriff Jim Katz told her over the phone.

Amy snorted disgustedly. When it got to be thirty below in the dead of winter, she would have to remember to ask the sheriff if it was cold enough for him yet.

"Man's got a job to do, y'gotta give him time to do it, Miz Becker."

"How long is that, Sheriff?" One glance at Jody's anxious face reminded her to curb the bitterness that burned the tip of her tongue. For the moment, anyway.

"I'd say ol' Tate oughta have them sheep penned up by eight and be warmin' up his innards at the Jackalope not long after. Once you start callin' the bars, if you can't track him down by midnight, you give me another call."

"Midnight. I'll make a note of that, Sheriff. Thank you."

"I understand you bein' touchy, Miz Becker. You've had more'n your share. But you gotta understand, I can't send out a search party every time a man rides out in his pasture."

"It's mostly my pasture, and it's dark and Tate's not familiar with—"

"Tate Harrison knows his way around, Miz Becker." Katz chuckled. "Give him a little more time. Then give a holler over to the Jackalope."

Amy wasn't tracking *anybody* down at the Jackalope. Men never took anything seriously until the situation was long past serious. She went about her business, and feeding her children came first. Twice during supper she jumped up from the table to check on the noise she thought she'd heard outside.

After she cleaned up the dishes she congratulated herself for getting the laundry done during the off-peak hours when electricity rates were cheaper. She left the baskets of folded clothes downstairs, thinking she would ask Tate to carry them up. Not that she couldn't lift them herself, she mused as she glanced out the window for the fifteenth time, but knowing Tate, she would be in for a reprimand if he caught her at it.

He would tell her it was too soon for her to be hauling heavy loads up the stairs.

She was the perfect image of calm, repeatedly reassuring Jody as she bathed both children. After she'd put them to bed, she showered and dressed for bed herself, even though she fully intended to keep vigil. She turned the lights out so she could see through the window, but nothing stirred in the bright circle cast by the yard light. Nothing—absolutely nothing. She folded her arms on the back of the sofa, rested her head in the nest they made and kept watch out the side window.

The yard light was a homing beacon, but Tate was disappointed to see that the house was dark. Not even a light left on in the kitchen. The vehicles were all lined up in a row, present and accounted for. No one was looking for him. That was a relief, of course. It didn't make any sense to take the kids out on a cold night and drive around looking when she wouldn't have had a prayer of finding him, anyway. Not on the trail he'd taken. He had half a mind to backtrack tomorrow and see just where in hell he'd been.

He got the sheep bedded down and his horse rubbed down. Outlaw deserved that and then some for getting him home— getting him *back,* back to the house. When he'd first seen that yard light, he'd really felt as though he'd found his way home. He'd had to remind himself that it was the Becker place. Just a house. Just a dark house, where everybody was tucked up in bed, nice and cozy the way they ought to be.

Amy sat bolt upright when the back door opened. Somehow she had let herself doze off, lost track of time, neglected her fretting. She sprang to her feet, but she managed to affect some measure of composure by the time she reached the kitchen.

"Tate?"

There he stood in the shadows just inside the door. He

was safe. He was home at last. He was unscathed, breathing normally, filling her kitchen doorway with his broad shoulders and the fresh scent of a winter's night.

He glanced up from pulling his gloves off. "You still up?"

"I've been waiting, but I guess I dozed off." She crossed the cold floor on bare feet, stopping short of arm's reach. "Did you have trouble?"

"Damn dogs wouldn't listen to me," he complained. She could tell his lips were stiff. "Other than that…I kinda got lost. Whole countryside's crusted over with snow. Looks like a huge white lake. You try to set your course, and just when you think you've got yourself lined out, you cross your own tracks. Pretty soon you start talkin' to yourself, tryin' to keep your brain from wanderin' away from camp."

Now that he was inside, his teeth had started chattering. "I brought 'em all back, though." He fumbled with the buttons on his sheepskin coat. "Every last bleatin' one of 'em. I counted."

"Let me help you." Her heart pounded out a jubilant rhythm as she took over the job of undoing his buttons. "Are your fingers…?"

"A little stiff, is all."

She pushed his jacket off his shoulders, then reached up to take his hat, then the scarf he'd tied under it. "How about your ears?"

He groaned when she put her hands over them. She knew the shock of her warmth must hurt, but he stood still for her inspection. There was even an indulgent smile in his voice. "They're still there."

"Oh, but so cold, and your cheeks…" Vulnerable places, all. She cupped her palms over his cheeks. If she turned on the light, would she find a healthy flame in his skin, or dark discoloration? She could feel his body shaking. Hers joined in, whether from relief or panic, she didn't know.

He put his hands over hers, sandwiching her warmth and pressing it to his face. She ached sympathetically with the stiffness in his hands.

"I don't know if I can get my boots off without a crowbar. My feet have turned to ice."

"I'll take them off. Sit here." She dragged a chair back from the table. The offer seemed to surprise him, but he complied, raising one leg so she could get a grip on his boot heel. "Can you wiggle your foot just a little?"

"Sorry, ma'am. 'Fraid I'm plumb out of wiggle."

"Okay, then, just hold still while I—" She turned her back, straddled his leg and tugged. His foot was forced to bend as the boot came loose, and he sucked his breath quickly between his teeth with the pain.

"If it hurts, you're starting to thaw," she said as she stepped over one leg and on to the next.

"I'm thawing, then. Hungry, too. Anything left from supper?"

"I'm going to fix you something, and it's also my turn to fill the tub for you, and I want to make sure…"

When the second boot came off, she found herself sitting on his knee. He settled his hands over her hips, and she looked at him over her shoulder. It was her turn to be surprised.

He grinned. "Why are we sittin' in the dark?"

Smiling shyly, she felt like a child sitting on Santa's knee. Partly uneasy, but mostly delighted. "Because I was watching out the window."

"I thought you'd gone to bed." He toyed with the white sash of her robe, tugging, turning her toward him. "The house was dark, so I thought…"

"I didn't know what to do. I took the kids and drove up

the road. I called the sheriff, but he said to give you…to wait a while, to…" She closed her eyes as he touched her cheek. "Oh, Tate, your hands are still so cold."

"Your face is warm."

"I wasn't sure—"

His arms encircled her, and his kiss put an end to uncertainty. He was there, in the flesh. She touched his face, his ears, his neck, hoping to transfer her warmth to his chilled skin. But his lips were warm. His embrace tightened as he tilted his head for a new angle, for better access to her lips and the recesses of her mouth. She welcomed his tongue's gentle onslaught. She was more than glad to have him home.

She tucked her hands into the open neck of his flannel work shirt and smoothed them over cool combed cotton. He had the neck and shoulder muscles of a breeding stud. The feel of him thrilled her, and when he broke the kiss, she knew he could read that weakness in her eyes. He could hear it in every fluttery breath she took.

She traced his collarbones with her thumbs. "Just a plain T-shirt instead of long johns, Tate? What were you thinking?"

"It started out to be a nice…." He closed his eyes, and his mighty shoulders quivered beneath her hands. "Oh, God, Amy, if you wanna undress me all the way…my fingers are still pretty stiff."

It would hardly be a difficult task, she thought. She could easily warm his body with hers. She could readily banish the chill from his bones and ease whatever stiffness plagued him. It was so good to have him safe in her arms that it was hard to remember any doubts she'd ever had about holding him close.

About trying to hold him at all.

"Let me start the water." She got up quickly and pulled him

out of the chair. "We need to get you into some warm water right away."

"I think I'm gonna like this part."

"It's all part of thawing out. How do you like it so far?" It was impossible to interpret his low groan, so she tackled another subject. "Jody was awfully worried. He couldn't help thinking about what happened to Ken, you know? And he kept asking and asking, 'Where's Tate?'"

She turned the hall light on. He blinked and squinted like a man who'd just awakened.

"I'll go in and tell him I'm back. Would it be okay to wake him up?"

"I think it would be a good idea. I made him go to bed, but if he's asleep, he's probably not *sound* asleep, because there's that—" She touched his sleeve, pressed her lips together briefly and nodded. "That worry."

Tate nodded stiffly. She wanted to say what he wanted to hear, what she had not quite managed to claim—that it was her worry, too. He turned on his sock-clad heel and made his way down the hall. She listened for the low creaking sound she identified with Jody's door. Even with the bathwater running, she was able to tune in to their voices—one small and high, the other deep and comforting. Tears stung her eyes. She wiped them away quickly and made herself busy. Busyness kept sentimentality at bay.

"You were right," Tate said when he returned from his mission. "He was awake. I think I lost a few points with him when I told him I got lost. He says if Santa Claus brings him a real horse this year, he's goin' with me next time, because he knows the way home." He smiled as he tackled his shirt buttons. "I think that's a hint."

"I've heard it before. That broomstick is the only kind of horse Santa Claus is ever dropping down *this* chimney." She hand-tested the temperature of the water. "I'm surprised he didn't pounce on you the minute you walked in."

"He heard us whispering, and he couldn't make out who it was. He was afraid to come out and see." He pulled his shirttail free of his jeans. "Sometimes a little kid gets scared when he hears adults whispering. He's afraid something bad has happened." He shrugged as he unbuttoned his cuffs. "Or he *knows* something bad has happened, and he's afraid of what might come next."

"You're still talking about Jody?" she asked carefully. She remembered Ken telling her that Tate had lost his mother when he was a boy, but she knew nothing about the circumstances.

"Sure, Jody. Or any little guy." He shed the plaid flannel shirt and whisked his T-shirt over his head. "He thought maybe the sheriff was here."

"He remembers the last time I called the sheriff," she said absently. She was staring. Tate's chest seemed so much bigger now that it was bare.

"So now he knows it doesn't always end up like that." He unbuckled his belt and gave her a crooked smile. "You wanna stick around and wash my back?"

"I'm sorry. I didn't mean to keep…" It wasn't easy to tear her eyes away. "I want to get some hot food in you, and this is one time I wish I had some liquor in the house."

She supposed she had that sinister-sounding chuckle coming.

He supposed turnabout chest-ogling was fair play.

"I think there's a bottle downstairs with a genie named Jack inside who could grant you that wish." His favorite brand. He hadn't brought it in, but she didn't need to know that. He figured Kenny had left it right where Tate would find it, in a drawer in the gun cabinet, alongside the liniment and the Ace bandages.

"Then we'll break the seal and let the genie out." She waltzed out the door, adding cheerfully, "For medicinal purposes, of course."

"Of course."

The water burned like hell at first, even though he knew it wasn't that hot. But he closed his eyes and rubbed it over him, letting it do its work. He didn't see any sign of frostbite, which was good, but restoring his circulation was a painful process.

"Tate?" It was Amy's voice, calling out just above a whisper. "I brought you something to put on. Ken's things. Is that okay?"

"Sure. The door's unlocked." He slid the shower door closed. "There. I'm behind glass. Just set it inside."

But she came into the room. "I found your genie, too."

"The one in the gun cabinet?"

"You and Ken must think alike. I mean, the two of you must *have thought*…"

"Like two pups in a basket, in some ways." Through the opaque glass he could see her, an obscure shape in a white robe, hanging some sort of reddish stuff on a hook on the back of the door. "Maybe we're still on the same wavelength. I knew right where to look."

"So did I." She gave a small laugh as she left the room, closing the door softly behind her.

After he toweled off, he debated with himself about putting his own clothes back on. It bothered him that the maroon terry-cloth robe smelled like somebody else's shaving lotion. And plaid flannel pajamas. He never wore pajamas. He figured for the sake of decency he ought to put on the pants, but the hell with that shirt. He couldn't believe Kenny had worn such a thing to bed. The sheepskin slippers were pretty dudish, too, but they were warm.

Tate tied the belt on the robe and checked himself out in the mirror. He needed a shave, but his razor was downstairs, and he didn't want to use the shaving cream in the medicine cabinet. He didn't like the smell of that, either. It wasn't his brand.

He shuffled into the kitchen and enjoyed having Amy wait on him at such a late hour. Beef stew and homemade bread warmed his shivering insides. Her robe was similar to his—or Kenny's—but hers was long and white. He wanted her to sit down with him without having to ask her to, but she kept bouncing in and out of the room.

Then he heard a crackling sound in the living room, and he turned to find her standing in the doorway and looking strangely hesitant. "Would you like to sit by the fire for a while?"

"Not alone."

"No." She watched him wash his soup bowl. "I'll have to feed the baby soon anyway."

He glanced at the clock.

"A couple of hours," she amended.

"A shot of whiskey and a warm fire would do me just fine, then."

He pushed the sofa closer to the fire. She poured him a shot of whiskey. She even warmed it over a flame before she handed it to him. "Dr. Jack," he said as he raised his glass to the fire.

"Was there water in the stock tank?" she wondered as she joined him on the sofa.

"I ran the pump."

"And how about the barn? And did you open the door to the shed in the far pen, in case—"

"I opened the door."

"I should have put fresh straw—"

"I put down fresh straw." He glanced askance at her. She was back to testing him. "I took care of it, Amy."

"I wasn't sure you'd think of—"

"I damn near froze my tail off getting your sheep back to the fold, lady. You think I'm gonna leave the job half done?"

"No."

She turned quietly to watch the fire, and he watched the firelight burnish her face while the flames danced in her eyes. He sipped his drink and toyed with the thought of going to bed with her. Not seducing her. Just getting up off the sofa when the time came and going to bed with her, as if he were her man.

"You think nobody else can do it quite as good as Amy can," he observed flatly.

"I couldn't have…" The words got stuck in her throat.

"Go on." He waited, then coaxed with a gesture. "You couldn't have what?"

"Well, I probably couldn't have—"

"Uh-uh, it was better the other way." He smiled, enjoying her struggle. "Come on, now, I worked hard for this."

"I couldn't have done any better myself."

"Damn right you couldn't have. I froze my—"

"I know, and I do appreciate that special sacrifice."

"I fed them and watered them and tucked them in for the night. I was gonna sing to them, but they said not to bother. They'd heard enough of that on the way home. On the way *back*." He drained his glass, and she poured him a refill in what he figured to be her bottom-line show of appreciation. "Hell, I don't even like sheep, and here I am, treatin' 'em like—"

"Children?"

"Cattle." He had half a mind to push his luck and light up a cigarette. "I'm a cowboy, remember?"

"I remember." She set the bottle on the hearth and studied it for a moment. "And I remember how I used to treat you after I married Ken."

"You always invited me to stay for supper. I always knew I could bunk in here for a night or two as long as I wasn't raisin' any hell." He smiled, remembering. "If Kenny and me went out and tied one on, I knew better than to set foot in your kitchen. I didn't blame you for that."

"You always saw that he got home."

"This was where he belonged. He had somebody waitin' for him."

"In most ways he was a very good husband. He didn't spend much time in the bars, except…"

"Except when I was around. Right?" She didn't have to answer. She was still staring at the bottle. "You know why married women are always tryin' to fix the single guys up and get 'em married off?" She shook her head. "They think their husbands envy our freedom. And maybe they do sometimes."

"They probably do."

"But it works both ways. We envy them, too, sometimes. Like when it's time to go home." He laid his arm along the back of the sofa and leaned closer, changing his mind about the cigarette. He liked the fresh scent of her hair. "How come you never tried to fix me up with somebody, Amy? Why weren't you introducing me to your sister? 'Fraid I'd ruin her?"

"My sister is older," she said evasively. "She was already married."

"A friend, then. Somebody just like you."

"It wouldn't be fair. You only want a home *sometimes,* Tate. Like when you're cold and tired."

He wasn't listening. "You don't have any friends just like you." He touched the softly curling ends of her hair. "There aren't any more like you, Amy. I've looked."

She looked at him skeptically. "Where?"

"Church socials. PTA meetings. Choir concerts."

"Don't you mean truck stops, rodeos and bars?"

He grinned lazily. "Don't tell me I'm lookin' for love in the wrong places."

"Don't tell me you're looking for love."

"Just lookin' for comfort tonight," he said lightly. "A warm fire and a hot meal." He sipped his whiskey, thinking maybe there was some kind of love to be found somewhere in the whole combination.

The baby's soft cry from the back room made him smile again. "Sounds like I'm not the only one." He caught Amy's hand as she started away. "You comin' back?"

"I'll bring her in here."

He poured himself another drink, resettled himself on the sofa and watched the sparks sail up the flue while he waited.

"I had to change her completely," Amy explained when she came back with the baby. "She was soaked through."

"Thought maybe you'd gone shy on me and decided to stay in the bedroom."

Baring her breast, she held his gaze with eyes that said she kept her promises. She'd promised to sit next to him while he warmed himself with fire and whiskey. And now she warmed him with a special intimacy.

"I like to watch you feed her. I haven't spent much time around babies. Or mothers feeding babies this way." He set his glass down and leaned over Amy's shoulder to watch the busy little mouth. "Not human mothers, anyway."

A feeling of possessiveness surged through him, and he wanted to physically become a shelter around this little family so that he could keep it safe from the cold night. He cupped his big weather-roughened hand over the baby's tiny head. Her downy hair felt precious and delicate against his palm. He remembered his first glimpse of it, what a wet, sticky, welcome and glorious sight the top of this little head had been, and it occurred to him that he'd put the cart before the horse. He had never made love to Amy, but in a sense he'd given her this child. He hadn't planted the seed, but he'd delivered the baby into her arms.

Little Karen drank herself to sleep, which was what Tate thought he would do, right there in front of the fire, after Amy took the baby back to bed. But Amy came back and sat beside him, as though it were her place. He tried not to think about the fact that he was wearing Kenny's robe, which smelled like Kenny's after-shave.

"You have a wonderful way with Jody," she told him. "I don't know whether I've mentioned that."

"No, you haven't."

"You seem to know all the right things to say. He's had to grow up a lot these past few months. He's been my strong little man."

"He still needs time to be your little boy. I'm not sayin' you don't do right by him, because you do. And you've had a lot on your mind. It's just that—" He shook his head. He knew he had to be half-shot if he was coming up with advice about raising kids. But she was looking at him as though she thought *he* thought she'd done something wrong, so he had to explain. "Sometimes when you get a new baby in the house, the older kid gets to feelin' like a milk bucket sittin' under a he-goat."

"While the mean old nanny—"

"Now, I didn't say that at all." He drew a deep breath and sighed. "And I don't wanna be buttin' into your business. I especially don't wanna be buttin' heads with you right now. I might crack."

"So enough about goats?"

"Enough about goats," he agreed. He dropped his hand on his thigh and rubbed his palm against the terry cloth. "I've got no right to talk, anyway, after the way I got after the little fella the day I was unloading hay."

Amy touched the back of his hand. "How old were you when your mother died, Tate?"

"Ten." He wasn't sure where that question had come from, but her touch would be his undoing. He could tell that right now. "She had some kind of routine surgery—gall bladder, I think—and there were complications. But I was almost grown. It wasn't like Jody, losing his dad before he even had a chance to—"

"Ten is hardly almost grown."

"When you live on a ranch, it is. The gospel according to Oakie Bain says that twelve is old enough to do a man's work." He turned his palm to hers, and their fingers seemed to lace together of their own accord. "All I'm saying is, just don't rush it. It'll happen soon enough. Once you give him a man's responsibilities, he won't be a boy anymore. And there's no such thing as a *little* man."

"You had a younger brother, didn't you?" He turned his face to the fire. "Ken told me."

"He told you what happened?"

"He said that your brother was killed in a farm accident

when he was quite young. That's what you're thinking about, isn't it?"

"I'm talking about Jody." He tried to shrug it off. "Just making a simple observation. Take a look at it, or leave it alone."

"I'll take a hard look at it, Tate. It's a lot more than a simple observation." She paused, but it was too late to step back. "What was his name?"

"Jesse." His voice became distant, alien, drifting in desolation. "My brother's name was Jesse. Half brother. Oakie was his father, not mine." That was enough, he told himself. She'd only asked for his name. But his mouth wouldn't be still. "Jesse was only nine years old. By anybody's standards, that's still a boy."

"What happened?"

"I backed over him with the tractor." Damn the whiskey and damn his thick tongue. "Ran a 4020 just like yours right over his…right over him." He heard the catch in her breath. She didn't need any more details. "I figured Kenny must've told you the whole story."

"No." She squeezed his hand, and he could feel the pressure in the pit of his stomach. "Can *you* tell me?"

"I just did. I killed him. That's all she wrote."

"But it was an accident," she assured him softly.

"It was a crazed tractor," he countered. "One like you read about in a horror novel." With a look, she questioned his judgment. He studied the contents of his glass as he recalled some of his best recriminations. "Or else it could have been a booby trap that some prowler set to trip Jesse up. Or an earthquake sort of threw us both off balance. Anything but an accident. Accidents happen when people get careless."

"How old were you?"

"Twelve." He gave a long, hollow sigh. "I remember it like it was last night's dream. Real vivid, you know, but just beyond your grasp. Just past the point where you can turn it around and shake it up and make some sense out of it. All you can do is let it play itself out. You open your mouth to scream, and nothing comes out. You watch yourself slam on the brake, and you see the look on Oakie's face, and he's waving his arms. Is he saying go forward? Go back? And you get that awful, sick feeling all over again when you realize your brother's under the tire."

He saw it all again in slow motion, for the umpteen-hundredth time. His hands were shaking, foiling his attempts to make the throttle work, to find the gear that would change the course of more than the tractor. He didn't see Oakie coming, and suddenly he was trying to turn a fall into a jump, then scrabbling out of the way. That was when he glimpsed Jesse's brown hair, and the outstretched hand, and the blood, just before he buried his own face in the alfalfa stubble and tasted dirt and bile and tears.

He felt untouchable, the way he always felt when he remembered, the way he had felt that day. He remembered thinking they would put him in jail, which was where he belonged. But instead, the sheriff had asked Oakie all the questions, sparing Tate a glance once in a while as Oakie had given the awful answers. "Is that right, son?" the sheriff kept saying. Tate didn't know; he'd just stared at his useless hands and nodded. His whole worthless body had gone numb. And no one had tried to touch him then.

But Amy touched him now. He wasn't sure what had happened to his drink, or what he'd said last. Suddenly Amy was holding both of his hands. He hated the way they were shaking. "One minute he was playing with a spotted pup Oakie had given him," Tate said distantly. "The next he was underneath the damn tire."

She bowed her head and pressed the back of his hand to her cheek. "You saw him, didn't you?" she whispered. "You found him broken and bleeding, the same way..."

The same way Kenny had been when she'd found him. Another shared intimacy. They knew the same nightmares.

"It wasn't your fault, Tate."

"How do you know?"

"You were only twelve years old," she reminded him. "Still a child yourself. You didn't kill your brother. It was a terrible—"

"Accident," he recited. "Tragic accident, horrible accident. I hate the word. It grates on my ears like somebody grinding his teeth." He watched the fire. "The sheriff said it was an accident. The neighbors, when they brought over their hot dishes and offered to help with the chores, they called it an accident. Oakie didn't say much of anything, not for a long time. Kids from school said, 'Sorry about what happened, Tate' and that was that. Nobody talked about it much after we buried Jesse. Or if they did, they talked around it."

"It's always in the back of your mind when you farm," Amy said quietly as she rubbed her thumbs over the backs of his hands. "You like to think it's a good way to raise kids. And it is. You want them to take part in the work because it builds character, and they learn so much."

She closed her eyes, and a lone tear slipped down her cheek. She shifted a little, hoping he hadn't seen it. "But there are the accidents. They happen, Tate. They happen more often than most people want to realize. They happen with adults at the controls. You were only—"

"A boy?" He shook his head. "I was doing a man's job. I was expected to act like a man. Stand up like a man. Own up to my mistakes like a man, meaning you don't make excuses and you keep your blubbering to yourself." He was quoting now, almost verbatim.

"You weren't allowed to—"

"Cry? No way. Not unless I wanted Oakie to, uh—" He recalled his stepfather's favorite warning. "Give me something to cry about. The only person I ever talked to about it was Kenny, and that was only after I'd had a few drinks, like now." Still staring into the fire, he gave a humorless smile. "Ol' Kenny and me, we learned to act like men. Drank and smoked like men. Cussed and scrapped it out like men. Chased us some girls and had us some women, just like real men."

With a groan she tried to be subtle about drying her cheek on her own shoulder. "Now you're beginning to sound like the other Tate."

"What other Tate?" He took her chin in his hand and made her look at him. "There is only one Tate Harrison."

"Maybe so." She took a deep, steadying breath. "But he has an outside and an inside."

"Just like everybody else." He found the dampness on her cheek with his finger.

"You've worked hard at toughening up the outside. You've done a better job than anyone I know. But when the chips are down, you always come through. You'd go out drinking, and Kenny was always the one who got plastered. You were the one who brought him home. You were always watching out for him."

His mouth quirked slightly as the knowing smile flashed in his eyes. "Hornin' in on your territory?"

"He was my husband."

"Kenny had his head in the clouds most of the time, but he didn't worry much since he had us both watchin' out for him." He raised one brow. "Trouble is, he got away from us one night. And you've been thinkin' you should've gotten to him sooner, while I've been thinkin' I should've been here."

"Crazy, isn't it?"

"It'll drive you crazy. Believe me, I know."

"I want Jody to be…different. I don't want him to *act* like a man. I want him to *be* a man. Independent. Responsible."

"Like his mom?" She was all set to take exception, but he laid a finger against her lips. "Relax a little. Let him be a boy first. I told you about Jesse because…" The name came hard, as always, but this time he had Amy's hand in his, and her acceptance. "Because of Jody."

Which wasn't the whole of it, and she knew that as well as he did, but it was easier to advocate for the boy. "He watches you with the baby," he said, remembering, looking down at their clasped hands, now lying in her lap. "I told him how the baby wasn't going to be much fun for a while, and he's trying hard to understand all that, but he needs—" She looked up, and he looked into her eyes and said almost inaudibly, "He needs you to hold him."

"I can do that," she said gently. He leaned closer, and she put her arms around him and laid her cheek against his chest.

A man's need to touch a woman was a given, but the need to be touched by her was something else. He felt the need so strongly, he was almost afraid to return the gesture, afraid he would give himself away.

They wouldn't touch him. He'd done an awful thing, and nobody wanted to touch him.

"This isn't what I learned about acting like a man," he said as he slid his arms around her. He closed his eyes and nestled his face in her hair. "Hangin' on to you for dear life like this."

"Is that what you're doing?"

He didn't think he could hold her close enough, but she found a way to surround him with more warmth than the fire in the hearth radiated. He breathed deeply of the sweet strawberry-and-smoke scent of her. "I feel like the kid who got lost in the woods. It sure was dark out there."

"Could you use a kiss, too?"

"Not the kind you'd give to a kid."

She slid her fingers into his thick hair and pulled his face down to hers, kissing him as hungrily, as greedily, as fervently, as he'd ever been kissed. He'd never wanted anything more desperately than he craved her touch right now, but not if he had to ask. And he didn't. Suddenly her hands were all over him under the robe, caressing his hair-spattered chest, his shoulders, his flat nipples. He sucked in a deep breath and offered her access to his belly. He was on his way to heaven when she touched him there.

He untied the sash and drew the robe back, trying to shrug out of it without changing her course. "This thing smells like somebody else, Amy." Her fingertips curled into his waist, and she went still. He dropped his head back against the sofa. "Is that what you want?" he demanded quietly. "You want me to be somebody else?"

"No." She pressed her forehead against his chest and breathed soft words on his skin. "God help me, no."

"I want you so bad. You know that, don't you?" She nodded against him. "But I'm not Kenny. I don't own a robe and slippers. I don't wear pajamas. I'm not—" He couldn't be, not even if he had the heart to try, and she had to accept that. "I don't ever want you to call me by the wrong name."

She sighed. "Tate, I know who you are." She lifted her head and met his gaze. "I'm beginning to, anyway. You're the man who delivered my baby, the man who fixed my son's broomstick horse, the man who—"

He touched his finger to her lips. He didn't want her gratitude. "I want to make love to you."

"It's too soon."

"Because of the baby?" He searched the depths of her eyes for her answer. "Or because of Kenny?"

"Both," she admitted. She closed her eyes against the disappointment she saw in his. "Both."

He nodded and withdrew.

"That doesn't mean we can't give each other—" She extended her hand to him quickly, then closed it on a second thought. "I started to say 'what *we've* been giving.' But you've been giving, and I've been taking."

"It hasn't been easy, has it?" She looked at him, perplexed. "Taking help from Tate Harrison."

"Oh, Tate," she said as she took him back in her arms.

It had been *too* easy. Too quickly she had come to rely on him. Too readily she had let him lay claim to a too-large piece of her heart. She'd made it all too obvious. She hugged him, but she gave him no more of an answer. At least she could try not to show him *how* readily and *how* easily and *how* much.

He kissed the top of her hair and held her close. "It hasn't been easy givin' it, either."

Chapter 8

Thanksgiving seemed to creep up overnight, but it did not pass without a traditional dinner. Tate was invited to carve the turkey and sit at the head of the table. He obliged. Even though he hardly considered himself a jack of the turkey-carving trade, he figured it out without asking for any pointers. Sitting in Kenny's chair at feast time felt a lot like wearing Kenny's robe and slippers, which Tate had quietly returned to the bedroom closet and never worn again. The prospect of an opportunity to play Santa Claus would have held considerable appeal except for the idea of filling someone else's boots again. Tate had his own boots. They were broken in nicely and fitted him just fine.

Amy hadn't been into town since the horse sale. The roads were icy, and she was glad when Tate volunteered to drive her in for the requisite six-week checkup. She had to take Jody along for a throat culture, and he and the baby were both fussy. The waiting room at the rural clinic was packed with whining children and cranky mothers. Tate excused himself to do some errands and promised to meet Amy and the kids at the Big Cup Café, two doors down the street.

It bothered her to find him sitting at a booth with her sister-in-law and Patsy Drexel. Marianne was working her way through a club sandwich, and Tate and Patsy were sharing a laugh and a cigarette. She was just passing it back to him, and he was about to take a drag when he saw Amy. One quick puff and, to his credit, he put it out before she brought the children to the table.

Patsy eyed the ashtray regretfully, as though she hadn't gotten her fill. Too bad, Amy thought.

"You guys ready for lunch?" Tate tipped his hat back and smiled. "I've been waitin' to order."

Amy shook her head. "We can wait 'til we get home. I have plenty of—"

"Mom, can I have a hamburger?" Jody pleaded.

"You can sit right up here with me and have anything you want, partner." Tate reached over the backrest and nabbed a booster seat from the empty booth on the other side. "We're too hungry to wait, aren't we? How's your throat?"

"They stuck a stick down it." Jody demonstrated with his forefinger. "Yech!"

"What you need is a big, fat hamburger and maybe some hot—" Tate glanced at Amy "—soup? Some orange juice?"

A little late to be asking my opinion, Amy thought. Jody had already scrambled into the booster seat, which Tate had pulled close to his side. She sighed and nodded, eyeing the remaining space on the horn of the half-moon booth. "Whatever he orders will be hard for him to swallow, and it's coming out of your wages, Harrison."

"That's all right," he said, chuckling as he signaled waitress

Madge Jensen. "I've been meaning to suggest a pay cut, anyway. The seconds are killing my boyish figure."

Marianne offered to hold the baby, and Patsy spared the bundle a cursory glance as Amy wearily took a seat. She felt as though she'd just been to the doctor for anemia and he'd prescribed leeches. The bill—like all bills these days—had been higher than she'd expected. It worried her that she hadn't been able to pay it in full. She needed the cup of tea Tate suggested. She *wanted* the lunch he offered that she wouldn't have to prepare herself.

"We need anything from the store?" Tate asked.

The question surprised her. Tate had been picking up milk and eggs when he went to town, and he knew how well stocked her freezer and pantry were with her own produce. Now that she was doing the cooking again, she made everything from scratch. No more canned soup.

"Thought maybe I could take you grocery shopping." He sipped his coffee, then offered a teasing grin. "Wouldn't that be fun?"

Compared to what? Amy wondered. Delivering babies? All the fun things he could do with Patsy?

"I don't have my coupons with me." She glared at him. *How do you like that for mundane?*

"Amy and her coupons." Marianne chortled. "Bill, Sr., never had to bother with coupons and weekly specials until Amy moved in and started talking it up. But since our store is a franchise..." She smiled sweetly. "Well, we went along with it, so everything's up-to-date in Overo now. I just don't see where you find the time to mess with all that stuff, Amy. Clipping coupons and watching for bargains."

"I'm organized," Amy said dryly. A quick glance at Tate forced her to add, "Usually. And I don't buy what I don't need."

"What do you need for lunch?" Tate's nod turned her attention to the waitress, who was standing near Amy's shoulder, pencil and pad ready.

"Just a glass of water, please, Madge."

"You are the stubbornest woman I've ever known," Tate grumbled under his breath after he and Jody had put in their orders.

"I'll have to agree with that," Marianne put in. "Have you given any more thought to having a geological survey done? Tobart Mining is still interested."

Tate tucked his cigarettes into his jacket pocket. "They've approached me, too."

"What are *you* going to do?" Marianne asked.

"I don't know." He picked up his coffee cup. "I've been thinking about selling out altogether. If I do, I guess I'll hang on to the mineral rights."

"So in a year or two I'm likely to be looking at a strip mine right down the road," Amy surmised with blatant disgust.

"Just because you let them take core samples doesn't mean you're asking for strip mining."

"Really?" The look she gave him was cold enough to freeze beer. "What do you think they'll find in our basin, Tate? Gold nuggets?"

"Well, there could be oil, natural gas. There could be a lot of things." He dismissed the possibilities with a disinterested shrug. "They reclaim the land."

"We're ranchers." Amy turned to her husband's sister. "That was all Ken ever wanted. A working ranch."

"I think you mean a working *wife*," Marianne said. She shifted the baby to her shoulder. "Ranches don't work. *People* work. And you work too hard, Amy."

That was her choice. "Your father left Ken his land and you his money." *Mine gave me a strong back.*

"I also own half the mineral rights."

"Which are useless to you unless I agree to exploration. The land is Ken's legacy to his children," Amy said firmly. "It won't be mined. Now, can we talk about something else, please?" She offered a tight smile as Madge appeared with coffee refills. "I believe I will have a cup of tea and a BLT, Madge. Are you ready for Christmas, Marianne? How about you, Patsy? Have you done all your shopping?"

"I've done some," Patsy drawled. She glanced Tate's way and sighed. "Seems like I'm always shopping around."

Amy had turned the heat down before she left, and the house was cold. Almost as chilly as the attitude she had given him since they'd left the café, Tate thought. It couldn't have been over the comment about stopping at the store. Hadn't she been the one wishing aloud for some fresh fruit just the other day? Besides apples, she'd said. She had apples in the pantry.

He wasn't just sure what he'd done, but he figured it had to do with Patsy Drexel. If that were the case, he could afford to feel a little smug, considering his innocence. He went about his business, feeding the livestock, mending a hasp on one of the gates and sneaking his morning's purchases down to his room when everyone was napping. He was feeling pretty damned organized, too, now that he'd done some Christmas shopping. He'd never wrapped a Christmas present in his life, and he'd thought about leaving the stuff with Marianne or Patsy, along with a hint that he hadn't used a pair of scissors since he was in grade school. But he'd missed his chance.

The gun cabinet had obviously been one of Kenny's places for secreting things. Since Amy hadn't disturbed Kenny's whiskey stash or checked the guns, Tate took the cabinet to be property left untended, now that its owner was gone. It wouldn't hold everything he'd bought, but there was plenty of room for the things he didn't want Amy to find. He heard her footsteps on the stairs just in time to shut the door and lock it.

"Another drink to warm up?"

He didn't know why the question stung him. He'd thought about it himself, actually, but he'd changed his mind. He didn't like the way she was standing in the shadows at the foot of the stairs and looking at him like he was some kid who ought to know better. Maybe he'd just change his mind back again.

She wagged her head and sighed disgustedly. "Ken always thought he was so clever. If you insist on having it in the house, you might as well keep it in the kitchen and use a glass."

"What's left from Ken's stock *is* in the kitchen. I just needed a place to stash a few things under lock and key." Working hard to keep his cool, he bounced the key in his hand for her benefit. "The lock doesn't do much good with the key sittin' right in it."

Slowly she walked over to the gun cabinet, stared at the glass door for a moment, then ran her hand over the carved molding. "It's been a slow process, dealing with Ken's things—his drawers, his side of the closet, his boxes and boxes of keepsakes. He never threw anything away." Her hand dropped to her side. "I haven't gotten to this yet, but the guns aren't loaded."

"The .22 pistol had two rounds in the clip."

"Oh, Ken." She drew a deep breath and cast her glance heavenward. "Why were you always so…?" With a quick shake of her head, she took the blame herself. "I should have thought to check. I should have been more careful."

"Everything's unloaded now. If you don't have any use for them, you could probably get a good price for some of them. Maybe keep one around for—"

"They're Jody's." She folded her arms and turned away from the cabinet. "They will be when he's old enough. Some of them belonged to Ken's father. One was his grandfather's." She stepped closer to Tate, distancing herself from the Becker family heirlooms. "Otherwise, I wouldn't have them around."

He wondered whether she'd ever told Kenny any of this. He remembered that the cabinet itself had been in Kenny's family forever, as had the love of guns. Tate owned a couple of hunting rifles, too. He figured most guys did.

"Out here alone, you've got predators to worry about, maybe prowlers." No surprise to her, he thought. If Kenny had been good for nothing else, he'd been capable of protecting what was his. "If you don't know how to use a gun, I can sure teach you."

"You're going to sell your land, aren't you, Tate?" The question came out of left field. He missed the catch, so she pitched her charge again. "You're just going to sell out to the highest bidder."

Was she kidding? For years the bidding had been closed to anyone but Kenny. "I've only kept it this long because Kenny wanted it. When you guys dropped the lease, I kinda figured—"

"It's been in your family. It belonged to your father."

"Yeah, well, he died young because he worked too damn hard. He had a bad heart. This is no life for a man with a weak heart." He thought better of adding, *Or a woman with two little kids*. "That's about all I know about him, too. He died when I was even younger than Jody."

Damn, he was at it again, spilling personal history like a leaky washtub.

"Jody won't remember much about his father, either, but he'll have the home his father left him."

"Forever and ever, amen?"

"A home is important." She jabbed his shirt button with her forefinger. "Roots, Tate. Roots are important. They give you a strong sense of who you are."

"You have a strong sense of who *you* are." He closed his hand around hers. "You've only lived here since you married Kenny. Where are your roots?"

"They're here. They grew fast, once they had fertile ground."

"Like the tree you fed from your own womb?" He didn't realize he was going to take her shoulders in his hands until he felt their slightness. "Aren't you afraid this land might suck the life right out of you, maybe through those roots you put down?"

"No," she said, standing her ground without pushing him away, as he might have expected. "I've brought new life here. I've made a home. A permanent home. You sold your family's house, and now you're going to sell the land it sat on."

"I don't have any use for it."

"They'll rape it, Tate. The speculators, the investors, the miners. They'll strip it down and violate it."

A caustic comeback sprang to the tip of his tongue, but he couldn't quite spit it out. He couldn't accuse her of being melodramatic, not with that look on her face and the image that the word *rape* brought to his mind. It was more than a risk to the land. It was a threat to Amy, to her power to make life flourish, to the essence of her femininity. In her eyes he revisited her pain and her triumph in the moment she'd given birth.

"You want it?" he demanded flippantly. The life force burned so strongly in her eyes that he was forced to turn away. "Take it," he said, his bravado deflating. "Christmas present, free and clear. I'll sign over the title."

"Don't be ridiculous," she tossed back.

He turned like a cornered gunfighter, the words piercing him as sharply as any bullet could have. "You've said that to me before, Amy. Remember?" *Remember the night I drove you home? You made your choice that night.* "'Don't be ridiculous, Tate.'"

She stared, frowning slightly, trying to dredge up some recollection of the details in her mind. Clearly it wasn't an easy task for her. Maybe it wasn't much of a memory for anybody but Tate.

"There was no way I was gonna hang around this town after you married Kenny and set up your *permanent* housekeeping with him. *That* would have been ridiculous."

"So you chose to live like a gypsy."

"A cowboy," he corrected with a cocky grin. "Don't gypsies raise *sheep?*"

"I don't know. All I know is that they wander from place to place, and their children just—" she gestured expansively "—wander with them."

"I don't have any children, so what difference does it make how I choose to live my life?" His eyes challenged her. He folded his arms and braced his shoulder against the gun cabinet. "What difference does it make to *you,* Amy. Why should you give a damn?"

"You were my husband's friend."

"It has nothing to do with Kenny, and you know it. It has to do with you and me, and it always has."

"There was no 'you and me.' You weren't really—"

His hand shot out and grabbed her shoulder again. "The only thing I wasn't really was the kind of man you were looking for. You chose your husband carefully, didn't you?"

She stiffened. "Yes, and you were his friend, which made you *our* friend."

"Give me a break." With a groan he released her and turned away, patting his empty shirt pocket. His cigarettes must have been in his jacket. It was about time for a smoke and the drink she'd first accused him of sneaking.

But at his back, she persisted with her crusade. "You know, you could have built something on that land instead of tearing down what was left and going off—"

Great suggestion. "You would have enjoyed that, would you?" He confronted her again, trying hard not to sneer. "You married to Kenny, and me living just down the road?"

"It wouldn't have bothered me."

"Yeah, right. Well, it would have bothered the livin' hell out of me."

"I just meant that…" They stood face-to-face, but they were talking past each other. Intentionally. He knew what she meant, and he could tell by the look in her eyes that she knew damn well what *he* meant.

She shook her head and softened her tone. "You don't understand about the land because you've never been one to settle down. It's just not in you."

"I understand something about the land, Amy. I grew up here." He glanced away. He didn't like that soulful look she was giving him. "I guess I don't understand about the roots. Mine must have eroded. What was left after Jesse died was me and Oakie. Two people who tolerated each other. Barely."

"Why do you keep coming back, then?"

"To see Kenny." *What, was she blind?*

"Kenny's not here anymore."

"I'm stickin' around to help his wife and kids get through the winter."

"I'm his *widow*."

"Which means what? Besides the fact that you need a man?"

"I *don't* need a man!" Fingers rigidly splayed, she swept the idea away with an abrupt gesture, then calmly echoed, "I'm not talking about that. I'm saying you've come back to—"

"No, let's stop talking *around* it, Amy. I'm living under your roof, and Kenny's dead." He braced his arms on the gun cabinet, trapping her between them to keep her from turning away. "Several years ago you said it was wrong. Several cold nights ago you told me it was too soon. What are you tellin' me now?"

They stared at one another, and finally it was he who had to turn away. If he got hold of her again, he would begin trying to shake some sense into her. Or he would be kissing her senseless—one of the two. He sighed. "What do you want from me, Amy?"

"I haven't asked for anything."

"Doesn't it mean anything to you that you haven't *had* to?"

Her lips parted. He arched an eyebrow, waiting, but she pressed those lips together again. He gave a dry chuckle, as short on patience as she was on answers.

"I'm goin' out for a smoke," he told her as he headed for the stairs. "Call me when supper's ready. Whatever supper you think you can spare your hired *gypsy*."

Tate thought a lot about "roots" when he and Jody rode into the hills—*his* hills, on his land—and selected a Christmas tree. He'd taken it as a somewhat positive sign when Amy hadn't refused to let Jody go along after Jody assured her that his throat wasn't "one bit sore anymore." The horseback part of the journey would be short, Tate had promised. They had trailered Outlaw as close in as they could. Then he'd put Jody in the saddle and mounted up behind him.

Maybe he did have some roots in the foothills, he thought.

The huge, pale winter sky rose high overhead and slid down in the distance behind the snow-capped western peaks. The morning freshness was filled with sage and pine. It felt good to fill his chest with something besides smoke, to get himself light-headed on pure air.

"What we're gonna end up with is a juniper or a ponderosa pine. You think that's okay?" Tate wondered as he surveyed the snow-spattered red cuts and the flat-topped slopes.

Jody nodded vigorously, the bill on his little flap-eared plaid cap bobbing up and down like a barfly's eyelashes.

"They don't make the best Christmas trees, but we'll find a good one. We can't use a limber pine. See that one up there?" The boy nodded again. "The wind's turned it into a pretzel."

"Mom and me bought our tree last year," Jody reported. "Did your dad used to go cut your Christmas tree himself?"

"My stepdad did, yeah."

"Did he take you with him?"

"He did. This is where we'd always come lookin', too."

He remembered the year a bobcat had spooked the horses. Jesse had been just about Jody's age, and Tate and Jesse had been riding double. Their sixteen-hand palomino had laid his ears back, and they'd gone streaking across the flat, with Jesse hanging on to the saddle horn and Tate, mounted behind him, gripping the swells. He could still see that jackleg fence up ahead. Just when he'd thought they were goners, the big horse had sailed over the rails like a trained jumper and kept right on galloping until he wore himself out. Oakie's face had been whiter than the December snow cover, but he'd said he'd never seen any cowboy stick a horse better, and he'd been looking Tate straight in the eye when he'd said it.

"We always found a good one out here," Tate said, surprising himself as he echoed Oakie's annual pronouncement. "You can't get 'em any fresher."

They chose a small juniper. Even though it didn't have the pointed crown they were looking for, it had a straight trunk, and it was already decorated with cones that looked more like pale blue berries. Entrusted with Outlaw's reins, Jody was content to stand back and watch Tate cut the tree down. But the notion of roots bedeviled Tate as he swung the ax. He would take the tree away, but the roots would remain. If he came back to this spot years later, he knew he'd find juniper saplings. For every one that he pulled down, Amy would probably plant two more, with or without a placenta to nourish its roots. That was the way she was. A nester, like his mother, whose life had been hard and brief. His mother hadn't lived long enough to see the get of her womb reach manhood.

The tree went down, and Jody cheered. Tate straightened his shoulders and flashed a smile the boy's way. It was good for a boy to have a man to look out for him, too, Tate thought. And it was good for a man to remember that times weren't *all* bad when he was a boy.

Amy had been keeping to herself a lot lately, spending hours behind closed doors in the bedroom with the sewing machine whirring. The tree pleased her. She emerged long enough to give it her special homespun touch, adding brightly colored calico bows, along with small hanging pillows shaped like rag dolls and toy soldiers and teddy tears. She gave the top berth to a lacy angel, then stepped back and announced that she'd never seen a prettier tree.

After letting it be known that offers to entertain the baby would be more than welcome, Amy went back to her sewing machine. Tate and Jody discovered that Karen had an ear for harmonica music. Now that she could hold her head up, she liked to bob along with their songs.

After several hours of late-night work, Tate managed to get his packages wrapped. The paper was cut funny in places, and he'd had to use a lot of tape, but he felt good when he arranged the gifts under the tree. He'd saved all the receipts. Half the stuff probably wouldn't fit. The other half was probably purely frivolous, but he didn't care. He'd picked out things he wanted his...he wanted *them* to have.

Amy didn't say much when she saw all the packages, but Jody was bursting with excitement when he asked, rather cautiously, whether any of the packages might be for him. Tate pointed to his name on one of the tags and challenged him to find the others.

Jody found one small box to be especially fascinating. He kept checking it over, shaking it, staring as though he were trying to develop X-ray vision, and muttering his guesses as though the package might respond if he hit on the right word. By Christmas Eve he had almost become a fixture beneath the tree.

After a supper of what Amy called her Christmas Eve chowder, she disappeared into the bedroom one more time and emerged with an armload of packages and a broad smile. "I have some things to add to the booty," she told Tate as they met in the hallway.

"Can you use some help?" Karen had fallen asleep in his arms, and he'd just put her down in the crib in her nursery. "Looks like you've been busy."

"You guys probably thought I was avoiding you these last couple of weeks. I wasn't." She let him take the top half of her pile of packages. "Mine are all homemade."

"Makes them more special."

"Jody's too young to see it that way. I know he's excited

about your gifts, and I'm trying not to be an old Scrooge about it."

With a quick frown he questioned her choice of words.

"What I mean to say is, I'm sure you bought him the kinds of things a little boy wants for Christmas."

"I was a little boy again when I did my shopping. You don't begrudge me that, do you?"

"No." They stood across from each other in the narrow hallway, his armload of boxes touching hers. A big red bow grazed her chin. "I appreciate it. It's the first Christmas without Ken, and I dreaded it. But you're here, and I'm glad, and—" She shrugged. "I guess I feel a little guilty about being glad."

He groaned. "You are so full of—" With a soft chuckle he tipped his head back against the wall. "The word that comes to mind...well, you'd take it wrong."

"Baloney?"

"That's not right, either. I know how you feel. I miss Kenny, too. Maybe not the same way you do, but I miss him." He ducked a little closer to her ear, as though he was sharing a secret. "I think it's okay to be glad about some things at Christmas, and still be sad about others. And I'm glad I'm here."

"Where would you be if you weren't here?"

"No place special." Probably hanging around Reno or Denver, or maybe working the holidays for some trucking outfit, but she was looking at him as though she thought he was sitting on the keys to some pleasure palace. "That's the truth, Amy. No place anywhere near this special."

Jody had fallen asleep under the tree. Quietly Tate set his armload of packages aside and knelt beside the boy. The colored lights from the tree cast a rainbow of soft hues over his soft blond curls and his sleeping-in-heavenly-peace face.

The warm glow seemed to seep into Tate's skin, like the gleam of approval he'd been seeing in the child's eyes lately.

That was a gift, he realized. The best gift anyone had ever given him. Nobody had ever accepted him unconditionally, the way Jody did. He imagined himself claiming his gift from under the tree as he lifted Jody into his arms, carried him to bed and tucked him in.

Amy had a steaming cup of apple cider waiting for him when he came back to join her on the sofa. "Homemade," she said as she watched him take a sip. "But it doesn't have much kick to it."

"I like it the way it is." He pressed his lips together, savoring the cinnamon flavor. "Homemade."

She nodded toward the packages under the tree. "It's that small box that fascinates him, but I don't think it's sugarplums he has dancing in his head. What's in it?"

"A gift for him and a surprise for you."

"The day you don't surprise me will be a surprise, Tate Harrison. I hope you didn't go overboard."

"I didn't." Not as far as he was concerned. "Anyway, what's done is done, and you're long overdue for a few pleasant surprises. And I'm just the man who can provide them, because you don't expect much." He gave her a mischievous wink. "I can look pretty damn good just by taking some time off from being bad."

"I wouldn't say that."

"You wouldn't say I look good?"

"You look—" she gave him a pointed once-over "—the way you've always looked." The observation made him squirm a little, which made her laugh. "Truthfully, I've always thought you looked good even when you were being your baddest."

"Baddest man in Overo?"

"Sometimes. You know darn well you turn a lot of heads, cowboy. You always have."

"But not yours."

"You know better than that," she admitted. "But I've always managed to be fairly practical."

"*Very* practical."

"I'm certainly not going to be unrealistic about a cowboy whose pickup odometer turns over every year." She glanced away from him, her attention drawn to the lights on the tree. "I do hate to see you sell your land, though. Someday you might wish you had a familiar place to park that pickup."

"I'm familiar with a lot of parking places."

"So was my father." She sighed deeply, and the lights twinkled in her eyes like distant memories. "My family moved all the time when I was growing up. When people ask me where I'm from originally, I still get all flustered with the need to explain. I used to launch into a complete history, but I've learned to simply pick a place." Her wistful smile seemed almost apologetic. "Or just to say that I'm from here now, because I *am*. I really am."

"Permanently planted, I'd say." Slipping his arm around her shoulders seemed a natural gesture. "Was your father in the military?"

"He should have been, but that was probably one of the few things he didn't try. He never held a job very long. He got bored." His hand curved comfortingly around her shoulder as her voice drifted and became almost childlike. "And I was never in one school for more than a year. He left us one winter when my mother decided that the trailer court we were living in was going to be home." A deep breath and a quick toss of her head grounded her in the present again. "She's still there, in Florida."

"Smart woman. I wouldn't wanna leave Florida in the winter, either. Where was the ol' man headed?"

"Who knows? I haven't seen him since."

He started to drink his cider, but a word from a previous conversation nagged at him. "Would you call him a gypsy?"

"Among other things." She offered a knowing smile. "He was a rover. He was a jack-of-all-trades. He was a lovable man in his way."

"Would you say he was a dreamer?"

"Oh, yes, he was that."

He looked her in the eye. "You know, you married a dreamer, too."

"Ken was not at all like my father. He may not have been much of a businessman, but he gave his family a home." She shrugged. "I'm surprised my father didn't try cowboying. It would have suited him well, I think."

"It would suit me well, too." Suit him just fine, he thought, as he drew his arm back and cradled the warm mug in both hands. "Except that I've been stuck with a damn flock of sheep lately."

"You're not stuck with them." She bit her lower lip, and he knew damn well she was thinking up a good one. Without looking up, she said quietly, "You're free to leave anytime."

"I was just…" *Damn*, she was a tough nut to crack. "I've made up my mind to see you and the kids through the winter, and that's what I'm doin'. I'm not sellin' any land before spring, and I'm not in any hurry to hit the road." He slid her a hard glance. "Unless you want me to."

"I just don't want you to feel obligated."

"I don't. I've got nothin' better to do. Simple as that."

Simple, hell. They stared at the Christmas lights until he couldn't stand the silence anymore. It was loaded with complications.

"Can't think of any place I'd rather spend the winter than Montana, freezin' my damn—" He glanced at her, and he thought he detected the hint of a smile in her eyes. "I don't know anyone in Florida who'd put me up for the winter, do you?"

"Not a soul."

"Besides, it's Christmas." He reached for her hand. "I'm not goin' anywhere at Christmas."

"Peace to you, then, cowboy." She gave him a peck on the cheek and whispered, "And merry Christmas."

Chapter 9

Jody didn't see Tate sitting at the kitchen table when he rode his broomstick horse into the living room on Christmas morning. Tate had already made coffee, and he was quietly biding his time as he sipped the first cup of the morning. Just waiting. He smiled to himself when he heard Jody's, "Whoa." There was a pause, and then, "Whoa! Mom! Tate! Hurry, come look!"

Tate hitched up his beltless jeans and poured coffee into a second cup, which he passed across the counter to Amy as she came around the corner carrying the baby against her shoulder. "Santa even made coffee this year?" she marveled with a sleepy smile. "What a guy."

"Special Christmas service for people who do two-o'clock feedings," Tate returned as he walked around her and touched the baby's cheek with one finger. "Happy first Christmas, little darlin'."

Eyes as big as saucers seemed to be asking him what all

the fuss was about. "This is Christmas," he explained, sliding his finger under her soft baby chin. "Are you ready for all the excitement?" She bounced her head up and down over her mother's shoulder and rewarded him with a smile.

Her brother galloped onto the kitchen scene, waving both arms wildly. "Come on, you guys! Hurry!"

Amy gave a throaty, morning laugh that sent shivers down Tate's back. "There's nothing in there that's about to run away, Jody." On second thought she cast Tate a warning glance as they headed for the living room. "Better not be anything on the hoof."

"There might be a few little tracks on the roof, but no new livestock this time around."

"Look at me, Mom!" Jody bounced astride the small saddle Santa had left under the tree. A small gasp escaped his mother's throat. "Just my size. Maybe there's a little horse for me outside!"

"Santa always takes these things one step at a time," Tate said. "I know for a fact that he never brings live animals without Mom's permission." Amy's soft sigh of relief made him grin. "But Santa knows every cowboy needs a good saddle, just in case."

A soft-body baby doll that was bigger than Karen earned a discreet test squeeze from her mother. The fancy stroller that could be converted for half a dozen uses obviously pleased Amy, too. "Santa heard that the stroller Jody used was ready for retirement," Tate said.

"Santa's insight was remarkable this year." Amy lifted the padded seat out of the stroller frame. On the floor it became a handy infant seat with handles that also served as rockers. Karen settled into it comfortably and quietly watched her first Christmas morning unfold.

No one tore through the gift wrap faster than Jody. He

announced what each gift was, barely able to contain himself as he pulled it out of the box. "Cowboy hat—thanks, Tate! Cowboy pajamas—thanks, Mom! Record player—thanks, Tate! Monkey with a button nose—thanks, Mom!"

Amy opened a box and lifted out the ruffled dress he'd picked for Karen. He blushed when she held up the frilly bloomers. "I liked the bows on it." He shrugged and sipped his coffee. "The one you made for her is prettier, though."

"This one is fancier." Amy's eyes glistened. "I love it, Tate. It's just darling."

"Well, see what you think of this," he said, urging her to open another box. He'd decided that a woman who'd just put aside her maternity clothes probably needed some pretty new things in her normal size, and he'd chosen a sweater, slacks, blouse and a down-filled jacket with fur trim on the hood.

"I saved the receipts in case there's something you don't like." He reached behind the sofa and pulled out a huge fruit basket, wrapped in red cellophane and tied with a green bow. "Except this. We're eatin' this."

"That's enough for an army!" It made him feel warm inside to hear Amy laugh so readily. "I like everything, but we'll see what you guys think about the clothes when I try them on. I can't even guess what size I am now."

"I don't know if the styles are right." Tate eyed her appreciatively and gave a slow smile. "But I'll bet you two oranges and a banana that I didn't mess up on your size."

"You sound awfully confident." Her smile was coy. "Did you seek expert advice?"

"Didn't need any," he drawled. "Got a damn good eye."

She ducked under the far side of the tree and delivered a gaily wrapped box into his hands. "There aren't any receipts for yours. About all I can alter is the fit."

He couldn't believe she'd made the Western shirt herself,

with its piped yoke, pearlized snaps and crisply tailored collar and cuffs. And the plush royal-blue robe she'd made was monogrammed with his initials and a tiny horseshoe. Tate smiled a little self-consciously as he tried the robe on over his T-shirt and jeans. He'd never been big on clothes to wear around the house, but he could see how it might come in handy for a guy who had a house to hang around in. He thought about breaking it in with his own brand of after-shave.

"Do you like the color?"

"It's a great color." It didn't look anything like Kenny's. "We knew you were busy back there, but we had no idea *how* busy. Did we, Jody? Ma'am, you sure outdid yourself on that sewing machine."

"I'll take that as the stamp of approval." Admiring the way it looked on him, she assessed the sleeve length and adjusted the fluffy lapels, smoothing her hands over them to make sure they lay just right over his robust frame. "Does it feel comfortable in the shoulders?"

"It fits great."

"I thought you'd like a pocket," she said.

With two fingers he traced the large *H* in the middle of the monogram. "How did you know my middle name?"

"I sneaked a peek at your driver's license."

"Picked my pocket, huh?"

"You're an easy mark," she said lightly. "You left your pants in the bathroom. But your license only says 'Tate C. Harrison,' so I'm still wondering what the *C* stands for."

"Carter," he said. "After my father."

Their eyes met briefly, exchanging myriad feelings neither dared name. He wanted to kiss her, long and hard. She wanted to put her arms around him and hug him in the new robe she'd made for him.

But she smiled and patted its single pocket. "This isn't made to hold cigarettes."

"What's it for?"

"I don't know." She gave him a saucy smile. "Maybe your billfold."

"I do like to keep that handy."

Amy sat on the floor next to the baby and tested out the rocker as she surveyed the colorful torn-paper chaos. "What was in that small box, Jody? Did I miss that?"

"Didn't open it yet," Jody said as he withdrew the last box from underneath the tree. "I was saving it."

"Well, let's see what it is." Tate's eagerness shone in his eyes as he watched Jody unwrap the gift.

"The harmonica." With wide eyes and a voice full of wonder, Jody took the instrument from the box. "The silver-and-black one."

"Is that yours, Tate?" Amy asked quietly.

"I have a couple of them," he said absently. He was busy cherishing the look in the little boy's eyes. "This is Jody's favorite. Right, partner?"

"Tate's gramma gave him this," Jody reported. "It was his grampa's."

"Oh, Tate—"

"Jody has a surprise for you." He gave an encouraging nod. "Go ahead, son."

The word *son* was out before Tate knew it was coming. Jody didn't seem to notice, and neither did Amy. She was too intent on listening to Jody play "Jingle Bells" and "Frosty the Snowman." Tate figured he'd only used the word because right now it suited the way he felt. He wasn't trying to take anybody's place. But he was just as proud of the boy's accomplishment as any father could possibly be.

* * *

By afternoon the snow was falling thick and piling up fast. By nightfall the wind had picked up. When Tate went out to the barn to put the sheep to bed, he found that the snowdrifts were getting bigger. He hadn't thought it possible, but the sheep were getting stupider. The shed was three-sided, and the solid wood doors on the barn had to be left open whenever the building was used for a sheep shelter. There were no deadlier conditions for sheep than moist air in close and closed quarters. He'd been meaning to build slatted doors for the barn, but he hadn't gotten around to it yet. Now the dumb beasts were huddled in every corner of the pens outside, and the drifts were mounting around them.

Daisy and Duke seemed to realize right off the bat that this was no time to play games with the cowboy, even if his signals were a little off the mark. They took the cue to drive every last woolly creature under a roof. Tate couldn't help marveling at the dogs' work. He vowed that the pair would feast on T-bones or soup bones, whatever he could rustle up from Amy's freezer. After supper they would be bunking in his room for the night. When the chips were down, the cowboy and the sheepdogs made a remarkable team.

Amy didn't object when the dogs stumbled in the back door with him, blown in on a big wind. He could tell she'd been waiting anxiously, just as she had the night he'd trailed the sheep back from his pasture. Not that he wanted her to worry, but there was something pretty nice about being met at the door.

"Visibility must be down to zero out there," he announced as he shooed the dogs down the basement steps to keep them from shaking snow all over the kitchen. "Ol' Daisy and Duke sure did earn their—"

"Where's Jody?"

The question slammed the brakes on Tate's heart. He stared dumbly.

"He's not in the house, Tate. I was ready to brain you for taking him outside in this, but…" She kept looking behind him, as though she expected the boy to appear at his heels. "He's not anywhere in the house."

"Get me the biggest flashlight you've got." Tate jerked the back door open and whistled for the dogs.

"I'll get dressed."

"You stay with the baby. We'll find him."

It was the kind of windy whiteout that spawned Western disaster tales, and the worst kind was about the child who slipped outside unnoticed and froze to death only yards away from the house. Galvanized by fear, Tate called out as he followed the fence line toward the pens, but the dogs bounded through the drifts in a different direction. They seemed to be headed for the machine shed.

With every inch in every direction turned completely to snow, there were no directions. There was no order, no sense to anything. A mere man was almost useless. The snow stung Tate's face as he followed the two canine tails, which were about all he could see. The flashlight probably wasn't penetrating more than a few feet, and the wind had his lung power beat all to hell. He had to trust the dogs' keener senses.

But when he ran smack into the chain-link fence surrounding their kennel, he cursed the dogs roundly. "I said find *Jody* you dumb sons of—"

"Here I am!"

Daisy and Duke were already digging the snow away from the doghouse door. Jody emerged like a snowball, tumbling into Tate's arms. He'd had the good sense to dress warmly, and he'd found a snug place to take shelter. Throat clotted with a burning flood of relief, Tate hugged him close. A whistle for the dogs was the only sound he could manage.

"He's okay," Tate announced as he came through the door again, his legs considerably less steady this time. "He was in the doghouse."

"In the doghouse?" Laughing and crying at once, Amy reached out like a desperate beggar and took the boy in her arms. She sat him on the kitchen counter and peeled his ice-coated scarf away from his face. She laughed again, relieved to uncover a cherry-red nose and quivering lips. "How was it in there?"

"Cold as ice," Jody blurted out.

"I guess one trip to the doghouse is enough for tonight." She took off his hat and combed her fingers through his matted curls. "Oh, Jody, I was so scared."

"M-me, too. I was worried about Tate. Th-thought I c-could help him get done with his chores f-faster." His teeth chattered. "I couldn't f-find the b-barn."

"You didn't know how bad it was out there, did you, partner?" Tate offered as he glanced anxiously at Amy.

The looks they exchanged over Jody's head acknowledged the internal mélange of emotion that defied words. Terror was slow to give way to complete, bountiful relief. Amy didn't know whether to scold her son or simply hug him to pieces, then do the same for his rescuer. Tate didn't quite know what to do with himself, either, other than to try to shake off most of the snow in the vicinity of the scatter rug by the back door. Amy handed him Jody's jacket, and he hung it on a hook next to his.

From the back room came Karen's call for her supper. One look in Amy's eyes and Tate knew that the woman had finally reached her limit, emotionally and otherwise. She couldn't stand the idea of coming apart in front of anyone. She needed a few moments to herself.

"I'll give Jody a bath while you feed the baby."

"Are you—" She pressed her lips together tightly and cupped Jody's cheeks in her hands. "Toes hurt?" she croaked.

Jody shook his head. "I just went out…'bout three or seven minutes ag-go."

"I don't think he was out too long," Tate said. "We'll go in the bathroom and get ourselves thawed out."

Amy nodded and fled to answer the baby's call.

Jody pulled one of his boots off and dropped it on the floor. "She's real mad, ain't she?" he asked quietly.

"*Isn't* she." The correction rolled off Tate's tongue as though teaching the boy proper English was something he did every day. Where had *that* come from? he wondered as he hunkered down to pick up the boot. Jody handed him the second one. "She's not really mad. She was afraid you were lost in the snow, and I was, too. It was a mistake to go outside, Jody."

"A bad mistake," the boy agreed.

"But it's not like you were being a bad boy. The rule is that you don't go outside without asking. Right?"

"She wouldn't have let me go."

"And now you know why." He set the boots by the back door, then turned with his big hands outstretched. "Come on up here, partner." They traded bear-and-cub hugs. "Oh, that feels good. A bath will warm you up just fine. I know that from experience. First you, then me."

But it was a couple of hours before Tate got his shower, and by then it wasn't quite as much of a treat. He'd said good-night to Jody and left him to make peace with his mom, who offered to read him three stories instead of the usual one long one or two short ones. Tate had used the little shower downstairs, trying not to use up too much hot water, in case Amy still wanted some, and he'd wrapped himself up in his brand-new bathrobe. Then he'd plunked himself down on the bed with a magazine and sat there listening to the wind whistling above the window wells.

Since he'd taken up residence with Amy and the kids, he'd made a point to limit his smoking to the great outdoors, but this was one night when he figured he'd earned a shot of whiskey and a cigarette. Trouble was, even though the whiskey felt good going down and the smoke steadied him some, it made him feel lonely.

It was Christmas, and here he was sitting on a single bed in the basement of the first place that had felt like home to him in one hell of a lot of years. It was *Christmas,* and he was indulging himself in two of his favorite vices. Big thrill. Daisy and Duke were curled up as close together as cloves on a Christmas ham, and Tate felt like a man who'd been relegated to the doghouse.

His blue mood didn't make much sense. This was the spare bedroom, after all. Hired hand or guest, this was where the Beckers had always put him up. It was comfortable enough, and he had his privacy. It didn't make sense that the four white walls made him feel so damn lonesome, not with Amy and the kids right upstairs.

But he'd spent this Christmas on an emotional roller coaster. His head was spinning with a hundred joys and fears, and there was no such thing as sense. If truth be told, he would have to say he'd started losing touch with his faculties the day he'd knocked on Amy's door and offered her a hand.

Offered to *be* her hand, and for next to nothing. In lieu of flowers, just the way he'd planned, just as the obituaries always said. Hell, he'd turned himself into a living memorial. Now he was turning himself inside out, like the kid looking for one last piece of candy in his Christmas stocking.

Pathetic. He damn sure didn't need steel guitars whining in the background to put him in a melancholy mood. But, then, he was a cowboy, and all a cowboy had to do was pour himself a drink and *think* lonesome. He finished his cigarette, tossed back the last of his drink, turned the light out, took his clothes off and crawled into bed.

Damn, those sheets were cold.

Three quiet taps on his door brought him up on one elbow.

"Tate?"

Just like a woman. She could smell smoke in the middle of a blizzard, and she'd come to give him hell about it. Man, she'd sure tiptoed down the steps quieter than a feather duster.

"I'm…here."

The door opened slowly, and there she stood in her nightgown, backlit by the light in the stairwell. "The kids are in bed, and it's so quiet upstairs," she said in a small, shy voice. "I…well, I thought…the lights look pretty on the tree, and…it *is* nice and quiet." She paused, obviously waiting for him to jump at the chance to go up and sit with her. "I guess you're tired."

"Yeah," he said finally. "I'm tired." Seeing the way her shoulders sagged slightly brought him a small surge of satisfaction. Minute, actually, compared to the surge of hot current that was suddenly running strong and lusty through his body and heading straight for his lightning rod.

Amy stepped back as though she'd felt the shock. She was about to retreat just as quietly as she'd come.

He turned over on one hip. "Amy?" She paused. He could almost hear her misgivings, but he could see they weren't strong enough to take her away. She was caught in the balance.

"Amy, you gotta know that I'm down here bunkin' in the

same room with two wet dogs who are huggin' each other up somethin' fierce, and my nerves are wound tighter than a spring, and I'm thinkin' if I could just get close to you right now…"

She went to him. Drifted across the floor like an apparition and knelt beside his bed. He swung his legs over the side of the bed and sat up, pulling the sheet over his lap. "Honey, I don't wear…any kind of pajamas."

"I noticed you were uncomfortable in them before."

"Amy, what I'm trying to tell you is I can't—" With her back to the dim light, he couldn't see her face. He could smell that strawberry soap she always used, and he forgot all about wet dogs. He took her face in his hands, touching the soft contours of her cheeks with his thumbs. "I want you so bad, I can hardly…"

"Hardly what?" She slid her hands over his upper arms, caressing hard muscle. "What would you be doing if you could get close to me tonight?"

"I'd be lovin' you up so good, you'd stop—" He drew her into his arms, lifting her into his lap. "You'd stop thinkin', stop worryin', stop—"

"I should warn you, Tate, I'm not very good at this."

"Good at what?" He knew damn well what, but he was going to make her say it. Here she was, cuddled against him like a kitten, and she was taking that instructive tone with him again, the one she used to protect herself. He'd always been a threat to her somehow, and, as always, she was trying to keep one foot on the floor, just in case she decided to run. Well, he wasn't about to *let* her run. Not tonight.

"I'm not the best lover." She drew a shaky breath. Tate wondered when and how she'd arrived at that conclusion. "I want to be good at it, but I know I'm not."

She just knew, and that was that. The rest he would have to figure out for himself.

"I am." He lifted her hair and traced the delicate arch of her ear with the tip of his tongue. "You want me to show you how?"

"I don't know." She shivered when he blazed a damp trail down her neck. "You probably think this is a funny conversation to be having with a woman who's somehow managed to produce two children."

"You hear me laughin'?"

"No. I appreciate that." She slipped her arms around him, shifting in his lap. "Is there room for me here? With you?"

"If we stick close together." He slid his hands up and down her back, teasing himself with the feel of soft flannel and the knowledge that there was nothing beneath it but Amy. "Is it still too soon? I know how to make love to you, Amy, but there are some things about a woman's body that are still a mystery to me."

"You've seen me at my...well, my least appealing."

She couldn't stand the idea of coming apart in front of anyone.

Oh, Amy. Her struggle with words and images touched him almost as deeply as her struggle with pain. "Why do you think of it that way? Because I was there?"

"No. I guess I shouldn't think of it at all." She pressed her face against his neck and kissed him there. "I guess I'm afraid it might bother you, and I'm afraid I'm not pretty enough or sexy enough or—"

"You trusted me then because you had to." He slid back, cradling her, entreating her as he took her into bed with him. "Trust me now because you want to. Let me decide how beautiful you are."

He peppered her face with kisses while he unbuttoned her

nightgown. "I want to kiss your breasts," he whispered, sliding down into position. "I'll be gentle."

He laved each one carefully, nuzzling, kissing, making them tighten. He could feel the passion rising in her, but he knew from the tension he felt in her body that she struggled still. Her instinct was to hold back. "I taste milk," he said.

"I'm sorry. I can't—"

"Don't keep it from me." He swirled his tongue over her peak, relishing it like an ice-cream cone. "Amy's milk. It's the only kind I like."

"Oh, Tate, you'll make me…"

"Does it feel good?"

"It makes me want…"

"Good." He kissed the valley between her breasts. She buried her fingers in his hair and held him while she gulped deep breaths, struggling to regain control.

He wasn't going to give it to her. He knew damn well it was the last thing she needed right now. She needed to *lose* control, and by damn, he was just the man. He was *just* the man. He whisked her nightgown over her head and slid down more, licking a stray drop of milk as he kissed the underside of one breast. "Do they hurt?" he asked. "Are they too full?"

"No, I just fed…but all you have to do is…"

"Shh, don't worry about that." He kissed her, sharing the sticky sweetness that clung to his lips. "Just tell me if anything hurts you. I'd cut off my arm before I'd hurt you, sweetheart, so just tell me."

"Your arm?"

Okay, so the protrusion straining against her thigh wasn't an arm, but he wasn't going to hurt her with it, either. Damn, she was teasing him. She touched her lips to his forehead, and in the dark he could feel the curve of her smile. "You don't get to laugh, either, woman." He slid his hand over her belly and kneaded gently, the way he had weeks ago. "Is it back to its normal size?" he wondered.

"I think it's—" She caught her breath as he caressed her, his hand nearly bridging the span of her pelvic cradle. "I'm flabby there," she said, but her soft groan told him that she was also aroused there. And lower. He sensed that the tension inside her was drifting lower, and he chased it with a slow hand. He didn't have to hurry. He knew where it was going, and he knew he would catch up.

He kissed her tenderly and hungrily, supplicating and demanding, and gaining wondrous kisses in return. He was gaining on her. "Relax for me, sweetheart."

Ah, her thighs were strong and stubborn, but her need was growing stronger. His tongue stroked hers, while down below he explored her springing hair, her damp folds, her soft, warm secrets. Deep in his loins he throbbed like a swollen thumb, but he knew what Amy's body had endured, and self-restraint was within his power. "Tell me when we have to stop."

With a delicate touch he stroked her until she responded urgently, pressing herself against his hand, inviting a deeper touch. "Don't stop," she pleaded. "Oh, Tate, don't stop."

He hovered over her, brushed her hair back from her face and kissed her. He was fully prepared to make the magic just for her, but he wasn't prepared for her quick gasp when he tried to slide his finger deeper. "Oh, sweetheart, I'm hurting you." He withdrew, stroking her thighs in the hope of comforting her.

"No, it's okay. I'm okay, Tate. My checkup...I'm—"

"Shh, you're not ready." He wasn't sure where it had come from, but he kissed away the dampness on her cheeks.

She groaned, running her hands up his back, digging her blunt nails in when she reached his shoulders. "That's for me to decide," she said huskily. "It might have to hurt a little."

"I can go as slow as you want."

"How about as fast as I want?"

"That, too. But if I hurt you inside, you tell me, okay?" As he spoke, he reached into the drawer in the nightstand and withdrew a foil packet. "You don't have to be strong for me, Amy. If I can't give you pleasure now, I won't—"

"I can't get pregnant now, Tate. At least, I *probably*—"

He smiled, palming the packet as he smoothed his thumb over her forehead, hoping to banish all probably-nots. "This doesn't sound like my cautious little Black-Eyed Susan."

"I told you I wasn't very good at this." She slid one tentative hand over his hard buttock. "But I want to be. I want to be… memorable for you."

He would never forget her shy, gentle hand on his hip. "Keep touching me, and I'll remember."

She did, and he returned the favor. He caressed her until she lost the last vestige of tight control and quivered in his hand, entrusting him with a rare moment of complete vulnerability. She was eager for him now, open to him with no reservations, no limitations, save the one he willingly placed on himself for her protection. She greeted his penetration with a soft, welcoming sound.

He groaned with the pleasure of immersing himself fully in her warm passage. "Put your hands on my chest," he implored. "Feel my heart beating and touch my…" His own nipples were sensitive, as she discovered with her fingertips. "Mmm, that's good. You can talk to me, Amy."

"I don't want to sound—oooooh, Tate."

"I want you to sound 'oh, Tate.' I'll remember every soft, sweet word."

"I'm afraid to talk," she whispered as she rolled her hips to meet the thrust of his. "This feels too good."

"Ain't that the…" The truth, which was ecstasy, which

was bearing down upon him faster and without regard for...
"Come with me, Amy."

She drew a quick breath, coming apart, shattering deliciously in his arms. "Stay with me, Tate."

"Like this, yes," he crooned close to her ear as he drew her knees up to his waist. "Let me take you with me."

She clamped her legs around him as she arched and lifted, unfurled and set sail.

Neither could move at first, and when they stirred, it was like a dance in slow motion. They nestled together, eyes closed, hands languidly touching damp skin, ears hearing the soft whistle of cold winds and hearts content in the shelter of a loving embrace.

"You okay?" he asked finally.

She nodded, and then in a small voice asked, "You?"

"Oh, yeah."

Over in the corner, one of the dogs yawned.

"Who asked you?" Tate's chuckle rumbled deep in his chest. "I'd have to say this is the best I've been in I don't know how long."

"That's for me to say, isn't it?"

"Pardon me." He traced his finger along the top of her shoulder before he kissed it. "Was I okay?"

"Best I've ever—" she pressed her face against his neck and whispered "—*had*, and I know I shouldn't say that."

"Give it a rest, honey." He caught himself and groaned. "I didn't mean 'honey.' I meant—" he kissed her again "—for both of us to give it a rest. This whole routine between us. Just give it a rest and let ourselves be together the way we've both been dreamin' about lately." He brushed his lips across her forehead. "Haven't we? I know I have."

"And now you know I have. And I shouldn't." He groaned, and she stretched her arm around him, hugging him close.

"I'm not regretting anything, except… Well, just look what happened tonight. Jody got out of the house without my knowledge. Where was my head?"

"Were you thinking about me? Were you thinkin' that the weather was bad, and I'd been outside for quite a while, freezin' my—"

"—tail off, I know. It's a nice one, too." She reached down and patted one rock-hard cheek. "Yes, I was thinking about you, hoping you were all right, wondering any one of the many things I've been wondering about you."

"Satisfy any of that curiosity tonight?"

"Satisfied…something. Not the questions, but—"

"The woman." Thank God. He'd been a little worried at first. "That's good. You're more woman than anyone I've ever known, my pretty Black-Eyed Susan, and you're a challenge and a half."

"Really," she said lightly. "I don't know who you're comparing me to, but when I said 'the best I've had—'" She huddled against him, as if she wanted him to hide her from something. "I didn't mean it the way it sounded."

"It didn't sound any *way*. I knew what you meant." He turned her in his arms, belly to belly, knees to knees. "You need a man, Amy. There's no shame in that."

"Then why does it sound so…shameful?"

"Maybe because—" he kissed the soft swell of her breast, and she sighed "—you know I'm the man you need."

She groped for a denial, but none would come when he touched her breast as reverently as he did. Silence, followed by soft, mingled breaths and appreciative sighs, spoke of sweet accord. He claimed his point with a kiss.

Chapter 10

As quickly as it had come, the Montana blizzard blew across the Dakota plains to become a Minnesota blizzard, leaving drifts of snow glistening in the morning sun. Jody had already forgotten the terror of blowing snow sweeping him across the yard on Christmas night. Snow pillows were friendlier, and he was ready to play in them. Amy bundled him up in his snowsuit and sent the dogs outside with him. "Stay right in the yard," she warned.

"I'm going to make a snow castle."

"I want to be able to see it from the window, okay?"

She later took her coffee into the living room, tapped on the window and waved. Jody waved back and pointed his mittened hand at the snow angel he'd just made. Then he waved again, and Amy turned to find Tate standing just behind her, waving back.

"You certainly move quietly," she said.

"Not as quietly as you do." The smile in his eyes said they

shared some new secrets. "Did you find the quarters a little cramped last night?"

She glanced back out the window. New secrets posed new problems for her this morning.

"I didn't expect you to stay," he said quietly. "Just wanted you to know I missed you."

"I don't want Jody to think…" She kept her eyes on what was going on outside the window. Her child was playing with his plastic snow-block maker, thinking only that his mother and his new cowboy idol were inside watching him. "Obviously, he knows that moms and dads sleep in the same bed. I don't want to confuse him with other…ideas."

"You're still a good mother, Amy. A good woman." Tate stepped up close behind her and laid his hands on her shoulders. "What happened last night didn't change that."

She closed her eyes, allowing the light, woodsy scent of his after-shave to fill her head with erotic images of the night before, but only briefly. It was as risky an indulgence as enjoying the feel of his strong hands. She opened her eyes wide and trained them on her busy little boy as she gripped the warm stoneware mug in both hands. "You mean, what happened last night with Jody?" she asked tightly.

"You know what I mean." He leaned close to her ear, his chin brushing the thick braid that lay over one shoulder. "I mean, what happened with me."

"I went looking for it, didn't I?" Her voice went a little hoarse. She cleared her throat, determined to be nothing more than matter-of-fact. "I asked for it."

"It?"

"You." She set her coffee on the lamp table and turned to look him in the eye. "I went looking for you, Tate. I wanted *you.*"

It galled her that the confession clearly pleased him. He

tried to take her in his arms, and she saw the confusion she caused him when she stepped out of his reach. She bolstered her resolve by telling herself that he was taking certain things for granted after just one night. He didn't understand her situation at all. Just like a man.

"I've decided to sell out, come spring."

He stared, confounded by the news. "When did you make that decision?"

"To sell out?" She shrugged, turning to the window again. "It's always been one of the options under consideration. Lately I've had to think about it more seriously. I have two small children. It's foolish for me to think I can give them the attention they need while I'm trying to run a business that demands…" She spared him a glance. "Well, you know what it demands."

"A lot of work. You need help." *You need me, Amy.*

"Hired help isn't always reliable." *But I do need you, Tate.* "If I can get through lambing, I'll make some money. My herd will be worth more with the lambs on the ground. But I need to know—" Watching Jody arrange a row of snow blocks gave her time to swallow some pride. *I need you, but how long can I count on you?* "How long can you stay, Tate?"

Now he was watching Jody, too, and his answer came without emotion. "I told you I'd get you through the winter."

"Last night complicated things, didn't it?"

"How so?" He gave a mirthless chuckle. "You think I'm gonna require more than room and board?"

"You didn't require anything." She faced him. "I was the one."

"Amy—"

"I want to pay you, Tate." She *had* to pay him. She knew it wouldn't keep him there any longer than this whim of his lasted, but it was the only way she could make peace with the way she felt about their tenuous arrangement. He was doing her too damn many favors.

"For what?" he demanded.

"For all that you've done."

"I've done what you needed me to do."

"Yes." She folded her arms, hugging herself tightly. "More than you bargained for. More than you hired yourself out to—"

"Stop it!" he growled. "Why can't you just ask me?" He closed his hands over her shoulders and recited the words carefully, as though she might be hard of hearing. "'I need you, Tate.' Is that so hard to say?"

She lifted her chin and turned her face away. One, two deep breaths helped her fight back the tears that threatened to betray her. She'd admitted to the mistake of wanting him, but *wanting* was different. With the exception of an occasional human indulgence, she routinely did without many of the things she wanted. Wanting could be kept under control, but needs had to be met. The children's needs, her own needs—it was up to Amy to provide for those. It always had been.

"Ken left some good horses," she told Tate in her most controlled, informative tone. "All registered stock, but they're not saddle-broke. I know horse prices aren't great right now, but I want you to take your pick. For every month that you've been here, every month that you stay, I want you to have one of those horses."

"What kind of services are you trying to pay me for, Amy?"

She pressed her lips together firmly. She wouldn't let his anger scare her. She could feel the power in the hands that gripped her shoulders, but she could also feel his restraint. He couldn't intimidate her. No man could. He could leave today if he wanted to, and she would get along fine without him.

"I'll stay. I told you that." He released her, his arms dropping heavily to his sides. "I'll stay and do what needs doing. Herd your sheep, deliver your baby, have a talk with your son—whatever."

She stared, startled by the knowledge that deep down she believed in his promise.

"Oh, yeah, and I can also take you to bed and give you the best damn lovin' you've ever had." He quirked a cocky smile. "Jack-of-all-trades, that's me. All that for a few broomtails?"

She affected a careless shrug. "It's all I can come up with right now."

"Well, I ain't that cheap, lady. I'm gonna cost you dearly."

"The wages of sin, I suppose."

"What sin? You mean what I got last night? Was that supposed to be my wages and your sin?" He took advantage of the momentary paralysis of her tongue. "Or was it the other way around? Damn, you've got me confused."

"I don't want to take advantage of you," she said tightly.

"Likewise," he assured her with a smug grin. "So I'm not about to take my wages out in trade. You'll have to come up with something better."

"I wasn't *offering* to pay for your…" She was tempted to put a bag over that grin. "I need your help, Tate," she said, forcing an even tone, "and I'm not suggesting anything—" *Stop that aggravating nodding.* "—unseemly. I'm only trying to—"

"That's a start. 'I need your *help,* Tate.'" He was on his way out of the room, wagging his finger and being a damn smart aleck as he went. "I like the sound of that. That's gettin' there."

"Where are you going?"

"The baby's cryin'." He paused. At first it was quiet, but

then came the muffled squall. Tate's tone mimicked her at her most indulgently instructive. "I'm going to pick her up. And if I had the equipment," he said, hands on his T-shirt-clad chest, "I'd feed her, too. But even a jack-of-all-trades has his limits."

He knew she didn't want to need him. Needing his *help* was difficult enough for Amy, but needing *him*—needing Tate Harrison—was like having the flu. She figured she would get over it. And maybe she would. If she did, hell, he'd never really pictured himself being tied down, especially not to a bunch of sheep and a piece of ground just outside Overo, Montana, and halfway to nowhere.

The Christmas blizzard gave way to a January thaw, and Tate used the respite to his advantage. He built the slatted barn door he'd mentally devised before Amy had declared her intention to sell out. His design allowed for a choice of doors. Amy was impressed. She also liked his wall-mounted hayracks and grain feeders, which he modestly claimed were "real easy to knock together." She was less excited when he rigged up a corral, using portable steel fence panels, and began breaking horses.

He figured he could have at least four or five green-broke by spring thaw. He didn't have time to make good saddle horses out of them, but some of them had potential. He enjoyed lecturing Jody on the subject, pointing out each animal's strengths and weaknesses, from conformation to temperament. He predicted which ones would really be worth something when Amy decided to sell them and lamented the fact that they would be worth even more if he had more time to work with them. The summer, maybe.

Given the chance, Jody would make a good horseman someday, if Amy would ever ease up on the rules. He had to stay off the fence, stay in the pickup, stay away from the horses when Tate wasn't around, stay away from the hooves, stay away from the teeth, and on and on. To her credit, Amy never said, "Your dad was killed by a horse," but her distress was apparent every time she came out to the corral when Tate was working the horses. And it annoyed the hell out of him every time she called Jody into the house because he'd been "bothering Tate long enough."

"Nobody in this house bothers me except you," he told her privately when she came out to the corral one day. "And you bother me plenty."

"Nobody's got you tied to the hitching post, cowboy. You can mosey on anytime."

"Cute." He watched the boy and his trusty stick-horse disappear into the toolshed, where he'd been sent to fetch a leather punch. "Are you trying to keep Jody away from me?"

"Of course not. He loves you like a brother."

"Brother?" He felt slighted, and feeling slighted made him feel mean. He gave her a mean-spirited smile. "What's the matter with *uncle?* You don't like that word?"

"Big brothers eventually move on, and they never realize how much little brothers miss them."

"Yeah, well, Kenny was like a brother to me, so the analogy doesn't quite work."

Jody appeared in the doorway of the toolshed. He waved the leather punch in the air, and Tate nodded his approval.

"You're right about one thing, though," Tate confided absently. He was pleased to see that Jody wasn't forgetting to close the door, and that he was carrying the tool back at a sedate walk, exactly as instructed. "The boy loves me. Unconditionally, no questions asked. And I love him right back the same way." He adjusted his hat as he looked Amy in the eye. "Believe it or not, I am capable of that. I don't care whose kid he is, I love him like my own."

She believed him. Now that she knew he was capable of giving more of himself than she'd ever thought possible, her heart ached all the more with the need to ask for another little piece of him for herself. But she was too proud. He'd been spending more of his evenings in town lately, which she regarded as a warm-up activity for a man with itchy feet. She tried not to lie awake and listen for the sound of his pickup. When she heard it, she tried not to notice what numbers were illuminated on her bedside clock. And when she didn't hear it, she tried not to imagine what or who might be keeping him out so late.

The month of February was torn off the Overo Farm and Ranch Co-Op calendar, and March came in with a lamb.

"We've got a baby comin'," Tate announced from the back door as he pulled off his work gloves.

"Already?" Amy pulled the plug on the dishwater and reached for a hen-and-chick print towel. "You're sure?"

"I suspect the signs are about the same for a ewe as they are for a cow or a mare." Tate tipped his hat back and grinned. "Human females like to keep you guessin', but you take their clothes off, the signs are probably pretty much the same."

"That's true. That's absolutely true." From the look in his eye, she could have sworn he was just as excited about the prospect of lambing as she was. Maybe he was the wolf at her door. "Your lunch is ready."

Tate's news seemed to wake up the house. Jody turned off the Saturday-morning cartoons, and Karen called from her crib. But Amy had to hurry out to the barn and see for herself what was going on. She'd counted the days and figured on almost another week before lambing would start. Now she would have to count on Tate, who was helping himself to a cup of coffee, and Jody, who was slurping up a bowl of cereal. They would have to spell her from a few duties while she did the job she felt called to do.

"You'll change your mind about sheep when you see the lambs, Tate. They're just as cute as—" She put Karen in his arms and smiled when the baby grabbed his chin. "Well, not as cute as *human* babies, but cuter than calves. I forgot to tell you about the lambing pens."

"I found them," he said. "I've already got a couple set up, and as soon as I have a cup of coffee…" He smiled down at Karen, who was trying to examine his teeth. "A cup of coffee and a couple of little baby fingers…"

"Lambing is my job."

With a glance he questioned her good sense.

"Your hands are too big, Tate." To emphasize the contrast, she put her hand over the back of his just as Karen laid claim to his thumb.

"Hey, that looks like Papa Bear, Mama Bear and Baby Bear," Jody managed to announce despite a mouth full of milk.

The look in Tate's eyes softened as one dilemma crowded out another. Amy nodded, smiling wistfully. "Mine are just the right size, you see. I have to help my mamas get their babies born. That much I owe them."

Tate had been party to many a calving, but delivering Karen had changed his outlook on the miracle of birth. Amy was right about the lambs. Those little wobbly-legged woollies were irresistible. Her skill and patience as a midwife were remarkable. Tate was content to observe the process while he tended the children. Some of the ewes required Amy's help in delivery, which often meant slipping a deft hand into the birth canal to assist a lamb in making its debut.

Most of the ewes produced twins, and one even had healthy triplets. Amy determined that the runt of the three would have to be bottle-fed. The death of three young ewes left orphans, two of which were successfully "grafted" onto ewes that had lost their lambs. Amy wrapped the pelts of the dead lambs around the orphans so that the adoptive mothers would accept them as their own. She graciously accepted Tate's offer to do the skinning.

That left two lambs to become "bottle babies," which pleased Jody immensely. Amy confided that raising orphans on the bottle was never profitable, and most sheep men didn't bother. "Sheep *women*," she said, "are different. When we sell the herd, we'll be keeping those bottle babies."

They were different, all right, Tate thought. She tried to talk offhandedly about selling her sheep, and she probably could have fooled almost anybody else. But Tate saw the pain in her eyes. Once lambing was over, she would use up what feed she had, and then she would put the herd on the market. Before the fields were lush with grass, she would sell out. She wouldn't have to worry about predators this year, she declared with artificial cheer. And shearing would be someone else's problem.

Leaving Amy and the kids would be Tate's problem. The more she mused about making her own preparations, the less he had to say about anything at all. The ground had thawed, and the first pale blooms of camas and sego lilies were beginning to dot the hillsides among the first green spikes of new grass. If he were planning to graze the livestock, he would take note of the poisonous camas and keep the animals away from them. He would be looking for coyotes, and he would be thinking about replacing a couple of sections of fence with the lamb creeps he'd been building. He'd modeled them after a picture he'd found in one of Amy's sheep-raising books. Not that he'd *read* it; he'd just sort of flipped through the pages. And not that he was thinking seriously about *any* of this stuff. A grazing plan had just sort of crossed his mind.

When he ran into Marianne and Patsy at the bar one night, he quietly took exception to a comment Marianne made about his "cozy little arrangement with Amy." But he wasn't about to tell the women that Amy was talking about selling out. Marianne would have been on the phone with her lawyer in a New York minute, trying to find out how soon she could get her damn core samples taken. Not that he cared about a few holes punched in the pasture, but Marianne's claim that there was money lurking below ground didn't impress him much, either. If they found anything, it was likely to be coal. And he had to agree with Amy about strip mining. It wasn't a pretty sight.

Faced with Amy's quandary, he'd forgotten all about his own plans to sell his land. When Marianne brought that issue up, he paid for his drink and called it a night. He wasn't sure why he was grinding his back teeth as he left the bar. Probably had something to do with the smell of Patsy's perfume.

It was almost midnight, but the kitchen light was still on, and Amy was still up. She was sitting at the table paging through a magazine, a steaming cup of tea close at hand. If he didn't know any better, he would think she wasn't planning to be up at her usual predawn hour.

"Waiting up for me?" He was trying for a touch of sarcasm, but it just wasn't there. He liked the idea too damn much to make light of it.

"The baby's been fussy."

"Seems pretty quiet to me." Little Karen had been sleeping through the night for weeks now.

"Would you like some coffee?"

"No, thanks. I'm awake enough." He tossed his denim jacket over a hook, thinking that if he couldn't work up any sarcasm, maybe he could bait her just a little. "You've got no business waiting up for me, Amy. What I do is my business."

"I wasn't waiting up for you. But you're early."

"Compared to what?" He pulled out the chair across from her, spun it around and straddled it, folding his arms over the back. "Compared to last week? Last month?" She glanced up from her magazine. "Compared to when Kenny used to come home?"

"Kenny always came home." She gave him a pointed look—though what her point was, he wasn't sure—then turned a page and found something that seemed to interest her more than he did. She tore into a corner of the page as she rattled on. "Ken had his faults and his weaknesses, but he gave us a home, and he was part of it. Always."

"Good for him." She glanced up, and he nodded. "I mean that. He inherited this place. Big deal. The truth is, *you* were good for *him*. How good was *he*, Amy?" Her eyes betrayed nothing as she carefully laid the coupon aside. "How good was he for *you?*" Tate demanded quietly.

"I don't see how his best friend could ask a question like that." She turned another page. "He gave me two children."

"*I* was here the night Karen was born," Tate reminded her. Her hand went still, the page stalled at an angle. "I was with you that night. She came—" Amy looked into his eyes as he gestured poignantly "—from your body into my hands. I've never felt so…"

"So…what?" she asked, as mesmerized by the memory as he was.

"Yeah, so what." He stood abruptly and jammed his hands into his front pockets, bursting the bubble with a shrug. "I shouldn't have said 'big deal.' I didn't mean to knock Kenny or anything the two of you…had. Okay?"

"I think you misunderstood, Tate. I meant…" But he was done. He was getting his jacket back off the hook. "Where are you going?" she asked.

Back to the Jackalope, he should have said, but her question had sounded sufficiently meek to warrant an honest response. "Out to the barn." Downstairs first, for something to keep him warm. Maybe blankets would be enough. "I need to take care of some things before I turn in."

She should just leave him alone, she told herself as she headed across the yard. He hadn't been out there very long, and he was probably having a cigarette. It was a clear, crisp night. Nice night to be outside. She visited Daisy and Duke in their kennel, then told herself to go back into the house. But herself wasn't listening very well. The light was still on in the barn. She pushed the side door open.

"Tate?"

"Up here." She saw his black cowboy hat first, then his face, then his denim collar turned up to his jawline. He peered down from the loft. "What's up? Kids okay?"

"They're fine. They're sound asleep." As she closed the door behind her, she noticed a pair of green feline eyes peeking down from the loft, too. "What are you doing?"

"I had a crazy yen to sleep out here tonight."

"In the barn?"

"Ol' Cinnamon Toast has been up here cleaning out the mice, and I just mucked out the pens today. Put down fresh straw." He flipped open a green wool blanket. "It's aboveground, which is a real plus. I feel like campin' out tonight." The hat disappeared, and there was some rustling of hay. "Could you hit the light on your way out?"

When the light went out, it was pitch-dark for a moment, but then her eyes adjusted to the dimmer light emitted through the clerestory windows directly across from the loft. The moonlight would be nice, she thought. It would flood across his makeshift bed like stardust. She climbed the steps quietly, although she knew he heard her coming.

"Tate? You'll get cold out here."

"If I do, I know where the house is."

She climbed over the top of the ladder and stood at the foot of the pallet he'd made. He'd pulled the blanket up to his chest, pillowed his neck in his hands and covered his face with his cowboy hat. His boots stuck out at the end of the blanket. He looked incredibly long. And he was ignoring her.

Amy cleared her throat. "As long as you've declared a truce, maybe we could…"

"Have ourselves a roll in the hay?"

"Have a talk about…the best way to go about selling the livestock." She knelt on the corner of the pallet. "I'll need your help, but I don't want you to think you have to—"

"I don't think I *have* to. Go back to the house, Amy. Give me some peace."

"It's too cold out here," she insisted. "I won't have you sleeping in the barn."

"What're you gonna do about it?"

"Well…" Good question. "I'm just going to sit here."

He shoved his hat back as he braced himself on his elbows and gave her a cool stare. "You can't control me the way you did Kenny. That's what scares you about me, isn't it?"

"Control? I couldn't control Ken. He puttered around with his horses and talked about all the things he was going to do around here, but I couldn't get him to make a *real* decision about anything important to—" her hands flopped against her knees in frustration "—to save his life."

"Kenny was my friend. He was a good-hearted guy, and we had some good times together. But he never took charge of anything." He sat up, leaned across his own knees and reached for her hand. "A woman wants a man to take charge once in a while, doesn't she?"

"Yes, but not—"

"Not to push her around." He tugged on her hand, cautiously reeling her into his bed. "Not to take her security away, but just to say, 'Lean on me for a while.'"

"That would be nice."

"Damn right." He lifted the edge of the top blanket and drew her underneath it. "So I'm gonna show you just how a man takes charge."

There was no more talk of selling anything. There was very little talk at all, and when they spoke, it was only of what was happening between them at the moment. They didn't undress completely. Instead they delighted in undoing buttons, one at a time, and finding places that needed kissing. Each piece of clothing became an envelope to be expertly unsealed, the contents to be secretly investigated without being removed. They were like first lovers, exploring one another, sharing secrets in a secret place. They teased one another about wanting to get into each other's pants, tortured each other by dragging zippers down and touching warm skin with cool hands. Inevitably the torture became exquisitely sensuous as hands and lips sought the deeper secrets nestled in the wedge-shaped envelopes of open zippers.

He had not hoped to love her this way again. Reckless as he was, he had never been the right man, but he would do for now. And for now, he would do well.

She had not expected to be held and touched this way again. Sensible as she was, she always sought moderation, but not tonight. Tonight she abandoned caution and demanded no compromise. Tonight his way was better.

Tonight she whispered love words while she suckled him. Tonight she made him moan as relentlessly as he did her. They kissed and touched with feverish abandon. He called her *honey,* because, he said, she tasted like honey. "And I've never said that to anyone before."

He was, she told him, a man for all seasons and all times of the day, but especially beautiful in the moonlight. Her hands cherished his every contour. "Like polished marble all over, all over, all over."

"We're going to shoot the moon," he promised as he eased himself inside her. It took some ardent stroking, some rhythmic pumping and some zealous writhing, but they did. They not only shot the moon, they made a whole new crater.

"Don't go yet," he said when she'd recovered strength enough to move. "Stay with me a little longer."

"We should go inside. We could…" She wanted to take him to her bed, but Jody might find him there. His room was right across the hall. Amy's good judgment put her wanting in its place.

And Tate didn't need any diagrams. "We'd have to get dressed," he lamented as he cradled her against his chest. "I'd have to fasten this." He couldn't locate a bra cup without brushing the back of his hand across her nipple. "And then I couldn't do this anymore." He smiled when he'd coaxed her nipple into a bead.

"You're a tricky one, Tate Harrison," she whispered contentedly.

He tongued her nipple gently, just one more time. Just for good measure. "How long will you nurse Karen?"

She answered with a soft groan.

He tightened his arms around her hips, holding her to him

as he pressed his face between her breasts. "Who gets weaned first, her or me?"

Like his lovemaking, his teasing hurt sometimes, but she could hide the hurt as long as he couldn't see her face. She tunneled her fingers into his hair and held him, his ear a scant inch from her thrumming heart. "Whoever grows up first, I guess."

Chapter 11

He woke up shivering in his blankets, and Amy was gone. Responsible Amy. She had children to look after—thank God she was responsible. He would have kept her up in that loft, rolling in his arms, halfway into summer. A loft was much better than a pumpkin shell, not that he owned either one. But he had a pickup, a passbook savings account and a piece of Montana ground. He was worth *something,* anyway. If the woman couldn't see that, it was time to point it out to her. The sun would be up soon. He decided that sunrise would be a damn good time.

He showered and shaved, and while he was getting himself dressed in the shirt she'd made for him, he could hear activity overhead. Karen was making those cute little baby noises. She was just naturally an early bird, but it was unusual for Jody to be clomping around the kitchen in his prized cowboy boots at this hour.

They were all outside by the time he got upstairs. He could

see them through the front window, Karen all bundled up in her stroller and Jody standing out there hipshot like a cool cowhand, leaning on his broomstick horse as if it were the gatepost on the approach to a ten-thousand-acre spread. Amy was dragging something out of the back of her pickup, which she'd backed up to the edge of the yard. Early-morning light brightened the sky all around them. The lavender hills sloped in silhouette against the pale yellow dawn.

Tate grabbed his hat and headed out the back, slamming the storm door shut behind him. Amy looked up and smiled. "We were just about to go looking for you. We're planting Karen's tree."

"You're gonna plant a tree just before you move out?"

"Whether we're moving or not, these things have to be done in their season, and it's the season for tree planting." She hooked a stray lock of hair behind her ear and pointed across the yard. "Jody's tree is that paper birch. See how nice and tall it's growing?"

Jody trotted across the yard to reacquaint himself with his birch tree. "It's budding, too," he boasted.

"We thought Karen's should be a Christmas tree." Tate took over the job of unloading the young nursery-raised blue spruce from the back of the pickup. "I don't want to block the view from the window, though," Amy mused as she surveyed the yard.

She wore an old yellow sweatshirt and faded blue jeans, and she looked as fresh and naturally pretty as the morning sky. She caught him staring at her, though, so he had to tear his eyes away and give some serious consideration to the problem at hand.

"I've been thinkin' we needed a windbreak over there by your garden." He quirked her a questioning brow, and she nodded. He carried the tree and pushed the stroller. Jody and

Outlaw, Jr., galloped along behind, while Amy donned her gardening gloves and brought up the rear. She carried the shovel.

Jody cut a wide circle around his sister's stroller. "Remember when we went out and got the Christmas tree, Tate?"

"I remember." Along with Christmas trees past, he thought. Trees had a way of making nice memories. He set the tree down close to where he wanted to see it take root, then he turned, eyeing the shovel. "You gonna let me do the digging on this project?"

"If you want to."

He took the shovel from Amy's hands and stabbed the ground with its point. He could feel her watching him with those earth-mother eyes of hers. When she was satisfied that he could handle the job, she dashed into the house and came back with a bucket of water and a plastic sack.

"Does that look big enough?" He knew it was plenty big, but he wanted to make sure she was satisfied with his work. This was one morning he wasn't giving her anything to complain about.

"It looks perfect." She knelt beside the tree and started tapping the pot to loosen the roots.

"Here, let me help." Tate hunkered down beside her and took the plastic pot in his big hands, breaking it down the side. Then he took out his jackknife. "The tool-of-all-trades for the jack-of-all-trades." He was really going to impress her now. He'd had a seasonal job with the Forest Service years ago. He knew that a competent planter of trees always scored the root ball.

The sun appeared in a crotch in the foothills, spilling fruit-basket colors across the sky as Tate lifted Karen from the stroller. They all gathered around Tate's hole in the earth and watched Amy empty the contents of the plastic zipper bag.

There was nothing unbeautiful about the blood from Amy's body, the tissue that had nourished her unborn baby. Tate held the tree steady with one hand. With the other he raked black loam into the hole. Other fingers plunged to his aid—Amy's slender ones, Jody's short ones and Karen's chubby ones. They pounded the first layer down, added water, and dug in again.

"Who's going to tend it?" Tate asked after the job was done.

"God takes care of the trees," Jody reported confidently. "Doesn't He, Mom?"

"The trees and the sparrows." Amy squinted against the sun's glare as she looked up at Tate. "Who's tending yours?" He looked at her questioningly. "The ones along the driveway that used to lead to your old house. There's a huge clump of daylilies that blooms there every summer. Did your mother plant those?"

"Probably." He remembered his mother's daylilies and her hollyhocks. He'd had to weed them every damn spring when she was alive. "They're still there?"

"Like Jody said, God takes care of them." She shifted Karen from one hip to the other and started toward the house. "Besides, you can't even get rid of daylilies with an eight-bottom plow."

Jody fed his orphan lambs with a huge plastic baby bottle. Amy and Tate sat side by side on the back step and watched them romp around the yard together. From their backyard kennel, Daisy and Duke let it be known that they were ready to romp, too. The lambs ignored the barking. They listened only to Jody, the voice of the milk supply.

"When Jody goes to school, he'll have two lambs on his tail," Tate said with a bemused smile. "Think that'll make the children laugh and play?"

Amy laughed as she bounced Karen on her knees. "You've been eavesdropping on the bedtime reading again."

"Karen and me both, right, sweetie?" He chucked the baby under her chin. "One night last week I walked the floor with her a little bit, and Jody's door was open just a crack. We didn't wanna interrupt, but we heard something about little lambs, and we were just curious."

"Tate, about last night…"

"You let me say something about last night, okay?" He detected an unusual timidity in the look she slid him. "Short and sweet."

"Yes," she said quietly. "Short, but very, very sweet."

He whispered in her ear, "I kept it up as long as I could, boss lady," and she closed her eyes and smiled. "I meant that my say will be short and sweet. *Maybe.*" She glanced up, and he chuckled. "Why is it we're always explaining what we meant after we say what we say?"

"To each other?" He nodded. She shrugged. "Maybe we don't speak the same language."

"We did last night," he recalled. The blush in her cheeks was so pretty, it stung his eyes. He had to look at something else while he said his piece. He chose Jody, tumbling in the new grass with a leggy lamb.

"I've been doin' a lot of thinking lately," Tate began cautiously. "You know, you can keep horses and sheep together real easy. They complement each other well, the way they graze. Sheep will eat plants that horses don't like, and sheep dung is good fertilizer for horse pasture. They seem like opposites, but each improves the pasture for the other."

"You have to separate them at lambing time," Amy pointed out quietly.

"So you make a few allowances." He turned to her. "You really plannin' to sell this place?"

"You really planning to sell yours?" He was ready to tell her that he wasn't sure, but she had a piece she had to say, too. "If you'd stop running long enough, you'd realize how useless all this running is. You were born to this land, Tate, this life, and it still shows, no matter how far you've tried to put it behind you."

"You wanted something different from the life you grew up with," he reminded her. "So do I. I want—"

"What?"

He smiled. "Listen to me, now. I'm trying to draw you this harmony-between-sheep-and-horses comparison."

"And I want you to tell me straight-out," she insisted. "What are you looking for, Tate?"

"I want a home and family. I want to feel like I belong, like I'm wanted and needed." He looked across the yard at Jody again. "Like somebody believes in me, trusts me. I screwed up bad once, but—"

"You were just a boy."

"I didn't know that. I thought I was supposed to be a man." He paused for a moment, thinking about that ghost and a few others. Here was an opening for him to try to put their ghosts to rest. "Kenny thought it was still okay for him to be a boy, even after he was married. He let you carry most of the load." He turned to her. "I wouldn't do that, Amy. I'm just as strong-willed as you are. We'd put it all together—what's mine with what's yours. But you'd have to be willing to share decisions with me, fifty-fifty."

She was doing her damnedest to bank up the coals on a warm smile. "Would you be wanting a few cows, too, cowboy?"

"I might. But if I can live with sheep—"

"I think I could live with cows if I had a real cowboy around," she said, too quickly, too eagerly. It was as though she'd caught herself on the verge of being happy, and it scared her, made her feel guilty. The implicit contrast was like a bucket of cold water dumped between them.

Dredging up a somber note, she glanced away. "I did love Ken."

"I know." Tate slipped his arm around her. "He was my best friend. Always." *Even when I wanted his girl for my own. Even when I wanted his wife. Even when I wanted to punch him in the face because he didn't know any better than to take the woman I wanted for granted.* "I loved him, too, Amy, but that doesn't have to come between us. He loved us. And we both did right by him."

"What you said about why we haven't always gotten along… Why I might have been…afraid of you in a way." She looked up at him again. "You might have a point."

"I might have a point." He claimed the baby, who shrieked with delight as he lifted her toward the sky in a joyful toast. "Ha-ha, I might have a *point!*"

"There's a chance we could become great compromisers," Amy said tentatively.

"We'd probably butt heads once in a while, but we'd take care of each other, too. You'd lean on me, and I'd lean on you, sort of like a jackleg fence." He was riding high now, with a pretty girl tucked under each arm. "And the kids, they'd be like the cross pieces, you know? There's a lot I could teach Jody."

"You've been like a father to him these last few months."

"I thought it was *brother.*"

"Father," she amended belatedly. "And there aren't too many fathers who can say they've actually delivered their daughters into the world."

He bounced Karen in his arm. "You remember that night, little darlin'? You popped your head into the world, and this was the first face to greet you." She patted his smooth-shaven cheek with a chubby hand. "It was a little bristly that night, as I recall."

"She was glad you were there." Amy put her arm around his waist and smiled up at him. "So was her mom."

"I know you needed me that night," he said. "How about now? Not just my help, Amy. *Me*." He needed to hear her say it. "It's not a weakness to need someone," he professed, as much for his own benefit as for hers. And suddenly, for better or for worse, he didn't mind saying, "I need you."

"For what?"

"For a companion," he offered. She wasn't buying yet. "For my partner, how's that?" Better, he could tell. "For my lover," he growled in her ear. "How's that?"

"It would be a lovely thought." She challenged him with a look. "If you loved me."

"I don't remember when I didn't love you."

Now she smiled, and the light in her silk chocolate eyes was like sunrise at sea.

"And I always will, Amy. How's *that?*"

"Is it…really true?"

"You know it's true."

She did. She'd known it for some time. And she'd known there would be heartache if he left her and risks if he stayed.

"I think my father loved my mother, too, in his own way. And we loved him, but…" Oh, God, could she keep a man like Tate happy? If she gave him a place in her heart and her home, would he find it too confining for his long, tall cowboy form and being?

She sighed. "I can be good in all the roles you named, but I'm not a good gypsy. You'd have to—"

"Settle down, I know. I'm feelin' pretty settled. I've been

a pretty good hired hand, haven't I?" She nodded slowly. "Fire me."

"What?"

"I want to be your husband. I want to be a father to your children." He searched the depths of her eyes. "If you think you could love me."

"I've been afraid to love you, but I've been loving you anyway. It couldn't be helped." She lowered her head and rubbed her cheek against his shoulder. His heart swelled when she finally confessed, "I need you, Tate. If you ever left me now…"

"I would die inside." She lifted her chin, then lifted her eyes to his. He smiled. "I've been runnin' in circles, endin' up back home every time."

He dipped his head, and their lips met for a long slow kiss. Karen smacked his cheek once, but it didn't faze him. Not when he heard the catch in Amy's breath over his fancy tongue stroking.

"Oh, mush," said a voice at his knee.

Tate groaned. He opened his eyes and reluctantly broke the kiss. Amy giggled as he turned a sheepish glance Jody's way. "Mush?"

"You guys gotta get married if you're gonna be kissin' like that."

"You think we'd better?" Tate asked expectantly. Jody wrinkled his nose. "Do I have your permission to marry your mom, partner?" Tate's nod summoned Jody for an exchange between cohorts. The boy leaned in closer. "Say yes, and I'll see what I can do about a horse to go with that saddle."

Jody's pogo-stick legs sprang into action. "Yes! Whoa, can you marry her today?"

"Jody!" Amy complained buoyantly. "You probably could have bid him up. I'm certainly worth more than one horse."

"I only want one." He grabbed Tate's knee, anchoring himself for one quick, anxious inquiry. "Will you be my dad then?"

"I will if your mom stops playing hard to get and says yes."

"Can we still be partners?"

"We can always be partners." He looked into the face of the only woman he'd ever petitioned for such an agreement. "You wanna be partners, Amy?"

"Kiss her again, Tate! She'll say yes if you kiss her again."

So he did kiss her. And she did say, "Yes."

* * * * *

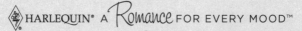

HARLEQUIN
Ambassadors

Want to share your passion for reading Harlequin® Books?

Become a Harlequin Ambassador!

Harlequin Ambassadors are a group of passionate and well-connected readers who are willing to share their joy of reading Harlequin® books with family and friends.

You'll be sent all the tools you need to spark great conversation, including free books!

All we ask is that you share the romance with your friends and family!

You'll also be invited to have a say in new book ideas and exchange opinions with women just like you!

To see if you qualify* to be a Harlequin Ambassador, please visit www.HarlequinAmbassadors.com.

*Please note that not everyone who applies to be a Harlequin Ambassador will qualify. For more information please visit www.HarlequinAmbassadors.com.

Thank you for your participation.